Hypocrite

NATALIE NICOLE NEVERMAN

Natalie Neverman

Other books by Natalie Neverman

Veiled

Generations

Coming Soon:

Weathering The Storms Series

Hurricane

Summer Thunderstorm

The Aftermath

Chapter One

Declan swung the creaking garage door open and walked into his kitchen, calling for his wife. He was exhausted with an aching back from a long day on his feet, smelling like raw meat, ready for a beer, and a home-cooked meal. When she didn't immediately answer, he instantly knew something was wrong. She was always waiting for him, knew how important it was to be waiting and ready for him; it was her duty as his bride.

He dropped his wallet and lunch box on the kitchen table and headed back towards the bedroom, hoping she was in the bath, was sick, or perhaps had lost track of time. He would have to punish her for it, but he could go easy on her as long as she had a reasonable excuse. As he went down the hallway, the stench of death overwhelmed him like a tidal wave, and he knew all too well what waited for him. He stopped, steadied himself against the wall, and refused to believe it could be true.

Opening the door to the master bedroom, he heard the music, piano in sharp and flat contrasts on low coming from the speaker on the nightstand, angry, bitter, and sad. She'd been listening to Tori Amos lately, no matter how much he warned her not to, made her pay for it, or tried to keep her from it. 'Crucify' played on repeat, stinging his ears, burning his soul. Somehow this artist spoke to her, though he couldn't relate, she needed what the melodies held.

As sweet as the day he'd met her, in a pretty pink dress, his wife rested dead on their bed. He stared in awe, unable to process as disbelief reverberated in his mind. He was unsure whether it was fear, dread, anger, or insanity. She was so beautiful. She was all he had left. He went to her, collapsed beside her, reached for her but recoiled, torn and in denial, pain twisting his face, hate burning in his mind.

How could she do this to me? Betrayal as hideous as being unfaithful.

Nauseated, overcome with grief, unable to breathe, kneeling beside the bed, he saw the note on the nightstand. Taking the paper with a trembling hand, he read the sad words as the music pierced him, drove deep into his psyche and his soul with the agony. Reading what she had written, seeing her last words to him, something shattered inside him.

My handsome Dec,

I didn't know how to explain it to you. I just couldn't do it anymore. Losing Candy, it changed us. It changed you, you became stronger and more determined to make the world pay, and it changed me, made me bitter inside like a toxic weed. I can't keep up anymore, with what you're doing, how you're doing it, who you're after, I can't let go of her while you're on this path, even if I believe in it. I miss her so, I can't heal, I won't heal, and I didn't find the purpose you did. Fly, right the ship and lift the rain, the world needs you, and you can't do what you need to do with me as your anchor. I love you more than I can ever put into words. Don't weep for me. I'll see you on the other side.

Love even in separation, Eda Jean

As he read it, he collapsed onto the floor, screaming, rocking against the edge of the bed, banging his head on the metal frame until his brow bled. He couldn't do it. He couldn't live without her. He couldn't go on the way the music did.

Exhausting himself, he wept on beside her, unable to sit up, incapable of accepting the truth. His mind wouldn't let him process, and it wouldn't let him rest. A culmination of the last two years swelled inside him, dark and sinister, reminding him what he now knew was his purpose for being on Earth. He had the God given talent to find the truth, and he had. Now he had no reason not to bring light to the reality, to make those with power wilt in the face of knowledge.

He and Eda Jean had fought about it, he hated it, feeling at odds with her, but she was different. He was strong in ways she wasn't. He thought she would have the power to heal, to move on, and he had found himself obsessed and dwelling, unable to live without vengeance. Not that it mattered now, his lovely bride had taken her own life. It was too late.

He sprawled on the floor beside her until darkness consumed the room; until he could no longer stand the smell, and the hate inside him began to burn like a torch. Dragging himself to standing, he stared at her, empty of tears, his heart numb, his soul blank, he still couldn't bring himself to leave her like this, alone and cold. If he was meant to bring their story to the world, to make the people responsible for their daughter's death pay as dearly as they deserved, he needed to know his girls were together. They needed each other now. He needed to make sure the world would know their story.

Chapter Two

The Hypocrite case, as it was being called, was national headlines, and FBI Supervisory Special Agent Ethan Hartman understood why. Six surgeons, all female, had been gruesomely murdered in less than five weeks in cold blood. Another, victim number seven, had gotten lucky and been left for dead but survived.

He hated cases the media penned a name for, it made them seem dramatized and blown out of proportion, but this one made sense. Someone killing people who devoted their lives to saving people seemed pretty hypocritical. Quite fitting. He wasn't surprised when it landed on his desk. With a track record built mostly on finding suspects who maneuvered as well as ghosts, he figured it was only a matter of time before the case became his to crack.

The first thing he had to do was build a profile, not of the murderer, but the victims. All seven women were in their mid to late thirties no more than six years apart. All had been employed at or attended Johns Hopkins University at the same time, though in different points in their career either for bachelors, residency, or post graduate work, including research. That left a mere four hundred and fifty-seven other physicians and medical personnel to be next in line for the chopping block. None of the victims had similar physical traits, so interactions with one another had to play a more significant role.

Mounds of research and paperwork stacked up in front of him, and he was just starting to get an image of the depth and scope of evil. All these victims were upstanding, competent physicians doing their best for their communities. He couldn't imagine someone wanting to thin out the upper echelon of medical talent for half the country. One of the first items to check off his list was a hunch, and as the phone on his desk in his San Francisco office rang, he was relieved to get it out of the way sooner than later.

"This is Agent Hartman."

"Good afternoon, Ethan. This is Director Gordon returning your call, what can I do for you?"

"Thank you for getting back to me so quickly. I appreciate your being prompt as I need to get ahead of a mess with a new case sooner rather than later." Ethan shuffled some paperwork on his desk and paused to load a file on his computer screen.

"Sure, my pleasure, I'm especially happy to help if you're concerned it might involve my wife."

"I'm hoping not, but it's a possibility I have to get out of the way so I can focus on other leads. The case involving your wife last year, was with the Gulf Cartel, correct?"

"Yes, her name was Eva Burke then."

"Has there been any backlash? Any threats or contact of any kind since Antonella Cruz was convicted?" Ethan asked.

"Not that we are aware of, of course, with the resources available to the Gulf Cartel, there is always a possibility something slips past us. That case, in particular, was heavy on threats, coercion, and bribes. Do you have any reason to believe the organ theft ring has resurfaced?"

"No, not specifically. I'm concerned about the similarities with this recent rash of murders of female physicians."

"Ah, yea, I read the notes on that. I keep an eye open for similar things since I have, well, vested interests at this point." Ben cleared his throat awkwardly. He still couldn't believe he got to go home to one of the best pediatric trauma surgeons in the state of Arizona every night because he broke protocol with a victim, who became a witness, who became his wife.

"I would do the same thing. It's smart. Since you're aware of the case, does anything stand out to you? Anything at all similar to the Cruz case in Velado? Names, weapons, a similar style of abduction?"

Ben let out a loaded sigh, thought hard about what he had read. It wasn't a stretch by any means. Antonella Cruz, leader of the largest known group of organized abductions to traffic human organs, was identified by his, then, girlfriend and incarcerated based on her testimony. Less than a year later, suddenly female surgeons all over the country are being murdered. Revenge is a dish best served cold, and he would have been dishonest to say the case hadn't spooked him.

"No, nothing I could say for sure. Overall, I don't think it fits. Trust me; it crossed my mind." The concern was evident in Ben's voice.

"What makes you say that?"

"Think about it—if the Gulf Cartel was blanketing female surgeons within a specific age range in retaliation, hoping one of them is my wife, why would they spread out the attacks? Wouldn't something like that be more effective if it came all at once? Plus, I think they could have pinpointed Eva's age better, this span of almost seven years doesn't make sense."

"Good point."

"Do you have any hard evidence left at the crime scenes?"

"Not much. Certainly no DNA or fingerprints, the perp has been careful so far, but he seems to be escalating. A couple of witnesses came forward, but they're sketchy, nothing rock solid. I'm anxious to talk to the one survivor, but she's still in a coma in Portland. The nanny came home unexpectedly during the attack and let the dog in from the garage. In the scuffle, the nanny retreated, and the dog was shot…"

"What kind of dog?" Ben interrupted.

"A very large, well trained Doberman pincher, not a German Shepherd, I caught that part of the Cruz case." Ethan could hear the relieved exhale on the other end of the line. "Dr. Eleanor Walker, our survivor, was hit over the head and shot three times after her dog died defending her. She wouldn't have survived if the nanny hadn't called the police. We haven't released that she's alive, she's in protective custody, still in the hospital."

"What a mess. Glad it's your case and not mine. I still have to believe if it were the Gulf Cartel, there wouldn't be any slip-ups. We gutted a large arm of the cartel, but it was still a fraction of their reach. These cases where someone needs round the clock protection, they get messy quickly. I speak from experience." Ben sighed with a thorough understanding.

"I bet. Hey, thanks for the quick call back, do me a favor and keep an eye on the notes just in case anything comes up that looks familiar. I feel confident enough I can cross this off as a possibility, and I hope it stays that way. Take good care of your wife." Ethan hung up after Ben said goodbye, then made some notes in the file. Rolling up the cuffs of his sleeves, he pushed back from the desk and strolled over to the window.

Staring out over the city skyline from his eighteenth-floor corner office, he could see the silhouette of the Golden Gate Bridge in the distance, shrouded in late afternoon mist. Commuters trying to get ahead of the rush hour were just starting to clog the lanes. The water shimmered as the sun slid sideways over the Pacific Ocean. Hues of melancholy aquamarine blended into glimmering rainbows as waves splashed in the wind throwing spray into the air. Sailboats cruised in what seemed like slow motion as the wind whipped through the bay.

It never ceased to amaze him how much he loved this city—the melting pot. Nowhere else ever felt quite so much like home.

Having grown up in Ukiah California, less than three hours north of the city, he remembered every trip here as a child. Every baseball game with his dad and two brothers, every trip to the zoo, countless days at Stinson Beach, meals at Fisherman's Wharf while his family watched the street performers, every memory stood out. He couldn't walk the streets without thinking about something from his past.

Today this case had him reminiscing about darker times, and it was hitting closer to home than he wanted to admit. He tucked his hands in his pockets, staring out at the horizon, and let his mind drift. He could just see the pillars of St. Mary's if he leaned against the glass. Memory led him through what had felt like endless hours in that church sitting with his father in a corner pew. His sister's birthday would have made her twenty-one three days ago, were she still alive. Lost in the recollection of days gone by, he was startled by a knock at the door.

"Come in," Ethan said.

"Sorry to disturb you, boss, but we just got a call I think you'll be interested in." Tom Quillet came darting in with a little note pad and headed towards Ethan's computer. With sandy blond hair, brilliant green eyes, a sharp nose, and angular jaw around an oval face with fragile features, Tom was lean and a couple of inches shorter than Ethan. His thin frame on long legs loped around the desk to the chair.

"You'll probably want to log into your email to review in detail, but we have what I feel could be a threat to a female physician here in the bay that might be related to the Hypocrite case. I figured I should bring it up since Allie would normally... but isn't..." Tom trailed off. The recent sudden departure of Ethan's personal assistant was a sore spot.

Allie had emphatically promised, even sworn up and down through her pregnancy, that she would return after maternity leave. Less than a week ago, she had called in an emotional, ranting state, begging forgiveness and gave less than the cordial two-week notice. Her desk had been packed up for her by her fourth-floor friend, Jenna, from the cybercrimes unit while Ethan avoided eye contact. It left him, in more ways than one, disorganized and disgruntled, and though he had wanted to be angry, he couldn't. He had adored Allie, her leaving him felt personal and stung more than he wanted to have known around the office.

Ethan sat on the edge of his desk as Tom opened his email and searched for a recent file. "What makes you think it's related?" he asked.

"The administration office at UCSF reported Dr. Aurora Soileaux attended Johns Hopkins during the timeframe in question for the adjacent victims. They haven't told her about it yet because they wanted to make sure it was credible. Local police called it into me about an hour ago, and as soon as I saw it, I forwarded it over. Check this out..." Tom opened a photo file of a handwritten note scribbled onto a three by five-card. Ethan squinted to make out the scrawling letters on the overly bright screen.

I saw you. I know you were there. Shining star as you are, I'm sure you remember. I haven't found the proof you're responsible yet, but I know you know who it is. Be prepared to pay the price.

"Well, it's simple, short, and straight to the point. When did it come in?"

"Yesterday, based on how the hospital processes mail, postmarked from Portland, where the last attack is still under investigation."

"It was mailed to the hospital?" Ethan frowned and flipped the screen to a photo of the envelope in which the note had arrived.

"Apparently, yes," Tom said.

Ethan began to run through the scenarios of why a suspect who had previously been silent, would do something so public, to be seen by others before even the victim. Would the suspect even know it would be screened?

"Do you know where this doctor is now? Does she live in the Bay Area?"

"Yes, boss. She has privileges in nearly a dozen hospitals on the West Coast. I ran a quick background on her but couldn't get a permanent address. She is a pediatric neurosurgeon specializing in oncology, like, one in five in the whole country. Someone in the credentialing department happened upon the conversation when the note came in and insisted on turning it into authorities. I guess they recognized her history and felt it significant in light of recent news reports."

A chill ran down Ethan's spine. She was too young, undoubtedly much too young, with the timelines from other victims, to have crossed the path of his sister over twenty years ago, but hearing the specialty hit home for him. He couldn't deny, it felt a little like fate.

"You said they haven't alerted her?" Ethan asked.

"Correct, they wanted feedback on authenticity. I guess these things aren't too infrequent, however credible, creepy, or wrong."

"There's a lot of money, a lot of power, in people who wield that kind of intellect and skill. We should have a conversation with her to see if she's received anything at her home or other threats recently. Do you know where she is now or how to contact her?"

"Yes, the hospital left a contact and said they know what cases she is on at all times. She's on-site through the end of the day tomorrow."

"Get them on the phone. I'd like to meet with her ASAP. Once you have her location call me, I'll go now."

"You boss?"

"You have someone better than the lead on the case?" Ethan's tone was sharp, he only had a temper for certain things, and having his authority questioned never sat well.

"No, sorry. I didn't mean it that way. I just thought maybe there was someone more… disposable than you, with Allie gone, so to speak," Tom stuttered.

"Send me the details." Ethan jumped to his feet, slipping on his dark navy suit jacket.

"Yes, boss. I'll call now."

Tom was out the door in the opposite direction as Ethan headed for the underground parking garage. The UCSF campus wasn't far. If he was lucky, he could catch her and the administrative personnel who chose not to inform her of her situation before everyone called it quits for the day. Having a motorcycle in California where splitting lanes is allowed would make his chances all that much better. He wasn't about to have a doctor in his city become next on the chopping block.

The late June air was crisp, chilly, and damp as he strapped on the black helmet while his bike purred beneath him. Backing out he admired, as he always did, the light and easily maneuverable Ducati. A long sought-after reward for years on a bicycle, he still felt the thrill of it every time he started the engine. Zipping his armored Kevlar jacket, he was glad for a chilly day since the material didn't breathe well, and he wasn't keen on showing up in a rumpled suit.

A few blocks later, downhill from Golden Ave, he tucked his jacket back into the seat compartment with his gloves and locked his helmet to the rear flare. Strolling into the main doors of the hospital, he was glad in the absence of Allie that Tom was on his team, a solid choice, he reminded himself. Tom's text read: *ask for Theresa Thirston in the medical staff office she is expecting you, fifth floor in the admin wing.*

He sauntered over to the information desk and, within five minutes, was greeted outside the elevator by a short, grey-haired woman with soda bottle glasses who introduced herself as Theresa. She had quiet grey eyes, and her hair tucked back into a neat bun at the nape of her neck. A shiny silver chain draped from the earpieces of her glasses behind her neck, and they hung loosely at a robust bosom as she removed them.

"Agent Hartman, I presume? Thank you for coming." She was terribly nervous, and her hand trembled as she shook his.

"Yes, thank you for being so responsive and for reporting the incident right away, it could prove pivotal in apprehending the suspect."

Ethan turned to follow her as she began to scurry down a hallway lined with plain doors. Her chunky heels flopped slightly too large on swollen ankles encased in thick caramel-colored pantyhose.

"Dr. Soileaux is just finishing up a surgery. I'll take you to her right now. Please follow me. This way is faster." She handed him a manila envelope. "This is the original letter, and some others received in the last year or so that I don't believe are related, but I felt the need to include just in case."

"Much appreciated. Tell me, Mrs. Thirston, why do you not report all the threats? My colleague informed me you said you get these types of things rather often."

They passed through a wide set of double doors, and the wing changed immediately from administrative to the typical linoleum floors of a sanitary hospital, fluorescent light washing out the lavender blue of her dress to a drab grey.

"Not all of them are threats, by any means. Most of them are regarding payment issues or things we refer to malpractice. Rarely are they anonymous, and they were never previously accompanied by verified violence against other physicians. Additionally, we don't get many for Dr. Soileaux; this level of anger is a first for her."

She glanced over her shoulder at him with concern as she led him down the hallway at a brisk pace. Heels clicking on the hard floor, she was wringing her hands in between shoving doors open.

"I see. Was there anything in particular that made you think this threat to Dr. Soileaux is more credible, specifically?" he knew part of the answer, but he wanted to hear it from her.

"I've worked here for nearly forty years. I started right out of high school as a secretary, and I've worked my way through dozens of physicians. I knew Aurora's father well. I've known her personally since she was a child. He practiced here for twenty years. She mentioned to me a few weeks ago how she knew, from the news, two of the other victims herself, it didn't seem to bother her terribly, though we all feel it's a crying shame. For someone to rip such talent from the world and extinguish hard-working, devoted, caring people," she choked up, her soft voice cracking as she brought her hand to her lip to steady it from quivering.

They were passing staff now, physicians and nurses in long coats and scrubs. She pushed a button for the elevator, and they paused while he patiently waited for her to regain composure.

"Well, needless to say, once she mentioned that, I began to worry. She said she knew them because they were with her several years ago working briefly on a clinical trial at Johns Hopkins," she said.

They stepped into the elevator, and as it closed, she looked him over, thoroughly judging his appearance, clearly skeptical of his trustworthiness. Though he stood much taller than her, at six foot three inches, and his solid and muscular two-hundred-and-thirty-pound build towered above her, she kept her chin high, clearly confident in her assessment and control of the situation. Her demeanor changed quickly, and before the doors opened, he felt as though he'd become privy to very personal information and chastised to protect it at all cost, at the same time.

"I'm an honest person, and I will take responsibility for my actions. I breached a certain level of confidentiality when I called Johns Hopkins and used my professional authority for personal reasons. I'm not sorry for it, and to keep our physicians safe, especially Dr. Soileaux, I would do it again. It didn't take much digging to find out all the physicians who have been murdered to date so far, shared cases during the time Aurora was researching there. Only a select few people have overlapped multiple cases with her. I warned her, I feel she didn't take it seriously, but now, I refuse to allow additional risk. If I lose my job but save her life, it would be worth it." She turned tersely on her heel and led the way out of the elevator.

"Mrs. Thirston, I can assure you…" She cut him off.

"Please, call me Theresa."

"Theresa, I don't see any long-term consequences from you reaching out to Johns Hopkins. As long as the information you've discovered stays squarely between you and the FBI, there's no breach of confidentiality. Especially if it does lead us to resolution, I'm sure there's a level of forgiveness afforded."

They paused at the edge of a large half round desk staffed with attendants.

"I need the status of Dr. Soileaux's case. I need to see her immediately," Theresa interrupted one of the employees at the desk with authority. Ethan thought the skin of her hands might begin to crack and bleed if she wouldn't stop wringing them so severely. He reached out to comfort her and placed one large hand over both of hers. She immediately inhaled intensely, and her shoulders relaxed as she breathed out.

"We're going to do everything in our power to prevent another attack. I give you my word. If there's protection I can offer, she will have it." His voice was low as he stood over her and released her hands. She let her arms fall to her sides and shook her head, stress falling away from her.

"It's very personal to me. Not that I wouldn't want to see any of our doctors safe. This... this is different, it just is." She looked to him imploringly, and he smiled as warmly as he could. Though in his heart, putting the pieces together, he realized the possibility this doctor was somewhere near the top of the list as the next target was highly likely.

The desk clerk put her call on hold and turned her computer screen slightly, motioning to Theresa.

"She just closed about ten minutes ago. She'll need a few minutes to clean up. I can call into the OR and have her meet you in the back-corner conference room if that's suitable?" The clerk pointed towards a door behind the counter to the left. Theresa nodded, and he followed her through, instantly overpowered by the strong smell of antiseptic.

Everything felt sterile, and he became temporarily caught up in memories from his youth. He hadn't been back in a surgical wing in decades, and his stomach threatened to lurch out of his mouth before he regained control. All this time, it still upset him. He could again see his tiny, frail sister withering away like it was yesterday. He tried to focus elsewhere, out the windows, shake off the heavy emotions he sometimes worked hard to keep at bay.

They entered a small corner conference room with several tall metal cabinets, a couple of computers on a table lining the far wall beneath exterior windows, and a kidney bean-shaped conference table with chairs strewn haphazardly around it. The room seemed, in general, sparsely used. Ethan sat at the table, opened the manila envelope, and began reviewing some of the other notes inside. Nothing jumped out at him. Whether it was a gut feeling, instinct, or just luck, he felt like Theresa hit the nail on the head with sending this new note. She didn't sit but instead paced in front of a door at the opposite side of the room.

Within moments he realized the conference room separated an area frequented by patients and a hallway that was staff exclusive. When Theresa stopped pacing, he sat upright in anticipation as Dr. Soileaux entered through the staff door. For a brief moment, he felt awkward, as if intruding in a personal family moment. Theresa threw open her arms and clasped onto the young physician as a loved one sorely missed for an extended period.

The young woman, wearing typical blue surgical scrubs right down to the booties on her feet, was not what he expected. She had just let her hair down, and the thick, shining, dark walnut locks tumbled over creamy caramel skin, throwing a lovely spicy scent he caught even from five feet away. He stood up and noticed she was a mere two or three inches taller than Theresa, petite but curvy with a slender build distinct even through the baggy scrubs.

"Tee-Ta," Dr. Soileaux said warmly to Theresa and embraced the woman as someone might hug a grandparent. She closed her eyes and seemed only to enjoy the moment, ignoring Ethan entirely at first. Theresa held her tight, rubbing her back for a moment and whispered something in her ear, clearly a very personal greeting. Even as they stood back from one another, Theresa held her arms before brushing a thick lock of hair from her forehead. He understood now she had been genuine in the elevator when she had said she was prepared to lose her job to protect this woman, and wondered to what extent she had breached confidentiality.

Theresa turned to him, extending an arm as he offered a hand to shake, and he was stunned when the doctor's eyes met his. She locked on his face with a smile that could have stopped traffic on a busy street, and her eyes, a unique blend of bright emerald and gold with what seemed a backdrop of honey, distracted him. She was beautiful, absolutely breathtakingly beautiful.

"Aurora, this is Ethan Hartman, Special Agent with the FBI." Theresa's face changed as quickly as did Aurora's, and while shaking Ethan's hand, she turned to look back at Theresa with shock apparent on her face.

"What in the world kind of worry has brought this on?" she spoke to Theresa without letting go of Ethan. Her grip was firm with long, elegant fingers and oval trimmed, perfect nails.

"It's a pleasure to meet you, Dr. Soileaux," as he said it, he tripped on the vowels. It came out sounding more like "soil-low" than "swallow," and a flush of red darkened his face. She didn't seem to notice, or mind, and merely smiled at him again as she finally dropped his hand.

"Under these circumstances, I highly doubt it," Dr. Soileaux said. Both ladies pulled chairs back, and though Theresa stayed tense as she sat, Aurora seemed to plop herself down with relief, though curiosity was still in her expression. "What has she told you that brought you here?" The inflection in her voice was of genuine surprise. Theresa didn't look up, allowing him to take the lead.

"It isn't just what she's told me that I'm concerned about, it was what she received in the mail." He slid the note across to her and gave her a moment to read it.

"It didn't come to me. It was an act of God, Aurora, I swear. I overheard them talking about it, and it hit me in the gut like a punch. I just knew it was about you before I even saw the address." Theresa clasped her hand over her mouth again, clearly in distress, before Aurora could look up. While still reviewing the note, she reached over and gently put her arm over Theresa, rubbing her upper shoulders sweetly.

"Ne t'inquiète pas," she said. *Don't worry.* Aurora whispered to her softly, surprising him again. *What was that, French?* He wondered silently. Tears welled up in Theresa's eyes, and she reached for Aurora's hand.

"What do you think this is about? It doesn't make any sense to me. I can't imagine why it would be addressed to me." Aurora continued to hold Theresa's hands like she knew if she pulled away the woman would twist them to breaking.

"I've been working this case for two weeks now, and unfortunately, I have good reason to believe, at this time, it is a credible threat. Between what we've discovered in your professional history and what Mrs. Thirston has provided, there is adequate evidence to believe whoever sent this is involved in the previous deaths," Ethan said.

"How do you know this?" Aurora frowned, not yet convinced but open to the possibility she might legitimately be in danger.

"The letter was postmarked from Portland only a day after the last incident. I can't reveal any details of that…"

Aurora interrupted him, "Portland? I didn't see any attacks on the news regarding Portland."

"We've kept that one out of the news, that physician was not killed, she is in a coma currently in round the clock protective custody, which is where I would like to see you as well." Trying to keep his tone light, he could see he'd failed as shock lit up her face.

"I'm sorry, what?" Aurora asked. Ethan could see Theresa squeeze her hands as an attitude of dispute trickled into her tone of voice.

"We are coordinating with a half dozen other offices across the country and have nearly eleven other physicians under watch based on similar threats. Until we can pinpoint the specific event or situation linking all of the cases," he chose to use the word murder minimally, "it's the best we can do."

"I don't understand. If this person actually knew where to find me, wouldn't they have done so? Doesn't this mean my personal information and whereabouts are mostly, if not completely, safe?" It was a logical thought, but not thorough.

"You're smarter than that, Aurora, please," Theresa snapped at her the way she might scold a child. Aurora looked to her in slight surprise. "After everything that your family went through with your mother, the addresses, the lengths they went to for their privacy? Well, of course, you'd be more difficult to find but not impossible. He knew you would be here at USCF this week. Hopefully, all their efforts pay off and keep you safe until they catch this maniac."

"Oh," the air slowly left Aurora's lungs, "I suppose you're right." She looked to Theresa thoughtfully.

"May I ask what specifically you are talking about with addresses and privacy?" Ethan straightened in his chair, aiming to appear as professional as possible.

"My parents, my father has passed, but my mother is very wealthy. My father was a surgeon here for years, and my mother was a CEO for Boeing."

"And royalty," Theresa added with tartness. Aurora flicked her eyes towards the ceiling without turning her head towards Theresa.

"My mother was brought up in Egypt in what was considered, two hundred years ago, a royal bloodline. Many of those ways died in the last century, and she wanted nothing to do with it anyway. She moved here for college, met my father, and shortly after graduating, was hired at Boeing. Her parents were killed in a private plane crash shortly after that, leaving her as the sole heir to a good deal of money, not that she didn't make plenty of her own.

"She also had," Aurora paused, unsure how much to reveal, "corporate publicity issues. She didn't like the attention, so Dad created a company within a trust, or some arrangement, and put the family properties in it as a shield. No one could find any of us by mere means of a phone book, that's all."

"She also had some... scuffles," Theresa added with indignance.

"And you still live in a residence that does not, in any way, bear your name?" Ethan asked.

"Yes, I—we," she stuttered. "We have multiple residences I often travel to and from for work and pleasure, and none of them bear a family name. Because of how often I travel, the majority of my mail comes to the hospitals for management. Unless it's very personal from a friend or family, my mail is handled by hospital staff, office staff, or my personal assistant."

"Who is we?" he stayed professional, cold, but was secretly hoping it wasn't a husband.

"My sister, Donia, and I—we both have unrestricted access to all the properties," she said.

"And these scuffles? Could this have left you as a target to something else I should be aware of?" he watched Theresa's face closely, but she kept her expression guarded.

Aurora again rolled her eyes, "No, it was a long time ago. My mother was a shark in the business world. Mergers, acquisitions, international corporate strategy, things like that left her very unpopular, but nothing I think would be an issue after all this time. She's been retired for years."

"I see." Ethan retrieved the note and gathered the remaining slips of paper back into the envelope.

"Is all of this still really enough to justify protection of some kind?" Aurora seemed ready to push the subject.

"Unfortunately, with the severity of recent attacks and the high-profile victims, I believe so. It's a liability for the Agency if we don't take necessary actions to protect anyone believed to be a target."

"So, what does that involve? An escort to and from work, around town?" she asked.

Ethan contemplated how much to trust the feeling in his gut. He wanted someone with her, at all times, keeping her in sight unless she was dressing or in the shower. He didn't want to admit it, but he wanted it to be him. He just wasn't sure how to get the bandwidth, how to justify it, or if she would accept it.

"How rigorous is your schedule? You said you travel a lot?"

"Yes, after I finish surgery tomorrow, I have a day off, then office work in San Jose, then I report to LPCH for a couple of days, from there I spend a week in Laredo before traveling to Cleveland for a clinical trial follow up."

"It's going to be hard to keep an agent with you at all times with that schedule, is there anything you can cancel or put off for now?" he asked.

She shot him an indignant look that could have sliced an apple and sat up in her chair.

"No, Agent Hartman. My life isn't congruent with canceling on children dying of cancer." Her tone was sharp and held more genuine distaste than mocking, but the acidity of it was there, beneath the surface.

Theresa piped up beside her, "You could get Dr. Tremble to cover your cases in San Jose, if it's something that absolutely requires your attention, you're back here in seventeen days, it could wait, and you know it. If you can reschedule for a wedding, or a funeral, you can reschedule to keep your head attached."

Again, Aurora looked scolded and annoyed with the logic.

"So am I to understand that I am to cancel on the patients I can so someone can sit outside of my house in a car eating fast food?"

She was going to be a challenge; he could see that already. People like this slipped their detail without a second thought and became more hassle than they were worth. Only, he felt pretty sure, in this case, she was worth it.

"What I would prefer is that you have an agent with you at all times, not in a car, but at your shoulder. We typically set up a hotel room, move people around as needed to keep a decent level of anonymity and security." He could see her face turning to frown, and was anticipating her rejection. "In your case, with your specific line of work, I would be willing to accommodate someone staying at home with you—if you'll allow that of course—instead of displacing you to a hotel. Since you're confident your residences aren't easy to track using your name, and it seems the suspect has already proven you're difficult to locate by sending correspondence to the hospital, there's some wiggle room."

Theresa squeezed her hands and put a comforting arm around her, leaning to rest her forehead on Aurora's shoulder. She still seemed hesitant.

"Prunelle de mes yeux," Theresa whispered, and Aurora sighed. *Apple of my eye.* Leaning her head against Theresa's, they looked like dear inseparable friends.

"Pour toi, Tee-ta, seulement pour toi," Aurora said. *For you, Theresa, only for you.* Aurora tilted her head, spilling her gorgeous brunette hair in front of her as she kissed Theresa on the temple before turning to Ethan. *I'm going to have to work on learning French*, Ethan thought to himself.

"So, if I accept what next?" she asked him point-blank.

"I'll look into assigning someone right away."

"It won't help me sleep any better; nothing will. Lord, there aren't enough prayers." Theresa stood up from the table, clutching her chest.

"In the meantime," Ethan said, "I can give you my cell phone number. Please pay extra attention to people around you, cars around you, anyone parked where they shouldn't be for too long, so on and so forth. If anything suspicious occurs before I can get an agent assigned, call me directly and personally, first."

He searched the room for a piece of paper to write on, and to his surprise, Aurora produced her cell phone from a pocket of her scrubs, unlocked it, and handed it to him.

"Just put it in here, I'll lose it if you write it down anyway," she said.

Theresa had gone back to wringing her hands. "Perhaps I should come to stay? It wouldn't hurt, would it?" she asked.

"No offense, Mrs. Thirston, but having extra bodies in harm's way isn't my favorite idea. I would prefer that you not accompany her." He finished typing his number into her phone, called himself quickly, and hung up. At least then, he could contact her or would know when it was her calling if she had to call.

"Alright, well, thank you, Agent Hartman. I very much appreciate everything." Theresa held out one of her weathered, arthritic hands, and when he shook it, she closed the other around his. They were warm, soft as silk, and slightly squishy.

"When can I expect to see someone? Will you let me know when they are on the way, so I'm not surprised by their arrival?" Aurora was tying her hair back again, straightening her scrub bottoms from slouching.

"Yes, I'll call, and if I can't get someone assigned tonight, I'll be joining you myself. Might I have the address where you're staying at the moment?" Ethan asked.

She raised her eyebrows intrigued at the idea but didn't seem put off.

"I'll text it to you. I'll look forward to hearing from you this evening. Until then…" She extended her hand to shake again, and he couldn't deny that for a split second, he lost himself in her eyes before letting go of her hand.

"I'll be in touch," he replied.

"I'll show you out, follow me please." Theresa led him back through the patient portion of the surgical area while Aurora disappeared down the staff hallway.

"Just so I feel comfortable about certain parts of her daily routine, there are adequate security precautions in place here at the hospital, yes?" Ethan asked Theresa as they made their way back out of the building towards the parking garage.

"Yes, I believe so. If you leave me an email address, I can forward contacts for our security department. They would be able to provide more detail." As they walked, she pointed out cameras, where doors automatically closed if codes were called, emergency exits, and other limited details she knew from routine orientation. She talked his ear off, knowledgeable, and confident.

As she bid him goodbye, she unexpectedly hugged him, a warm and genuinely affectionate embrace that caught him off guard.

"If there's someone who has to be in charge of this, seeing her safe, chasing this lunatic, I'm glad it's you. I trust my instincts, and right now, they're telling me you are of excellent character. Of course, let me know if I can do anything for you at all." She smiled sweetly, and as she walked away, he could see her pace had changed from brisk to sturdier and more relaxed. Now he only had to get Dr. Soileaux to be just as relaxed.

Chapter Three

Aurora marched down the staff hallway back towards the elevators on the way up to a staff dictation room. She had mounds of charting to catch up on, results to check, patient charts to review for tomorrow, and it was already nearly six o'clock. She wished she had some green tea, the authentic kind, with a lot of caffeine.

Standing at the elevator, in an empty hallway, a chill ran down her spine at the thought that Theresa and the FBI Agent could be right. Could someone really be after her next in this ridiculous murder spree? Suddenly standing alone in the hallway was daunting, and she thought perhaps she should extend more of a welcome to the agent who would be assigned to protect her. If protecting her was even possible.

As a plus for her, if she had to have a protective detail, Agent Hartman was at least easy on the eyes. With his short, curly, chestnut brown hair, deep-set dark chocolate eyes, and muscular build, she thought she could keep an eye on him as well as he could keep an eye on her. Lost in thought, she recalled how he towered over her when he stood to shake her hand, how broad his shoulders were on sturdy hips and how thick his neck was right up to the muscles of his jaw behind a strong square-framed chin.

There had been something about him, something that though authoritative, wasn't forceful. Aurora knew he could probably force her to cooperate, but he let her agree willingly.

Respect was a significant deal to her. As a woman in a man's world, not having to demand it was attractive.

She cruised into the dictation room and grabbed a bottle of water from the mini-fridge at one end, admiring the shadows thrown across the bay by the sinking sun. The picture window spread out wall to wall behind a row of computers. How did they expect anyone to focus on work with that view?

Plunking herself down in a squeaky, rolling office chair, she logged onto the computer and committed herself to tasks at hand.

Though she flew through documentation and review at her typical focused pace, she couldn't help but stop to ponder, at points, if any of these patients were related to the Hypocrite case. Could she really have been at fault for something that would make a person angry enough to kill?

Her mind drifted away, mentally flipping through patients she had seen over the years. Her patients were always higher acuity, some of the sickest kids in the country, and usually with a poor expected outcome by the time they reached her. The possibilities were endless for someone to have been so depressed they would act out violently. The idea made her skin crawl.

As the sun sank, so did her energy levels. By the time an hour had flown past, she had the bulk of her duties completed and was starving, thoroughly, growling and grumbling, *hangry* starving. Glancing out over the bay, she could see the twinkling lights of Oakland were just starting to show in the fading twilight, cars clogging the bay bridge as late commuters fought with traffic.

It was time to call it a night, but the first thought on her mind besides her hunger was leaving the building alone. For some reason, she had expected to hear back from Agent Hartman sooner, leaving her thinking perhaps the threat wasn't as real as he described. Her steps were light as she bounced down the hallway to the locker room to change. The last thing she wanted to do was let the whole situation get her down.

As she changed clothes, she checked her phone and though she had expected him to contact her, was still surprised to see a text.

'Address?' Was merely all he sent. She shot him a quick reply with the address for the King Street apartment she planned on staying at tonight, suddenly nervous about making the brief ten-minute walk from the hospital. Like he read her mind, a reply came before she was on the ground floor.

'Walking?' He replied.

'Planning on it.' Shot off her fingers to him as she crossed the main lobby. Perhaps she would make her way to Little Skillet on her walk and grab a bite to eat while she waited for her impending shadow to arrive. The restaurant was a couple of blocks out of her way, but it was one of her favorites, and she'd been inside all day, the walk would do her good. The air was crisp, smelled clean in the whipping wind, and fog instantly dampened her cheeks as she

walked through the spotless sliding glass doors glancing over her shoulder. She wasn't paranoid, but she knew when to follow instructions.

Having an almost photographic memory couldn't hurt. She took mental notes of people behind her and crossing the street away from the hospital as she exited. There was no one she recognized, certainly no one that seemed to be paying any attention to her. Outside she turned left and headed out Third Street towards Townsend. Her stomach was calling for her favorite pulled pork.

Her phone buzzed in her pocket as she crossed at the signal. *'Do me a solid, share your GPS location? Are you headed straight home?'* Back on the curb, she tapped the info button at the top of the text thread and shared her location indefinitely. It couldn't hurt, she thought, he was a Fed after all.

She replied, *'Grabbing a bite at little skillet, then headed home.'*

The bay smelled of the familiar, slightly rotting fish with the usual faint hue of garbage as she crossed the bridge. *Why does it still feel so fresh?* She wondered. She loved the sound of the water lapping the walls of the inlet, and a roar came from the ballpark. Probably a home run, based on the sounds, making her smile. At Berry Street, she glanced around again, still no frightening faces. She made her way towards Townsend, and when she hung a left rechecked her surroundings, but saw nothing out of the ordinary. It never occurred to her to keep an eye on vehicles around her.

By the time she was strolling into the restaurant, waving at her favorite server, she was famished, and light-headed even. She peeled off her thin windbreaker and parked herself at the bar. Within ninety seconds, a glass of Cabernet arrived, and a wink from the bartender told her it would be on the house, as usual. She laid her phone on the bar and saw a new message had come in.

'I'll meet you at the restaurant, don't leave without me.' A slight twinge of a smile came across her face as she was pleased if someone had to follow her around like she was royalty at least he was eye candy.

She made small talk with Curtis, the bartender, and Carlie, the waitress, and watched the news and latest stats for the Giants as she devoured her BBQ Pork Sandwich with extra pickles. At the thirty-minute mark, a tall man in a black motorcycle jacket planted himself in the seat beside her, startling her out of her skin. She wasn't expecting Agent Hartman to arrive looking anything less than the professional FBI Agent he was. She quickly wiped her face with her napkin for fear of being covered in barbeque sauce.

"Am I supposed to shake your hand and act professional every time I see you?" she asked. The one glass of wine had her tongue loose, but he smiled. A crooked, dimple laden, genuine smile that had something in her fluttering.

"You could, but you don't have to. I'll try to be seen and not heard most of the time. Hopefully, I won't be around long enough for you to get tired of it," his dark eyes twinkled.

"Would you like food or a beer?" she asked.

"I'm technically on duty, so on the beer, thank you, but no thank you, and I already ate." He had grabbed a burrito on his way back to the office so he could focus on getting orders completed for her before the end of day deadline.

"Does that mean you can be my designated driver until no one is worried about me dying anymore?" She winked at him and waved off the ensuing comment as she was joking. "I'm kidding, and really, I appreciate whatever the government has to invest in me, I'll try not to take advantage of it, I promise."

"I don't mind being your ride once in a while, as long as you don't mind the motorcycle."

She laughed, "I'm not really a motorcycle kind of person. You know what they call motorcycles in my line of work, don't you?"

"Donor cycles, right?" he had heard it before.

She nodded before tilting her head back to finish the glass of wine. The restaurant had become crowded as the evening progressed and was now playing loud music and filled with boisterous laughter. She had to lean close to him to hear what he was saying and picked up an edgy, sexy scent.

"The bill is paid. If you're not going to eat, we can go any time you like."

"I'm ready when you are. Can I convince you to join me on the bike for the three blocks to your apartment?"

"Not a snowball's chance in hell, my friend." She tilted her head, and jovially laughed as she stood up and began to put her windbreaker on.

"Even if I let you have my helmet and promise to keep it under ninety?"

"What kind of bike?" She eyed him skeptically, and the thought was tempting, it was getting chilly out.

"Ducati Monster." He winced at the face she made, but as he held the door for her and the burst of crisp air hit her, along with the bumper to bumper traffic, he could see her shoulders shrug in silent consent. "I promise I haven't killed anyone in days."

She glanced over her shoulder with a sparkling smile, laughing as he followed her outside, and he resisted the urge to wink in an attempt to stay professional.

Crap, I'm going to have to watch it with this one.

"It's only a couple of blocks, so I guess just this once, but don't think it's going to be a habit," she shook her head at him.

"Noted." He looked around the poorly lit street, hovering over her shoulder, examining cars and passersby for a potential threat. Nothing seemed obvious, but he took quick stock of car colors and models anyway. Turning towards where he had parked on Clyde, the hair on the back of his neck stood up, though he wasn't sure from what, his instincts were telling him to stay alert. He planted his hand lightly in the middle of Aurora's back, urging her to walk more quickly through the dimly lit alley.

"How long have you ridden a motorcycle?" she asked in an attempt to make small talk.

"I've been *driving* a motorcycle of one form or another since I was about four, old enough to manage a 50cc dirt bike clutch."

"Really?" She was thoroughly shocked, not expecting to hear that at all.

"Yes, really. My brothers and I camped and rode trails constantly up in Mendocino county. I wanted to keep the first race bike my dad saved to buy me in my bedroom. I loved it so much." The thought of him as a child with a dirt bike in his bedroom made her laugh and put her more at ease.

"Well, I suppose that's good to know, at least with that kind of experience I feel safer you won't kill me." He laughed as they reached the bike where he unlocked and handed her his helmet.

"You know how to strap this, yes?"

"I've never been on a motorcycle and have never used a helmet like this, so sadly, no. Though I'm fairly intelligent so I think I can figure it out." The grin that spread across his face had her giggling. "Don't judge, you're lucky I'm doing this at all, I barely know you."

"I'm not judging, take your ponytail out and come here." He helped her slide the helmet on and adjust the straps, it was far too large for her but would be better than nothing in a pinch, if worse came to worst. As she wiggled it, slipping her fingers around to make her hair more comfortable, he swung onto the bike and lifted the kickstand. As he started the engine, she jumped a little and was glad he couldn't see her face with the helmet on.

He shook his head, grinning while he zipped up his jacket and said, "Trust me, you'll be ok." He extended his hand to help steady her as she climbed on behind him. Wrapping her arms around him, she realized just how big he was. She could barely clasp her fingers around him in the front.

"I suppose, in my situation, I'm going to have to learn to trust you with more than a motorcycle ride, so I may as well get started somewhere." She could feel his chest tighten as he laughed, but the purr of the engine drowned out the sound of his voice as he shifted into gear and started down the alley. They weren't even going twenty miles per hour, but her heart jumped at the sight of the ground zipping away beneath them. When he turned to pull into traffic, she found she had begun to squeeze him tight without realizing it.

Her stomach bubbled and fluttered, but by the third turn at their destination, she found herself unbelievably enjoying the feel of being behind him. He paused at the opening to the parking garage.

"Do you have a pass to get in?"

She was already peeling off the gear and dismounting. Handing over the helmet, she said, "I do have a pass, but because I walk so often, I keep it in my car, which of course, is already inside. Let me have someone at the desk let you in, and I'll meet you by the elevator inside."

She darted away, disappearing around the corner towards the lobby. Ethan waited only a minute before a car pulling up behind him triggered the gate. He pulled in and parked, at just after eight-thirty, full darkness setting in, shadows playing tricks on his eyes. A hint of urgency trickled over him as he slipped his backpack over one shoulder.

In the elevator, he got the first hint at what was ahead of him upstairs. The immaculately clean, chrome adorned, mirrored interior had some kind of iridescent stone for buttons. He punched the number for the lobby and was impressed by how quickly it took off. At the first step inside, he had a passing fear someone might mistake him for a less than welcome guest in his black, rough-looking attire.

The first thing he noticed in the empty gallery was that Aurora was nowhere in sight. His first thought, glancing back at the elevator, was that there was no way she went up without him. He broke into a swift step, and around the corner saw she was still not in sight of the front doors. He immediately asked the desk clerk in a loud voice, "Aurora Soileaux—has she been here?"

"Dr. S? No, I haven't seen her tonight," the clerk answered.

"She wasn't here two minutes ago asking for you to open the garage gate for a guest?" Ethan demanded and his pulse started to race.

"No, I haven't moved in twenty minutes, the last person I saw was Mr. Templeton leaving. May I ask what you're doing here, sir?"

Ethan dropped his helmet and backpack and dashed towards the doors yelling back, "I'm FBI! If you have security cameras, find her now! Call the police!"

The desk clerk immediately turned three shades of pale, his mouth falling open as he grabbed a set of keys and scurried towards an office behind the counter. Ethan shoved the doors open so hard he thought they might slam and shatter behind him. Out on the sidewalk, he turned away from the direction of the parking garage and began to run at full speed. Scanning cars from the restaurant paid off. At the corner, he caught a glimpse of a charcoal grey Toyota Avalon. An average height, robust man was accompanying a petite woman who appeared to need his assistance. She had one arm around his neck, and his arm circled her waist. It was Aurora.

"Freeze! Federal agent!"

The man spun around at the sound of Ethan's voice. Aurora flopped, clearly unconscious in his arm when he swung around. As Ethan bolted towards them, he could see dark hair, dark complexion, and a mustache, but in the low light, he couldn't make out features. Realizing Ethan would reach him before he could accomplish getting Aurora into the car, he roughly dropped her and fled. The assailant was across the street, gone, lost in the crowd before Ethan reached her.

A split-second observation of the situation left him with a losing hand. He couldn't leave her unconscious and vulnerable in the street, but he needed that suspect. He knew, in his gut, it was the Hypocrite killer—but he couldn't prove it unless he caught him.

Kneeling beside her, he drew his gun from beneath his jacket and aimed, but there were too many people. The baseball game was letting out, and with traffic and pedestrians flooding the streets, he didn't have a chance. All that was left to do was ensure Aurora was alright. He straightened her head out and felt for a pulse. She was breathing, but her heart rate was rapid and felt irregular.

"Aurora?" he spoke to her, tapping her cheek gently. "Aurora, can you hear me?" Nothing. She was out cold. Sirens blared not far from them, and a need to get off the street hastened him. He scooped her up from the sidewalk and dashed back inside, somehow surprised how light she was. With her tiny figure limp in his arms, his heart thundered. *How in the hell did this happen so fast?* He asked himself. Pushing through the glass doors, two wary and skeptical security guards met him.

"Sir, we need to see some identification," one guard demanded without confidence. Ethan ignored him, pushing past to deposit Aurora on a nearby couch.

"We'll deal with identification after I know she's alright. Only the authorities are to enter or leave this building without my consent, do you understand? Tell them we need an ambulance and lock it down, now." The desk clerk was still on the phone and stuttered instructions as Ethan brushed the hair back from Aurora's face, it was pale, and her breathing was shallow.

"Come on, talk to me, wake up," he began to unzip her jacket to check for wounds. He wondered if she was drugged, began to check for needle marks when she stirred.

"Hey, over here, wake up, Aurora," he spoke gently to her. Seated beside her, he leaned over her, still running his hands along her shoulders and arms looking for a wound. Her eyes opened, her arms flew up defensively, and he caught her left hand barely short of scratching him in the face.

"Easy, easy, relax, you're alright." He pulled her arms in close to him as her eyes began to focus, searching bewildered for reality as only waking from forced unconsciousness causes. She gasped and tried to sit up, clearly disoriented and weak, but he breathed a sigh of relief.

"Can you hear me?" he asked.

Her head swam. A ringing in her ears hushed the sounds of the world around her, and her blurred vision strained to clear. Ethan's large, warm hands were the first things she recognized. Two figures also dressed in black hovered behind him, and sirens blared louder. Everything tingled, her face, her lips, her arms, her hands were shaky and felt almost numb, and there was a pain in her side she couldn't explain. All she knew was she was with someone she recognized, and the trust he had earned on the short ride home had already proven crucial.

"My side," she managed to gasp out as she tried to shift to take the pressure off the stabbing pain. His hand quickly slid, welcome or not, up under her top and raised it so he could see. On her left side was a bright red, well defined slight burn mark from a taser.

Shit, Ethan thought, *that was too close for comfort.* He leaned on her while he fished out his ID and handed it to one of the security guards. Her fingers wrapped around his arm, startling him.

"I'm FBI Special Agent Hartman. I'm managing protective duty for Dr. Soileaux until further notice. I need you to help me get her into her apartment. When the police and ambulance arrive, send them up, I want her out of sight." The security guard handed him back his ID and nodded at the desk agent before heading for the elevator. Aurora still squirmed uncomfortably on the couch beside him, clinging to his forearm.

"Yes, sir. Follow me," he said. Ethan scooped Aurora off the couch. She panted and made little noises as if she were struggling to breathe.

"Hold on, we're almost home," Ethan said. "Grab my helmet and backpack." He barked at the other security guard who obediently dashed over to retrieve his things. Flashing red and blue lights streamed in from the floor to ceiling glass windows facing the street as the sirens closed in, but Ethan ignored them. The desk clerk shouted out a number, and the guard pushed a button for the twenty-third floor.

"What happened to her?" The guard asked.

"Stun gun, and attempted abduction," Ethan left it at that. He wasn't in any mood to give out information to a rent a cop.

"We have the building locked down. Do we need to add an extra person for tonight?"

"As long as she is here, I recommend adding an extra person until further notice," Ethan said.

The doors opened, and the guard led them out to the left and down the hall to a corner door. Much later, Ethan would look back on that moment and realize had he not been preoccupied with the stress of the situation he might have felt overwhelmingly out of place. The apartment was incredible, down to every detail. From the granite countertops to the slate tile flooring to the view through floor to ceiling and wall to wall windows in the living room, it was breathtaking. Focused as he was, he raced across to barge into what looked like it would be the bedroom.

"Agent!" Aurora gasped and stuttered. Her tongue didn't seem to want to cooperate with her brain. "I feel sick. I think I have to be sick." Her head swam, she felt dizzy, and she was sure she was seconds from vomiting on the hot FBI Agent whose first name, at the moment, was frustratingly escaping her.

While the security guards lagged, Ethan pushed the door to the bedroom open with his foot and darted for the bathroom, feeling grateful she was so light and easy to carry. Sliding in sideways, he set her on the floor beside the toilet as gently as he could, and she hung onto the sides just in time to vomit.

She heaved and heaved, and was glad her autonomous nervous system was still intact and functioning because the rest of her body wasn't cooperating. She tried clumsily and in vain to keep herself upright unsuccessfully and was thankful Ethan stayed with her, cradling her firm but gentle as her body retaliated against the vicious jolt of electricity she had endured. Before she was finished, breathless and weak, paramedics swarmed her bathroom.

As she sprawled out flat onto the floor, sweating and still feeling randomly numb, they began checking her vitals. Head swimming, ears still ringing, stomach doing hula hoops around her belly button, she succumbed to their care. For only a fraction of a minute, she had another jolt of anxiety as Ethan's voice faded into the bedroom before she again became unconscious.

Ethan pulled out his cell phone as he stormed back into the living room. With paramedics tending to Aurora, he wanted to get as close as he could to nailing this asshole. While he was dialing FBI backup, he barked orders at the security guards and the police who had just arrived.

"Put a canvas out for a male, approximately five foot ten, dark hair, skin, and eyes with a thick mustache. He was wearing a dark blue hooded blazer and jeans with black sneakers and was driving the Avalon parked across the street. I want security footage pulled for the last hour, and I want that Avalon dusted for prints ASAP, an FBI unit will be here shortly, keep the scene secure." Authority boomed in his typically mild voice, and before Tom answered the phone, everyone was in action.

"What's up, boss?" Tom sounded alert and ready for a task.

"There's been an attempted abduction on doctor Soileaux. I need a forensic team here ASAP." Ethan wanted his guys to beat the locals to the punch. Things got messy, having too many hands in the cookie jar.

"Right away, boss. What happened? Where am I sending a unit?"

"I don't even know the address, just dispatch to my location. There's a Toyota Avalon across the street that needs to be dusted for prints and run the plates, local LEO's are down there now. The guy took off into the crowd. I want the area canvassed thoroughly. He has to be close still, but he knows we're on his tail. I need security footage pulled, and you have full cooperation from the building staff. Make it happen, ok, Quillet? I have other things I need to focus on."

"Is the doc ok?"

"They're checking her out now, but she's alive, that's what counts."

"Good job, boss, I'll see you shortly," Tom hung up before even waiting for a reply. After covering a few more bases with local PD and getting a canvas set up for the area to try and snag the guy who wanted to snatch Aurora, Ethan headed back to check on her. She had managed, with the help of the paramedics, to navigate into bed to rest. Blood pressure cuff on, and pulse oximeter attached to a finger, her color was starting to return.

"How are you feeling Doctor?" Ethan asked as the paramedic shot him a quizzical expression, unaware he was treating a physician.

She took a deep breath and exhaled sharply, "Sore, scared, shocked, glad I'm alive, thanks to you." She smiled weakly, her honey-toned eyes beginning to clear.

"Glad I could be of service," Ethan grinned.

"Oh, it was more than that, and I think you know it. Isn't that why you decided to come today, and not send anyone else?" She hadn't lost a beat in all the panic. She propped herself up on a couple of pillows and tried to shoo away the paramedic.

"I recommend you let us take you to a hospital, ma'am, you've had quite a jolt based on the wound on your ribs, and with the subsequent symptoms overnight observation wouldn't be a bad idea." The young paramedic seemed to want to hold his ground.

"Don't call me ma'am, its' Dr. Soileaux, and I know, just from listening to you, that my vitals are stable, and I'm otherwise young and healthy. I know it's your job to try to convince me to go, but there's nothing else a hospital room can offer me. Thank you for your service. I appreciate everything, now please get out of my bedroom."

The paramedic looked shocked but dutifully wrapped up the medical supplies into a case. As they both readied to leave, Ethan couldn't help but lean in to whisper, "I'll call if she needs it whether she wants me to or not, if it makes you feel any better."

With the medical team cleared out, the local police working on securing the scene, an FBI team on the way, and building security busy dealing with all of it, Ethan took advantage of the calm before the storm. For the first time, he looked around the room, admiring what he saw. Its decoration was lavish, in deep hues of gold and purple, with the same floor to ceiling windows, every inch incredibly stylish and immaculately clean. He knew doctors made good money, but this was extravagant.

As if aware he was surveying the space in awe as he stood by the bed, Aurora stirred him by brushing her hand lightly over his arm.

"Thank you for tonight. I'm glad I wasn't more of a pain in the ass earlier because I'm pretty sure I'd be in someone's trunk on the way to my own grave right now," she squeezed his forearm gently.

"It's my job, but I'm glad you're safe. I'm only pissed I couldn't get a hold of the asshole."

"You will."

"I hope," he paused and considered her state of mind, "so, not that I want to invade your personal space, or add to your trauma in any way, but I need a photo of that mark. May I?" he waved his cell phone.

"I'd prefer not. Why?"

"Because different brands of taser leave different burn marks and if we're lucky we can pinpoint the model based upon the marks it left. I need to take a picture."

"You're truly going to find this guy based on taser marks?" she asked skeptically, frowning.

"No. But we might nail the bastard with a combination of the car with plates, taser in his possession, and fingerprints, among other things. It's always a web, never a smoking gun that convicts a person. If we find a guy with the same kind of taser, it's a good lead. If you're uncomfortable with me doing it, I would be happy to get the paramedics back."

There's that respect thing again, she thought. His mellow demeanor made her want to cooperate.

He patiently waited for her to consider the situation and was relieved when she rolled on her side and gingerly lifted her shirt partway, allowing him to observe the burn. He lifted it the rest of the way with only one finger, never actually touching her skin, and with his cell phone snapped a couple of quick up-close photos. It wasn't awful, but he was sure it would throb through the night.

"Thank you, get some rest, and I'll be back in a bit. I'll have someone posted to the door while I deal with the details downstairs." He turned to leave, and she took a breath as if to say something, causing him to pause. When she stayed silent, he simply said, "I won't be long, I need to get your statement documented too," and was gone.

She nodded, but a pang of worry washed over her to think he would be out of earshot. Burying the anxiety as best she could, she pulled the lavender-hued satin comforter over herself. Tingling was still coursing oddly through her limbs, and when she moved, nausea surged up. She remained light-headed, and she was regretting the large dinner and red wine, now that she had violently expelled it. Her mind wasn't agreeable to sleep, but her body was winning the battle as she began to doze and drift.

Chapter Four

By the time Ethan got back downstairs, the place was crawling with uniforms. Multiple police cruisers were parked in the alley and out front of the Avalon apartments. The young and naïve desk clerk still looked as if he'd seen a ghost and was overwhelmed by the incident. Tom Quillet was diligently interviewing the security guards and had efficiently dispatched a forensic team, and Ethan could see the white vans parked out front.

"What do we have so far?" Ethan asked Tom without typical greeting pleasantries.

"About twenty uniforms canvassing the area, five of our own organizing the pattern—we blocked off the three streets leading away from the alley based on security footage showing the direction he ran. The Toyota appears abandoned and didn't have much inside; the techs are sweeping it now. We'll have it towed, obviously. We've interviewed and screened a few people off the street who might have been witness, and three residents that were coming in and out in the last fifteen minutes or so, no solid leads or anything suspicious. Did you get a statement from the doctor yet?"

"I think she needs some rest, passed out again upstairs. She was still pretty pale, puked her guts out. She'll need some time for the fog to clear. I have photos though, of the mark, bastard used a stun gun." Ethan took out his phone and showed Tom the pictures before sending them to him.

"Nasty, that doesn't look like a normal taser burn."

"Agreed. It looks to me like it was set on high, and someone tampered with it. She's lucky she had a couple of layers of clothes on."

"She's lucky you were here."

"I don't know. I'm pissed. I should have had the prick. I don't know how I knew, but as soon as I left the hospital today, I knew I shouldn't have gone back to the office." Ethan tensed, felt angry, and responsible.

"Not your fault, boss, you saved the day. Thanks to you, we have living victim number two. By the way, the last one in Portland," Tom paused, hesitant and proceeding with caution, "we got a call late today, she took a turn for the worse. She started having seizures of some kind, and they're not sure she's going to make it."

"Son of a bitch," Ethan's stomach dropped, and his chest tightened. He could have had the bastard tonight. He *should* have had him tonight.

"I'll keep you informed of any changes," Tom fidgeted. He knew from working with Ethan for almost five years how he was internalizing everything.

"Alright. Do we have a link into BART and the busses, metro? Is anyone keeping an eye out on the transit cams?"

"Yep, I assigned one person at each entrance and stop within five miles in case the guy hopped an Uber before hopping a train. I'll make sure we get copies of the tapes too. I'll get The Fourth to start a file on facial recognition based on the security footage here, and maybe we'll get lucky and get a full-face shot." The FBI team in charge of cyber investigation was on the fourth floor of the FBI's main office on Golden Avenue. Agents in the building had, endearingly, begun to refer to them as 'The Fourth' after closing a big case one day in May. A joke circulated afterward titled '*may the fourth, floor, be with you.*' It had stuck.

"Good idea."

They chatted about a few other basic, routine requirements and details before Ethan headed back upstairs, glad he'd chosen Tom as his right-hand man. He had been missing Allie sorely with such a complicated new case, but Tom had absorbed her workload nicely, caught details he hadn't expected. He knew he would have to get to interviews to replace Allie sometime soon, but it occurred to him now with how well Tom was handling things, that perhaps he should let Tom do the interviews to choose someone.

Back upstairs, he relieved the uniform at Aurora's open door and slipped in quietly. Peeking into the bedroom, he noticed she had wrapped up and appeared asleep, allowing him a short reprieve. Pulling out his laptop and setting up at an oversized glass dining table with black wrought iron bottom resembling curling bramble, he mentally ran through the checklist of forms to file to get the incident adequately documented.

As the laptop booted up, he walked around a bit and studied his surroundings. The apartment, with its breathtaking views of the Bay Bridge and East Bay, was the largest he'd seen in the city. Aside from the bedroom Aurora was in, there were five more down a hallway, including one that appeared to be another master that took up the corner. The rooms flanked the side of the building to take full advantage of the view, and each had the same floor to ceiling windows. The decorating was all modern with either ornately designed interlocking hardwood floors of varying colors or top of the line stone tile.

Each room had a different color scheme, but all seemed to share warm golden hues tying them together. Overhead lighting, thermostat, and wall fixtures were all controlled by a shared smart home system, and panels glowed automatically in anticipation of orders as he walked from room to room. Bathrooms adjoined the rooms either dedicated to one, or shared Jack and Jill style, and all had heated floors, bidet, and showers boasting seats beneath multiple showerheads. In the second master bathroom was a tub with high tech jets and three fill faucets that Ethan imagined could comfortably bathe a baby elephant.

Very few personal items were to be found anywhere in the rooms or bathrooms, but the closets were nearly full, all with women's clothing though upon quick inspection some of the clothes seemed much too large for Aurora and some too short. In the medicine cabinets in the bathrooms were typical hygiene items, but they all lacked any kind of personal medication or other labeled items. The apartment, though it seemed she frequented alone, didn't appear to be often occupied otherwise.

Common areas were lavish with leather couches and recliners, televisions the size of most garage doors, and wall after wall of books and art. The place could have refilled a city library if the need arose. Rooms with hard floors had large plush rugs soft enough to sleep on, and other rooms had deep luxurious carpet. He wondered if he should have left his shoes at the door.

Back in the living room, he admired the open kitchen with its stainless steel appliances and marbled black and grey granite countertops with gold flecking. It looked barely used, not a dirty dish or crumb on the counter. Out of curiosity, he opened the dishwasher and wasn't surprised to find it empty. He looked next into the refrigerator and found mostly minimum essentials like milk, condiments, sodas and bottled water, and a few pieces of fresh produce to make a salad. It was almost like Aurora didn't live here, or at least spent very little time here.

He sat back at his laptop and logged on. It was after ten o'clock, and he had a lot to get through, first and most importantly, now that things had died down, would be Aurora's statement. He hated having to wake her, but it was imperative he got the details straight before she lost them. He opened a couple of forms and filled in minimal information to save time before knocking on the half-open bedroom door. He wasn't surprised right away that she didn't answer.

"Aurora?" he asked in a voice loud enough to wake her but hopefully not enough to startle her. She didn't move.

"Dr. Soileaux, I'm sorry to wake you, but I have some questions we have to get through." She still didn't stir, and his heart skipped a beat. Approaching her, he could at least hear her breathing, and she appeared fast asleep. He put his hand on her shoulder and shook her lightly, concerned when she was difficult to rouse. Her sleepy eyes strained to open, and even with how tired she looked, he could sense the worry in them.

"Aurora, are you feeling alright?" he asked as he squeezed her hands and rubbed her arms. Her eyelids were heavy, and she seemed to be struggling to wake up, reaching for him, her grip was weak. She rubbed her face and seemed drowsy, almost drugged. As she flipped the blankets off of her, he could tell she had been too warm.

"I feel nauseated again," she said sleepily, almost slurring, "can you help me up?"

"Sure," he helped her sit up, noticing her skin felt clammy. She leaned heavily on him as she tried to swing her legs off the side of the bed.

"Do you see a lot of taser victims?" she asked.

"I have in the past, my fair share."

"Do they get this many side effects? I felt better earlier, and now I feel worse." She started to stand up and swayed, clinging to him, grateful for his arm around her waist.

"It's not typical, no, but I don't think this taser was typical. I think he tampered with it." He helped her into the bathroom, realizing she wasn't capable of walking entirely on her own.

"Set me there," she pointed beside the toilet. She had broken out in a full sweat, but she felt cold and sank onto the tile, unable to sit up straight.

"Do you need me to call someone?" he asked, unwilling to completely let her go.

"I don't know yet, give me a minute. I think I just need to be sick again." She did her best to prop herself near the toilet, but even with both hands hanging on, she struggled to sit up. "My side, it hurts so much worse than I think it should."

"Can I take a look?" he asked.

She nodded, almost shy, "I guess so, sure." He lifted her shirt, and to his horror, the taser wound had swelled considerably and around it was a sizeable purple ring.

"I think it's time we call someone. I have never seen a taser wound do this," he brushed his fingers lightly over her side, and she winced.

"Hold up, let me get my bearings a little, that's a reaction to some kind of poison." She released her grip on the porcelain basin and sank to the floor, one arm draped over his knee as she continued to count on him to steady her.

"Poison?" he questioned. "And… we are waiting to call someone, why?"

She relaxed onto the floor, her face flush and damp with perspiration, holding onto him.

"It's localized, like a spider bite, and I'm probably just having some measure of anaphylaxis. A simple antihistamine might do the trick."

"Sorry, I don't speak doctor. Is ana-whatever serious? Do you have what you need here? You're worrying me."

She inhaled sharply, patted his hand, and said, "in the drawer—the far left-hand side there, you'll find diphenhydramine capsules, bring me one." Dutifully he got up and opened the drawer, fishing around amidst multiple boxes of medication. Here, he thought, was the proof she stayed at the apartment at least somewhat regularly. "It's in a pink box," she said.

"This one?" he held it up, and she nodded, "do you need water to swallow it with?"

"Ha," she huffed, "no, just bring me a capsule. I need you to open it and spill the powder underneath my tongue. I don't think I have the dexterity at the moment." Though he raised his eyebrows in doubt, he did as she requested. As he knelt beside her, she pushed herself up, halfway on one arm.

"Pull the pink and white apart but hold it vertical and try not to spill before you sprinkle." She opened her mouth, and though he would have preferred calling a paramedic, he dumped the powder as best he could beneath her tongue. She grimaced, squishing up her face in reaction to what was clearly a terrible taste, but held her mouth closed as she lay down on her side.

"What is that supposed to do?" he asked, trying to casually hold her wrist as he kept track of her pulse.

"It enters the bloodstream faster sublingually. It will halt whatever is going on sooner this way." Her speech was garbled, trying not to disturb the medication.

"And, dare I ask, do you know what is going on?"

She looked at him, rolling her eyes, not wanting to have to explain at the moment but understanding his anxiety.

"I know enough. I don't know what's causing it, but the symptoms are clear. There was something on that taser, something meant as a catalyst. Any ideas, Mr. FBI?"

"No, that's not my department, but I've got a guy. You want me to call him?"

"Let's not and say we did."

"As long as you stay conscious, I'll let you have some say, but if you pass out again, I get to make the decision, deal?"

"Deal."

He kicked off his shoes and sat beside her, quiet for a time, listening to her breathing, keeping track of her pulse. It was uncharted territory for him. Had it been anyone else, without a medical degree, he would have called an ambulance regardless of protest. With her, it was different. She had to know what she was up against and understand it as well as anyone he could take her to. It occurred to him that he was going to have to learn to trust her as much as she was going to have to learn to trust him.

After a few minutes, her breathing seemed to be less labored, her color was returning to a healthy rosy pink, and her pulse was slowing. She seemed more at ease, eyes still closed, calm flat on her back on the floor of the bathroom.

"Can I get you anything?" he asked.

"Maybe an ice pack, and I think I could use a drink of water from the fridge."

He went out to the kitchen, retrieving an ice pack from the freezer and filling a glass of water. He noticed the freezer was better stocked than the refrigerator, full of every kind of ice cream that contained chocolate. There had to be a dozen pints scattered throughout, and he wondered how she stayed in such good shape with that kind of habit.

Handing her the ice pack, he asked, "Anything else?"

"There's some Ondansetron in the same drawer up there, could you see if you could find it please?"

"Sure, what color is the box?"

At this, she laughed in a way that relieved him as she slid the ice pack under her shirt. "Is that like when you ask a kid what flavor they want and they reply with a color? Not everything works that way, look for a regular prescription box with the name on the label."

"Alright, how do you spell it?" he sounded snarky.

"Like, on dan set… something down," and she smiled, "don't worry about the end just look for on dan set." It didn't take him long to fish out the box with two sleeves of blister packs of small white oval pills.

"One or two?" he asked.

"One, for now, and if it doesn't work in the next ten to twenty minutes, I'll have another."

"You're the doctor." He said as he handed her a small pill, which to his surprise, she again set beneath her tongue. "I've never seen someone stuff so much medication under their tongue, is that normal?" he asked as he sat beside her again on the floor.

"You've never been really sick, have you?" her tone was dry, and he thought hard about it.

"Beyond the flu, no, you're right. I've never been *really* sick."

"Lucky you."

"How are you feeling? Any better?"

"Getting there. I don't feel so sleepy, but still not myself." He reached to check her pulse again. "Do I look as bad as I feel?" she asked.

He paused, *tread carefully,* he thought. He wanted to say that even stretched out on the bathroom floor, having been assaulted, having vomited, flush and sweaty, she was still the most beautiful woman he'd ever laid eyes on. This was work, however, a job he had to do and he doubted she would appreciate the personal sentiment.

"You don't look awful, a little flush still, but alright."

"Flush? That's good; flush is alright, pale is not." She sighed. "I think I'm ready to go back and lie on the bed. For how cool the tile is, it's rock hard." She reached up for him, and he instinctively helped her up, appreciating the slight bit of trust it represented.

He helped her back to the bed, and she flopped out like a drunk starfish, flat on her back, limbs out.

"Did you get any information on the guy that did this? I take it you didn't catch him?" she asked.

The thought of having to admit the truth irked him, but it was still the truth. "We didn't catch him yet, but we did get some information. Don't worry about it right now. My biggest task at the moment is getting you to feel better." He shifted the ice pack against her side to cover the swelling better, and she recoiled, obviously sore. "Does it hurt a lot?"

"It's no walk in the park, but I'll live. I've seen small children endure worse, so I feel like I can't complain."

"Your job must be stressful," he said thoughtfully, thinking of his sister.

"It keeps my blessings in perspective, that's for sure." She let out a long, deep sigh and seemed to be in less distress as he sat beside her on the bed.

"I can imagine," his tone was reflective. Somewhere in the apartment, a cell phone jingled a catchy pop tune.

"That's my cell, can you grab it quick, please? No one calls at this hour unless it's important." Ethan jogged towards the sound coming from her purse in the pile the security guard had left earlier on the couch. The call was from someone named Trent, and a photo of Aurora with a handsome blond guy was on the screen as it vibrated. *It figures she's got a boyfriend.* He thought as he simultaneously scolded himself for considering her as more than a professional assignment. He handed it to her, and she answered it quickly.

"Trent, darling, how are you?" Ethan cringed at the greeting. He couldn't hear the other side of the conversation and wondered if it was best that way, standing at her bedside he suddenly felt intrusive and so began to pace the giant wall of windows as he listened.

"Really? When did she start doing that? … Oh, that's creepy odd. It gives me the major heebie-jeebies … you're not going to believe the evening I've had… I have an FBI Agent pacing in my bedroom at the moment." She glanced at Ethan, and he feigned disregard.

"Theresa called him this afternoon, apparently I've received some kind of threat and it was valid enough I have someone protecting me. Luckily they got to me in time as someone tried to abduct me this evening… for real, a rather large man in a hoodie came at me with a taser on the way home from Little Skillet… yes, a real taser, and we think it was laced with something. I got so sick, and my ribs are all swollen, it's ridiculous… how could she have known?… that is quite a coincidence though, you're right, I have goosebumps! Is that why you were calling?"

A long pause ensued, and her whole demeanor changed. She had sounded glad, almost bubbly to answer the phone, and now a sense of regret seemed to wash over her. She had propped her head up in the pillows and now sank back sluggishly, as if going limp with bad news. Her other hand came up and covered her face as if to hide her emotions.

"God, that's awful." Her voice seemed thin, struggling to push back tears. "Well, I think with the condition I'm in, I would have had to cancel anyway, but I would have much preferred that to having to hear this… yes, please send something very nice, they had another girl in college, think of her as well. You're always good at those things." Ethan had paused without realizing it and was watching her intently.

"It's so nice to hear your voice. I'm so glad you called. It's been a day, and you always make things better, even from the sourest of situations… I'll try to come down tomorrow then, it would be nice to see you and just spend some time… Bastet, Mommy is alright, you be a good kitty, stop freaking … I love you … Bonsoir mon beau." She hung up, tossing the phone beside her on the bed as if discarding lousy news.

"Dare I ask who Trent is?" *Shit.* His tone sounded sourer than he intended it.

"Trent is my personal assistant. It's difficult in my line of work to balance cases and jumble patients with all my travel between multiple offices and hospitals. He is a registered nurse licensed in all five states on the West Coast, and he manages my schedule, and a lot more. We were friends before he came to work with me, I begged him, and he's wonderful. I don't know what I would do without him."

So I jumped the gun. Ethan felt slightly ashamed now, but she hadn't eliminated the guy as a lover either.

"He had bad news for you?"

"He did. Not only has my cat been on some bouncing, meowing, scratching, trying to escape freak out since—oh, about the time I got tased, but I lost a patient today." She wasn't looking at him, was lost in her thoughts, staring at the ceiling.

"I'm sorry to hear that."

"She was tomorrow's early surgery case, a fourteen-year-old girl. She was beautiful, smart, sweet, but she battled a difficult cancer and had been battling a long time. Tomorrow was going to be her fourth surgery," she covered her face again. "She killed herself today."

The thought stopped Ethan in his tracks. His mind flew back to his sister. The depression, the struggles, the false hope, the guilt, the tears, the grief and anger, all flooded over him, and for an instant, he felt bare. He knew what it was like to stand in the same shoes as the family of the patient she had just lost, but not exactly. Cancer took his sister, and that was bad enough. Aurora rubbed her eyes, and as she looked to him, he could tell he needed to get his expression under control.

"I'm even more sorry to hear that." He stared down at the floor, hoping she wouldn't see the regret in his face.

"Me too. There's so much I wish I could fix, or prevent, in what I do, but there aren't many times I wish I could take something back."

"I admire that," it came out before he even thought about what he wanted to say, "the world needs more people like that, like you."

She rolled to face him as he strolled towards her, hanging his head.

"It means I have tomorrow to recuperate, though I'd take it back if I could."

"If only life worked that way. Speaking of which, I need to focus on keeping you alive. That means I need to get this place buttoned-down and get a statement about tonight. I assume, for starters," he said, looking around, "you have a decent alarm system?"

She took a deep breath, "Yes, there's a panel behind a picture right by the door. Help me up, and I'll show you." Still looking fatigued, she sat up and held out a hand for his assistance. He held her arm as they went to the front door.

"Do you need the code or shall I just set it?"

"Just set it, and if you'd trust me, I'd appreciate it if you wrote the code down. In the event it is triggered, at least I can turn it off that way. Tuck it somewhere safe, and I'll only use it if I have to." At the front door, there was a painting of a beautiful, flame orange tiger lily in full bloom, and with one finger, she slid it sideways easily since it was on a roller. *How clever.* Behind it was a security panel with more options than he was used to seeing.

"So do you want to alarm the front door, or the staff access through the library, or both external doors, individual bedroom doors, what?"

"You have staff access through the library?" *How did I miss that?* He wondered.

"Yes, it's disguised. My father always thought it was fun to do things like that. Narnia, it's a long story."

"Arm all exterior entrances, please. Is it possible, with this eccentric smart home system, to set the lights to come on instead of a siren?"

"Yep." She punched in a code that was at least ten digits before accessing a menu for response options. The panel beeped three times, and she slid the picture back over the front. "It will still ring the police if it goes off, but instead of noise, every light in the house will come on."

"Sounds perfect."

"No, ice cream sounds perfect." She leaned into him more than he anticipated she would and when a sexy flowering scent hit him, his heart knocked hard a couple of times. "I think it will help settle my stomach. Would you like some? I've plenty."

"Yes, I saw it. And no, I guess I'm not much of an ice cream person, but I would take a soda if I could talk you out of it?" he smiled and enjoyed every second of her smiling back at him.

"Help yourself, what's mine is yours. I owe you, to say the least." He deposited her on the couch and went to retrieve ice cream and a soda.

"Any particular flavor?" he asked when he reached the fridge, snapping open a can to chug.

"Anything that has chocolate as the first word." She was already sprawling out in the plush pillows.

"Where are the spoons?"

She pointed and added, "The second drawer from the left on the island."

Stretching out on the couch next to her, they sat quietly for a few minutes. He downed the soda in long, refreshing gulps as he watched her eat timid bite after timid bite of ice cream. She scooped it then flipped the spoon over, so the ice cream met her tongue, and the spoon shielded the roof of her mouth as she sucked. It was all he could do not to stare.

"I know it's late, but do you think you could give me a statement describing the evening?" His soda was, sadly, almost gone. That meant it was either back to work or off to bed.

"There isn't much to tell. I went around the corner, and the guy was walking in the same direction as me. He stepped up next to me so fast, like someone hopping out of the street away from an oncoming car. He just calmly said, 'Dr. Soileaux' and before I could make out a face or features or anything, he had a taser in my side, and I blacked out. I may have seen more than I committed to memory, but that doesn't help if I can't remember."

"What was his voice like?" Ethan knew most victims would remember more by focusing on what hard details there were instead of fishing for things missing.

"Rough, husky, deep." She sucked on her spoon more, and he abandoned the soda can on the coffee table.

"Did he have an accent? Did you smell anything?"

She pondered for a moment and said, "I didn't pick up an accent, but I did smell garlic, perhaps onion, and some kind of East Indian spice. A strange mix of Thanksgiving and garlic. I don't know for sure; it was so fast, and my mind was elsewhere."

"What about the feel of his hands? Did he touch you?" With that, she frowned and put the empty ice cream pint carton on the table. The hands of her would-be kidnapper weren't the hands that had been occupying her mind throughout the evening, and she found herself glancing down at Ethan's.

"I didn't feel his skin because I had the long sleeves of my jacket, but his hands were smaller than yours, thin with pointy fingers that felt sharp and hard." She shivered and sat up. "Can we do more of this in the morning? I'm exhausted and looking forward to sleeping in for a change."

"Sure. I'm sorry I've kept you up this late already," he stood up and offered her a hand.

"It's not you. It's life, the tides, the moon, whatever is bringing all this to my doorstep I'm convinced it's not *your* fault," she sighed. "You're welcome to any bedroom you like and any of the creature comforts they contain. There are extra blankets in every closet. Please help yourself."

"I brought a few things, and the couch right outside your door is the best place for me, but thank you."

He walked her to the door of the bedroom, and she seemed comfortable leaving him there, didn't extend an invitation for him to walk her in. After he let her go, she held onto the door and turned to him, smiling sweetly.

"Thank you for being here, and thank you for all you did today. I know it's a job for you, but I hope you know it's much more than that for me, and I appreciate you."

He nodded before turning away as she closed the door. He retrieved his backpack and headed for the bathroom to clean up. If nights in the future were going to end anything like this one, he knew he would have to be on his best behavior.

Chapter Five

Silky light streamed into the room from the East. The sun shrouded with fog kept the room from feeling like day had set in, but it was well after sunrise. Ethan blinked blearily taking in his surroundings. He was a light sleeper, so the time surprised him at just after six in the morning. The couch was softer than he would have preferred, and his back reminded him he was still young enough to get through nights like this, but too old to skip the gym. He was going to have to figure that out in his schedule, right after coffee.

He padded on bare feet into the kitchen and began rummaging around for a cup, fumbling with a spoon and coffee grounds to fill the reusable pod. *Why would someone with so much money insist on reusable coffee pods?* He wondered, aggravated with the mess he was making. As he tried to scoop the grounds off the counter in an attempt to clean up after himself, a bright laugh came from behind him.

"First time making coffee?" he turned to see Aurora fully dressed with a shining smile.

"You're up early. I thought you were looking forward to sleeping in?" he felt his attempt at not being gruff had perhaps failed.

"I did sleep in, and it was fabulous." She came around beside him with a sponge from the sink and swiftly had the grounds under control as coffee sputtered from the machine.

"You normally get up before six?" he yawned.

"I am normally up between four and five. I could have used another hour today since I was up so late, but routine typically gets the better of me. How did you sleep?"

"Fine, thank you," he sipped the black coffee, and she made a face.

"Straight black? You're tougher than you look, and you look pretty tough." She eyed him from head to toe as he realized he was shirtless, wearing only a black pair of athletic sweat pants. He hadn't anticipated her waking up before him. *Why is that uncomfortable when I would typically relish having anyone as pretty as her admire me?* He wondered, as he stood up straighter and walked back to the couch to immediately put his shirt on.

"How did you sleep?" he asked.

"Like the dead, though, I'm glad I wasn't."

"That makes two of us. Do you remember anything more about last night now that you're well-rested and clear-headed?" he asked as he sat carefully on the white couch, making sure not to spill the coffee he was sipping.

"Sort of, though I'm not sure it's important."

His interest was piqued, "Do tell."

"Well, he did say my name quite perfectly, like he had heard it frequently or used it before. Most people get it wrong, so it stands out when someone gets it right." Ethan cringed, remembering his own poor pronunciation the day before. "But he didn't *just* get it right. He pronounced it perfectly. Like he had used it not once or twice before but regularly and was comfortable with it. Very few people say my name with the finesse he used." She had poured herself a cup of vegetable juice and joined him on the couch. Watching her set it on the cushion beside her nearly gave him a heart attack, and it wasn't even his furniture.

"So does that mean you feel this person has worked with you or is familiar with you in more than passing?"

"Possibly, I mean, he said it the way people close to me or even in my family would say it." She began picking at her fingernails absently.

"Well, I can adjust the investigation if you feel it's warranted. Is there a possibility you have a direct patient or someone in your family who might have that much of a beef towards you?"

"I don't have much family. I mean, my mother was an only child, and my dad's sister died a long time ago. I have no direct cousins, so it's only my mother and sister, and neither of them would have any contact with my patients. The guy is obviously after medical professionals, right? I think that rules out my family in general."

"Sounds like it."

"As far as my patients, I honestly can't recall any that would have major beef towards me. I mean, I deal with a lot of parents who lose children, but with those patients, it's typically undeniable by the time they even get to me that I'm the Hail Mary - the last chance. I've never gotten the idea anyone considered me at fault for anything that wasn't already going to happen. In general, anyway, I feel like I have more success stories than I do sad ones." She sipped the juice as her mind seemed to drift. "Unlike yesterday," her tone was sad as she stared blankly out the window.

He wasn't sure what to say or what would ease her discomfort. He remembered feeling distraught over his sister, and though he hated to admit it, he knew from personal experience nothing he could say would make her feel better. Some things in life were just inconsolable. He studied her briefly, her hair down around her shoulders in dark tumbling waves, her face sullen, eyes glowing with amber hues as they stared into space.

"Can't change yesterday," he tried to pretend it wasn't a pep talk, "so now that you have a change in plans today, what are you going to do with it? You mentioned last night going to Palo Alto?"

"Oh, yea," she pulled her phone out of her pocket. "I think we should go see Trent." For some reason, the thought wasn't appealing.

Oh, right, because this might be a lover of hers.

"Trent runs your personal and professional affairs, right?" he asked.

"Yes, and more than that, we're close, and with free time he cheers me up," she said. Ethan raised his eyebrows.

"A pleasure call, then?" he wasn't sure why he had said it out loud, or in the tone that he had used, but she smiled.

"Yes, a pleasure call, but more than just that. You can have access to my schedule and all my paperwork and patients, wouldn't that help you?" she had him there.

"As a matter of fact, yes, it would. But it might mean more to someone who can process the data quickly and appropriately. I'll make some calls. What time would you like to leave?"

"Are you hungry? I haven't eaten yet. As soon as you're ready we can hopefully beat the traffic and eat down there, Trent is an amazing chef."

Oh goodie, he cooks too. Ethan scolded himself. The caffeine hadn't totally kicked in yet.

"I'll waste no time," he hopped off the couch and went to put his coffee cup in the sink.

"Oh, and I'll drive this time. No motorcycles today." She followed him with a smirk on her face.

"We can take your car, but if we do, you're not driving. And do me a favor while I'm in the shower, don't answer the door. Or even go near it, for that matter." She wrinkled her nose up at him as he fished out his cell phone and headed for the bathroom.

Thirty minutes later, they were in her candy apple red Tesla roadster on Highway 101 headed south towards Palo Alto with Agent Ty Larson in the back seat and Agent Rick Jansen following them in the typical federal issue black suburban. They weren't field agents, weren't prepared for any kind of scuffle, and though they still carried guns for some reason, it didn't make Ethan feel better to have them along. He felt short-tempered as if having them around only meant two more people he had to worry about keeping safe.

The car was fun to drive, and it had been apparent Aurora thought it was amusing to see him tuck his oversized frame behind the wheel. He had been a little nervous. It was the most expensive vehicle he'd ever driven. He had never seen the inside of a second-generation Tesla, let alone one with all the bells and whistles. The car had all leather, heated seats and steering wheel, and was fire engine red with top of the line navigation software. It was quiet, much quieter than he could have imagined, and had the acceleration of an American muscle car.

It was almost as sexy as her.

While he navigated the five lanes of traffic, she was mostly quiet texting or doing something else on her phone. He had disabled her location services since he had zero intention of letting her out of his sight, but he still worried she was somehow leaking private details. Cases like this always irked him, needing to worry about someone's wellbeing while trying to alleviate them of a threat at the same time.

Ty sat in the back seat, seemingly happy as a lark watching the world go by, which for a reason Ethan couldn't figure out was all the more irritating. *May the fourth be with you, my ass.* He thought as he regarded the cyber nerd in the back seat disdainfully.

"There's a blue Chevy Bolt about six cars back in the left lane that has been with us for about four miles. It changes lanes and keeps speed with us, did you notice?" Ty asked. *Ok maybe I'm a little hard on them,* Ethan took a deep breath.

"I hadn't. I'll see if it stays at the next exit. Call Jansen and tell him to keep going." Ty pulled out his cell and sent a text. "A text, really? On the freeway?" Ethan scolded him in the rearview mirror, and Ty merely rolled his eyes.

Aurora smirked and said, "It is 2019, after all. Does anyone make a phone call for less than two hundred words?" Ethan just grunted and changed lanes, headed off the next exit.

After a few seconds, Ty shifted slightly and said, "It's still there, on the exit, about seven cars back."

"I see it," Ethan grumbled. His heart smacked hard into his ribs a couple of times as he noticed Aurora's eyes follow his arm down into his jacket to unbutton his shoulder holster. He glanced at her, trying to gauge her mood. She seemed calm but sat back in the seat and sank lower. Staying in the middle lane, which turned either direction, he sped up and at the corner turned right away from the highway.

Ty turned in the back seat, "Still there, looks like it might have pushed through a yellow light to keep up."

Ethan pulled out his cell and dialed Jansen. Hip hop music blared over the Bluetooth briefly as he answered.

"The tail still there?" Jansen asked.

"So far. Get off at the next exit and wait at the Shell station, I'm going to swing through and get back on. I want you to pull out behind that car, see if you can see the driver."

"Sure thing," he disconnected.

Ethan went left a couple of blocks up and driving parallel to the freeway kept a close eye in the rearview. Just as suspicion began turning to reality in the back of his mind, about a mile off the highway, the blue car changed lanes and turned right into a neighborhood.

"False alarm," he said. "Ty, send Rick a text and let him know he can just follow us back onto the freeway? That Chevy turned into a neighborhood a few blocks back."

"Sure thing."

Ethan couldn't help but notice Aurora had tensed but seemed to relax when they passed the Shell station, and Jansen got behind them again. She went back to texting, and as they closed in on the address she had given them in Palo Alto, she began to smile to herself as she fidgeted on her phone. They exited Middlefield Road and headed towards Stanford, passing the expansive campus and winding into the neighborhood of lavish homes behind it.

"Pull in the side, under this tree, and park between the houses on the left side of the smaller one." She pointed at a driveway that dipped down as if meeting a daylight basement that was between two homes, one on the right looked like it was worth a million, the one on the left looked like it was worth twenty million or more. He stopped in front of a three-car garage and waited for Jansen to pull in behind them before getting out. Before they were able even to grab gear from the trunk, the handsome Trent was dashing out to greet Aurora. He picked her up in a bear hug and swung her around off her feet when she threw her arms around his neck.

"Bonjour!" he said and laughed as Aurora kissed him on one cheek then the other before grabbing his hand and pulling him towards the back of the car where Ethan was taking out his backpack.

"Trent, this is Agent Ethan Hartman," she waved a hand at him, and Trent extended his to shake. Ethan found it challenging to smile though the handshake was firm.

"It's a pleasure to meet you, Agent, and your associates?" Trent nodded back at Ethan as he turned to introduce himself to Ty and Rick with a slightly hidden but sultry southern drawl. Ethan couldn't help but stand between Aurora and the street, glancing warily over his shoulder as he tried not to seem overprotective by ushering her inside too quickly.

"Welcome to Palo Soprano, as we like to refer to it." Trent almost giggled and gave off a strange vibe as he glanced over his shoulder and winked at Ty while opening a lovely glass double door into a game room. As soon as the doors swung open, a very loud 'meow' greeted Aurora as a silver-grey cat with black stripes dashed out from under a chair. Aurora lit up and began babbling something in French as she scooped the gigantic cat off the ground and into her arms. The cat greeted her with a series of follow up cries before curling in her embrace purring boisterously.

A pool table and a fully equipped bar were inside with large sliding glass doors on the left opening to an immaculately landscaped backyard with a pool immediately visible. It appeared to be a guest house or secondary living quarters of some kind and paled in comparison to the main home it undoubtedly belonged to, and still would have fetched a pretty penny. Aurora obviously owned the giant unoccupied mansion directly next door, and Ethan wasn't sure why he was surprised.

Across the room at the foot of the stairs that paralleled the front of the house, the cat peered over Aurora's shoulder, and its laser-focused ice grey eyes seemed to examine them each carefully. It was a beautiful but very odd-looking cat, like nothing Ethan had ever seen before. Its coat was superbly shiny, and it's spotting somewhere between a cheetah and a zebra with eyes more oval than usual. Its ears were twice the size of an average cat in a wide crescent shape and its muzzle more pronounced and shorter. It rubbed its head against her neck as she scratched it and cooed at it lovingly.

Here must be Bastet, he thought.

Trent led them up the stairs emerging into a great room that shared the living room facing the street, and a kitchen taking up the back corner of the house. In the center of the first floor were stairs ascending to bedrooms. On the left side of the house was a library that doubled as an office facing the front porch that also opened to an elegant dining room occupying the rear left-hand corner of the house.

The decor felt old school British with a modern flair and was classy and clean. Sturdy wood beams polished in dark stain crossed the ceiling and blended into railings, wainscoting, and lovely hardwood floors. It screamed expensive.

Trent led them into the library office and said, "Gentleman, from what Aurora has been telling me, you'll probably find this space most useful." Ty and Rick started opening laptop cases on a side table. The room was almost an oval shape the way the walls and windows were angled, and the bookshelves built. Ethan walked past a life-size framed, brilliantly colored portrait of Elvis done entirely in velvet. Aurora sat in a leather chair in the front window of the house and turned her attention to Ty and Rick.

"Trent is my right hand, personal and professional. Please feel free to access any patient records, emails, schedules, or anything else you think would be helpful. If you find anything you are lacking, he has the authority and ability to retrieve whatever you need. He will need to continue to work and monitor responsibilities, but hopefully, you won't hinder each other too much. Please know you have my full support and cooperation." Aurora sounded resolved, confident. She let the cat down, and when it darted to Ethan to curl around his legs, he caught her smiling as her eyes followed it.

Trent logged onto the computer but immediately got up to welcome Ty to sit in front of it.

"Now that your professional needs are taken care of, how about something personal – are any of you hungry? I have fresh coffee, fruit, pastries, and I'm happy to make eggs or bacon. What's your pleasure?" Trent stood at the threshold of the room beneath an ornately carved wooden arch with his hands clasped like a perfect host.

"I'd love some coffee," Ty said as he shoved his glasses up his nose.

"Make that two please," Rick smiled from over Ty's shoulder.

"Cream and sugar?"

"Please," Rick said. Ty nodded, and when Trent looked to Ethan, he also nodded, but Aurora interjected, "He'll take his black." Her sense of ownership in answering how he liked his coffee felt personal, and he enjoyed it.

As Trent disappeared into the kitchen, Aurora went after him and beckoned Ethan to follow her. As they reached the stairs, which led up and away from the front door, she paused with arms crossed, looking slightly uncomfortable. They were out of earshot of anyone else, but her voice was still hushed.

"So, I'm not sure how this all works, from here on out, but I assume you'll be around for a while?" she asked.

"I'll be with you as much as I can, and if I'm not, you'll have another agent assigned to you. Why?"

"Well, I just wanted to be sure you'd be as comfortable as possible," she headed up the stairs to the third floor, "follow me."

The floors were all hardwood on the second level, but as they rose to the third floor, it turned to a shaggy, plush mauve carpet. There was a long hallway at the top of the stairs with rooms on either side. It ended in what appeared to be another sitting room where all that could be seen through the door was a painting canvas and supplies against a far wall. There were four bedrooms in all, one master in the left rear corner, and three others of varying sizes. The master bedroom was obviously in use with a messy bed, and there were clothes strewn about, but directly across from it, as Aurora swung the door open, was a large room with two full-size beds. It had colorful walls and children's décor for a girl on one side and a boy on the other. It was clean and organized, but the toys stacked in a chest in one corner were well used.

"Trent's niece and nephew stay in this room when they visit, they're here every other weekend or so. He often keeps them for his sister since his folks live back in Tennessee. I asked him to pick it up and get it ready because I figured it would be more comfortable than the couch for you?" She raised her eyebrows, unsure what she was doing was the right choice.

Ethan shrugged and said, "Sure, if you're alright with both of us in the same room."

"It was actually Trent's idea; he was rather insistent. If whatever is going on is serious enough for me to get tased, then I should treat it as a threat to my life. Otherwise, you wouldn't be here, right?" She was standing close to him in the doorway, close enough he could smell her again, and heat in his chest made the moment feel personal.

"That's a good way to look at things, yes. How is your side anyway? Is the swelling continuing to get better?" he had to fight to keep from reaching out to touch her.

"Yes, it's gone down substantially, still sore to the touch, but better." She smiled, and her eyes locked on his, warm like a sunny beach. "There's a bathroom that joins through to the studio, but you may use it solely as yours, I'll use the one across the hall in the mistress quarters where I usually stay, all my stuff is there anyway."

"You don't normally stay in the master with Trent?" It was an out loud, automatic question. He didn't even know it was coming until the words were on his lips, and he instantly wanted to suck them back into his mouth. He tried to look away from her as his cheeks started to feel hot, but she laughed. Her expression flashed disbelief then amusement as her eyes twinkled at him.

"Oh, no," she chuckled softly, "Trent and I aren't, a thing, no—he's in a relationship and, um, he's gay." She bit her bottom lip entertained by his, incorrect, assumption.

"Sorry," his mouth hung open with embarrassment, "I shouldn't even have said anything. It isn't any of my business."

"It's totally fine. It's human nature. I get it." She stepped back into the hallway, brushing against him slightly as Trent started up the stairs towards them. Without turning back to Ethan she said, "It isn't private information, I'm single." She swirled around to face him again as Trent handed her a cup of coffee and offered one to Ethan as well.

"What do you think of the décor?" Trent asked. "I did almost all of it myself. I've been here for almost ten years, and it's taken me a while to get it to feel like home."

Ethan nearly choked on his first sip of coffee as it burnt his tongue, but he caught it, that vibe. He kicked himself for not recognizing it earlier. Maybe the accent had covered it up, totally gay. As it sank in, a strange wash of relief seeped through him, and he scolded himself again. It shouldn't matter; she was off-limits single or not.

"It's very nice, classy," Ethan cleared his throat as coffee blocked his windpipe, and he wheezed.

"I'm quite proud of it. Well, everything except Elvis," he rolled his eyes, "that's entirely Kurt."

"Never going to get past the velvet Elvis, are you?" Aurora giggled.

"I have to get past him every day he's right in the front hall, I can't get to my bedroom without getting past him," Trent said in a comical tone as he threw his hands in the air, rolled his eyes and turned to Ethan. "Agent Hartman, please allow me to extend my warmest welcome possible this woman means the world to me, and I don't know what I would do without her, so I appreciate everything you're doing."

"Awe," Aurora seemed genuinely touched, leaned in to kiss him on the cheek.

Ethan felt like an ass.

"Hold onto that sentiment because there's more." Trent put an arm around her lovingly as a brother would right before she pinched the back of his other elbow.

"Theresa called you, didn't she?" she asked.

"No, ouch! I called Theresa. I'll have you know."

"You traitor," she giggled again.

"Whatever, you got tased sister," they began to bicker like siblings and headed back downstairs. As Ethan followed them, the cat nearly tripped him and meowed sharply, twisting at his feet. Aurora looked back with an expression of surprise on her face, making a smooching noise with her lips and called to the cat in French. It reluctantly followed.

Ethan headed back to the library as Aurora and Trent retreated to the kitchen.

"Any preliminary thoughts on the software? Can you get any information out of it easily?" he asked Ty and Rick.

"There's one scheduling program, and it looks like it's been the same one for at least five years now, we should be able to download a decent amount of information from it. There's access to patient records but in over a dozen portals between offices and hospitals…" Jansen continued to chatter away about URLs, IP addresses, and databases while Ethan booted up his laptop.

"Make as much sense of it as you can start with cross-referencing the dates from Johns Hopkins." They both frowned at him. Cyber tech wasn't his thing. They only gathered the data, he knew, he would need to put the pieces together. It wasn't even nine in the morning yet, and he could tell it was going to be a long day.

Chapter Six

Aurora felt home. This house was one she'd known a long time in her life, and seeing the way Trent cared for it, how happy he was here always made her feel more at home than her own family had. She sat at the counter, sipping her coffee, watching him make fresh-squeezed orange juice and slice pineapple. She was overdue for a visit, she knew. She always gained a couple of pounds with his cooking, and recently, she could feel her pants getting loose. It was time to gain back what she'd lost.

"So how's Kurt? And Aubrey? The kids?"

"Kurt is Kurt, still off trying to paint the emotions of the world as large as possible for all to see. He's actually in Laredo right now meeting with some local artists he's connected with recently. He wants to get into a big gig at Burning Man." He rolled his eyes. "Aubrey seems happier since Jason got a new position in the Sheriff's office. She likes him off patrol with more dependable hours. He's home with the kids more, and for some reason, she thinks it keeps him safer."

"She's probably right, in some small way."

"Perhaps, whatever makes her happy is fine with me. She was thrilled. I kept Paul and Mary last weekend, so they had a night alone. She said they ate dinner at Nola's during happy hour and were home, in bed, asleep by eight. She said it was heaven."

Aurora laughed, "Parenting, that's the life."

"Indeed. The kids had a great time, and we spent the gift cards you sent for their birthday, they love the new clothes they got."

"I hope you got some play stuff in there too – I know Mary was eyeing that princess dress and was it the cape, for Paul? Or the mask he wanted?"

"Oh he got both, they drew pictures for you, they're upstairs. You'll find them when you decide you're ready for a nap later." She giggled as he retrieved a bottle of champagne from the refrigerator and popped it loudly. He poured her a stiff mimosa with the freshly squeezed juice and slid a thin slice of pineapple over the rim. He handed it to her before pouring one for himself, with which he promptly toasted her.

"I'm going out on a limb here," he glanced in the direction of the library with a silly grin, "but here's to fate, not only the foul but the friendly that it brings your way." He winked at her, silently saying he thought Ethan was hot, she could read his mind as they sipped. He busied himself with making an extravagant platter of food. Brie, blue cheese, fancy crackers, grapes, strawberries, honey, salami, and a plethora of other bite-sized delicacies began to stack up in front of her. She happily snacked as they talked, and as the morning wore on, she found her worries trickling away.

"Let me bring this into the guys in the other room, be right back." Trent trotted off with the tray full of food as Aurora let the champagne buzz swirl in her head. *A nap, perhaps, would be entirely in order today*, she thought.

Trent set the tray of food in front of Ethan on the table, carefully avoiding files and cords. He waved his hands over the small feast and said, "If this doesn't speak for itself, please help yourselves." He stood back and quickly stepped behind Ty at the desk, glancing warily in the direction of the kitchen. He made a motion with his finger beckoning Ethan to join them then placed it over his lips to ensure silence. The hair on the back of Ethan's neck stood up.

Trent reached between the two cyber techs and quickly accessed the desktop on the computer and opened a file titled with only a date.

"I haven't shown this to Aurora or even spoken to her about it yet," he whispered carefully, "this is why I called Theresa." He pointed to the screen and a file he had opened with contents Ethan instantly recognized. As Ethan stepped closer, Trent leaned in and spoke quietly into his ear with eyes trained on the hallway the entire time.

"The hospitals and offices Aurora works with scan and email her mail to me twice a week. These letters all arrived between Monday and Tuesday at every location she has privileges. I would have gotten the one from UCSF in the same batch if Theresa hadn't intercepted it already." Ethan's stomach churned. There were at least seven files, all appearing to be similar threats, all indicating the suspect knew at what locations she worked.

"And why didn't you say anything to her immediately?" Ethan questioned him.

"I would like to catch up with you later, Agent Hartman, perhaps just the two of us. Aurora is amazing in every way, but she's been through a lot, especially the last few years. Only about six months ago things started to smooth out for her again, she's had a couple rough patches in her life, but her father's death was very hard on her. She doesn't trust a lot of people, but she trusts me, and I won't jeopardize that, though I am choosing to trust you. This is your job, find this guy, and understand that *she is my job*. I'll do what I can to keep her out of harm's way while you work. I've canceled her office appointments in San Jose next week, and the next three days at Packard, I've found nearly enough coverage so that she won't have to work. She won't like it, but I can handle her."

"I'm going to go out on a limb here and say she's the final piece to this guy's puzzle," Ethan was studying the notes, flipping between the files. "Do you have any suggestions about where to start in all this?"

"Let's chat later, alone." Trent made it clear he wasn't up for entertaining questioning at the moment and hurried back to the kitchen to join Aurora again.

Ethan stretched between Ty and Rick, reading each note carefully before leaning back.

"We've got a lot to do, email those to me, and let's find the pattern. This guy is way too close for comfort."

By the time one o'clock rolled around, clouds had rolled in as well. The soft pitter-patter of warm, late June rain tinkled against the windows, and its fresh smell wafted through the open house along with the music playing in the living room. Trent had done an excellent job, so far, of keeping Aurora not only busy but entertained and relaxed.

The three agents had been mashing information for nearly four hours, and though Ethan was sure Ty and Rick were doing their best, he only felt pulled away from what research of his own he needed to work through. They fed him file after file, columns, and rows, dates, and locations, it all had to be pulled back apart and compared to the timeframes and his suspicions.

Ethan pushed back from the desk, hunger starting to get the better of his attitude when his cell rang.

"Hey Tom, what's up?"

Quillet sighed lightly.

"Hey boss," there was a pause that Ethan immediately recognized as bad news. "The doc up in Portland, she just passed away. Some kind of unexpected blood-thinning resulted in a problem in her brain. I wanted to let you know right away."

"Shit." Ethan sighed out the expletive as he leaned forward on the table with his elbow and put his head into his hand. One more piece of the puzzle he wasn't going to get, just as he was already starting to think this killer could be the first one to elude him. "Thanks for calling, I'll be back in the office later today for a bit, I need to grab some files I forgot. I also have to grab some stuff from home and figured I'd take advantage of Ty and Rick here."

Tom huffed sarcastically, "You're trusting those two? Did you see Larson's last firearms qualification? Eeek."

"I can't exactly drag her around with me, it's the middle of the day, and there are three other people here, two of them trained Agents. You have a better idea?"

"I could trade you for a couple of hours."

"No, not today. I'll probably need you the next couple of days if Aurora goes back to work. She had today free because of a cancellation." He hated calling a suicide a cancellation, but he didn't want to get into the details at the moment. "She had tomorrow scheduled off already, but then she's back at Packard seeing patients, as it stands now."

"You're the boss."

"I'll see you later," Ethan hung up.

"Bad news?" Ty asked.

"The last attack, the victim in the hospital, just died." He stood up and turned just in time to realize Aurora was standing in the entryway to the open library with a horrified look on her face.

"She died? The doctor in Portland? The one no one knew was alive?" For the first time, the expression on her face was one of genuine fear. Ethan froze. He wasn't sure how to react, so he silently nodded his head in confirmation. He didn't want to freak her out worse, but the damage was done, she knew now.

"And what do you mean 'if I go back to work, as it stands now'? Why wouldn't I be seeing patients as usual?" her emotions were on her face like a billboard as fear, shock, and anger all mixed up in her glowing eyes. Ethan's heart skipped a beat, he needed her to cooperate, now more than ever, and he wasn't sure what to say. Trent came sliding in behind her, and there was an audible sigh of relief from all three agents.

"Can we go for a walk?" he asked Ethan directly, and Aurora frowned at him.

"I'd prefer that you stay inside if that's possible," Ethan tried to keep his tone authoritative without being pushy.

"A walk is a terrible idea, at the moment," Ty piped in without regard for the delicacy of the situation.

"How about a soak in the hot tub? Outside but acceptably close?" Trent raised his eyebrows as Aurora crossed her arms over her chest in overt protest.

"Is the entire yard fenced?" Ethan asked.

"Yes, and there's a lock on the back gate at the moment." If Trent could feel Aurora's eyes boring a hole in him, he didn't show it.

"Alright, let me go take a quick look around out there first." Ethan headed for the back door as Trent put his arms around Aurora's torso as a child would.

"You're going to be mad at first. I'm willing to bear the brunt of the storm because I know after it all sinks in, you're going to be grateful." He tilted his head and made a face at her like a puppy as she scowled at him.

"Maybe I don't even want to know," she huffed and rolled her eyes as she squirmed away from him.

"Great, that makes it all the easier."

"Trent!" she used a snappy tone.

"Go get your bathing suit on!" he snapped back, and they both headed upstairs.

~

Outside, Ethan walked around the edge of the house to the corner of the property then followed the entire fence line. The yard was large, with old-growth Oak, Elm, and Maple trees and astutely manicured. Open grassy areas blended into ground cover then into tall grasses and bushes. Roses adorned raised areas giving the whole space a serene, private sense of depth. The pool area had all new furniture and a shady cabana with a fire pit and what looked like an outdoor pizza oven. A shiny grill set into the side of the stone countertop had cabinets underneath that were clean and latched shut.

For a salary that can afford all this, I should have been a doctor instead of an FBI Agent.

When he reached the hot tub, he felt better about the situation. It was on a second-floor deck that extended out the back door on the left, overhanging the exit from the game room below. With access only from a set of steep stairs and from the entrance to the house through the dining room, at least she wouldn't be a sitting duck from any angle. There was a gate, apparently installed to prevent children from falling down the stairs, and it latched soundly with a sturdy child lock. Anyone coming up would have to fidget with it or go over it, neither of which would exactly be easy.

As he stood surveying the view into the backyard, a meow and a loud purr startled him from his feet. The cat jumped up onto the edge of the hot tub and shoved a wet nose against his arm. He put his hand out to smell, and the feline promptly wrapped her head beneath it and into his palm, purring contentedly for the affection.

"Hey there, kitty, you're a pretty little thing, aren't you?" he massaged her head and oversized ears admiring how incredibly soft she was. When the door to the dining room swung open behind him, he was glad the cat was there to distract him as Aurora stepped out in nothing but a sparkly purple bikini under a sheer lace-trimmed kimono.

"Well, how about that?" she marveled at Bastet. He strained to keep his eyes on the cat.

"She hates everyone," Aurora smirked.

"Really?" he continued to stroke the cats back as Aurora came to stand beside them and offered her forehead, which Bastet promptly did as well.

"Yes," she made little kissing noises and scratched the cat's chin. "She does hate everyone, she doesn't even like Kurt, and he's lived here for almost four years. She won't let him touch her at all. She only likes me and Trent and well, my sister, but she's never around."

"Bastet – is it a boy or a girl?" he asked.

"She's a girl. She's an Ocicat, a unique and rare breed. I named her after the Egyptian Goddess of protection, the warrior daughter and defender of the sun God Ra, descendent of the lioness." She said it in a silky but silly voice as she nuzzled the cat's head, and it made Ethan smile. "Maybe that's why she likes you, protector."

She looked up at him batting her thick eyelashes and with her standing so close a flash of heat seared through him. Her dark, thick hair lazily and loosely pulled back left pieces falling around her face. Her creamy caramel skin so velvety and perfect, made him so badly want to touch her. She leaned towards him slightly as if tempting him, as if she knew she held him captivated. At the same moment that he realized he had stopped breathing, Trent came sauntering out onto the deck. He seemed not to notice the tension of the moment.

"Suitable, Agent Hartman?" he asked.

"Please, call me Ethan, and yes, it's fine for now, but I'd prefer not after dark. Please keep the gate locked and the door to the house open, enjoy your soak."

"Thanks," Trent dropped a navy pin-striped terry cloth robe onto a chair beside the tub as Aurora let her kimono fall over her shoulders onto the step. It took all of Ethan's willpower to take his eyes off her as he went back into the house.

He needed a break.

He took out his phone and texted Tom. *'I changed my mind, can you head this way? Keep an eye on things while I refresh?'* Within thirty seconds, Tom had replied, *'send me an address, I'll leave in 5.'*

Ethan dropped a pin for his location and went back inside to peruse the kitchen for food. The oversized side by side fridge and freezer combo boasted an incredibly organized, restaurant-quality selection of food.

He picked out some cold cuts and cheese and made himself a sandwich with sourdough bread that had him double-checking the brand on the bag because it was so incredible. Staying here for a few days surely meant he would have to hit the gym extra when the case was over. Retiring to the library office, he got back to work on deciphering what the cyber geeks had gathered. They would be on their way out by about four o'clock, so he sent them to eat in order to take advantage of a few minutes of quiet time.

The hot water was just what Aurora needed, she decided, as she examined Trent and his demeanor for hints of what was to come. They'd been friends for over a decade, and he'd been nothing, ever, except loyal and wonderful to her. Knowing their history left her feeling, momentarily, like her doubt and insecurity was in itself, a form of betrayal. She couldn't figure out why she felt her life was spinning out of her control as if people were keeping things from her and lacking trust in her ability to handle her own issues.

That's teenage, isn't it? She scolded herself.

As the bubbles caressed her from buttock to shoulder, she turned her eyes skyward, anticipating the next downpour, comparing her life to the weather. It was just a storm, wasn't it? She'd been through it before. Every storm ran out of rain, didn't it? But then there was Ethan, this new addition that had a spark blooming into an ember inside her. Every time she looked at him, it was like life was throwing all the things she was missing right in her face. Did Trent see it? She turned to him now, relaxed and ready for the worst, not sure if she was pleased or disgusted that he knew exactly how to handle her.

"So why are we soaking? What do you have to tell me?" she asked him lazily.

"You know I love you, right? Like, not just love you but love you like a sister, like someone I share half a soul with, right?" His head lolled to one side, resting on his shoulder above his outstretched arm, and his expression was relaxed but held finality. Whatever he had to tell her, he felt there was no coming back from it.

"Of course I do. And I love you so much I hate you for it. If you were straight, we would have been lovers, married, and happy somewhere living our days out in passion. Even though you're not, I can't deny we're soul mates. However much I would like to, so spill it, what is going on?"

"It's hard for me to explain to you that I know certain parts of you better than you know yourself. I'm sure as difficult as it is for you to believe or admit it. It's even more difficult for me to take certain actions to protect you while accepting that you may be so angry that you never forgive me. I face losing you, regardless of whether I chose to act or not. Can you relate to that?" His sincerity had her worried. His tone, his demeanor, the way he sat up to face her, it all made her shrink a little.

"Looking at your face, I can now," She sat upright, letting the water lighten her weight.

"I received threats against you, sweetheart. I didn't call Theresa because I had spoken to you. I called her before I spoke to you. I called her because the mail came in yesterday and had over a half dozen extremely creepy letters. Between your offices in California, Nevada, Oregon, Washington, and Idaho, whoever this person is, he has your number babe. Love me or hate me, I gave them straight to that hunky FBI agent."

He waited, soft blue eyes sullen in the weight of the moment, for her response. Her heart bubbled, skipped beats as it trotted faster than usual. The heat and the mimosa had her wits slow, her mind not quite prepared to absorb the full ramifications of what he was saying.

"I got more letters? Besides the one Theresa received?"

"Yes, honey, quite a few more."

"Oh." She sat back again, resting her head on the edge of the hot tub, the jets floating her slightly as she leaned into them while tiny bubbles raced up her back, tickling her. The sky seemed to mirror her mood, deep tones of watery grey and azure blended with a misty lining.

"You've been doing so well lately, after everything you've been through you shot up with flying colors and yet here you are, being chased by some demon that's no fault of your own. I know how the anxiety affects you, will you let me help you keep it at bay?" his tone was almost a plea.

"You mean my mother's betrayal, losing Dad, my whoring sister disowning me? Yes, I've had a rough few years that taught me how to handle myself, taught me how to *be* myself. You're right—of course, you are." She locked eyes with him, sad and suddenly overwhelmed and said, "You know parts of me better than I know myself."

"I'm glad you understand."

"So, you canceled my cases and got someone to cover the appointments?"

He nodded.

"I didn't bring the letters to you because when I reached out to Theresa, she had already contacted the FBI for the one she found. She was insistent they would get you into some kind of protective custody, so I gave her twenty-four hours. I told her if she didn't have you safe by this morning, I was going to tell you. And here you show up with Captain America. I think she did pretty good, sweetie." Aurora knew he was softening her internal struggle with Theresa. She loved the woman, more than she loved her own mother and for all the same reasons.

Children tend to strike out from their parents, demanding independence even when it's not good for them, but her mother wasn't her ball and chain. Her mother had always been so consumed with profit and loss reports, capital gains, and mergers, that Aurora often felt invisible. But there had been Theresa, following her father around the way a dutiful wife would. Theresa took care of his patients the way Trent took care of Aurora. She took care of his finances, his scheduling, his credentialing, and, ultimately, his family.

If her own mother had loved her the way Aurora felt she should have, perhaps she could have bonded with Theresa differently, in a healthier way. Because her mother couldn't have cared less what her life was becoming, and there was Theresa, molding her and shaping her, pushing her in her father's footsteps—the love was misguided.

Aurora sought independence from Theresa instead of from her mother and realized, perhaps much too late, how much she loved her. She shed all her teenage rebellion on a woman who was volunteering in place of an absentee parent. Still, Theresa had stayed strong. For all the bitterness Aurora had thrown at her in youth, Theresa somehow managed to forgive her, always to have her back and fight in her corner when she needed it most.

Aurora sighed in the hot water, stretching her limbs out to enjoy the feeling of weightlessness. Lost in her thoughts for a moment, a new sprinkle of fresh rain roused her back to reality.

"You're right," she said plainly. "Of course, you're right."

"Baby, I love you," Trent's voice was sad, yearning for forgiveness he shouldn't even be asking for form her.

"I know, and I love you too. I've grown up, thanks to you and Theresa, and I feel different now. You have every reason to be worried, and I won't lie, the anxiety rears its ugly head once in a while. But I know how to recognize it now, and I know how to deal with it, thanks to you. No thanks to my mother, and I hope we're still on the same page about that."

"Girl, you know I know where your limits are. But, for full disclosure, Theresa called her."

Aurora's face went blank for a minute, letting reality sink in as raindrops soaked her hair. "Tee-ta called my mother? The queen bitch of Egypt?" She was thoroughly shocked.

"Oh yea sunshine, I heard all about it. Ice queen was all karma ridden with 'I knew it would happen eventually' and 'she brought it on herself' so on and so forth. The usual." The thought stung. How much it must have pained Theresa to call the woman she essentially replaced, stung more.

"Tee-ta does love me, doesn't she? Like, through to her core? And more than my own mother could have," her tone was reflective, wise.

"Oh, hug me, honey," Trent was temporarily overcome with emotion as he reached for her. She settled her head on his shoulder, glad for the rock she had found in him.

"If you, and this FBI Agent, really feel like I should crawl under a rock, then I guess I will. No point in worrying about the patients in the next two weeks if I'm not around for the next twenty years." She felt depressed, and it showed in her voice.

"About you and this FBI Agent..." Trent shuffled her embrace to look down at her. "Bow chicka bow wow." He chuckled and made a mocking sexy face with pursed lips as he slurred the words. She laughed out loud, from her toes, a full belly laugh. Sliding down more in the water, she felt the rain increase as a new wave of showers threatened to pass over them.

"What about Agent Hartman?" she asked tauntingly.

"Uh, duh, he's hot. And, even though I'm gay, it doesn't mean I don't understand what men, even straight men, find attractive. Girl, he is into you."

Aurora rolled her eyes. "Based on what?" she asked.

"Did you see the way he was looking at you when you came upon him loving on Bastet? And, by the way, may I remind you that cat hates everyone." She laughed because he was right.

"It's true, Bastet hates everyone."

"Well, she doesn't hate him. He didn't even have to work for it. Kurt's going to be pissed."

"Oh, poor Kurt, I feel bad for him. He loves her. Why doesn't she like him?"

"Who knows? Really, who cares? All that matters is that she likes this guy and let's be real, don't lie, you like him too."

She sighed, leaned back, and opened her mouth to catch raindrops on her tongue. Blinking up towards the sky, she shoved hard against the pretense of relationships she was raised with and forced herself into a new, unknown realm. She did like Ethan. He was long-term material. Trent knew she liked him without her even saying so. She couldn't deny it was the first man she had thoughts about where he was more than a transient one night stand. In a decade, she hadn't considered a human of the opposite sex as worth more than eight hours of her time. But Ethan, this new kind of protective, professional sexy in her world, she couldn't explain or deny it, but she wanted him to stick around.

"I do like him. I'm just not sure how that works, you know? He's here for a job. I *am* his job. He's been assigned to me less than twenty-four-hours, how can you seriously say it's 'a thing' after only that short time?"

"Honey, Kurt and I knew within the first twenty minutes. It's reality—maybe not love at first sight, but enough to know you want more than just lust. And, you are my job too, but if I were straight, I'd nail you, you know he wants to. Maybe it's a matter of time. Use this situation, this free few weeks away from the stress of the real world, to get to know him a little. Maybe once it's all over, it won't 'be over' if you know what I mean."

"Dear Lord, I have missed you," she said. They both laughed, face to the heavens, inviting every raindrop.

Chapter Seven

Declan swerved the rented blue Chevy Bolt briskly through the yellow light cursing out loud. He was confident the man at the wheel of the red Tesla was the same one who had interrupted his attempt to kidnap his victim the night before. Now the hulk in a dark suit was throwing a wrench of a whole new kind into his best-laid plans. He had to be some kind of law enforcement, and though he anticipated the involvement of cops, he knew his mailed notes would bring attention from police or FBI as they drew Aurora out of the dark, he hadn't planned for them to intervene so quickly.

He cranked the Rob Zombie song blaring on the radio and screamed out loud, gripping the steering wheel with white knuckles. He had planned to intercept her as soon as he figured out which office called the authorities first. When UCSF didn't email his note to her personal assistant, he should have acted faster, taken a plane ride perhaps.

He should have just gone to the hospital and dragged her out by her hair with a gun to her head. Before long, everyone was going to know the truth anyway, and he would be joining his wife and daughter, so what did it matter?

Too late now.

Watching the crimson car pull off the freeway, he had known they were diverting from their destination in Palo Alto. The only person he'd been able to link to her was that queer assistant of hers. Since they changed directions, they had no doubt noticed his pursuit. He would have to delay his plans yet again. Scarlet faced and searing mad he considered whether or not he could draw her away from her knight in shining armor and threw his coffee cup at the passenger window.

He sharply turned the car and diverted down a side road. He needed someplace to aim the hate that had been boiling up in him steadily from the time he'd seen her ride away with someone else at the wheel. Pulling over, he popped the trunk and got out to retrieve the pistol he had brought just in case of a situation like this. He had to focus, and he had work to do. He wasn't finished, and he needed to accomplish what he had set out to do. Now he was just going to have to do it with extra collateral damage.

Chapter Eight

Tom knocked on the front door at one forty-five, almost exactly forty-five minutes from when Ethan had texted him. Relieved and already packed up, Ethan let him in, itching to get going.

"Do I get an introduction before you leave?" Tom asked.

"Ty and Rick can introduce you. I'll be back as soon as I can. I'd like to beat the traffic." As Ethan threw his backpack up over his shoulder, he was almost to the door when Aurora came down the stairs.

"Where are you going?" her voice held concern.

"Dr. Soileaux, this is Special Agent Tom Quillet, he's going to cover me for a couple of hours while I retrieve some personal items and a few files from the office. I'll be back later this afternoon."

"Someone couldn't retrieve those things for you so you could stay?" Anxiety shot through her, momentarily unchecked. Ethan stared at her, not sure how to react. He hadn't prepared for her to be nervous about him leaving. Trent came down the stairs behind her and threw an arm around her shoulder.

"Honey, how many people have a key to *your* apartment?" he asked.

"Oh, right, sorry. I didn't think of that. But how are you getting back? We came in my car."

"I was going to use the company car Tom came in. I'll bring it back later."

"But your motorcycle is still in the garage at Avalon. Why don't you take the Tesla? You can leave it there for me, retrieve your bike, and we can make room in the garage for it here. Then you aren't stranded when everyone else leaves." Ethan paused and considered for a moment. A company ride was never far away, but it would be nice to have the independence of his motorcycle.

"If you're sure you're alright with that, it would be helpful, thank you."

"She never lets *me* drive the new Tesla," Trent smirked as she went to retrieve the keys.

"That's because I bought you your own, you turd," she called back from the kitchen. Tom merely raised his eyebrows in a passing glance to Ethan, who returned a look of indifference.

"Well, there's that, but it's not a roadster." Trent rolled his eyes, and she poked him in the ribs as she handed Ethan the keys.

"Yes, well, you'll have to move your model three before he gets back, poor baby." She rolled her eyes in response and went to the front door beside Ethan.

"Agent Quilt, he can reach you if he needs to?" she asked.

Ethan smiled for a change and said, "It's Quillet, not quilt, and yes, he can reach me, but he's capable. I wouldn't leave you with anyone I don't personally trust. I'll be back soon." Her behavior warmed him and he felt her preference for him to be around was a sincere compliment.

He slipped his sunglasses on and noticed as he went down the front steps outside that it took her a long time to close the door behind him. Inside the Tesla, he cranked the air conditioning, enjoying the peace and quiet of only the fan. Traffic was light, and he began making a mental list of things he had to grab from home. The rain was falling in waves, and he was careful to watch his speed. The car seemed to have a mind of its own for speeding.

Passing Shoreview Drive, he happened to catch emergency lights in the rearview mirror, but as he changed lanes, he also caught sight of a blue Chevy Bolt about five cars back. *No way,* he thought, *it has to be a coincidence.* He slowed and waited for the ambulance to pass him before getting back into the second lane from the left, and sure enough, the blue car shifted lanes right behind him. He waited a couple of exits, and when he had a clear lane to his left again, he switched quickly and hit the gas, watching the blue car keep up with him perfectly.

The Tesla hummed along smoothly as he hit eighty, then ninety, and at nearly a hundred miles per hour, cars in front of him forced him to let off the gas. He switched lanes back to the right again, pulling out his cell phone. The Chevy caught up with him as dispatch for CHP answered. He rattled off his FBI badge number, hands tensing on the wheel.

"I need support on Highway 101 north at my location. I have a tail I believe to be a critical suspect." The dispatcher put him on hold a moment, and in front of him, traffic thickened and began to slow. Once connected directly with a unit, he rattled off the exit numbers he was approaching. The officers were about two miles behind him, not close enough.

Rain began to pelt again, thick and drenching. He fidgeted to get the windshield wipers on, and as traffic began to move again, he lost sight of the Bolt momentarily. Turning his head to search behind him, he almost missed a car cutting him off, and the collision alert system beeped, braking automatically. Traffic in front of him screeched to a halt. Before he could get his bearings to locate the blue Bolt again, it was in the blind spot on his left, and the windows of the Tesla popped loudly on both sides of him from a gunshot.

He closed his eyes instinctively and held them shut for a split second to shield them from flying glass, opening them just in time to see the blurry back end of the assailant's car speeding away in the breakdown lane. Officers still on the phone questioned what had happened, and though he tried to change lanes to pursue, he was already blocked in by civilian cars. They might get lucky enough to catch up to him with sirens blaring, but it was a long shot. People in the cars around him didn't even seem to notice what had just happened.

Ethan smacked the wheel hard, grinding his teeth in anger, screaming, "Catch him!" into the phone still on speaker. A minute later, the CHP passed him in the breakdown lane, impeded by the public. Traffic was moving just fast enough to give the bastard a good lead, and Ethan sagged back into the seat, feeling defeated. He didn't notice the sting on his chin until he began evaluating the holes in the windows, spider webs of broken glass radiating outward from the tiny punctures. Bright red soaked his white shirt as he took off his tie to stop the bleeding and check out the wound in the mirror.

Just a scratch, he realized as traffic began to regain speed around him. Too close for comfort, though, as he pictured what could have happened had it been Aurora behind the wheel, unaware of her surroundings. Whoever it was had decent aim and had he not been cut off, forcing him to stop faster than anticipated, it might have been the end of him. His skin crawled, and he unbuttoned his weapon from its holster if only to make him feel better.

The officers chattered without regard for him listening, so he interjected, "Call me if you catch him or at least get a plate," and without waiting for a response hung up. Rain seeped in the hole in the glass beside him, breaking off tiny pieces in the wind. He dialed Tom.

"Yes, boss?" Music played in the background upbeat and peppy.

"You're not going to believe what just happened."

"Try me," he said flatly.

"I just got shot at."

"No shit," the reply came with only the slight surprise of an affirming statement.

"Well, I got shot, but it's only a scratch on my chin."

"So you have an excuse not to shave for a couple of days? Sweet."

"Way to think on the bright side, Pollyanna," Ethan snarked.

"Polly-who?"

"Shut up, Quillet, never mind. I need you to see if you can get into any cameras on or near the freeway on my route back, get a look at the guy behind the wheel of a blue Chevy Bolt. It's a rental, I'm sure, but if we can get a face, it would help a lot. Oh, and maybe don't tell Dr. Soileaux her Tesla needs new windows yet, I'll handle that when I get back."

"Sure thing, on it, boss," Tom hung up. At least Ethan could trust the guy to do his job without being coached continuously, whether he knew his historical television greats or not.

He drove the rest of the way in silence, contemplating the actions of the suspect. It didn't all add up in his mind. Threats, with obvious intent to abduct her, had escalated into a severe attempt to snuff her out. Why? What had changed in the last forty-eight hours that would push the suspect from poking and prodding for information, to quick and straightforward murder? He became lost in scenarios, running through previous cases and possible motives. Before he could make any sense of it, he was pulling into her parking garage.

He went briefly to the front desk to let the clerk know the Tesla in the garage was damaged and retrieved a bag to empty the glove compartment and anything from the trunk in case anyone got the idea to rummage through it. He wasn't surprised to find it mostly empty. Other than a few napkins, a flashlight, some loose change, a spare pair of sunglasses, and the usual insurance information, the car was empty. She had said she didn't drive it much.

He returned the bag to the front desk for safekeeping and was on his motorcycle on his way to the office within ten minutes. It was almost three o'clock, and if he was going to avoid traffic, he needed to hurry. At Golden Avenue, he decided to keep his armored jacket on to avoid being questioned about the blood on his shirt. He was still stopped a half dozen times when coworkers noticed his chin. After quickly retrieving the files he needed, he was left with a half-hour to grab a few items from his apartment.

Dumping the rumpled contents of the backpack haphazardly onto his bed, he quickly threw in dress pants, jeans, a couple of shirts, and new underclothes. Stuffing everything in tight, he figured he would have to throw it in the dryer to avoid looking like he'd slept in it, but it couldn't be prevented. He quickly changed into a casual shirt, threw his bloody shirt into the sink in cold water and soap with the hope it would wash out, pulled on some jeans, and was out of the apartment in twenty minutes flat.

Back on the freeway, the feel of the bike raised his spirits, as did the fact California had a split lanes law so that he could bypass the bumper to bumper gridlock. Passing the spot where the killer had shot at him, he slowed down and paid close attention to surrounding businesses. There was a gas station on one side of the freeway, but most likely too far away to get any kind of detailed view of the driver. Cursing CHP, he sped on, anxiety about where the killer could be raising his blood pressure. *He thought he was shooting at Aurora, didn't he?* Ethan wondered, and a whole new set of scenarios began popping in his mind. What if the shooter knew it wasn't her behind the wheel?

Pulling into the driveway of the mansion, he was both relieved and alarmed the garage door was open, indoor lights on, with Tom and the cyber nerds waiting for his arrival. They were lost in conversation as he pulled in and dropped the kickstand.

"Hey, boss," Tom greeted him, "welcome back."

"Did you get in touch with CHP? Any luck on cameras with a view of the freeway?"

"CHP didn't get him. They're still looking, BOLO in place but no luck. There was a gas station, but it was too far off the highway for cameras to be effective if they even had working cameras."

"Of course," Ethan said sourly as he got off the bike and started taking off his jacket.

"How's the chin?" Tom walked closer, "Nice little slice you've got there."

"It's fine, just ruined a shirt, I think, no big deal."

"Fraction of an inch more, and that bullet would have taken off part off your jaw, to say the least."

"Yea, I was lucky. Not lucky enough to catch the prick, but I get to live to die another day." The garage door started to close, and they turned to see Aurora standing in the doorway to the house in a long, pale blue flowing maxi skirt with a slit to above her knee and a white form-fitting cotton shirt with a v-neck. She darted across the garage barefoot and immediately grabbed Ethan by the face, firmly clasping his muscular, square jaw in her long, elegant fingers.

"Shot at." She said sharply as she turned his face so she could see the cut in the light. "You got shot at because of me?" her face twisted, obviously holding back emotion she couldn't process. His hand came up and gently closed around her wrist. Tom and the cyber nerds had already made a swift exit back into the house.

"It's just a scratch, really, but I'm sorry about your car." Her fingers slid off his cheek, but he didn't let go of her. As his hand fell, it slipped into hers, and she squeezed, refusing to let go.

"I don't care about the car." She rolled her eyes, shaking her head as she continued to study his face. "I could buy ten of those cars over and never miss the money. My life hasn't been about money since I was fourteen."

"Still, it sucks. It's a nice car," he shifted to sling his backpack off his shoulder and began to lead her into the house. "I put your things from the glove compartment into a bag and left them with the front desk of the Avalon."

"I had things in the glove box?" she asked, genuinely surprised.

"Some sunglasses, napkins, nothing exciting." As he pulled the door to the house open, she caught him by the zipper on his jacket and held him back.

"I'm happy you're alright, and I'm sorry you went through that for me. Whatever you need, anything I can do for you, or to make things easier, just say the word." She stepped close, looking up at him with her tawny, emerald flecked eyes fixed on him, the knuckles of her hand pressed against his chest as she clung to his jacket zipper. She was so petite standing so close, like he could scoop her up, light as a feather, and hold her against him.

Career, professionalism, and wariness for their situation, blared in the back of his mind, but for a moment, only a short and scorching moment between them, he pictured what could be. In a split second, he imagined bending to meet her luscious lips to suck, soft and inviting, warm and willing. Her smell swirled around him again, citrus and spicy as her hair radiated the scent, fresh and robust. Trent called her name from the top of the stairs, and Ethan inhaled sharply, breaking his reverie.

He broke her grip, simply whispered, "Thanks," and started up the stairs ahead of her, feeling hot coals in his chest. The house smelled terrific; something with garlic and butter overwhelmed his senses as he ascended the stairs. The brightly lit kitchen welcomed him, and fresh flowers in a large vase adorned the counter. The dining table to the right boasted more flowers, fancy china settings with sparkling silver edges sat at every chair, and a salad, fresh bread, butter with flaked salt, and three bottles of wine already waited for guests.

"Agent Hartman, I'm glad to see you've sustained no major injury, welcome back." Trent had a plaid, masculine apron on, and was busy fussing around seafood at the sink. Ethan just nodded at him in acknowledgment.

"So much for not saying anything?" he sneered at Tom.

"She's quiet. She snuck up on us and has good hearing boss, I tried," Tom shrugged back. The cyber geeks had packed up and were ready to leave, black bags with laptops waiting by the front door.

"I need tomorrow to get organized. I take it you've sent me all you could find?" Ethan asked them, and they nodded in agreement simultaneously. "Alright then, get out of here, I'll be in touch if I need you, so make yourselves available," he said sternly.

"See you later, boss," Tom had already fished out his keys. A brief goodbye was said, and as Ethan went up to the third floor, he watched Aurora close the door behind them.

He dropped his backpack on the bed and his motorcycle jacket with his helmet onto a toy box beside it. After a glance in the mirror at his chin, he decided it wasn't even worth a bandage and headed back downstairs. A brief awkward feeling swept through him as he walked into the kitchen where Trent and Aurora were whispering, standing close to one another. When Trent caught sight of him, his eyes flashed towards Ethan before his eyebrows raised quickly, and Aurora turned to greet him.

"Are you hungry? Can I get you a drink?" she asked. She held out a hand indicating he could sit at the counter, and as soon as he slid into a barstool, Bastet was seated in the one beside him, meowing for attention.

"I'll have a soda if you have any?" Ethan asked as he began to scratch the cat tenderly.

"Soda?" Trent made a face of disgust. "Make him an Italian, with cream," he shot Aurora a sideways glance.

"I need wine," she said as she marveled at the cat. She twirled a few times and gathered a bottle of red wine, club soda, and a glass full of ice. "What's your favorite fruit or berry?" she asked Ethan.

"Um, maybe strawberries," he shrugged. He didn't care to admit that he didn't eat that much fresh produce. He was more of a fast food, take-out barbeque kind of guy. Trent opened the wine as she fiddled in a cabinet, clinking bottles before coming up with a strawberry Torani syrup. She poured club soda over ice in a fluted pint glass then added a shot glass full of the syrup. Aurora stirred it while she took her first sip of wine then poured a few tablespoons of cream over the top. The cream billowed into the glass like a cloud settling through the pink ice, and she handed it to Ethan carefully, obviously admiring the way it looked.

He was skeptical at first, as he couldn't imagine the taste of cream in strawberry soda, but at first sip, he realized it was something exotic. It was like drinking velvet. The cream blended on top of strawberries with just enough bubbles to zing his taste buds and was delicious. It was cold, refreshing, and unlike anything he'd ever had before. His face must have shown it as he caught Aurora studying him intently.

His stomach suddenly growled at the thought of food, the smell around him lifting his spirits. Trent was busy tasting a sauce on the stove, then turned to rinse clams in the sink and within a step or two had added some breaded kind of fish to a frying pan sizzling delicately.

"Alright, let's make it official, the night is coming to an end." Trent turned to Aurora, "Are all the doors locked?" he asked.

"Yes," she smiled.

"Are all the first-floor windows closed?"

"Yes," her eyes looked to the ceiling as if mentally checking off the task of closing each window.

"Are the doors downstairs all locked and the garage closed?"

"I'll double-check now," she started to stroll away, but Ethan caught her.

"No, you won't," he said tersely, "at least not alone." She shot him a skeptical look over her shoulder as she headed downstairs. She stayed by the landing and watched as he rounded the room, checking each window and door, pulling shades.

"I could have done that, I'm a thorough person."

We seem to have a thorough killer as well, he thought but kept his mouth shut, instead just smiling at her politely.

Back upstairs, Trent was swirling in the kitchen.

"Do you have any foods that you find repulsive like you just can't bear to put them in your mouth?" he asked Ethan.

"Brussels sprouts, Greek yogurt, and sushi," Ethan replied.

Trent's mouth fell open, a look of horror on his face. He blinked emphatically and shook his head in shock.

"We'll have to work on that, but for tonight I can deal." His fingers flailed in protest as his hands flew up between them as if flagging traffic. "This evening, we have steamed clams in a white wine garlic butter sauce, Aurora's favorite," he turned and winked as she smiled. "Along with fresh vegetable salad accompanied by homemade creamy balsamic vinaigrette. We have fresh cod in crusted Panko with remoulade and a fine drizzle of cilantro crème sauce, in addition to seared bacon-wrapped asparagus, mushroom risotto, and homemade bread, ending with another favorite of Aurora's—chocolate mousse."

"Do you always cook like this?" Ethan asked, and he could see a smile on Trent's face.

"Only as much as I possibly can." He spun around as Aurora came up behind him, planting a quick kiss on her cheek as she retrieved another wine glass and poured some for him. After toasting him silently, she rounded the counter to sit beside Ethan, eyeing Bastet in his lap purring contentedly, and the gun tucked under his arm timidly. He could tell it made her nervous, but that she accepted the need for it in the current situation.

"What do you think, little lioness?" she asked as she reached to stroke the cat's head sweetly, "shall we keep Agent Hartman around awhile?" Bastet stretched her paws out, kneading Ethan's stomach as she curled deeper into the crook of his lap. He wasn't sure what to say, so he said nothing, running his fingers through the silken fur of the pleased cat.

"Music!" Trent shouted, clapping his hands. Aurora stood on the rung of the stool to reach over the counter and retrieve her phone. Opening an app, she scrolled through a long list of songs.

"What do you like?" she asked Ethan, sliding the phone in front of him. He tried to sip the soda, but it went down so easy he realized he had already gulped half of it.

"Can I play anything?" he asked. Trent whipped around from the stove, shaking his finger furiously.

"Cheater!" he cried. Aurora laughed, and Trent said, "You have to show us *you,* and not worry about what we will think, music is the voice of the soul, be you, just play!" He giggled and sipped wine, spinning back on his tiptoes.

Lord he is so comfortable with who he is, I wish I could be that way.

Ethan wasn't sure why, but the thought of being judged based on the music he chose had him feeling self-conscious. It shouldn't have, but it struck him as personal and seemed daunting, causing anxiety to creep up in him. *Silly,* he thought, *there shouldn't be anything wrong with them knowing me on a more personal level, this should be simple.* He thought for a moment about growing up, about spending time with his grandparents' camping, about fishing with his dad, countless starry nights and hot days at the lake, things they would never see behind the suit of a hardened FBI Agent. For better or for worse, between these two very trendy people, he chose a childhood favorite.

Breaking the silence of the sizzling fish Alan Jackson's *'Livin' On Love'* blared out of the Bluetooth speaker. Ethan guzzled the soda as a rosy pink to match it unwillingly flared up in his cheeks. For an instant, he felt embarrassed like a simpleton, but in perfect time with the music, Aurora's voice sailed along at the very first word. Trent squealed delightedly, waving a spatula as he bounced in front of the stove.

Ethan was floored. He looked at her as if she were an alien as she sang every word, not only because she *knew* the words, but because her voice was incredible. Warm and inviting, powerful but smooth, her shoulders swayed to the rhythm confidently singing every word.

He stared at her in awe, hoping the amazement on his face didn't translate as creepy. At the end of the song, she paused it, and Trent swung around clearly enthused and snatched the phone.

"My turn!" he smiled as he typed something in, and Aurora giggled. "Sing it, sister! You know this is my favorite!" He danced, jumping back and forth with flair as Madonna's *'Vogue'* streamed out. They both made silly moves with their hands, and Trent teased her, "Don't poke an eye out!"

Ethan finally laughed, feeling more relaxed.

By the time the song ended, Ethan was thoroughly impressed with Trent's dance moves and hanging on the edge of his seat as to what would come next. Aurora took her time flipping through to find the next song.

"Well, there are so many choices, not one song speaks to me, but if we're going for something that speaks to me at the moment, I have to go with Mimi." Mariah Carey's *'Fantasy'* dominated the room as she turned the volume up. Trent spun around laughing so hard Ethan was worried he might pass out, wondering what was so funny.

There has to be an inside joke. Ethan thought.

Ethan watched them suspiciously, trying to pick up on cues that would tell him why that song, in particular, was so funny. He didn't catch anything telling. Wiping tears of laughter out of the corner of his eyes, Trent turned and scooped the fish out of the pan. Pulling the clams off the burner, he drained them, emptied them into a shallow dish where he promptly poured a sauce over them and began taking the food to the dining room.

Aurora sang beautifully at the top of her lungs as she helped him transfer food to the table. The two danced together and swirled around the room, and Ethan was caught up in the moment, amazed at how easy their friendship was. Some small part of him admired what they had in a vein of jealousy. Remembering his sister he couldn't help but wonder if he would look the same with her today if she were still with him.

As the song concluded, Aurora paused the music and poured him another Italian soda before waving him into the dining room with a spicy smile. As they sat and broke bread, hefted delicious food onto their plates, and shared stories, the weight of the situation disappeared for a short time. Trent asked questions of Ethan while expertly revealing small things about Aurora. As the evening wore on, Ethan felt he was becoming acquainted with them in far more than just his routine professional manner, and loved every minute of it.

Trent insisted on serving the chocolate mousse, topped with fresh whipping cream, in martini glasses in the living room. With cocoa sprinkled on top and fancy cookie straws sticking out, Ethan believed the man was a chef in a previous career. By the time they finished dessert, he was dreading the hundred pushups, sit-ups, and half-hour of jumping jacks that he would need to do just to work off the dessert. They all helped clean, and he couldn't help but notice Aurora tripped lightly in bare feet, swaying with the radio and the whirl of wine in her head.

A cuckoo clock he hadn't previously noticed chimed lightly from the dining room, signaling ten o'clock and Aurora sighed as she sipped the last of her wine.

"It's bedtime," she said in a sigh.

"Indeed, my love. You know how you are, don't push it," Trent shuffled her off as he took her glass.

"I'm going to check the perimeter one more time, I'll be back in a few minutes," Ethan retrieved a flashlight from his computer case in the library office. As he turned to go out the backdoor, Aurora caught him at the foot of the stairs.

"Should Trent go with you, strength in numbers?" she asked as she reached for his arm.

He smiled and said, "This is what I do all the time. I'll be right back, don't worry." He couldn't help but notice a concern in her demeanor and how she again studied his weapon in the shoulder holster intently. He slipped out the back door as Trent whistled while washing the last few dishes.

Just outside Ethan could hear him telling Aurora, "I'm not sure why you think I'd be any help to him, other than to perhaps explain why *'Fantasy'* was your song choice tonight. Did you see the look on his face? Clueless. We've got to work on that." They both laughed, and the inside joke dawned on Ethan.

Did she mean that I am her fantasy? That can't be right.

He pushed the thought out of his head and rounding the yard he made sure the gate was still locked and that no one was lurking on the premises. The night was crisp and fresh, the heat of the day had dissipated, and the rain had passed, leaving behind only the sweet smell of flower pollen lingering in the air. As he went back towards the house, a light in the upstairs came on, and he could see Aurora was in the studio, her silhouette well defined in the light. Pausing for a moment, he admired her shape. Her arms went up, lifting the hair off her shoulders, defining her slender neck.

He shook his head, trying to remind himself and his heart, this was not a woman with which he could have anything more than a professional relationship. At least not until the Hypocrite killer was behind bars, or dead. Heading back into the house, he was plagued with the memory of her smell, her touch, her laugh, her voice, how smart she was, even her choice in music. Everything about her drew him to her.

Back inside, he said goodnight to Trent, who was shutting lights off, double-checking that the doors were locked, and setting the alarm.

"If she snores, wake her up and make her drink some water," Trent winked at him as he darted up the stairs and slipped into his room. After a final pass around the house to double-check windows and doors himself, Ethan headed upstairs. Aurora had ducked into the room beside Trent's and closed the door, so he went into the bathroom in the kid's room and began to brush his teeth. He tried to flatten out his outfits over a chair, but they were hopelessly wrinkled. He plugged in his phone charger and sprawled out on the bed to catch up on emails and the day's baseball scores. It wasn't ten minutes before Aurora came tiptoeing in.

"Am I going to keep you awake if I'm on my phone?" he asked.

"Heavens no, I sleep like the dead." She set a bottle of water on the pink nightstand beside the other bed and pulled the covers back. She was wearing a pair of loose cotton pajamas that consisted of shorts and a tank top in a bright pink floral pattern and had her hair pulled back. Her skin looked damp from having just washed her face. She slipped off flip flops, slid beneath the covers, and rolled to face him.

"Are you going to sleep alright in that bed? It's small for you, I'm sure, but it's probably the best option in the house. Unless you want to sleep with Trent." She smiled a teasing, crooked smile.

"I don't ever sleep well, a side effect of the job, and yes, this bed is fine. It's quite comfortable."

"Well, for whatever rest you can get, I hope it's good, goodnight." She reached out and snapped off the pearlescent pink lamp beside her, and he would have sworn she was sound asleep within ninety seconds. Bastet came slinking in before long and hopped on the bed beside her, settling between the pillow and the headboard above her head, purring in a quick rhythm.

After catching up on the baseball scores for the day, reviewing the injury report, deleting some emails, and sending a text replying to his mom telling her not to worry as he was out of touch on a case, he plugged the phone in and shoved the covers back. He was still wearing sweatpants and a plain black t-shirt and loosened the holster around his chest to be slightly more comfortable yet practical. He usually ever only tucked his feet barely beneath the blankets in anticipation of having to jump up quickly, but they hung off the edge of the bed, so he left them off entirely.

Listening intently, he familiarized himself with the sounds of the house. Trent was talking softly, apparently finishing up a phone conversation, and the light chime of the cuckoo clock could be heard every half hour from downstairs. Other than tree limbs scraping the house in the breeze, and the purring of the cat, everything was quiet. Stretched sideways on the full-size mattress, he tucked a pillow beneath his head and rested in a light, undisturbed sleep.

Chapter Nine

Declan laid his laptop, tablet, and other equipment out on the small desk in the hotel room, checking everything for damage and battery life. Everything was irritating him. The hum of the freeway outside, the yellow of the bedside lamp, the cold bright white tile that transitioned from the bathroom too far into the bedroom, was all under his skin. He gritted his teeth. The last two days had not gone as planned.

Not only had he been prevented from capturing the sexy little doctor who was part of his plan, he'd missed eliminating the thug government official who had now become her shadow. He hated law enforcement. All he had ever seen of a jackass in a uniform was too much focus and time spent on good people in unfortunate situations and not enough time locking up real criminals.

He carefully organized his backpack, securing all his small devices and their controls back into the protective cases they belonged in. He then turned to the bottle of Jack Daniels he'd saved as a celebration for a job well done, that hadn't gotten done at all. It left him with a lot of surveillance work to do the next day.

Pouring a stiff shot into a plastic glass with soda and ice, he kicked off his shoes and chugged half of it, sprawling out on the bed, still fuming. He wanted to be done already, wanted to have the doctor in his trunk, and be on his way to Santa Cruz to finish the whole thing off. But apparently, that wasn't meant to be, so instead, he would have to make due. Knocking off a couple of CHP or an FBI Agent while he was wrapping up his mission would have been a bonus. Maybe tomorrow, he thought, as he rolled onto the blanket Eda Jean had made for their sweet Candice.

Chugging the last of the Jack and Coke, he snapped off the light in the cold, sterile hotel room, trying hard to smell a bit of each of his girls on the one thing he'd taken with him from both of them. Unable to sleep, his mind ran through corrections to his disrupted plan. The ideas popping in his head for sending a little extra terror through Dr. Soileaux pleased him as he drifted off to sleep.

Chapter Ten

Ethan wasn't sure what woke him, but cold sweat had soaked his back. He had been dreaming, a dream he hadn't experienced in a long time, wandering long hospital hallways trying but unable to find the source of weeping. His mind flashed back before coming to the present, in a bed too small for him beside someone he was trying to protect. Listening, he tried to get his bearings and heard the cat, purring lightly.

His heart was in overdrive, racing in his ribcage as he took a deep breath, trying to shake the emotion of the dream. His mouth was dry, and his head hurt, his throat was stinging and felt parched. Deciding he needed a glass of water, he sat up and swung his bare feet onto the plush carpet. As he stood up, Bastet promptly decided he needed company and jumped off the bed to dart behind him. He quietly went downstairs, listening for anything out of the ordinary, all was serene.

Finding the drinking glasses in the third cabinet he opened, he filled a pint from the refrigerator and promptly chugged half of it. Bastet meowed low and twirled in between his legs, rubbing against him, arching her back for attention. He refilled the glass and knelt to pet the cat, resting on one knee, still admiring how much softer she was than any other cat he'd known. Sipping the refreshing water, listening to her purr, he never heard Aurora slipping around the corner, and she didn't see him, kneeling with the cat.

As she came around the counter, believing he was still in bed, the figure in black at her waist height sent terror ripping through her as he stood. She jumped a foot straight up as he almost bumped into her with his head, and a shrieking scream escaped from her toes. Reacting lightning fast, he sloshed water all over just before dropping the glass, which instantly shattered into a thousand pieces, to grab her before she came out of her skin.

"It's me, it's Ethan!" he shouted as his arms closed around her to keep her from stepping backward into broken glass. Her instinct was to shove him away, so her hands came up in front of her, though it did her no good. He pulled her tight against him, securing her arms.

"Dear God and all that's holy, what the hell are you doing on the kitchen floor?" She demanded in a panting gasping voice, distraught, sweat bursting at her brow. He held her so tight she nearly came off her toes, but once she realized it was him, she exhaled, rested her forehead against his chest, and relaxed into his arms.

"Sorry," he gasped, "I just came for a glass of water, and I bent down to pet Bastet. I didn't hear you come down." Her arms came around him to steady herself as she began to shake and laugh at the same time.

"I thought you were still in bed, I didn't even look," she almost laughed. For a brief moment, they stood there together, embraced, solidly linked. For the first time, she could feel his strength, the muscles of his biceps around her, his back taut and hard as steel. She could smell him, as she let her face rest against his chest, his cotton shirt warm and clean. His heart thundered wildly, as did hers, both of them breathing too fast from the scare.

In between the fright, and recovering from it, was a brief moment of connection. His hands softened, caressing her without thinking about it, flat and holding her secure. Her fingers traced the small of his back before reaching up to pull his shoulder down towards her. For the first time, she noticed how his biceps filled out the sleeves of his shirt entirely, tight over his impressive muscles.

He could smell her hair, and for the first time, feel the softness of it, the silken locks loose over bare shoulders that resembled the texture of delicate flower petals. Holding her against him, he became aware of how petite she indeed was, curvy and beautiful, but frail. His fingers had found a small piece of skin between her shirt and shorts, and the electricity radiating off her was dazzling. Her perky, perfect breasts pressed against him, and as reality began to sink in that he was holding her, he snapped to attention. If he didn't let her go, something else was going to stand at attention.

As had been the case several times already, Trent saved the day. The lights in the hallway came on, and his voice came hailing from the third floor. His shadow bounced down the stairs, and he came sliding around the corner behind it, wielding a large flashlight as a weapon.

"What the hell?" he screeched. He snapped on lights to the kitchen and stood dumbfounded as Ethan raised a hand to stop him from stepping in the glass. Aurora noticed Bastet had leaped onto the counter and was licking her paws, utterly unaffected and unconcerned about the commotion.

"Everything's alright, just a misunderstanding. We startled each other. Sorry about the glass. If you can grab my shoes, I'll gladly clean it up for you." Ethan loosened his grip on Aurora. She refused to loosen hers as he lifted her easily to set her on the counter.

"Sweet Jesus, you almost gave me a heart attack! You're lucky I don't own a gun." Trent panted, standing in nothing but cherry red boxers covered in white and black lip imprints he clung to the wall for stability. "Hold on. I'll be right back."

He returned a moment later wearing flip flops with a royal blue silk robe on and rushed past them into a pantry closet built beneath the stairs. He unleashed a robotic vacuum and whipped out a regular broom and dustpan. After he cleared a small area, Ethan snatched the broom from him and continued cleaning.

"What the hell were the two of you doing?" Trent retrieved a bottle of brandy from the liquor cabinet, and crunching unconcerned over the broken glass poured a stiff double shot.

"I got thirsty, and I came down to get a drink. Bastet followed me, and I was petting her. I never heard Aurora come down," Ethan said.

"I wanted some ice cream. I thought he was in bed." Aurora averted her eyes to the ceiling as Trent looked to her with scorn.

"Midnight snacks? Are we there? Already?"

"Maybe," she refused to look at him. Without a second thought, he took a hefty drink of the brandy, then retrieved a spoon and a pint of ice cream from the freezer, handing both to her. After taking another sip, he got down a new water glass, filled it to the rim, and set it beside Aurora for Ethan, motioning to him.

"Let the robot do the rest. Cleaning isn't what you get paid for."

Ethan smiled, and after dropping his dustpan full of glass shards into the trash, sat beside Aurora. He was impressed she had quickly put a good dent in the ice cream.

"So, any flavor that starts with chocolate?" he asked as he drank more water.

"Mostly," she said, "my favorite is Chocolate Therapy, but I like Americone Dream, and what girl doesn't love Chocolate Chip Cookie Dough, and Cookies and Cream? Once in awhile, when I'm feeling randy, I go for some Tonight Dough, but Rocky Road and Chocolate Therapy mostly hold my heart."

He smiled ruefully at her, "Do you share your delicacies?"

She smiled back, and without a word, Trent tossed him a spoon.

The three of them chatted aimlessly about spooking other people and laughed over silly stories while they finished their midnight indulgences. After a half-hour, they were all ready to return to slumber. Trent swayed up the stairs first as Aurora and Ethan headed up the rear, flipping off the lights.

"Sweet dreams, ya'll. Stay in bed this time." Trent didn't look back but waved a hand high over his shoulder as he tripped into his room. Aurora turned off the light in the hallway as Bastet darted between her feet. Losing her footing, she reached for the door jamb and felt Ethan's hands steady her waist from behind. Spinning to face him as she pushed the door open, she reached for him, grasping his shoulders firmly even though she'd regained her balance.

In the darkness, he loomed over her entirely dressed in black, and she thought she should feel threatened. His sheer height and girth and the absolute strength in him should make her feel vulnerable, but instead, she felt reassured. Holding onto him as he held onto her, they took a few steps together towards the bed.

"You alright?" he asked in a hushed voice.

"Yeah," she whispered, "thanks to you." Without thinking about it, without considering consequences or the predicament she was in, her hand slid up to his face. Feeling the muscle of his thick neck, she pulled before sliding her hand to his cheek, gracing the wound on his chin with her thumb, she turned his face and kissed him softly on the cheek. She lingered and could feel him tense, could feel the wrought iron of his stature hold stone still, but he didn't recoil. He didn't make a move towards her but instead stood unmoving until she slipped away from him, whispering, "Goodnight and sweet dreams."

He had let her go, but he hadn't pushed her away. As he fell into bed, for the second time of the evening, his mind unwillingly drifted to her. He focused on the feel of her fingers, soft silky hair, spicy-sweet smell, and the light in her eyes that beamed sparkles when she laughed. As he drifted to sleep for the second time, his dreams turned this time to possibilities that he wouldn't allow himself to entertain while he was awake.

Aurora was surprised when she heard Ethan stirring upstairs, a little after six. She had slipped carefully downstairs less than a half an hour earlier and was sipping coffee, curled up in a plush Papasan chair, indulging in a book as she had not done in quite some time. As he came downstairs, she rose to get him coffee, meeting him in the kitchen.

"Good morning," she sweetly smiled as she pulled out a coffee mug.

"Good morning, again, I suppose." He smiled mischievously at her, watching her fill a reusable coffee pod and pop it into the machine.

"How well did you sleep for the rest of the night?"

"You mean after the heart attack wore off? Just fine." He stood across from her, specifically out of arms reach, not only because the feel of her lips was still fresh on his mind but because he didn't trust himself not to touch her. She wielded a power over him that he knew he needed more than willpower to manage.

"Did you get enough sleep through the rest of the night?" he asked as she handed him the cup of steaming black coffee. He was still wearing black sweatpants and a tight black cotton shirt. In the light of the kitchen, she couldn't help but remember feeling his arms around her and again admired the way his biceps filled out the short sleeves. She was beginning to look at him in a whole new way, and a flutter ran through her.

"I did, but I'd make it up some other way if I needed to. I could take a nap, and it's just as good as nighttime rest."

"I can relate to that," he sipped the coffee.

"So, what's on the agenda today?"

"Research, putting pieces of the puzzle together, trying to figure out next moves and get ahead of this guy." He tried to make it sound less intense than it was.

"Anything I can help with?" she asked.

He shook his head and said, "Other than staying put, maybe answering a few questions, not really."

"For right now that's easy enough," she shrugged, not wanting to let him know she was already feeling claustrophobic, "not that I want to rush you or anything but what do you think it's going to take to get this guy?"

"You mean, how long?"

She nodded at him as she poured herself another cup of coffee since hers was half-finished and had gone cold already.

"It's hard to tell, and I can't make any promises. I'd love to guarantee we'll catch him but I can't. All I can say is they haven't handed me a case I haven't closed, so far."

"Impressive," she smiled.

"It keeps me employed, and on that note, I think I'll get started for the day." He tipped the mug to her in thanks as she poured sweet cream in hers. She watched him turn and walk away, and it occurred to her had they put anyone else on this case she wouldn't have been nearly as content to put her life on hold.

He was as much motivation as murder.

He disappeared around the corner into the library office, and she went back to her book, unable to focus, knowing he was just in the other room. She wanted to pull him away, talk with him, sit close to him, get to know him more, but she resisted. After a half-hour, she gave up, abandoning her again half empty and cold coffee she slapped the book back onto the coffee table and went upstairs. She had plenty to do, but she had held a hardcore line that on scheduled days off, she did not work. The day before had been a freebie, but she somehow couldn't swap it for her actual free time. She'd learned a long time ago that if she didn't *schedule* enjoyment, she quickly lost her sanity right along with her drive.

She swung the door to Trent's room open, the light just starting to spill in from sunrise. She could see he was still fast asleep, breathing heavily. Changing gears, she went and threw on some old clothes and headed for the studio. She turned on lamps on the long butcher block work tables instead of the overhead light, the room was cold but felt warm, and comforting. She couldn't paint, didn't have much of a creative bone in her body beyond her ability to sing, but she enjoyed painting. She liked the feel of a paintbrush and the way colors blended, running together and flowing from the bristles.

She dug around for a new canvas and carefully set it up on the easel. Kurt was an excellent artist, and his work, some unfinished and others detailed elegantly and hung proudly, were scattered throughout the room. He was great at portraits, faces so real and authentic to life that she often felt as though she were looking through a canvas at an actual person. More than once, she found herself jealous of him, having the talent to spend his life doing what he loved. Not that she didn't love what she did, but it came with stress and consequences she would often prefer to avoid.

She grabbed an ice cube tray, as was Kurt's favorite tool to mix colors of paint, and pumped in a few squirts of the brightest colors she could find. A neon pink, daisy yellow, traffic cone orange, fire engine red, orchid petal green, brilliant aquamarine blue, and when she turned to purple found herself drawn to a dark amethyst. Purple was her favorite color, after all.

Digging out brushes, she laid them on the tray of the easel and, without much planning, began slapping color onto the blank white. Kurt would scold her, she knew, for not using a background color, no base for blending. But he was the artist, and she was merely a weekend warrior of paint. Her mood was light, with a fascinating man downstairs who made her feel safe, made her feel sexy, brought new parts of her to the surface, she chose flowers. Simple, easy, and a representation of her mental state, with so much in life left to watch bloom.

She blended, dripped, brushed, smeared, rubbed, slapped, splashed, and threw paint on the canvas, smiling and singing all the while. She lost track of time entirely and was startled to see Trent leaning against the doorway sipping coffee in his terry cloth robe. He smiled at her so warmly, with the love of family in his face.

"Good morning, sunshine," he said.

"Good morning," she smiled. "How did you sleep?"

"The first time or the second time?" he raised an eyebrow at her, and she laughed.

"Both."

"I slept well at first, but I drank too much brandy too fast the second time." He sauntered in to look at what she was painting and reached out lackadaisically to wipe away smeared paint she didn't even know was on her cheek.

"How about you? Were you able to rest after being heated up in the middle of the night by that handsome hunk of a man in black downstairs?"

"Was it that obvious?"

"Absolutely," he wrinkled his nose at her, "you two were lost in the dark clinging to only each other when I came around the corner, scared half to death," he feigned a sultry mocking voice.

"Yes, well, I started that way too."

"Good thing he was there, yes?" Trent snorted before sipping more coffee.

"So I like him, sue me."

"You know I'd much rather just see you with him."

"I'm not sure it's that easy," she brushed purple around the edge of a large yellow pansy petal. Bastet meowed from the door, and Trent shooed her away.

"No kitty footprints in paint," he closed the door. "Why can't it be that easy? You're both good looking, smart, and until further notice basically attached at the hip. Doesn't seem so hard."

"He can be funny, but mostly he's dry, stoic, professional. I think some code of conduct prevents him from consorting with victims."

"Well, first of all—you aren't a victim—yet, you're still only a target. If anything he's the victim, he got shot in the chin, not you. And secondly, when did rules ever stop you from doing anything?"

"True, but this is different. I like him, for real. Not like I like him enough to roll in the sheets, then kick him to the curb. I can't explain it. It's just different."

"Yes, more than a one night stand different, I can see it. You aren't respectful to the guys you look at as disposable, you've been different with him, I recognize it."

"Well, that's reassuring, at least. I'd hate to come off as my normal bitch self." She laughed as she stashed the paint and stood back to look at what she had created. It was messy, flowers spilling out of a royal purple pot that tumbled on its side cracked in half.

Petals were scattered loosely around the bottom of the canvas without regard to the container being on a table or the ground, but it was all bright, lovely colors.

"I like it," Trent rubbed her neck affectionately.

"Thanks," she smiled as she went to dunk the brushes in water.

"Now, are you ready for breakfast?" he asked as he headed for the door.

"You know I'm always ready for food."

"Good because I caught Captain America searching for cereal in the cabinets downstairs. I thought even straight men eventually grew out of that." He rolled his eyes as she laughed wholeheartedly, and he slipped back downstairs, closing the door behind him pretending it was to keep the cat out.

Ethan had sat for nearly an hour, finished a second cup of coffee, and was halfway through an analysis on patients cross-referenced between Aurora and one of the other victims when his stomach started to growl. Aurora had been upstairs for some time, seemingly unconcerned about food, and he didn't want to disturb either her or Trent, so he decided to go it alone. In the kitchen, he rinsed his coffee mug and put it in the dishwasher before going to the pantry to see what breakfast cereal or oatmeal was available for quick consumption.

What he found was, without preparation, inedible. Raw steel cut oats and grape nuts rounded out the dry goods section, and though there was peanut butter, he didn't see a banana or a slice of regular white bread anywhere. As he went to close the door, he found Trent staring him down, eyebrows raised, holding French vanilla cream.

"Did she leave you to your own devices?" Trent asked.

"It appears that way."

"Tell you what, if you can hold off for about twenty minutes, I'll make something fabulous. If you can't, have a pastry, and that should tide you over." Closing the fridge, Trent walked to the corner and opened up a roll-top cabinet that held bread and cardboard boxes. He pulled out a box and handed it to Ethan.

Inside were small croissant pastries containing fruit filling and drizzled with colored icing.

"Organic," Trent said as Ethan opened the box, "cherry, pecan, apple, and my personal favorite—lemon."

"Thanks," Ethan fished one out and realized he could finish the box in less than eight bites.

"Are you a big protein guy? Like, bacon and sausage for breakfast?" Trent asked.

"I like my protein at lunch. Carbs are more up my alley before noon, as a rule of thumb." The pastry was excellent, and he couldn't help but take another.

"What a relief," Trent turned and filled a pot with water and put it on the stove over a high flame. He began taking things out of cabinets and fished the oatmeal out of the pantry with a couple of other things under one arm. "How do you feel about coconut?" he asked.

"Fine."

"And almonds?"

"Just as fine."

"Man of many words, I like it," he laughed. Ethan put the box of remaining pastries reluctantly back on the counter. "Speaking of which, do you have a few minutes to chat?" Trent asked.

"Sure, what's on your mind?"

Trent dropped a cup of the oats into the water and stirred it briskly before turning back towards the stairs. He held up a finger, indicating he wanted Ethan to wait behind as he peeked up the stairs to where Aurora was painting.

Coming back, he shuffled Ethan downstairs into the game room, pulling the door closed behind them.

"I'm good with her, but I'm not a miracle worker, I'm only going to have a week, at most, before she starts to climb the walls. She has patients in Laredo in the last week of June, and she's not going to want to cancel on them. Those families have already had to travel extensively for care, and she only gets up there once every ten weeks or so. What are the chances of wrapping this up before then?" He had crossed his arms and gone into a fully professional mode.

"I have no idea. I wish I could tell you, but I don't have a crystal ball."

"Alright, well, the next thing is going to be managing her anxiety. I joke about it, make it sound silly, but it isn't. She'd kill me for sharing with you, so please, I beg of you, keep it to yourself." His eyes flicked nervously to the door, but he continued.

"She took nearly four months off after her father died. She and her mother haven't spoken in over a year, and she's been on the outs with her sister ever since. They only share a text message here and there, but her sister defended her mother, it was a big mess. I'm sure, at some point, she'll tell you all about it, and I don't want to violate her privacy any more than I have to. She got very depressed, she was having panic attacks, night terrors, and it took her a long time, on medication and with therapy, to pull herself together.

"It wasn't pretty, and she's learned how to keep it under control, but it isn't easy. When I heard her screaming at you last night, I thought for sure it was a night terror, and I immediately had visions of her needing her therapist. The midnight snacks are a bad sign because that's what she resorts to when she can't sleep, and when she can't sleep, she starts sliding into depression. I don't want this guy to be the straw that breaks the camel's back if you know what I mean."

He had begun talking very fast, nearly losing his Southern accent entirely, and seemed wary of her coming in and finding them talking in private. Glancing up the stairs again, he turned back to Ethan.

"Do you have your cell phone on you?"

Ethan pulled it out.

"Put my number in it please and text me, so I have yours, I'd like to be able to communicate with you in private. Put my name in as something else, and if I text you, please keep it to yourself." Ethan opened his phone and promptly saved the number Trent spouted at him, putting his name in as Sheila without showing him, though he wasn't sure why it felt safer to have him represented as a woman.

"Alright, anything else I need to worry about?" Ethan asked.

"Not until next week. You know her family has dozens of properties around the world. She could be in Venice tomorrow if that would keep her safer."

"Would she do that?"

Trent sighed, "Probably not, no."

"Well, I'll put it under my hat as a last resort anyway," Ethan winked.

"I'd better get back, thank you. Anything you need help with, let me know. I know her patients almost as well as she does, so if it keeps her from having to answer questions, I'm happy to intervene." He started back up the stairs in a hurry, and so Ethan followed him.

He stirred the oatmeal on the stove, turned towards the third floor, and said, "Let me get Aurora down here, and I'll have a feast in no time." Like flipping a switch, he went back to a jovial, fun-loving and carefree guy. Ethan wondered how much he held Aurora's world together.

Breakfast was incredible. Unlike anything Ethan had ever eaten, Trent served steel-cut oats cooked to a perfect texture, creamed with coconut milk, then topped with sweet coconut flakes and almonds both toasted to perfection. Trent had also taken some kind of generic croissant dough out of a can and worked a secret magic to make flaky, buttery, melt in the mouth cinnamon sugar twists of which Ethan ate far more than his fair share. He was going to gain a few pounds during this case.

As Trent served Aurora a fresh-squeezed strawberry Bellini, Ethan excused himself back to his laptop. The morning had felt so typical, eating with them, being with them. They were inviting and fun, made him feel at home. It seemed no matter how hard he tried, he was going to end up making this case personal.

Chapter Eleven

Thick layers of fog rolling off the salty sea obscured the Santa Cruz night sky. The day had been mild, but heat off of the water brought droplets of dew that itched on Declan's face. His target had been challenging to locate, primarily since she must have known he was in the wind after her. Cursed reporters and their half-assed coverage never did his mission justice.

He studied the screen of his tablet, carefully swinging the camera left and right to be sure he caught as much of the room she was sitting in as he could. *Fat, lazy, rich bitch,* he mused. She was supposed to be his last victim, but the Feds had messed up his initial idea, forcing him to formulate plan B. It wasn't turning out so bad he thought, when he finished, it would be even more artistic. She was sitting on a lavish couch with her sausage fingers around the stem of a fancy crystal wine glass with her disgusting, feet rough as pigs' hooves up on a glass coffee table watching television. Just seeing her, the surroundings she had bought with blood money, made him sick.

Not for much longer.

Stashing his equipment, he tucked the rolled-up photos and paperwork he wanted to leave as his mark into the front pocket of his hooded sweatshirt and scaled the fence. *Amazing,* he thought, *all these people with money for real protection, and they feel secure with nothing more than a six-foot fence.* Creeping through the rose garden, he quickly navigated to the back of the house, onto the deck of the second floor and located the window to the master bathroom.

Having watched her all day, he knew the window was left open a slight amount, and he was in luck. He slid his fingers into the small crack and lifted it quietly, slipping inside and dropping to the floor undetected. Being there, so close, made all the feelings real again, made everything sting as if it had been yesterday, he lost his daughter, yesterday he discovered the truth about the machine they'd used on her.

Slipping through the room and into the hallway, breaking in was even easier than he'd anticipated it would be. Retrieving the cord from his pocket, he wrapped the ends around his gloved fingers, his breathing quickening in anticipation. Feet fast and light, movements swift and soft within seconds he was down the hallway and behind the bitch holding his breath.

With one long lunge, he had the cord over her neck, cutting off air to her surfacing scream. The wine glass toppled to the ground, shattering as she flopped like a trapped seal in the cushions. Planting his knee against the back of the couch, he pulled her head back, securing it against the wooden edge. Her hands flew behind her, fingernails finding his double-layered shirt, attempting to dig in through the thickness to no avail.

He prepared for her protest, however energetic. She kicked and twisted as he held tight, a foul odor on her as she defecated even before losing consciousness. It took longer than he anticipated, for her obese and out of shape body to quit twitching. Lifeless at last, her throat sliced and bleeding, she sagged onto the couch as he released her. He snapped the television off since it was the only light in the room, and he wanted to be sure there was obscurity in the aftermath.

As long as there were no sirens, no authorities dispatched by a nosy neighbor, he would leave a work of art behind him to expose her selfish, evil deeds. Her rotten, greedy, black intentions would be splayed open, like her throat, for the world to see in death.

He sat in the dark, drinking the expensive wine directly from the bottle, and when no one showed up after twenty minutes decided he was safe to leave his mark. He dragged her to an upright position, retrieving the rolled stack of paperwork from his back pocket. Carefully he laid out each piece of evidence in chronological order.

From her first contact with the salesman to her private meeting with the CEO in Cabo San Lucas to her deposits from the manufacturer, and her email communications revealing stolen private and confidential patient records, it was all here. His heart broke all over again, knowing it included those of his darling

Candy. It couldn't be helped. His daughter was a martyr now, and he needed to make sure her death wasn't in vain.

He meticulously planned each page for the witch, showed her real purpose, exposing her most private and evil intentions. It was all he could do, as his last acts on the earth, to share what he had found, to show the world the devil in the details. He didn't have anything to prove, he knew hell would claim her charred soul, and he was here to help her meet her maker.

Standing back to admire his work, he was pleased, but he wasn't done. Retrieving spoons from his pocket that he had specially sharpened, he worked carefully, slicing her black eyes out of their sockets. It wasn't what he had expected. The muscle around the eye was far thicker than anticipated and took determination to separate carefully. He predicted it would be like popping them out of a doll and instead found himself working diligently around the edges, though the globes were firmer and more resilient than expected. Dropping them into the bag he brought, he tucked them safely away. He had plans for them.

Finishing the bottle of wine, as the moon loomed on the horizon over the ocean out the front window, he spat on her. Cursing her and the very air she had breathed, he smeared the blood leaking from the bleak and empty sockets of her eyes down her face. He paused and wondered if he shoved something through her eye sockets if her brain would ooze out.

He left the empty wine bottle, not caring if anyone found traces of his DNA. By the time they figured all of it out, he would be finished and wouldn't be worried about them finding him. His mission would be complete before the week was over. As his last act, he found the thermostat and turned the heat up to a balmy eighty-five, smiling.

Retrieving his backpack from the front yard, he walked calmly into the night, admiring his work. By the time authorities showed up, she would be so ripe the house would never be free of her stench.

Chapter Twelve

In the few days Ethan had spent with Trent and Aurora, the three of them had fallen into a good rhythm. Trent soaked, painted, did a little gardening, and played video or card games with Aurora to keep her from climbing the walls when she wasn't head down reviewing patient data and research. They had each found their time through the days for independence, and seemed to each equally relish setting the stress aside to eat and laugh. Trent continued to prove he could give Gordon Ramsey a run for his money, even on a bad day.

Friday beamed in sunny and warm with a hefty breeze outside. Trent had gone as far as to grill an incredible tri-tip for lunch and ever since had been busy in the kitchen cleaning, organizing, and baking something that smelled like blueberries in heaven. Aurora had indulged in a bloody Mary with her red meat and promptly retired, claiming she needed a nap. Of course, the only time he needed her for a couple of questions, she seemed not to want to be disturbed.

By two o'clock, Ethan was starting to wonder if she would sleep all day. When he stood up to go peek in on her, he was thankful for his terrible timing as a screech of anger followed by a slamming noise came resonating from upstairs. For the first time, Ethan was surprised by Trent's reaction. Rather than running to her aid, he simply set things he was working on aside, cleared a spot for her at the counter, and waited. Seeing Ethan peering out from the library, he shook his head solemnly 'No' and waved him back into the office.

Aurora came downstairs within a minute, huffing into the living room to Trent, who by that time had put on a tea kettle.

"Bitch!" She shrieked, slamming her phone onto the counter so hard Trent winced, and Ethan was sure she cracked it. Ethan couldn't see her, but he could feel the anger radiating off of her just the same.

"How can she defend her? How can she seriously expect me to forgive that woman when she won't admit, let alone apologize for her insufferable infidelity?" Aurora was screaming at the top of her powerful lungs. Trent pulled down a mug but was careful not to put it within her reach, yet.

"Donia, I presume?" Trent said.

"Who else?" she snapped.

"Well, it's always either her or the queen of Egypt; no one else ever gets your pressure up like this. What was it this time?" Trent's voice was level and calm as he had filled a tea strainer full and began dunking it in steaming water.

"How I have shirked my responsibilities as a daughter, of course. She acts like being completely free of responsibility, and spending the family trust makes her a better daughter. Whoring, drunken, floozy!" Aurora kicked as if to make contact with a barstool, but luckily for her foot, she missed.

"Do you know what she said?" she sneered across the counter with her hands flat, her face crimson.

"I can guess, but you should get it off your chest anyway, sooner rather than later." Trent kept his voice flat and almost unconcerned as he continued to dip the tea strainer and turned to face her across the counter.

"How I am such a spoilt rotten little brat because I didn't call our mother to tell her that a psychopathic killer is hunting me. What an ungrateful little twat I am to make our cheating, dishonest mother, who hasn't called me in over a year, worry for me." She said it in a tone of angry sarcasm as she sat, presumably beginning to run out of steam.

"You know better." Trent slid the mug across towards her but left it far enough away that she would need to sit forward to reach for it.

"I do, but it still makes me so damn mad! Furious!" she clamped her head between her hands as if to keep it from popping off her neck. "If my mother is so concerned about me, cares about me so much, why hasn't she reached out to me at all since I called her out for cheating on my dying father? Hypocritical, stuck up, arrogant, deceitful, stubborn, know it all wench!" The escalation in her voice indicated some kind of climax, and after she had it out, seemed to begin the process of letting go.

106

"Why do you even answer the phone?" Trent sounded sympathetic in his questioning as if he couldn't understand why she wasn't protecting herself.

"I was half asleep. It came from a number I didn't recognize. I wasn't thinking. Use any excuse you like. It's my fault, and I know what you're thinking." She slumped briefly before reaching for the tea.

"It's not your fault that your sister and your mother lack common morals. It's only your fault for letting them into your heart to break it. Fool me once..." Trent came around the counter now to sit beside her and draped an arm over her lovingly.

"You know the worst part?" she asked.

"She wasn't sober?"

"Ha," Aurora made a sound resembling bitter, tired laughter before shaking her head and leaning it against him. "I could tell she was at a party. There was music and laughter in the background, and she started out so bubbly like she used to be as if she really just missed me. Then I realized it was a ploy, her usual cry for attention under the 'my spoiled, ungrateful sister' banner." Sadness seeped into her voice, and after a single sip of tea, her hands fell to her lap.

"You can't blame her for being jealous. You are prettier, smarter, more successful, and accomplished, and get more attention from the right friends and men than she will ever get from the wrong ones." He rubbed her shoulders reassuringly, squeezing her to his side.

"I should have put the phone on silent."

"Then you would have been down here an hour later with a nasty message that would have made you just as upset. Don't let the ten dollars stolen ruin the million that remain; you know this." He kissed her head kindly, and she took a deep breath, slowly exhaling as she again reached for her tea.

"You're right. You're always right. What would I do without you?" she asked.

"Be way too damn skinny, for starters," he laughed and got her lips to spread a thin, weak smile. "Now, I had just the plan in action for a moment like this. Don't be sour, but you need your hair done. And, how about these nails? Sister, you have not been taking care of yourself."

She fanned her fingers in front of her, clearly questioning his judgment but smiled playfully. He whipped out his phone, and as she sipped the tea, he sent a half dozen text messages.

"Red and blond? Or more on the violet side?" he asked.

"Red, like Zinfandel red, of course."

"Go get into the bath then, soak your cares away, and by the time you are out, you will be able to pamper them away as well." The timer on the oven loudly beeped, and he swirled away to retrieve the heavenly baked goods as she reticently went back upstairs.

Within thirty seconds of her retreat, Trent marched into the library office to Ethan.

"Do I need permission to have friends over?" Trent asked. Ethan shook his head, no.

"Good, then I'm having some friends over in about an hour. We'll have a sort of semi-party this evening. I'll warn you," he glanced warily upstairs again, "this is usually a downward spiral, so tread carefully with her. She's delicate now." Without another word, Trent disappeared back into the kitchen and was on a phone call within seconds.

Aurora filled the gigantic tub in her mistress quarters with water as hot as she could stand it. She dumped in Epsom salt and a pink bath bomb that fizzed and smelled of pomegranate. She felt exhausted. Though she had learned to recognize the kind of exhaustion brought on by having to deal with her sister and mother, she was still never quite able to figure out *why* they wore her out so. She knew them, through and through. She knew what they would say, how they would act, their jaded and twisted opinions of the world stained by far too much money.

Why did she allow them to affect her so?

She dropped her clothes and dipped into the stinging heat, pleased she could get both her knees and her shoulders beneath the surface at the same time.

If not just to show off to her friends what an awful sister Aurora was, why would Donia bother to call her? Did Donia not realize it was like wallowing in her cursed narcissism? Did her friends understand that? Then again, Donia didn't have real friends, not like Trent. Of course, she'd only known what was going on in the first place because Theresa had called her mother, who had undoubtedly called Donia to wallow in the same misguided pity. All because her mother refused to admit she'd been shown up by someone who had years ago replaced her.

Aurora felt the urge to call Theresa, to connect with her, to soothe her internal struggle, but she didn't want to dump more on her. After soaking for a few minutes, as her skin began to wrinkle, it dawned on her that Theresa would not look at it the same way she did. Theresa would be glad to hear her voice and to know she was alright, she would be delighted for the update.

As soon as she was out of the tub, Aurora dialed Theresa, Tee-ta, as she called her so much after having been her lifelong nanny. Aurora couldn't pronounce her name when she was small, and Tee-ta had been the best she could do for a long time, it had stuck. It was like a nickname, and had always been a sign of affection for her. She wished she had called her that more often as she sat, solemn on the side of the tub listening to the water drain and the phone ring.

"My princess!" Theresa exclaimed as she answered.

"Hello, Tee-ta, how are you?" A smile spread across Aurora's face, and her mood brightened just to hear the voice on the other end of the line.

"I'm alright, darling, how are you?"

"I'm doing alright, thanks to you and Trent and this Agent Hartman I was lucky enough to get in my corner." Aurora headed back to the bed and sprawled out as the conversation bloomed. She was glad to connect again, grateful for her dear friend, and enjoyed a long conversation. As the discussion came to a close, however, her good mood came to a halt.

"We should do lunch when I am back next time, at UCSF, I don't know for sure when but I'm sure Trent can set some time aside."

"Oh well, darling, let's not worry about that. I can come to see you anytime." Theresa's voice cracked a little.

"What do you mean, why wouldn't we just meet up where it's convenient?"

"Promise me you won't be upset, darling."

"I'll do no such thing, what's wrong?" Aurora sat up in bed.

"Nothing is wrong, I just…" she paused, and the silence jacked Aurora's heartbeat up. "I don't work at UCSF anymore, dear."

Aurora was dumbfounded, at a total loss. Shock didn't even remotely describe her reaction.

"What do you mean you don't work there? You've been there for forty years. You were less than four years away from retirement. Why would you quit?" The ensuing silence made Aurora's anxiety creep up another notch.

"I don't want to lie to you, but I also don't want you to feel responsible, I knew very well what I was doing, and I'm glad I did it. I wouldn't take it back for the world. I want you to know. But, dear, the hospital let me go." Aurora's heart threatened to stop on her completely.

"They *fired* you?" Her tone became terse, "Are you serious?"

"Yes dear, but it's no matter, I should have retired last year anyway, I've plenty to get me by, and I'm happy, I don't need the money, you know that."

"That isn't the point. You haven't needed the money in thirty years. You loved that job. You were excellent at that job. Who do they think they are going to get to replace you who will do half as well, let alone any better? What was their reasoning?" Aurora demanded, but the line was silent for a long time.

"It was my own doing because I put family first," she said, and it immediately sank in. Theresa had told Aurora she had violated some kind of privacy policy to contact Johns Hopkins on her behalf. As it all became clear and concise, the reality was like a hammer on her heart.

"Me. You got fired because of me." A sinister, vengeful tone snaked out of Aurora from somewhere deep she hadn't even known existed.

"No!" Theresa interjected, "I was let go because there are parameters to my position, and I violated them, willingly. And I would do it again, don't you for an instant think I wouldn't. You're more important a thousand times over, and I don't regret it," she insisted. But Aurora did.

"This won't stand. I won't let it. I love you too much." In one searing moment, the weight of the entire week came crashing down on her. The anger, the fear, her trust issues, her blessings, and lack of gratitude where it counted most all slammed into her like a tsunami.

"Oh darling, don't worry, please don't be upset. I'm just so glad you're safe. It's so good to hear your voice and know you're well. I just get to catch up on some of that, what do you call it? Binge-watching? Yes, I've started Game of Thrones, you know? You were right, it's quite intense, and I've loved every minute of it."

"That's what you do," Aurora's voice shattered as tears threatened to consume her. "You take the heat and the hard hits for everything so I can be happy, and I've never been good at telling you how important you are to me. I've never shown you how much you mean to me. I love you so much, Tee-ta."

"Oh princess, don't cry," and suddenly tears of her own consumed Theresa. Aurora wanted to unburden herself of the weight of her mother and sister, to tell her all about everything and tell Theresa she had done the right thing since the day she was born. But she didn't. She left all the distress and trauma out and merely washed Theresa with affection and praise. It felt good, but in a way reminded her, it wasn't enough. It had never been enough. By the time they hung up, Aurora had managed to restrain her emotions enough to put Theresa at ease. As soon as the screen went dead, confirming the call was over, the flood engulfed her.

She sat on the edge of the bed, staring out into the wild and whipping wind of the sun-drenched afternoon and cried her heart out.

After the way Aurora blew up, anticipating additional guests, Ethan felt the need for back up. He had already been thinking about taking a break, his mother's birthday was coming on Sunday, and he would need someone else up to speed, just as comfortable there as he had become. So he called someone he had found he could always count on, Tom.

"Hey, boss," the familiar greeting was a welcome sound.

"Can you grab some stuff and come back me up tonight? I've got, well, the target—has company coming in."

"Sure thing. What kind of company?"

"I'm not entirely sure yet, but I take it a few guests. More than I can keep an eye on solo, so I'd appreciate it if you could join me tonight."

"I'll be on my way momentarily. Anything you need from the office or otherwise?"

"Just you, thanks," the quick call ended, and Ethan turned back to his files. He had been making excellent progress, had isolated what he felt were top contenders for being the suspect.

After the tantrum Aurora had about an hour earlier, things had been quiet, almost too quiet. Trent had busied himself with food, as seemed to be his style in moments of stress, and Aurora had disappeared entirely. With a stack of questions for her on his plate, he assumed it would be better for him to get them out of the way now, so she could enjoy the evening, while he and Tom stayed out of sight.

Taking some pictures and a few notes, he went upstairs. Seeing the room they'd slept in empty, he next knocked on the door across the hall that she had called, surely in jest, the Mistress quarters. The door was cracked open, so he swung it carefully and realized she hadn't been joking as there was a door linked directly to the master bedroom. The room wasn't large, filled with a couple of dressers and a queen-size bed, but had lavish decor.

Aurora sat in a bay window on the far side facing away from him, dressed only in a thin silk robe. She had her knees pulled to her chest and rested against the glass, lost in the view outside. Bastet was curled at her feet on a velvet pillow, watching her intently. He softly knocked before stepping in, not anticipating any issues, but as she heard him, she hurried to wipe her face and leaped to her feet, facing away from him. Instantly he knew he was on thin ice. The cat jumped down to swirl around his ankles, purring enthusiastically before darting away.

After her hands were at her face for a moment and she blew her nose, she turned reluctantly only halfway. What he could see of her face was red, her eyes puffy, her hand holding wadded up tissues.

"I'm sorry, the door was open. I didn't think you needed privacy. I can come back," he said, stepping backward in the hope of escaping any drama.

"No, it's alright," she turned towards the bed, tightening the robe around her without looking up at him entirely and motioned for him to sit at the foot. There was no avoiding breaking the ice now, may as well dive in like the polar bear he had trained to be.

"Are you alright?" he asked tenderly and surprised even himself when he felt it, he genuinely cared.

"No, but I'm used to it. It will pass." She pulled a thin blanket over her lap and bent her knees up, draping her arms over them.

"I couldn't help but overhear about your sister earlier," he sat on the bed beside her, "I'm sorry about your situation."

"Yes, well, I'm even sorrier." She fought back more tears, wiping her eyes in vain, wanting to avoid spreading her sour mood as much as possible. "It's not about my sister or my wretched mother this time, but it is my burden to bear, for better or for worse. I just wish sometimes I had a crystal ball to help avoid the worst parts." He felt for her, truly and deeply as she sat so frail, and exposed.

"Sometimes, God gives the strongest of us the most difficult burden to bear." He wasn't sure where it came from, but it fit. Something he had once been told in the trials of his life which had helped him. She reached out and put her hand over his.

"That's very sweet. Don't worry about me. What can I do for you?" she asked.

"I have a few photographs of people connected to you as well as several of the other victims. I have patients, some staff with a previously violent history, and a couple of professors, unfortunately. I was wondering if you remember any of them or could tell me if there's more than meets the eye, any kind of temper, or inclination towards violence to you specifically." He handed her a stack of a dozen photographs, each one labeled. As she began to flip through them, he explained how each had crossed paths with her and the other victims. About halfway through, her expression changed, and she paused to set a photograph squarely in her lap.

"Something familiar?" he asked.

"Maybe, yes… I don't know for sure." She held the picture up in front of her examining it. "I think this might, just possibly, have been the man with the taser." His heart skipped a beat.

"Alright, take a breath, take your time. There's no need to rush to a conclusion, and we don't have to act rashly. What is familiar about him?" Ethan slid the other photos away.

"Well, I don't know, I can't explain it. I've seen him before. I know that, but I can't precisely picture where. Are you sure all these people were in my past?" She dropped the photo and looked to him for guidance.

"This one, in particular, he was the father of a patient who passed away, one who was in a clinical trial. He has a rough history of mental health issues and some domestic abuse infractions, but because his daughter came up as treated by multiple victims, I pulled him out."

She continued to stare at the photo, lost in her own world. The man in the photo had a dark complexion with black hair and eyes and a sinister look on his face in the picture Ethan had managed to find. There was no mustache, but that was easily adjusted. Maybe it was just his expression that had her creeped out.

"I can't put words to it, I know him, but I don't know from where. You said he was the father of a patient? Treated at Hopkins?"

"Yes, a girl who passed away at about two years old. Her chart has lots of big words, but forgive me, that isn't my forte." He sorted through a stack of paperwork and handed her an abridged version of the chart from the daughter. She intently read over a dictation that was partially redacted, reviewing a face sheet with the patient's personal information.

"I'm sorry. I just can't pull this case to mind. I'm trying to recall, but based on the dates, this was just under two years ago, and any cases during this time frame wouldn't, or shouldn't, have been mine." She frowned. "I did see a handful of patients in the crossover at Hopkins after a clinical research trial I was involved in publishing, but that was…" She trailed off thoughtfully, and her face became sad again.

"You didn't take cases during research? It has your name on it as the attending." He flipped to the back page, and sure enough, the dictating physician name stamped in a corner said 'Dr. Soileaux' but she just couldn't remember the patient.

"Research cases, the kind I have worked on, are extremely complicated and in-depth with dozens of qualifying factors and requirements. We were working on cutting edge cancer treatments. This patient had a very severe form of cancer with a survival rate of less than ten percent within a year of diagnosis. Patients are often born with it, and the family doesn't know it because there aren't developmental symptoms until it's too late. If I treated her, if she were involved in the trial, I would have worked closely with her and her family. I should remember this." She was becoming frustrated.

"It's alright. No one expects you to remember everything. Half the time, I can't remember what color boxers I put on in the morning, and without checking, I couldn't tell you what I'm wearing now if my life depended on it." He shrugged and made a funny face, and it seemed to ease back her agitation. "You have a lot going on right now, it's understandable. Take some time, if other details come to you let me know. I still have a lot to get through, so it will only narrow the pool." He gathered up the papers while she looked through the other photos. When she handed them to him, she noticed he lingered a moment.

"You sure you're alright?" he asked again, locking on her gaze with concern. They were sparkling emerald as if the tears had rinsed away another color that had been covering it. She hesitated. She liked this man. She liked his mannerisms, his sense of humor, the way he dripped with stability and dependability, his focus on the case, and ultimately, on her. She sighed heavily, trying to gauge how personal he intended the question to be.

"UCSF fired Theresa," her voice cracked.

"What?" The tone of disbelief with a hint of anger told her she had gauged the moment appropriately; it had been a personal question. "On what grounds?" he asked, furrowing his brow.

"Me. It's all my fault." Tears stung the back of her eyes again, and her throat tightened.

"That's ridiculous, Aurora."

"It is, but it's still true. Whatever she went to Hopkins for was reported back to the board of directors, and they let her go. She worked there for forty years. It was all she knew. I'm so mad. Mad at them, mad at myself, mad at this whole situation, and I want so badly to fix it, but I feel like all I do is make things worse, even when I do what I'm supposed to."

"That doesn't mean what happened was your fault." He wanted to comfort her, slid closer as the tears began to course freely again down her cheeks. She reached to cover her face, and he caught one of her hands, holding it in his he caressed her fingers gently, suddenly overwhelmed with a desire to scoop her into his arms.

"I want to call and scream at the board of directors. I *will* call and scream at them, and I'll make them take it back, once I'm not a blubbering mess anymore." He leaned closer to her, laid a hand on her knee as he continued to hold her elegant long fingers.

"You're not a blubbering mess," he chuckled lightly, "trust me, I've seen blubber and messes, they're nowhere near as beautiful as you." Her hand fell from her face, and she looked at him, suddenly smiling through the tears. He warmed her, he made her heart flutter, made her feel all fuzzy inside.

"Why are we blubbering?" Trent demanded from the doorway behind Ethan, and a feeling of being caught in a compromising, unprofessional situation had him tensing.

"Why would I *not* be blubbering, my life is a mess!" Aurora squeezed but released Ethan's hand as he pulled back to stand up.

"It's nothing a margarita or two can't fix, trust me."

"I don't know that I have the energy or the mood right now," Aurora said as she flopped over on the bed, thoroughly defeated.

"That's why you have me. I do have the energy, and I do know how to fix your mood. And, I know Mario and Crystal, and Wade…" he continued down a long list. "I ordered catering, and I have my specialty margarita with Casamigos Blanco on the rocks chilling downstairs. All we need is a playlist, which is all you sister. Come on; you need some pampering." Trent went to the bedside and pulled her up clearly against her will.

"A manicure wouldn't kill you either Captain America," Trent shot a flirtatious look over his shoulder that had Ethan instantly examining his fingers.

"What's wrong with my fingernails?" he asked indignantly, making Aurora laugh and the moment instantly lifted.

Still smiling, she said, "There's nothing wrong with your fingernails, but it's lucky you can't drink on duty because, after one of Trent's margaritas, they'd be hot pink." Trent squealed as she said it, and Ethan just raised his eyebrows and shrugged. Snagging his paperwork off the bed, he left the photo she thought she recognized, doubly glad Tom was on his way, the evening sounded like it was rounding out to be quite the party.

Chapter Thirteen

Within an hour, five guests had arrived, and Ethan couldn't wait for Tom to show up. Listening in on some of the conversations from the library office Ethan was sure it would be a night to remember. The chatting flowed from stories of times the friends had spent together, through catching up on love lives and family. Aurora spelled out all her distress, and they cooed and coddled her and before long had seemed to lift her spirits. When the subject changed from things he mostly already knew or didn't care about—to Aurora's love life—he couldn't focus anymore and found himself hanging on every word.

"What happened to that baseball player?" One of them asked.

"She only saw him the two nights, and that was a record." Ethan recognized Trent's voice.

"Two nights was plenty, I like baseball, but that guy wasn't good for much else, trust me," Aurora answered.

"Really?"

"Yea, I mean, he was fun, and at the time, I was bored, so it worked. But he had the conversational skills of a rock plus a total lack of heat, no passion at all." Grumblings came from the group.

"That was like six months ago, has there been no one since then?"

"Oh, several, but no one noteworthy," Aurora's voice was casual, non-committal.

"Come on! There was a time that you were the queen of one-date-wonders. You had a different guy for every day of the week and two on Saturday. There have to be some good ones recently. Dish it!" A female voice that Ethan suspected was Crystal chimed in.

"Oh, there was a radiology tech in his early twenties, but he acted like it. I took a charming bartender home earlier this spring. He was entertaining."

"But you never called him again, did you?" Trent asked. "And there's a reason for that. None of them are worth your time, and you know it."

"True, they're all fun, just fun until I'm done." Ethan felt a little tug at his heart. He liked her, or at least he thought he did, but hearing the way they were talking about her love life made him feel like she went through men like toilet paper. Struggling to ignore it and focus elsewhere, he found himself repeatedly lost in scenarios of her chewing him up and spitting him out.

When Tom rang the bell, he didn't hear it, but the shadow at the front door had him hopping up, glad for the distraction. Having come straight from the office, Tom wore the typical ebony suit, and the guests instantly began to whisper. Ethan shuffled him back to where his laptop sat with only a wave towards the group, all watching while pretending not to.

"How's it been going, boss?" Tom asked, chewing a large wad of bright pink bubblegum.

"I think I've made some headway. Did you get the backgrounds on the five suspects I sent you?"

"Sure did," Tom dropped a backpack and fished out a thumb drive.

"Anything on the surveillance of the area?"

"Nothing concrete." Before they could both sit back down, Trent popped in.

"When are you two going to join the party?" he asked.

"We will probably keep our distance so we can keep a good eye on the surroundings, but thank you."

"Spoilers! The food will be here soon. You'll at least eat with us, won't you?"

"I'm always hungry," Tom piped up.

"Excellent, wrap up what you're doing then." Trent waved his hand, and Ethan noticed for the first time he seemed thoroughly relaxed as if he had been carrying some level of professionalism he shed when his friends arrived. As he turned to go, he winked at Tom, looking him over from head to toe. Tom frowned, confused, and looked at Ethan.

"They're a couple of pitchers of margaritas down already," was all he replied, and Tom just shrugged. "Did you bring the monitoring review from the nerds on four?" he asked.

"Yes, it's on the flash drive. I took a look at it quickly, and it looks clean. They didn't find anyone listening in on her cell, they checked a couple of office lines, and those were clear. Her email accounts appeared untouched, all the patient information is secure under hospital protocols, and they were all intact, so the computers she's using are clean. A team was out yesterday, and her car was clean too. It seems like whoever we're dealing with is either way ahead of the game and untraceable or pretty old school, finding her without tracking tech."

"So maybe we're looking at someone older?"

"You never know, boss, it could just be funds too." The two of them sat and began going through new information collected, trying to eliminate suspects. There was still a mountain of work ahead of them.

At six o'clock, enough food for an army arrived, as did a flurry of additional guests. After Aurora had her hair highlighted and cut into a new, shorter, sassy style that framed her face, but still brushed her shoulders, she had gone to freshen up. When she came back, she was wearing a sexy summer gown in pale periwinkle that had Ethan double-checking to make sure his mouth wasn't hanging open.

The dress dangled off her shoulders, leaving every vanilla bean tanned inch of her back exposed, but clung to her waist and butt like it was painted on, made of a material that billowed and swung gracefully, she was a vision. Just barely, when Ethan looked closely, he could still see the yellow remnants of bruises from the taser a few days earlier, reminding him why she was off-limits.

There was Thai food, a variety of pastas, lots of fresh fruits and vegetables, some spicy Indian dishes, and a whole corner devoted to dessert. As it turned out, Trent was just as good at ordering catering as he was at cooking. Ethan and Tom called it quits about seven, just as things started to wind up. They helped themselves, at Trent's encouragement, to more food than either of them needed.

They had agreed that once night fell, they would stand guard outside to watch the front and back of the house. The music was loud enough that conversation had to be close to an ear, so small groups had gathered, and as evening set in, even a little dancing was going on. When 'Worst Nites' by Foster the People came on, everyone sang the chorus in unison.

Aurora had loosened up and was twirling, laughing, and Ethan found himself watching her, glued to her every move, and it wasn't going unnoticed.

"I could give you a few pointers if you need to get your crush on her under control," Tom said.

"What?" Ethan snapped out of his reverie, and Tom just smiled sarcastically at him.

"Let's get out of here before you get yourself into trouble," Tom shoulder bumped him as he headed for the door.

Ethan followed him, wondering if it was so noticeable what he thought of Aurora. As he navigated the crowd, he caught sight of her again, and the answer was clear. Yes. Yes, it was undeniable how taken he was with her.

She was dancing with someone he didn't even notice as the movements she was making held him captive. She swayed, swinging her hips and shoulders, dipping and bouncing with the beat. Her curves moved in perfect time with the rhythm, her thigh slipping out of the slit in her skirt, her leg bending below a perfectly round butt that balanced her perky breasts. He was mesmerized. There was no denying he was insanely attracted to her. He tried to remind himself of the earlier conversation where it had sounded like she pretty much went through men like toilet paper, but it wasn't a deterrent.

Thank heavens, he had the sense to call Tom. Though the night air outside was still warm, the sting of the afternoon heat had faded with a comfortable breeze. The front entrance had a covered porch and a small array of furniture, and as they walked out, Tom peeled off his coat and loosened his tie.

"I can see why you wanted an extra set of eyes, but I'm guessing this wasn't what you meant?" Tom bent down over the stairs as Ethan shut the door.

"What wasn't?"

Tom stood up, holding a glass mason jar a little smaller than a coffee mug with his tie so as not to touch it directly. Inside it was a pair of deflated eyeballs suspended in a pink liquid. On top of it was a small folded note. They both looked around as if they would see the person who had left it standing somewhere close, but the street was empty.

"Shit." Ethan said, "Let me get a set of gloves from the briefcase inside. Wait here." Tom nodded, he had a good intuition, and for some reason, his gut was telling him the events of the evening would be anything but boring as they unfolded.

Ethan came back with gloves and an evidence bag.

"You think we should send everyone home, boss?" Tom asked.

Ethan thought for a moment, glancing around again. "No one's been back outside since they arrived, and someone would have seen it walking up the stairs as they went in, so we know it isn't anyone in there, at the moment the crowd is probably safer. Let's just get it hidden and into evidence to see if we can get any prints off of it."

Pulling the gloves on, Ethan took the jar studying it, pulling the note off the top. He handed Tom a pair of gloves and said, "Here, put these on and take some pictures of it. Let's get it put away before anyone sees it. I would have to guess everyone in this crowd will freak." Ethan read the note as Tom snapped pictures with his cell.

"Do you think the eyes are human?" Tom asked, thoroughly creeped out.

"I hope not."

"Aurora would know, wouldn't she? Being a doctor?"

"Not going there."

Ethan flattened the note out, it read:

Remember when my daughter's eyes looked like these? I know you do, and I know you know who was at fault. Time is running out.

"Well, that's not helpful." Ethan handed Tom the note and asked, "Can you get this all back first thing tomorrow morning?"

"I can take it tonight if you want," Tom was sealing the evidence bag now containing the jar.

"No, I want you here. Let's walk the perimeter."

"What are we going to do with this?" Tom handed Ethan the jar as he picked up the note to put it into a separate evidence bag.

"Do you think it needs to be kept away from any heat to preserve the parts inside?" Ethan turned the jar around in his hands, grimly examining the eyes.

"If you're not going to ask the doc if the eyes are human, I doubt it's a good idea to stick it in the fridge."

Ethan shrugged, "Let's stick it inside a paper bag so no one can see it and put it back into the briefcase." Tom draped his jacket over it and went back inside, stashing it quickly before drawing any attention.

"Do you have an extra flashlight in your car?" Ethan asked from behind him. He nodded and fished out his keys, "go get it, and let's make sure this creep isn't lurking around somewhere close."

They walked around the property, careful not to be out of sight from the front or back doors, and found nothing. No footprints, no garbage, no indication of anything out of the ordinary, and so went back and kept watch as guests began to leave.

Aurora's head was swirling. As she had gotten dressed, Wade doting upon her as if she were in one of his photoshoots, she had admired his handiwork. Her hair was shorter, but not drastically. He had created layers, choppy and thick, to hang framing her face well without much need for styling, which she loved because she was often too busy to spend time doing anything with her hair. The colors of auburn, gold, burgundy, and a hot plum were fabulous, blended as highlights, but also draped at the ends of the cut in balayage. He was indeed a miracle worker with hair.

The dress Crystal had brought her was stunning. Though it looked in many ways like any old casual summer dress, the cut it had made it look like something she could wear to a night club, and the specific shade of blue lit up her eyes like the sun did the clouds in the sky. The material was so soft, silky, but velvet at the same time, she found she enjoyed being touched just to feel it pressed against her skin. Throughout the night, she sought to be touched, and no matter which direction she turned, in a room full of people, her eyes kept coming back to Ethan.

In navy Dockers and a black cotton polo shirt, which she was sure he chose so the shoulder holster he wore wouldn't stand out as much, he still stood out like a sore thumb amidst her colorful and jovial friends, but she found it alluring. After all, he wasn't there for the party. He was there for her. With tequila tantalizing her senses, a new haircut, new manicure (that would last less than twenty-four hours if her track record stood), and a sexy dress, she expected him to be drawn to her. In her buzzed brain, she imagined he should be by her side, protecting her like the secret service, wasn't that why he was there? Every time she honed in on him, however, he was lost in conversation with someone else, peering out the windows watchfully, or conversing in private with the other agent.

She almost felt like he was *trying* to avoid her. He had questioned her about possible suspects that afternoon, and though she had done her best, she hadn't been much help. She thought back to her outburst after the call from her sister. She mulled over his behavior when he had questioned her about patients, how concerned he had been about her when he learned about Theresa. She wondered now if it was all an act, or if he had been put off by her behavior.

Her thoughts turned to his training, to how he was supposed to handle people like her, and suddenly a dreadful insecurity was dominant in her mind, plus by nine o'clock she hadn't seen him in an hour or more. She wondered if she was mere bait while he watched and waited for some psycho to lunge at her. *There are the trust issues*, she thought, *rearing their ugly head.*

As the clock swept past nine pm, she had been sipping cocktails for nearly four hours. She was growing tired, and the house felt stuffy, tight, and overcrowded. When she went to refill her drink, she swapped the vodka soda for only soda and slapped a lemon slice into it before slipping out into the night air off the back porch. The breeze felt revitalizing on her face as she leaned against the railing, swaying lightly with the alcohol buzz.

Bastet, her trusty sidekick, jumped up next to her, nuzzling her furry head against Aurora's bare collarbone. She stroked the cat lovingly, running her fingernails along her back as she arched and purred appreciatively. She took a sip of her soda and set the glass down on the railing so she could scratch the cat's ears with both hands. Bastet put her paws up on her breasts, leaning into her, happily soaking up the attention.

"What do you think, my little lioness?" Aurora bent her face down to put her forehead against Bastet's. "What shall we do about our predicament? Mommy dearest has forsaken us, sister blames us for everything, and Tee-ta has taken ruin for it all, but here we are, with a soul mate and warrior. What do we do now?"

"Does she ever talk back?" Ethan's voice scared the living daylights out of her, and as she nearly jumped a foot in the air, the cat leaped into her arms. She clung to Bastet for a moment waiting for the stars in her head to simmer, breathing entirely too fast, wondering why he was holding a flashlight sneaking around the backyard.

"Is it something they train you for, in the FBI, creeping up on and scaring the bejesus out of people?" She was having trouble catching her breath. Ethan had come around the deck on the side of the house, past the hot tub. In the shadows and dressed all in black, he loomed authoritatively over her.

"Sorry. I was just checking things out, making sure everything is still secure. You really shouldn't be out here, especially not alone," his tone was soothing as he spoke and walked towards her.

"You've got to stop scaring the crap out of me, and I'm not alone, I have Bastet and a house full of people." She let the cat down to run off into the night and grabbed her drink. Being startled had made her throat run dry.

"I didn't mean to spook you. It certainly isn't on purpose." He strolled over to stand beside her, tucking his thumbs in his front belt loops.

"I'd hate to think what you could accomplish if it were," she took a couple of long sips, and he laughed lightly.

"We all have our talents, I suppose."

"Well, you're more than talented at it," she laughed, shaking off the jitters. "I suppose it helps you learn a lot, yes? Like, how you were just eavesdropping on me talking to Bastet?" A little embarrassment flushed her cheeks, and she was glad it was dark, preventing him from seeing her expression too closely.

"I did, but I promise to hold it in the highest of confidences. You know I have top-secret clearance, right?"

"You do?" For a second, the slight buzz she still had and not seeing his expression in the darkness got the better of her as she stared at him in wonder.

"No, not really. I'm kidding." He leaned on the railing beside her, and she laughed, smacking him playfully on the arm.

"Come on. You're in the FBI, that has to have its covert advantages, doesn't it?"

"Oh, it does, and I could tell you, but then I'd have to kill you," he smiled. Even in the dim lack of moon glow, it lit an ember inside her.

"Alright, Bond, James Bond, tell me something you *can* tell me."

"Oh, that's MI6, closer to CIA than FBI. Totally different bag of tricks."

"Like the watches that shoot little poison arrows and boats that pop out of suitcases?" Now she had him laughing. "Did you eat a lot of the alphabet SpaghettiOs when you were a kid? Is that what made you want to be in this line of work? Risking your life for other people?"

"Oh, no, in general, there's not as much risk to my life as you'd think there is. It isn't like television, you know?"

She sipped her drink, spun around to lean her elbows on the railing to face him, lost in him momentarily.

"No? Not like The X Files, Agent Mulder?" she made him laugh again.

"No," he leaned on one hand, opening his stance to look at her. "We have training and face people who are generally untrained, so it's not a fair fight, usually."

"That training makes you superior?" she leaned into him ever so slightly.

"In some ways, superior, I suppose. We have academic requirements, weapons training, and physical testing."

"I'm sure you pass everything but the physical, right?" She was joking, of course, as she reached out and brushed her hand over his chest. She trailed from his pecs down over his rock-hard abs, and when he didn't recoil, she stepped closer to him, sliding her hand around his waist to find the incredible muscles of his back, which led to the canyon that was his spine. She couldn't remember ever being so attracted to someone so physically dominant.

He was impressively tall, steady, and rock-solid, as though he could be a threat, but she wasn't in the least bit anything but incredibly attracted to him. Rising on her tiptoes, one arm around his waist and the other sliding over his shoulder to pull down on his neck, she stretched up and pressed her lips to his. For a split second, he was still and unresponsive. A flutter crossed her as she widened her mouth slightly to peel his bottom lip away, and as she sucked on it, flames took hold.

Like a vice, his arms came around her, pressing her against him as she welcomed the heat. She licked at his lips, inviting his tongue to dance within her mouth, and as he accepted her invitation, he ravaged her as if he'd been starved. He was powerful, she was like a petal in his palm, and he lifted her, hands around her waist and straying to the curve of her butt to grip it entirely. He set her onto the railing to sit as he devoured her uncontrollably.

She tasted like citrus and salt, margarita still on her lips. The music, the night, the stress of her life completely disappeared while she clung to him. Her arms around his neck, her fingers entwined in his thick, curly hair she made a fist and pressed him as hard against her as she could, letting the searing passion of the moment cloud her decisions.

It was a decision, however, and though his body responded to only his attraction, a nagging in his mind surfaced as he remembered the conversations from earlier that day. He slowed the kiss, brought his hands tight around her waist barely above her hips, and used all of his willpower to pull back.

For a single hot and dry bewildered moment where her mind was in disarray, she didn't understand until she saw his face. In the dim light spilling from the windows, she could see the expression in his deep chocolate eyes, and it was regret. She let her hands fall away from his broad shoulders, and as he backed up, he gingerly helped her off the railing.

Unable to accept his action, she clung to his forearms, wondering what was going through his mind. Her thoughts raced a hundred miles an hour, but rather than know, rather than face whatever sad reason he had for not wanting her, she decided she'd prefer to just go to bed.

"I'm sorry," he said, stepping back from her. "I shouldn't have let you do that... I, I shouldn't have done that," he tripped over his words.

"You shouldn't have let me? You shouldn't have done that? Why? I'm a grown woman, and I know what I want, I'm not going to accuse you of anything or cry foul. If you don't want to kiss me, you're right, you shouldn't have, but you did."

He stared, unable to compose a single rational thought in his mind while blinded by her beauty. His heart was slamming against his ribs, blood pulsing in his ears. Every inch of him was drowning in the feeling of kissing her. Standing in the romantic half-light glowing from the house in a dress that could make a man melt with looks to kill, he was stunned.

She had come after him, without hesitation, to kiss him and he couldn't deny he wanted her, didn't want to lie and claim he didn't want her. He wanted very much to admit that he was desperate to have her, only he didn't want to just be another notch in her belt.

"You're right, I did. I," he hesitated, wasn't sure how to place his next words.

"You what?" her tone had changed. Though strength was still leading her emotions, a hint of anger, of rejection, was bubbling underneath.

"I'm not interested in passing flings, and I'm not sure we're on the same page, that's all." He wasn't good with words, and as soon as they came out, he was kicking himself. She frowned at him, her face confused and contorted with disbelief.

"You think I just want to sleep with you and move on? That you would be fun because as soon as you accomplish, whatever there is to finish in the transient situation, you'll be easy to dispose of?" She was sincerely dumbfounded as to why he would think of her that way. "Do I seem like that kind of person?" She almost laughed as she said it, reading into his expression and his tone.

"No," she held up a hand to stop him from speaking and turned towards the house, "don't answer that. I don't want to know."

"Aurora, don't, that came out wrong, I'm not good at these things and, well, you've been drinking. I only came to get you inside anyway. It's not safe out here."

"You're right, I have been drinking, but I'm not drunk. I'm certainly not inebriated out of my wits. I knew what I was doing, I've been thinking about doing it for days, and I don't regret it. So I'm wondering why you – sober as a stone – seem to have done something *you* regret, but I will hand it to you, you're absolutely right, you do suck at these things. If you wanted me to go inside, you should have just asked." She turned curtly on her heel and went back inside and straight upstairs. The reality stung for her that the only way he could have hurt her is with precisely how he did, rejection.

Ethan leaned heavily on the railing, kicking himself. He had landed somewhere between professional 'not going to happen' and 'enjoying going too far,' not achieving success at either one. He realized if he was going to stick with professional, he needed to keep her lips off his in the first place, but once they had landed and the damage was done, he at least should have let it play out instead of offending her. As he stood, in the buzzing hum of crickets and the breeze in the trees, he had accomplished neither professionalism nor landing the girl.

Immediately looking for things to blame, he questioned his stupidity in accusing her of being drunk, and in the same breath, stared at the drink she left on the railing. Picking it up, he could tell it wasn't margarita though her lips had tasted so sweet of citrus, and taking a sip realized she was drinking only lemon-flavored carbonated water. *Damn it.* There had to be a way to backpedal and he realized he had better think of it fast.

Chapter Fourteen

The party started wrapping up around ten as even though Trent was a master entertainer, he also respected his neighbors. Aurora had slipped upstairs and into bed without anyone noticing, the heavy fatigue of alcohol drowning out the regret of a fantastic kiss, and the stress of the day. She was sober enough, but the tequila certainly did its job in temporarily quelling her anxiety. As soon as her head hit the pillow, she fell asleep. By eleven, the last guests were trickling out, and Trent turned his energy to cleaning up what couldn't wait until tomorrow.

Since Aurora was tucked soundly in bed upstairs, Ethan decided to help Trent, considering he looked dead on his feet. The three busied themselves putting furniture back, sealing food away, taking out trash, loading dishes to be washed, and mopping up sticky spills from clinking glasses. By the time midnight rolled around, the place wasn't looking half bad, and Trent was ready to collapse.

"Thank you, Captain America," Trent gave Ethan a high five, "and thank you, Mr. Incredible – I know it's a cartoon, but it's as close as I can come in my exhausted state." Tom just laughed, said thanks as Trent waved goodbye, clinging to the railing as he headed to bed.

"Well, boss, that was fun but not as exciting as I expected after we found the little housewarming gift," Tom shoved his hands in his pockets.

"I'm relieved of that, aren't you?" Ethan asked.

"Oh, all is well that ends well, I suppose. Shall we do a final walk around?"

"Probably not a bad idea, then you could help yourself to the drink I know you've been coveting all night before you turn in."

Tom tilted his head, "You know, I just might do that, those margaritas he stashed in the five-gallon pitcher looked pretty darn appealing." He rocked back on his heels, considering how much he wanted to pour for himself.

"The empty room is up on the left, take your stuff up, but don't wait for us in the morning, head back with the new evidence as soon as you can," Ethan told him.

Ethan started into the office library, checking that the windows were securely closed and locked. He ran a quick survey of the backyard, locked up, and poured Tom a drink, also tempted to pour himself one, but he knew better. He handed it to Tom, and they quietly stepped out onto the front porch.

The heat of the day had dissipated entirely, and slight moisture in the air held a chill that was pleasing compared to the evening full of people. Ethan sank into a chair and propped his feet up on the table, wondering if he should admit his mistakes and woes to Tom. They trusted one another but had yet to cross solidly into a personal arena.

"I'm fairly good at reading people, but I'll admit you tend to be a challenge for me," Tom said as he sipped the margarita.

"Yea?" Ethan was reflective.

"In general, but not tonight. What's on your mind, boss?"

"Why do you call me that? I mean, I'm team lead on the case, and I get it that I'm technically the decision-maker, but I'm not officially your boss."

"I like to think of it that way. Anything I do at your request that goes wrong, you would take the heat, so to me, that's a boss."

"I guess," Ethan leaned his head back.

"Well, I'll be real, that's leadership, and I respect you, so I guess my way of showing it without being a brownnosing follower, is to call you boss."

Ethan chuckled, "I can appreciate that."

"So, let's have it, what's going on? I can't see emotion, but I can see the wheels have been spinning for a couple of hours now."

"It's that obvious, is it?" Ethan asked. Tom just laughed and nodded, yes. "And it can stay between us, and no one else?"

"That goes without saying. At some point, I'm sure I'll need the favor returned."

Ethan sighed heavy, settled down in the pillows in a vain attempt to relax and said, "She kissed me."

Tom nearly spit his margarita out of his nose and said, "What? Dr. Soileaux? When?"

"Earlier tonight, right before she went up to bed. I was sitting out back, keeping an eye on things when you were out here, and she came out, didn't see me. One thing led to another, and I'm probably screwed. I was stretching this protective detail anyway, I pushed it through against policy."

"Start from the beginning, did you initiate, or did she initiate?"

"She did, but that shouldn't matter, she's off-limits, she's a target I have to protect, and I should have kept my head clear."

"Did she pull away first, or did you back off?" Tom wasn't letting any details go.

"I backed off, with every last inch of my willpower. It wasn't easy."

Tom swirled his drink and said, "So she came at you, a grown woman who, by the way, is stunningly sexy, incredibly smart, and seems to have a great personality, and you're kicking yourself for not shooing her away like a fly?"

"It should just be work, shouldn't it? No funny business of a personal nature should be involved."

Tom laughed again, "Funny business? What are you, twelve? Whoppie cushions and clowns are funny business. A woman like her coming on to you is anything but funny."

"Still, there could be a reprimand from superiors, and I could get pulled from the case for conflict of interest, or worse."

"They would have to hear about it first, and she doesn't strike me as that type. If she does, you're probably better off not working the case since it would give you a chance to spend time with her, and I can consider a lot worse scenarios for conflict of interest. It isn't like she paid you for a sexual favor," Tom paused to take a sip, "I mean, she didn't actually offer to pay you for sex, did she? Because with the money she has, I could support you skipping out to make that happen."

"Jesus, Tom," Ethan shook his head, rolling his eyes. "No, she did no such thing. She seemed genuinely attracted to me, and it caught me completely off guard, and ultimately I probably acted like an ass."

"How so?"

Ethan exhaled hard, reliving his stupidity, and the stress of the moment made his skin crawl all over again. "I basically blamed her for coming onto me because she was drunk, which I then realized she wasn't after I kissed her like she was the only woman on the planet and sort of accused her of not being interested in commitment."

"Good one." Tom snorted, "Where'd you get that idea? The Bachelor? Dear God, in aiming at being offensive, you pulled out all the stops."

"Very funny," Ethan mockingly sneered.

"Sorry, boss," Tom couldn't help but laugh, "you're right, it's not funny for you, but in my shoes, you have to see it is slightly amusing. I mean, she's hot, and there is a level of professionalism which you can set aside, temporarily, but also used as a defense so, yea, not sure why you thought to criticize her decision making after a couple of cocktails sounded like a good idea. Let alone accusing her of being able to use you without remorse. Which, might I point out, says just as much about how you view yourself as it does how you anticipate her opinion of you."

"Damn it."

"You want me to stick around for breakfast?"

"It might not be a bad idea."

Tom polished off the margarita and set the glass aside, "So you've been here a few days, you've got to have some inclination of her personality beyond a passing conversation, you think you can fix it? Like, did she slap you and call you a bastard as she dumped a drink on your head?"

"No," Ethan sat up, "she just sort of pointed out what an idiot I am and stormed off."

"She accused you of everything you actually did and just bailed?"

Ethan thought hard about it for a moment, trying to recall what she had said precisely. "Umm, yeah, pretty much exactly that."

"Well then, I think there's hope on some level, there's always room to backpedal if she hasn't called to have you removed from the premises by dawn."

"I guess," Ethan didn't feel confident in any of it.

"Regardless, if she's in bed, now is not the time to breach the subject. Maybe after a good night's sleep, and an apology, a little groveling will be appealing. In my experience, smart women are faster to hand out appropriate forgiveness."

"I suppose. I think I'll head in, speaking of a good night's sleep I could use one, what's left of it anyway." Ethan stood up and, through the window, caught a glimpse of a light in the kitchen. "I might get that chance sooner rather than later. Someone's up." His phone flashed, signaling a call as Ethan went back inside.

"Good luck boss, I'll see you in the morning."

Aurora woke in a cold sweat, tongue slightly pasty from drinking all evening, her head beginning to pound. Tequila was one of those drinks with which she had a love-hate relationship. Thankfully, she hadn't had enough of it to bring on a migraine or worse, a spell of sickness or hangover, but she needed some water and a couple of ibuprofens. Sitting up in bed, she was doubly relieved there was no dizziness. The thought of staying around too much longer, with Trent's lifestyle, was becoming less appealing.

She slipped on a pair of socks and padded downstairs to get a drink, noticing Ethan was not yet in the bed across from her, wondering why. As the memory of the kiss she initiated earlier that night came flashing back in vivid detail, her heart galloped in her chest, and she instantly wondered if he'd decided to let Tom take his place. *Alright*, she thought, *I wasn't drunk, but I wasn't using rational thinking either, alcohol blocks my inhibitions, and I should probably own up to it.* She started down the stairs, and upon seeing the whole first floor dark and quiet, a flash of anxiety had her worried Ethan had left.

In the kitchen, she grabbed a glass and filled it with water, noticing Bastet had not come to bed with her. Thinking the cat must be outside and knowing the fresh night air would also do her some good, she glanced to be sure the alarm was off and stepped outside. The evening breeze was delightful, sweet, and moist as she strolled to the railing. The starry sky was dazzling. There was just enough stirring around her, just enough breeze to shake the bushes and trees that she didn't sense she wasn't alone.

Her thoughts turned to Ethan. He had been so willing to hold her, remembering his hands warm and rough on the bare skin of her back sent a flutter through her. It couldn't be that simple, she thought, she couldn't believe what he had said, there had to be some hidden motive. The way they had caught fire in the darkness was not her imagination. Drinking water like she had to put out a flame, the feel of his taut waist between her thighs when he had lifted her sizzled in her mind.

A blood-curdling sound from Bastet startled her. Beyond where starlight blended into pitch black, there was a cry she wasn't familiar with hearing. The cat was hissing, screeching in a nasty and violent way that sent shivers down her spine. *Could it be a catfight?* She wondered, but that had never happened before. Turning to open the child gate, Aurora shouted, "Bastet? Here kitty," but before she could even reach the latch, a leather-gloved hand wrapped around her face smothering her mouth and nose. A beast of a man had swiftly and silently come around the corner of the second-floor deck and had a hold of her around the waist before she could get her bearings.

Her water glass dropped from her hands, shattering as she reached to peel the fingers away from her mouth to breathe. Trying as she could to scream, all that came out was muffled panic in panting breaths. Lifted off her feet, her attacker overpowered her. Opening her eyes in a vain attempt to get her bearings, she could see another large man bolting across the grass towards her. Terror kicked in with the realization Ethan might not be there, if she disappeared no one knew she was outside, no one would know where she went or what happened.

Adrenaline surged through her veins, and with her mouth open from the failed attempt to scream, she bit down as hard as she possibly could. Her teeth found a knuckle joint of the first finger, and a satisfying crunch accompanied a grunt. Her hands flew above her head in an attempt to find flesh of any kind, and though she felt a knit mask, she got lucky and also made contact with an eye. Her assailant cursed in Arabic, and before it could register in her mind, his partner was grabbing hold of her legs. Kicking for all she was worth, she screamed and twisted, and though her strength was waning, her mind stayed sharp. Her first attacker tried to shove her over the gate, but she curled a knee up and let loose with a hard heel to his throat. It didn't take much strength as the blow was well placed, and he coughed immediately, losing his balance on the steps.

Just as her mind started to race through scenarios she might be facing to escape from these men, the hands loosened around her, and she smacked, head first, onto the deck. Her legs hung at her knees over the gate, and she fell sharply, landing on the back of her skull. Her vision immediately lit with stars, and not the romantic constellation kind. With the attacker on the stairs having regained some balance and refusing to give up entirely, the gate was now open, and he reached to drag her out by her legs.

Struggling to get her wits back after the nasty whack to the head, she twisted and latched onto the railing, unwilling to let herself get dragged down the stairs without protest. Only peripherally aware of the fight happening on the deck beside her, she clung to the post and recognized the language flowing freely between her attackers was indeed Egyptian Arabic. It stunned her, why would these men after her be speaking her mother's native language?

A light in the house flashed on, and another person darted out the back door in a white shirt. *Tom*, she recognized as she saw the sheen of his blond hair in the dim. He made a swift move towards the man who had a hold of her feet, pulling a gun and shouting for him to freeze. There was no response and no hesitation from the man still pulling on her legs. Seeing Tom's weapon and anticipating shots would be fired, Aurora took it upon herself and screaming in Arabic shouted for them to freeze, or to be shot by a federal agent. To her immense relief, the man on the stairs released her legs.

She continued to yell, telling them to back away or face consequences of arrest or even death, to raise their hands and lie face down on the ground. Tom bent down to check on her and lifting her as she leaned on him for support, she could see Ethan clearly for the first time. He was kneeling with one knee in the back of the man she had bitten who was face down on the deck. At first glance, she didn't recognize the mess, but as soon as she stood on her own two feet, it became clear. Blood. The entire deck was splattered with dark red and shimmering blood.

The entire attack happened fast, and as Trent came running out flipping on the backyard floodlights, cell phone in hand prepared to call for more authorities, a chill fell over Aurora that she was afraid to admit even to herself. Ethan and Tom cuffed the assailants and left them face down on the back deck. Tom called for reinforcements as they went into the kitchen. Realizing the whole incident was over took a minute to set in, and she had to push herself to process the situation. As reality settled in, the bright and drenching light of the kitchen revealed the pale in Ethan's face.

His shirt and the front of his pants were drenched in blood, completely soaked in it. His hand rested at his shoulder just above his left collar bone, and even though his knuckles were white with pressure, a steady stream of fresh blood oozed from beneath it. Other than the wound at his shoulder and a few superficial cuts, he seemed otherwise unharmed. Aurora stared at him in awe, unsure what to say or do, glued to his dark and steady eyes.

"I have a team on the way. These two won't say a word." Tom had been asking questions and stood in the doorway to the deck, disheveled but calm.

"I, maybe, I'm not sure, but," Aurora stuttered, "I might know why."

"Feel like sharing?" Tom raised his eyebrows.

"I don't think they speak English," she said, somehow not wanting to admit it.

"Really? Then what do they speak?"

"Egyptian Arabic," she paused and took a deep breath. "I heard them speaking instructions to each other before the one dropped me on my head."

She looked to Ethan, as he leaned against the counter still a couple shades too pale, unsure what to do. She wanted to go to him, to dote on him and worry about him but he didn't appear to want her near him. He was exuding a significant amount of aggression in an apparent 'stay the hell away from me' mood.

"And you speak this language? It's what you were shouting, wasn't it?" Tom pressed her.

"Enough."

"Not the time to be humble, honey," Trent piped in.

"Can you ask them their names and what they're doing here, trying to kidnap you? I mean, we were worried about a serial killer, but these two professional hitmen were not what we expected."

"Hitmen?" Aurora gasped.

"Yes, Dr. Soileaux, I searched them thoroughly, and I've seen the type before. They came prepared, in stealth, with binding and weaponry to support kidnapping and torture. They certainly weren't here for a holiday brunch."

Something in her blood ran cold. The language, the dark masks, the sneak attack brought her back to her childhood.

But it couldn't be, could it? She wondered.

"So, can you talk to them or what?" Tom persisted.

"What do you want to know?" she asked. Tom went quickly into the office and came back with a paper bag. He waved it at Ethan as if asking for permission, and Ethan nodded approvingly.

"Ask them about this first," Tom took out the jar, and nausea rolled through her.

"Are those eyeballs?" she recoiled.

"Yea, we're not sure if they're human or not, though."

Trent gagged a little, "Where did those come from?"

Tom again looked to Ethan for permission first.

"Your front steps. We found them earlier tonight during the party."

"I'm sorry I asked," Trent turned to go lie down on the couch. Aurora was feeling green, but she went outside with Tom anyway. The fight had shaken her, but the jar had her unnerved beyond her ability to cope. The two men stayed silent, still face down on the deck. One was bleeding profusely, and it struck a chord with her that she had zero instinct to help him. Whatever moderate wound he had given to Ethan, he had suffered tenfold in return, and she was glad of it.

"Let's start with names and whether or not they're alone," Tom stayed close to her as she knelt. Out of nowhere, Bastet came strolling onto the deck, planting herself stiffly beside Aurora in an apparent act of sinister support. Aurora asked, in Arabic, who they were, if they were alone, and what they wanted. Neither responded.

Tom sat the jar down on the deck between them, carefully gauging their reaction. One looked away, and the other twisted his face up in disgust.

After a few seconds, she asked again. This time she asked if they knew anything about the jar, with more authority in her tone. One of them looked sideways at her and spoke back.

"This one says he doesn't know anything about the jar, but they still won't tell me their names." When she asked the next question, carefully, she knew she wouldn't like the response. She knew it would be the final cut in a long-strained relationship, and there would be no recovery from the truth.

"Did Rashida Soileaux send you?" she asked carefully in Arabic, pointedly in a cold but quivering voice. The man Tom had apprehended responded, and a full verbal onslaught ensued. The two men argued between each other before Aurora interrupted, and when she did, it was with a temper from hell.

Down on both knees, she screamed at the one she had bitten only inches from his face with a fury she didn't know her soul possessed. Years of betrayal, lies, and neglect snapped something inside her, and when one of them admitted they had been sent by her very own mother to remove her from the situation *she had gotten herself into*, she knew she would never be able to forgive.

Once the admission was out, once the truth shone like a beacon in the night, everything changed. She stared at them, unwavering and bitter, and hate swelled up in her that had to escape, or else it would consume her, and had nowhere else to go.

"Dr. Soileaux, what did they say? What is going on?" Tom asked, completely unaware of the torrent of revenge welling up inside her like a hurricane.

"I know who sent them, you were right, it's nothing to do with the jar." Her voice was shattering as tears threatened to overwhelm her.

She *wanted* to scream, and for the very first time in her life, she *wanted* to cause harm. These men were here to take her against her will, as was her mother's typical controlling style. They had caused her only a few bumps and bruises, but Ethan was hurt. She cared for him. He came to her rescue and had sworn to protect her without knowing her a day in his life. He stood in the other room, bleeding from a wound one of them inflicted. The thought wholly and entirely removed all sympathy and empathy she had ever possessed in her soul.

The man Ethan had neutralized clearly led the mission her mother devised, and a stare from Aurora that could have melted steel zeroed in on him. In a lightning fasts movement she reached out, laced her hands in the hair at the back of his head, and pulled hard, craning his neck to a point she hoped it would snap. With her face only inches from him in a clear, slow, perfect Arabic, she told him in no uncertain terms that she hoped the wrath of her mother would punish him with the intensity he deserved.

Right before Tom reached her, she had just enough of her balance to slam the man's face into the deck as hard as she possibly could. She was seething, seeing red. Tom grabbed her hard then, pulling her to her feet, and she forced herself to calm as he restrained her.

Dragging her with his arms wrapped around her, Tom pulled her back into the kitchen. Her whole world felt different, looked different through her eyes, and as they met Ethan's, she accepted change wholeheartedly for the first time. She knew it was truly time to let go, and she was truly ready to move on.

"What the hell?" Tom asked as much in surprise as frustration.

"You were right. They're hired kidnappers. There aren't any more of them. The one on the left blames the one on the right for screwing everything up. They've been watching me since Wednesday morning," she seethed as Tom released her. "The Egyptian bitch who gave birth to me sent them to kidnap me, and I want to press charges, as many as I possibly can."

"What?" Trent reeled. "Are you kidding? That can't be. I mean, we've always known she's ruthless, but for you? Kidnapping?"

"Believe it." She turned to Ethan, noticing his color wasn't improving, blood still trickling in a steady stream from where he held pressure on his neck. "When the time comes, for them to cooperate and confess, feel free to research and use the Gearhardt-Townsend bludgeoning of Mexico City for a little motivation. You'll want to have an interpreter ready. It isn't a good idea for me to be in the middle anymore."

"Obviously," was Tom's only reply as he stood in shock.

She walked to Ethan, concerned for him, angry, bent on making sure her mother's mistakes wouldn't impact him long term.

"You don't look so great, Captain America," she smiled weakly.

"I'm alright, nothing a few stitches won't fix." But his breathing was labored, and she could tell from his shirt he was losing more blood than was safe from a reasonably small cut.

"Come on, let me take a look, I'll save the federal government a few bucks if I can." She took him by his free hand and pulled him away from the counter, "Sit here on the floor, then lie down; that way, we can keep the mess contained."

As he sat, she marveled again at his sheer size. Once he was horizontal, she called to Trent, "Have any random supplies still hanging around?"

"Of course, you know me. I'll be right back." He went into the other room and came back swiftly with a large red kit holding a decent spread of professional supplies.

"Can I buy you a new shirt?" she asked Ethan.

"Why?" he asked.

"Because I have to cut this one off to get a good look at what's going on. Standard protocol, it's either the EMTs or me." She was sitting on his left side and straddled his arm as he continued to hold pressure on the wound on his shoulder. The bastard he had interrupted in the process of kidnapping her had stabbed him with a small long knife. He had a clean but deep wound.

She slid her fingers up beside his and pushing his hand aside, maintained pressure on the gash with one hand while Trent stepped in and cut away his shirt. She pulled back only briefly to see the size of the cut before applying pressure again with gauze.

"Looks like you've got a pretty straight forward stab wound, deep but clean."

"It's bleeding a lot," Trent looked at her concerned.

"Yes, thank you for the observation, Nurse Baldwin. I'm guessing he's got one or more superficial clavicle arteries intersected." Aurora shot Trent a look that reminded him of how to behave while managing a patient.

"Is that bad, like surgery or something, bad?" Ethan asked in a calm though concerned voice.

"We'll see when the paramedics get you to the hospital," she looked to Tom, sitting on the floor beside the door, who had lost a few shades of his own. "You did call paramedics, right?" she asked him.

"Yes, sorry, I don't do great with blood, they're on the way."
He wiped a clean sheen of sweat from his brow. Aurora kept her
thumb tight on the small wound on Ethan's shoulder and waited
patiently. There wasn't much she could do without some anesthetic
and better supplies, so all that was left was manage the bleeding as
best she could, and wait.

Time seemed to slow to a halt as they sat, silent, waiting for the
FBI team and the paramedics to arrive. Kneeling over Ethan in the
blanching light of the kitchen, it was like her brain was in
overdrive. The events of the week, of her life, zoomed through her
mind at high speed, and as she struggled to control them, one thing
became crystal clear—she wanted this man to continue to be a rock
for her. There was something about him that just set her world
right, and set her heart booming like fireworks.

"For a minute, when I came down, I thought you had left," she
said to him to pass the time and keep him focused. A spry smile
spread on his face.

"Why would you think that?"

"You know, my bad behavior."

"That's ridiculous, first of all—it wasn't bad behavior, second
of all—even if you did misbehave, I'm here for the duration of the
case. I'm not a quitter," he smirked.

"I should have known," she said as his hand brushed the inside
of her ankle as she straddled his arm. "How's the feeling in your
fingers?"

He looked at the ceiling, opening and closing his hand,
evaluating it as he made a fist between her feet.

"Good, I think, it only tingles a little, not bad." The glance
Aurora shared with Trent was telling. "Why? Is this little knife
wound going to give me more trouble than you care to share with
me?"

"Maybe, we'll see," she said as sirens wailed in the distance.
"Whatever needs to happen, I'll be sure you get the best care
available."

"Whatever happens to Ethan I guarantee these guys are
regretting setting foot here, he kicked some ass, they don't look
good," Tom was watching the men outside.

Aurora sneered at him for even bringing up the state of her
attackers.

"Not to mention, I'm pretty sure you broke this guy's nose, maybe a cheekbone," Tom gagged and looked away.

A few minutes later, the FBI and a team of paramedics were swarming the house. Aurora was insistent that Ethan would be taken care of first, so she stretched the truth. The paramedics were familiar with the terminology enough to know she was seriously concerned, which she actually wasn't, but she wanted them to think so. They loaded Ethan into the ambulance first, and after racing to change into something more appropriate than her silky pajamas, she joined him.

"Stanford ER," she barked as they slammed the doors behind her. She placed his IV and wasn't trusting anyone else with his care. As soon as the ambulance was in motion, she knew she wouldn't have long. She pulled out her phone and made a call.

"Beckworth, are you running the board tonight?" she asked into the receiver. "Yea, I have a favor to ask." She was silent for a minute. "Remember when your kid had that funky fainting thing, and you called me? … I thought so, can you scrub in on a little project? … Yes, it's important, I have an FBI Agent who needs the best vascular surgeon Stanford has to offer, I'm concerned about nerve damage … I do believe that, and you know it because I called your cell directly. Can you prep, please? I don't want anyone else." She smiled, and after saying thank you, hung up.

"Vascular surgeon?" Ethan asked with eyebrows raised. "Isn't that heart stuff?"

She laughed, "No, vascular is the entire system, not just heart but close, good observation of vocabulary," she winked.

A team of staff and surgeons were waiting in a trauma bay when they arrived, to Aurora's delight, and they whisked Ethan upstairs for what was actually a minor repair as if he were the President. She got herself a cup of coffee, caught up with friends on the night shift, and was grateful for the professional distraction from her personal world amidst the stress of the evening.

Ethan was out of 'surgery' in less than thirty minutes. She knew they would give him only a light anesthetic to repair the small puncture wound efficiently, but she liked being able to pull rank and clout when it counted, and she rarely asked for special attention. She also wanted him to heal quickly and was worried he would be out of commission during his recovery.

She slipped into the recovery area to check on him just after one in the morning, finding him peacefully sleeping relieved her. He was so tall his feet nearly hung off the end of the gurney. He had been changed into the standard-issue hospital gown and looked so relaxed she couldn't help but let some of the stress of the day fall away. She sat beside him and trailed her hand lightly over his arm, remembering the kiss from only hours earlier. *Slow it down, sister, you have a real chance here,* she told herself.

At her light touch, he roused to look at her, taking a deep breath slowly.

"Hello, Agent Hartman, how are you feeling?" she asked.

"Oh, now that I'm in a hospital bed where it's professional for you, you're going to be all 'Agent' this and 'Agent' that?" he made a cocky grin that had her smiling.

"No, Ethan, I just like the sound of Agent Hartman off my lips occasionally."

"Well, that's nice to know."

"How are you feeling?" she asked.

"Relaxed, good actually. Whatever drugs they gave me are pretty slick."

She continued to caress his hand and was glad he accepted her touch, not breaking his gaze from her face.

"We aim to please," she shifted onto the bed more and put her fingers in his hand, admiring him, silently relieved her mother's mistakes hadn't landed him in a worse situation. He shifted the pillow to look at her better and pulled the blankets up, never letting go of her hand. She set her paper coffee cup aside on a metal tray by the bed and tucked her leg beneath her to face him.

"How's your head?" he asked.

"Oh, it's fine. A small egg maybe but nothing permanent."

"I'm glad. About earlier," he began.

"How much earlier?" she interrupted. "We have a lot of earlier today. Was it earlier when you heard me lose my shit about my sister, or earlier when you found me crying about Theresa, or earlier when I kissed you like I wanted to make money at it, or earlier when you saved my life, for the second time? Or is it the third time now?" He squeezed her hand and caressed the back of it with his thumb, grinning ear to ear.

"Earlier when I kissed you like you were the only woman on Earth," he said and she rolled her eyes and smiled, pink seeping into her cheeks. "I'm sorry," he said. It wasn't really what she wanted to hear, but she figured he had to get something off his chest.

"Yea? About what part of it?"

"I'm sorry I pulled back, and I'm sorry I said the things I said. I heard you talking with your friends about men you've dated, and I guess I was a little gun shy because the truth is, I don't want to just be another notch in your belt. I didn't do an awesome job of explaining where I was coming from or why. I've never been good at relationships because I always want more than the women I date seem to want. I get caught up quickly, too quickly, more often than not. And, I guess I was afraid—*I am afraid*—of what could be between us."

She wasn't sure if it was the drugs talking or the late night, but his sincerity and insecurity pierced her.

"You don't need to apologize. You're right; I'm forthcoming, unusually more so with men. I know what I want, for better or for worse, and most men don't mind when I only want something physical. I'm not fake or false. At the very least, the men I go out with know what they're getting. That's probably the part missing from your earlier eavesdropping." She shot him a raised eyebrow glance that said 'caught you.'

"I tend to lead with what I want and have time for, which is hot and fast, and you're not that kind of guy, which is all the more reason I like you. You don't seem like the kind of guy to go for fun but fleeting. So don't apologize, consider it a learning curve for both of us, if you're still interested," she batted her eyelashes at him.

He smiled at her, lost again in her eyes, unsure if it was the pain meds or a part of his heart that had him feeling drugged. Dizziness had him wondering if he was having this conversation at all or if he would wake up having dreamed it.

"I'm not sure interested is quite the word for it, but I need to get this case wrapped up, with you alive and well before I can spend some time on that 'learning curve,' as you call it."

So you're telling me I have to keep my hands to myself for a while? She almost said it out loud and was utterly relieved when her cell rang, interrupting the conversation. It was Trent.

"Hey, the sidekick back here wants to know if he's coming to get his boss, or what's going on? He survived, right?" Trent was teasing, and she could hear Tom, worried, questioning him in the background, which made her giggle. She got up and strolled away from Ethan's bedside.

"Yes, he's fine, quite well as a matter of fact. He's all done. We're just waiting for the IV antibiotics to finish. You can send him to get us in about a half-hour if you want. Is the house still swarming with people?"

"It's like CSI. Only they're all grumpy, and none of them are attractive," Trent huffed and sounded tired.

"Alright, well, get to bed as soon as you can. I'll catch up with you tomorrow sometime."

"Sure, Sugar, see you later."

She interrupted him, "And Trent, I'm sorry about all of this, I never meant to drag you into a complete nightmare."

"I still love you, but Kurt's home tomorrow, you know."

"Yes, I've been thinking about it, I'll see what I can do about getting out of here, maybe take a drive."

"Is that going to be alright with Captain America?" The sarcasm in his voice was dry.

"I don't know, but at this point, I feel like it's the right choice for me, I'm not sure he's going straight back into action anyway."

"Well, good luck, we can talk about it later," he said goodbye, and she hung up. When she turned back to Ethan, he had fallen asleep again. She paused to admire him. In the too-small hospital gown that was surely not covering his backside, he looked awkward but peaceful, breathing deep and steady his color had returned. He had a small purple mark on his cheek where he had taken a glancing blow, and a cut on the outside of his left forearm. Thinking of how he had jumped in harm's way for her only hours earlier, wholeheartedly and without a second thought, tugged at her heart. A hot feeling she hadn't known in a long time simmered in her belly, and was drawing her to him.

He had been right when he had singled out the conversation points from earlier that day. She did tend to go through men like

French fries. Hot, salty, easily accessible, and cheap, she hadn't dated anyone worth a second look in so long she couldn't remember. Whether she considered them gold-digging, trying too hard to show off their own spoils, shallow or egotistical, she had written off the idea of a fruitful long-term relationship some time ago.

She couldn't figure it out now, standing over this incredibly handsome, smart, somewhat shy but heroic man. Did she open herself to him because of the way he came sliding into her life uninvited? He hadn't come onto her like all the other guys she'd entertained. He had kept his distance, professional, and polite while she had begun to admire everything she saw. Looking at how attached she had become to him over the last week, she felt like it was almost a trick, fate's trick. Trent had been right—the foul and the friendly.

Realizing it was probably going to take a while to get him out of there, even with the pull she had in the situation, she logged on to the nearest computer and texted Dr. Beckworth. Within minutes all his orders were signed, including discharge, so she went out to the nursing station to retrieve his personal effects. In a large bag, she found his pants and cell phone. His shirt had been discarded as she thought it too damaged and dirty to bother keeping.

She sent a quick text to Trent, *'have Tom call me, Ethan needs clothes, see if he can grab some'* only to receive a reply promptly, *'he left, something about a chain of custody, blah blah, I can get you.'* She didn't want to inconvenience him again, so she decided to call him off. Typing quickly, she replied 'no, absolutely not, we'll figure it out, I'll call an Uber or something, go to bed.' Knowing it was the right call anyway, she was relieved just the same when a text, with only a thumbs up, arrived in response. Thinking fast, she darted out to the nursing station, again flagging the first male nurse she recognized.

"Derek!" she grabbed him quick, "can you do me a favor pretty please?"

"Sure, Dr. S, what's up?"

"Can you grab me an extra pair of the double XL scrubs from the men's staff locker room?"

He frowned at her, "Sure, but what for?"

"A friend of mine, I need to get him home in something besides a hospital gown." She smiled sweetly, and he nodded, darting in the opposite direction. Half an hour later, she had Ethan dressed in standard-issue blue hospital scrubs and was loading him out of a wheelchair into the backseat of an SUV with Uber.

"Just don't pass out on me, alright, big guy?" she said.

"Pass out?" he frowned down at her.

"Yea, you're still rather loaded on pain meds, and you're far too big for me to carry." The medications and lack of sleep had loosened him up. He leaned on her a little in the car and pinched her bicep, making a 'that'll do' kind of expression.

"I'd put money on you. I think you'd figure it out." He smiled drunkenly, and she couldn't help but laugh. They sped along the freeway, and the driver turned up the radio just enough to spill into the back seat. The DJ announced the song coming on next as *'Wrecking Ball'* by Eric Church, but Aurora wasn't familiar with it. Ethan was leaning against the window, and she sat in the middle, close enough she could get it down fast if he became nauseated from the anesthesia. As the beat of the music bled out of the speakers, he sat up, leaned on her, and looked at her like no man had before.

The song drifted into the back seat like honey, thick, sticky-sweet, and sexy. She didn't recognize the melody, but Ethan seemed to know it, and at the chorus, he began to mumble the words. The man's voice in the music echoed. He had a twang, but she liked it, and she especially liked the way Ethan was staring at her. He put his arm cautiously up around her shoulders and caressed her tenderly, shifting to face her more.

She rested her head on his uninjured shoulder, a little thrill coursing through her, electric and breathtaking. He stroked her face then down the nape of her neck, light as a feather, bending his head to her, lost in her eyes. Time froze as he stared at her, studying every little bit of her features in the glow of passing streetlights. His sideways smile, smooth and sweet, had her heart sighing in her chest.

She felt like it was the first time she was seeing a private side of him, something he kept hidden. The song swayed, the words describing the artist destroying a house while consumed in the throes of passion from missing a lover so dearly, it was almost as intoxicating as the dreamy way Ethan leaned closer to her. The way his lips met hers had her breaking out in a sultry, searing sweat. Lingering and sure, intentional and confident, he took his time exploring every bit of her luscious pink mouth. She couldn't breathe, felt held between the real world and some fantasy, melting into him like ice cream on a hot day. His fingers were strong, on a hand large enough to cover her whole shoulder, trailing along her skin so gently, tickling and tantalizing her collarbone and jaw as he consumed her as if she were a vital cure to what ailed him.

Lost in him, enthralled by him, she succumbed to his desire and fed her own like she was famished. He burned like a torch on low, a blue flame set to last the night, impossible to deny and satiating. The way he kissed her, steamy and eager but not demanding, had her clinging to him, numb to the outside world. Her hand flattened against his chest, feeling the warmth of his body, sliding up and over his shoulder, into his hair thick and curly. He pulled her into his embrace, his hands gradually soaking in every inch of her, and had her wondering why she had ever entertained another man in her entire life.

The driver slowed to a stop at a light, and the bright red of the lamp had Aurora gasping, taking stock of her surroundings. Without letting go of Ethan, still enjoying his breath raspy in her ear as his kisses glided down her neck, she realized they had driven past the exit on the freeway only to double back. The driver had missed it or had perhaps realized how the two were enjoying one another in the back seat. He had allowed for an extra three or four minutes in the car, but now they were at the last streetlight before the house.

She couldn't let go of Ethan, couldn't bring herself to sit up. Her legs draped over his, his arms solid and tight around her felt so right. When they finally pulled up in front of Trent's house, she climbed out of the car over his lap, thanked the driver twice, and added a tip that was four times the cost of the ride. Being careful to test that Ethan could effectively stand under his own power, she accompanied him into the house, straight upstairs, and to bed.

After freshening up and changing, she went to check on him. A small part of her wanted to crawl in beside him and snuggle in the crook of his shoulder. She couldn't bring herself to do it. He was injured, and they both needed sleep. With glowing numbers on the clock showing just past three in the morning, she decided there would be plenty more time to nourish what was going on between them later. Crawling in bed, she drifted off to sleep with Bastet beside her on the pillow, purring sweetly and dreams of Ethan's lips on hers swirling in her head.

Chapter Fifteen

There was a loud crash, something breaking upstairs, and it sounded like an entire table of glass had been knocked over. Aurora could hear her sister screaming as she huddled behind the arm of the big black couch in the living room. Her mother was shrieking something in her native language she couldn't understand. Tears stung her face, and she heard from somewhere deep in her memory a cappella singing, *hallelujah*.

The lovely, deep voice of a woman rolled through the back of her mind as if she were in the same room. The words enveloped her as would arms in a hug, she covered her ears. *Where's Daddy?* She wondered, trying to remember what day it was. A door slammed, and another crash ensued, something splintering and tinkling to the floor like tiny pieces of metal. Aurora closed her eyes and focused on the song, *hallelujah*.

The sky outside was dark, the wind was blowing the curtains through the windows, and it made her imagination jump with fear, someone was watching. Someone was coming. Her heart raced, her throat felt dry and sticky, panic rushed up in her, and she began to picture all of her favorite spots to hide when she and Donia played hide-and-go-seek. Donia never found her. She had all the best hiding places. She could hide for hours, and Donia never knew where she was. She hid so long she got bored but hearing the woman's voice piqued her curiosity, where had she heard it? *Hallelujah*.

The screaming continued, thrashing and slamming still loud above her. She squeezed her eyes tighter and pictured a place she was happy, the water. Crystal clear blue waters of Tahoe, where the beach sand was rough, sharp, and hot beneath her feet. She couldn't really build nice sandcastles in Tahoe sand. Tahoe sand is made of decomposed granite, Daddy said, it makes better mountains. She could see his face, see his smile, and he made her feel better. But he wasn't there now, and he wouldn't ever be back, she felt so sad, *hallelujah*.

Silence. Were her hands over her ears drowning out the yelling and anger? Aurora opened her eyes gingerly, timidly, weary, and fearful. Her mother sat at a desk in a big office, her office at Boeing. The windows were so wide, and the sky outside was watery grey with clouds, and rain dripped down the panes. There was no yelling, but she could tell her mother was mad, angry like she always was.

"Get her out of here. I have work to do." Her mother snapped, and a part of Aurora's heart broke. Why was she always in the way? Why was she never good enough? Tears stung her face, itching and burning as they streaked her cheeks. She closed her eyes again, where could she go now? Anywhere but here, she imagined. Where her mind took her was worse.

"What's wrong with Dad?" Her voice didn't sound right. She was staring at herself, and she recognized herself, but it wasn't her, it was someone else, someone older. She had to be someone else, or she wouldn't be able to stand the pain. Her mother didn't care, never had cared, she had another man, and he stood beside her, bald and ugly like a vulture. *Rashida replaced Dad with this ugly ass clown? Before he was even sick?* Aurora's heart pounded, threatened to explode inside her as if she were outside her own body, and she watched herself crumble as the monitors sang a solid tune. *Hallelujah.*

Anger swelled in her, regret and bitterness stabbed as hate formed a hard knot in her chest. She breathed deep, too fast, she felt light-headed. Why wasn't her sister crying? Why wasn't her mother even upset? She squeezed her eyes shut and leaned, feeling the cold leather of the arm of the big black couch again. Rashida came back downstairs and didn't even look at her, didn't look *for* her, didn't *care* for her. She was alone, and the only person who had loved her was gone. *Hallelujah.*

"Aurora," Ethan's hand was around her shoulder, another at her cheek. "Aurora you're dreaming, wake up, are you alright?" Aurora peeled her eyes open through salty, sticky, stinging saline. The room was pale, but the day had sailed in at full speed. She gasped. She had been dreaming but the tears, they were real. The emotions in the dream were more than real, overwhelming her, rendering her helpless to fight them or recover from them.

"Aurora, good grief, what's wrong?" Ethan's face twisted with concern, his touch firm as he leaned over her distraught. She tried to breathe, but it was no use, sobs railed in her chest, and she surrendered to them, hard and rough, her body reeled. She shook her head. She couldn't tell him, even if she wanted to, she couldn't get the words to form in her mouth. She reached for him, pulled on the pale blue scrubs he still wore, and remembered him in a hospital bed before putting them on.

"Hey, let me help you, can I help you? What can I do?" He looked so worried it pained her even more. She wiped her face and rolled towards him, into his embrace, clung to him like a drifter in the ocean would cling to a raft and continued to sob. She let him lift her, let him scoop her into his arms and buried her face in his shoulder. Her throat was scratchy, her nose was running, and she couldn't control the tears.

"Easy, try to breathe; it was just a dream, easy, easy." His voice was so kind, so reassuring, but she couldn't get a hold of herself. As she sat in his arms crying, reality began to sink in, bit by bit, piece by piece. She wanted to let go, wanted to be free of the burden, but she had no one else. Her mother and her sister were her only family, and fear held her back, years of neglect held her feet fast like concrete shoes.

"Alright, I'm here, and I'm going to wait. When you're ready, I'll still be here. Take your time; easy now." Ethan whispered to her and held her while her body heaved a kind of hiccup, reacting to the heavy sobs and the fractured emotions. Her body shuddered and shook, and she let him hold her steady, let him be her harbor in the storm.

Ethan inspected the bandage on his shoulder in the mirror, unsure what to think. It wasn't throbbing, not like other wounds he had in the past. He'd been shot in the leg a few years back, and this paled in comparison, but he had a strange hot sensation that shot down his arm when he moved wrong. It was like a nerve was pinched or caught, and his instinct was to hold his arm entirely still. He finished shaving and replaced the towel around his waist with a pair of navy blue Dockers, his go-to business casual, and went back out into the bedroom.

Aurora was still soundly asleep on the bed he'd been sleeping on alone, seemingly peaceful again. He watched her out of the corner of his eye as he slipped a tan polo shirt on, still a little wrinkled, but it would have to do. She had fallen back to sleep nestled beside him after whatever nightmare had consumed her, and he decided that if she started to show the slightest sign of agitation in her slumber, he would wake her up promptly. As it was, he felt ready for breakfast but was afraid to leave the room.

At just after ten in the morning, Trent's warning from only a few days earlier echoed in his memory, *'a downward spiral, so tread carefully with her. She's delicate now.'* At the time, he had taken it seriously but hadn't remotely anticipated the kind of behavior he had seen after waking her up that morning. She had cried for a solid twenty minutes, breathless and uncontrollable sobs he hadn't been able to ease. Now he remembered being told that when she slept late it was a precursor to depression of some kind. *Was that it or was it the late-night snacking?* He couldn't remember, but his gut was telling him to wake her up.

He checked his phone to find several messages and texts from Tom, other people at the office wondering if he was alright, his boss and his mom included. He only considered one from Tom that said new intel had come in, and one from his mom, wondering how he was doing as remotely important. It was Saturday; could he hold them off at least until after he had his first cup of coffee? Yes, he made an executive decision and stuck the phone back in his pocket, still on vibrate.

He sat on the bed beside Aurora, tracing a finger along her cheek and down her arm, and she roused, rolling toward him. As her eyes opened and she focused, her face was at least relaxed and free of panic, but her eyes were puffy and red with dark circles.

"Good morning," he said softly. She winced and stretched.

"Don't give me that crap. You know very well it has not been," she stretched then rubbed her eyes. "I don't think it's been a good morning since just after midnight when you got stabbed. I mean, the kiss was a highlight, but the rest of it has kind of sucked, you have to admit."

He shrugged, "There's a little bit of it left, so let's try and pull it out of the gutter then, shall we?" He took her hand and intertwined his giant fingers in hers. "And we can repeat the kiss anytime you like. You just let me know." He leaned closer and dropped a little peck on her forehead before pushing himself back off the bed, attempting to pull her with him.

"I'm sorry about this morning," she said, her expression suddenly turning sulky.

"You want to tell me what it was all about?" he asked without expectation, and she appreciated that.

"At the opportune moment, yes. I think I need some time right now."

He smiled and helped pull her up, admiring her figure in the spaghetti strap pajamas.

"Well, we have plenty of that." He expected a smile of some kind from her, and when it didn't come, his heart sank a little. "Coffee first?"

She nodded and, once on her feet, went to retrieve her robe. "I'll be down in a minute," she said as she slid on the sapphire blue silk. He turned to head back downstairs but took a second look when he reached the door; something in him was nagging that she shouldn't be left alone. They weren't at that point emotionally, however, and he knew not trusting her to herself would be a nasty faux pas if he was wrong. Knowing who *could* handle her that way, he rushed downstairs, hoping Trent was up.

He was in luck. Trent sat at the counter reading a magazine, sipping from a mug twice the size of any standard coffee cup.

"Danish are in the roll-top, help yourself," he said without looking up and frowned as Ethan came to stand close beside him.

"Thanks for that, but I have more pressing concerns. Aurora had a nightmare." Trent immediately set the magazine aside and his expression became worried and focused. He glanced around Ethan to the stairs. "She'll be down in a minute."

"What kind of nightmare?" Trent's voice was hushed.

"She wouldn't tell me, just tears, a whole lot of uncontrollable crying."

"She wouldn't say anything about it?"

Ethan shook his head, no.

"How is she now? Did she wake up alright, for the most part, or is she sulky?" Trent asked.

"Sulky is probably putting it lightly."

"Shit." They could hear her feet on the stairs, "I'll make some calls. Let me handle it." Trent whispered, shooing Ethan away with his hands. He went back to his magazine and his giant cup just in time for Aurora to come around the corner and see Ethan grabbing two coffee mugs.

"I'd like extra sugar in mine, please." She looked utterly exhausted, not just physically, and heavy emotion was radiating off of her. She wore it like lead at her ankles.

"Sure, a teaspoon on top of the French vanilla?" Ethan asked.

"Two," she replied as she plunked down beside Trent immediately flopping her head down onto her folded arms.

"It was a rough night, but was it that bad?" Trent asked.

"Can we talk about it later? I'm not in the mood," she didn't lift her head. Trent raised his eyebrows and looked at Ethan, mouthing the words *'this is not good'* over the rim of his coffee mug. Ethan slid a steaming cup towards Aurora, leaning on his elbows, watching her intently while his coffee sputtered and spat as it filled. Before he could muster anything to say, her phone was ringing in her pocket, and she sat up quick, seeming to expect the call. She snatched the coffee and turned away, answering quickly.

"David," she answered in a relieved tone, but the name had a French accent to it, sounded like *'Da-veed,'* and she followed immediately in fast and fluent French. She took a sip of the coffee and disappeared around the corner upstairs.

"So that's not good, at all, in any way," Trent dropped his magazine again. "David is a good friend of her dad's, is like an uncle to her, worked with him for years, and tends to be someone she runs to when she feels like she's coming unglued. And the nightmare, with nothing but tears, last time that happened she ended up locking herself in her room for almost three days. I almost called the locksmith."

"So, what now?" Ethan asked as he took his first sip of coffee, thinking there might not be enough of it in the world to get him through the day.

"Go after her. Convince her she needs to stay with you, in protection."

"That sounds easier said than done."

"She likes you a lot, and you've got a better shot at it than I do. Make it personal if you have to."

"That's the advice you have?" Ethan scoffed.

"Trust me. If you're smart, it's all you need." Trent's response was almost a sneer which surprised Ethan. He'd never seen the man dig his heels in. Heading to the stairs, he could tell she was still on the phone, and he didn't figure interrupting her was the best starting point. He diverted towards the library office to pack up his laptop and files. After shuffling around for about twenty minutes, eavesdropping and wishing the entire time he spoke French, he finally became confident her call had ended and went upstairs.

He found Aurora in the mistress quarters, suitcase open, packing with furious speed.

"Going somewhere?" he startled her.

"Yes, actually," she barely looked up to him, barely missed a beat. "A good friend of my dad's, he has a cabin on Tahoe, I could use a few days in the sun on the beach or a boat in the dog days of summer, especially how I feel right now I know my soul needs some rest."

Ethan leaned against the doorframe, sinking his hands into the deep pockets of his pants and just watched her throw clothes haphazardly. He had never heard her call her mother 'mom' so hearing her refer to her father as 'dad' clued him in about her feelings. She was barefoot, wasn't folding anything, and was leaving a trail of items strewn on the floor as she selected her favorites, discarding others. He thought about her emotional state, considered what she had been through not only in the last week but throughout her life. He'd gleaned her family wasn't a cakewalk, and considering what he would be without his own family, his heart ached for her.

"Do you need to go alone?" he asked in an unassuming tone. She stopped dead in her tracks, turned and looked at him with a blank stare that reassured him he had hit the nail on the head. She slid a silky garment of some kind through her hands, examining it, thinking.

"I won't be alone, not most of the time anyway. He said he would join me next week."

"Alright, that's good, but it isn't what I asked you. Do you need to go, wherever you're going, alone?" He could see something tense in her, something tugging at her decision making. She strolled over to the nearly full suitcase before looking at him.

"No," her body relaxed. "I don't suppose I *need* to go alone. I don't need to *be* alone. Why?"

"Other than the fact you had eyeballs delivered to your doorstep last night, had an attempted kidnapping from the back porch, there are a few other reasons I could list off. Can you make room for an FBI Agent?"

She smirked at him, "You want to go with me?"

"I would like to. I won't lie. But with a bum shoulder I might not be the best choice plus, my mom's birthday is tomorrow, I had planned to take some personal time this weekend so it wouldn't hurt my feelings if you weren't up for specifically having me as your shadow. I do think it's best if you have someone from the Bureau with you." He stayed casual, relaxed, having tossed the ball back into her court.

She looked at him then turned sharply and began picking things up off the floor, throwing them back into drawers without rhyme or reason. He could see the wheels turning in her mind.

"What were the eyeballs all about anyway? We never really discussed it."

"There was a note. It didn't make much sense." He wasn't sure, with her current behavior, that she was stable enough to handle more information about the case.

"What did the note say?" She pressed him, stopping to stand beside the suitcase, her eyes laser-focused on him, her body rigid and confrontational. His gaze dropped to the floor, and he shifted uncomfortably.

"You sure you want to talk about it?" he asked.

She frowned, her expression hinting she might start to get angry, but concern on his face stopped her. The tension in her stance faded, and she softened against the bed, ruffling some of the clothes in the suitcase to make extra space.

"You're concerned for me, I appreciate that, but there's only so much you can protect me from. The truth isn't one of those things," she said, and he hated to admit he couldn't argue with her.

"Assuming it was from the Hypocrite killer, it said you would remember when his daughter's eyes looked like the ones in the jar, and that you know who was at fault for causing it." Ethan was relieved when she didn't have much reaction besides a grimace.

"Was there anything about the eyeballs that was odd or stood out as abnormal? It was a bit much for me to take in when Tom put them on the deck." She put her hand over her stomach and frowned at him.

"Well," Ethan thought hard, "they seemed not so round, a little flat and deflated. They were floating in a pink fluid, but that's maybe not what you need to be worried about right now."

A chill ran through her as she remembered the eyes in the jar, haunting and familiar. She felt like she recognized them, though she couldn't figure out where from, and she had no intention of admitting it to anyone. She rubbed her temples, thought hard, but couldn't pull anything up from the depths of her memory.

"I'm not sure *worried* effectively covers the bases with anything I feel right now. I just want this guy to go away. I want to go away in the hope he'll forget me," she said.

"And on that note, am I going with you, or am I assigning someone to you?"

"Well, David has plenty of space, I would be happy to have your company, and I'm sure he would be fine making room for you. I can't say I feel like sharing my time with a stranger, again, for an unknown duration. For that matter, having to be with people is driving my departure. I adore Kurt but he is due back tomorrow and for how much I enjoy him, three is a crowd. I always prefer to stay with Trent when he is alone."

She sailed away from him into the bathroom and began talking to him from where he couldn't see her as she opened and closed drawers and cabinets. Ethan considered what it took for her to no longer consider him a stranger and contemplated if that was a good thing or not.

"That being said, I don't want to take you away from family by any means. I can only imagine how important things like birthdays are to someone like you." She hid it well but the bitterness was there, lurking just beneath the surface, ready to snarl at the slightest emotional turbulence. "I could go without you a couple of days, and you could join me if that is agreeable?"

She was using every ounce of professional tone she could muster, but he could still see grief in her body language as she dumped a load of cosmetics and personal items into a smaller bag, glancing up at him. Taking his time to figure out the most advantageous approach, he simply watched her.

"Would Trent mind if I left my motorcycle here awhile?"

"I'm sure he wouldn't, it's a large garage after all, why?"

He thought carefully about his response and what he knew he would need to say afterward. "My shoulder isn't terrible, but I don't think I'm up for a long drive on the bike. If we could stop by my place to grab a few things and, if it's alright with you, if I ride along with you in your car, I'd like to go with you, wherever you're going. Tahoe doesn't sound like a bad place to hang out, hiding."

"What about your personal time? Your mother's birthday? I can't justify taking you away from that. I'm confident where I am going I'll be untraceable for at least a few days. I'm sure I'll be safe. You could take the weekend to recuperate, spend time with your family, meet me on Monday."

"If that's what you want, I could do that, but I'd still prefer to assign an agent to you in the meantime." As the sentence came out, he strolled towards her unassumingly, and with as much affection as he could portray without touching her said, "It isn't only due diligence for your safety, but I wouldn't personally relax unless I knew someone was with you. So, it's either me or someone I assign. Your choice."

There's that damn respect again, she thought.

She sighed, flipped her suitcase closed, leaned on it with one hand, and faced him.

"What about your mom? Birthdays are important."

"She's my mom, she loves me, and she knows I love her, she'll understand. We'll celebrate when this is all over. She guilt's me into a nicer gift that way anyway." There it was, the crack, the rift in her heart that had her waking up in tears. She didn't have that, the mother who loved her and the accepting, supportive family waiting for her. All the genuine love from family she had known was her father, and he had passed away. A little piece of Ethan's heart swelled, seeing the underlying ache in her expression, and he reached for her hand.

"You're sure?" she asked.

He nodded, steadfast, and unwavering.

"Absolutely."

With her free hand, she ran her fingers through her tousled hair but didn't release his grip until she turned away.

"Alright, I need to shower. I told David I might not be there until late. He texted me the code to get in and said the place is all stocked for guests so not to worry about bringing anything besides personal items. It's almost a five-hour drive, as long as we leave the bay by three we should be there in plenty of time to get a good night's rest. Lord knows we both probably need it." She sighed heavily and headed for the bathroom. "I'll be down shortly. I would like to take Bastet with me so I need to pack for her as well. Don't say anything to Trent, please. I'd like to talk to him myself."

Ethan nodded, grabbed her suitcase for her, and went across the hall to prepare his bag. He had calls to make with explanations, probably a few expletives, and a lot of begging for forgiveness.

Chapter Sixteen

For a Saturday, the traffic was light, and as Trent maneuvered his Tesla on Highway 101 north, Ethan was regretting not taking a pain pill. Waking up, he hadn't felt much pain, but now that he had generally been active, there was a sharp stabbing throb beneath his collarbone. He tried to ignore it and strived to hide it, as he worked through emails on his phone in the back seat.

He had managed to call everyone he needed except his mom, so he shot her a couple of texts, and backed them up with a couple to his dad also. He wasn't in the mood to have the conversation within earshot of Trent or Aurora as he sat beside Bastet. The cat peered at him calmly through the carrier window, curling her tail back and forth, more relaxed than he imagined any other traveling cat would be.

Trent and Aurora chatted in the front, for the most part, light subjects, though Trent seemed bound and determined to get a better read on Aurora's intentions and emotional stability while he still had the chance. Ethan stayed out of the conversation unless one of them requested interjection, but they arrived at the Avalon before any discussion with repercussions had ensued.

Ethan was surprised to see the Tesla repaired in the short amount of time it had been parked there. New windows were rolled up, and the thought of racing the car up the Sierra Nevada's to Tahoe sent a thrill through him. Like a child excited for a new set of hot wheels. Maybe holding off on the pain pill would end up worth it in the end.

Aurora hurried upstairs to grab a couple of things while Ethan and Trent moved bags, and the cat. He'd never seen such a lavish cat carrier, or a cat so comfortable and accustomed to traveling as this one. Aurora had added two more bags while he had waited for her to shower, and he wondered how long she thought she would be staying away.

"So, what happened between you two?" Trent asked as soon as the elevator doors had whisked Aurora out of earshot.

"What do you mean?"

"Don't play coy with me. I've known her for a very long time. She has agreed to all of this without firing a shot. That's not like her, so spill it before she comes back down."

Discussing his love life wasn't something Ethan did, ever, with anyone, regardless of how close they were. Yet, something about Trent and the weight of the situation pried open his nervous, clammy heart, forcing him to admit what he would usually never put into words.

"It was just a kiss," he thumped luggage into the trunk, "or two."

Trent grinned from ear to ear. "You burly thing you, did you go after her, or did she take the reins?"

Ethan considered the question, grudgingly, probably turning red at his collar. "Both, sort of, I guess. She made her intentions clear last night at the party, outside by the hot tub and I..." for a split second, he wondered if it was wise to reveal his weakness and poor judgment to Trent. Ultimately, there wasn't anything but the truth in his arsenal. "I guess I sort of blew it, at first. I backed off, she kind of freaked me out. But then after the intrusion and everything that happened, we sort of met in the middle."

Trent reflected on him thoughtfully, raising Ethan's blood pressure a couple points.

After a pause, he said, "You're good for her, you know?" It wasn't what Ethan expected to hear.

"Yea? How's that?"

"She's used to guys who are self-centered, egotistical, sort of in the moment to score with the rich, hot, smart girl, you know? A notch in the belt."

Ethan shrugged; he'd never been that kind of guy and found, more often than not, that most women treated *him* that way. Skepticism was still like concrete in his heart that a woman even existed who shared his outlook on marriage and life.

"That's too bad. She's better than that."

"I'm so glad we agree," Trent smacked the trunk shut. "So while we're on the subject, do me a favor, don't react to everything. I mean, she's a hard nut to crack, and she's used to taking care of herself. She's going to balk a little. So when she lets you in, accept it. She doesn't open up to a lot of people, and if, or *when,* she opens up to you, just know you've only got one shot."

Ethan was impressed with how open Trent was, and realized what a bridge he had been to Aurora's private life, silently supportive. Even though Trent had expertly navigated withholding anything substantial about Aurora, Ethan also realized that without him, there would be some significant holes to maneuver around to understand some of her kinks.

"Speaking of balking," Trent leaned on the trunk. "Did you see the Cubs game where Descalso scored on a balk?"

How did he know I was a Cubs fan?

Ethan was impressed; Trent had flipped from hardcore emotional territory, without incident, to baseball.

By the time Aurora came back down, they had run through the last weeks' worth of National League stats, and Ethan was relieved to find Trent was not a Giants fan. Having grown up in Tennessee, the team his family related to most was the Braves. Ethan found he could deal with that, at least it wasn't the Cardinals.

Aurora handed Ethan the keys, deciding it would be easier for him to drive than to try and take directions from a man. Besides, she hated city traffic. She hugged Trent goodbye warmly, and with a quick kiss on each cheek, they headed in separate directions.

"So, you're a Cubs fan?" she asked skeptically in the car as they pulled out.

"Yep. Die-hard."

"How did I not know this?"

"Because we hadn't talked about it, I guess. But you know it now."

"Well, we're talking about it now, so since we're on the subject—you know my parents met in Chicago while my dad was doing his residency at Shriners."

"And… how would I know that."

"We hadn't talked about it, I guess. But you know now," she winked at him.

"So, what does that mean? That your dad was a Cubs fan?"

"As a matter of fact, he was a phenomenal Cubs fan. He had an entire room dedicated to his memorabilia, photographs, autographs, all kinds of gear, and silly things."

"Really," Ethan tilted his head, trying to imagine her dad.

"Really. I have most of the stuff, packed away, I kept it all after he died. He used to love to go to games wherever he could. He had a dream of visiting all the ballparks to see the Cubs play and getting a ball from each game. Call it something on his bucket list."

It was the first time he heard her discuss her father in detail.

"Did you ever go to games with him?"

"I did, when I was a teenager, we went quite a bit. I was too young to appreciate it until I was in high school. We had a few years where things worked out, and we went a lot, but then when I moved to college at sixteen, it got hard, and we didn't go as often." It took Ethan's brain a block to process what she had said.

"Wait, did you say college at sixteen?"

She squirmed a little, seemed uncomfortable. "Yea, I was in the gifted and talented, blah blah. Mostly Dad made sure I absorbed everything he could throw at me. I was a couple of years ahead in school and graduated with some college credits. It's mostly juggling classes, that's all."

"I wouldn't say that. I'd call it quite the accomplishment." She didn't reply, instead stared out the window blankly.

"Well, you're wrong. It's just time management," she sounded sour, and whatever had changed her mood, he couldn't pinpoint. He decided it was treacherous waters to tread in and let it go as they were pulling up to his apartment.

"Well, I think it's impressive anyway," he said. She didn't look at him, so he gently put his hand on hers. "You're impressive." When she turned back, she seemed to have smothered whatever was bothering her and flashed a shy smile. He slowed the car and crowded the curb to park.

"This is where you live? I thought it would be farther away," she peered out the windows studying the street.

"Home sweet home. You're welcome to come in for a bit. I won't take long." He parked in the shade beneath a large tree by a church with a park beside it.

"Will Bastet be alright in the car?" she hesitated. It wasn't a hot day and still early, but too warm in the car for more than a few minutes.

"We'll leave the windows open, it's in the shade, I shouldn't be more than fifteen minutes," he said, and so they headed in together.

He led her across the street and up a flight of wooden stairs that seemed as old as the city, rickety and squeaky, to a small balcony entrance. He unlocked it and inside she was surprised to find a lovely space. It was large, especially for the area of the city, and she wondered how he afforded it. Most places had been chopped up into the smallest apartments possible to utilize the maximum rent, but this loft was spacious.

"Nice space," she said.

"Thanks, uh, my family is close friends with the woman who owns the building and the lot across the street the church is on. Old money, but I get a deal because of the relationship. She likes having an FBI Agent living above her, and I help her with heavy lifting sometimes."

"Sounds like a win, win," she said as she continued to stroll through absentmindedly.

Maple hardwood floors gave the kitchen and great room a warm and inviting tone even though the walls remained white. It had ornate crown molding but otherwise wasn't decorated lavishly, with utilitarian appliances that seemed antique, though very well restored and maintained. To the left of the kitchen was a door that had a laundry room and a flight of stairs to a garage. The space to the right opened into a small corner living room and bedroom beyond.

The area was large and, at first glance, revealed a set of love seat couches facing a corner television cabinet. As a makeshift living room, blending personal space into the great room, it worked well. Around the wall that separated living area from the master bedroom was a dresser set adjacent, back facing the couches, and beyond it, a California king-size bed and corner bathroom on the left. The television could be seen from both the sofas and the bed, *how creative*, she thought.

She didn't want to intrude into his bedroom while he packed, but she was surprised how personal and trendy the whole studio felt. Dressed in colors of muted grey and dusty blue, it was mostly white but felt relaxing and inviting. It was tidy and neat, and even the couches were a light cream color, like new, and the room was without clutter on the center and end tables.

"Have a seat, help yourself to a soda if you want, I'll only be a few minutes." Ethan went into the bedroom area, and she heard drawers and doors opening and closing. She began to poke around the kitchen, opening cabinets, peeking into the fridge. The kitchen had an island, similar to Trent's house only smaller, and opposite the cooking area were bar stools. Behind it, beneath the windows on the opposite side, was a desk with a long table beside it.

She snooped a little, trying not to be obvious, and noticed an empty dog food dish on the floor near the washer and dryer units, though there wasn't a dog anywhere. She meandered in and noticed that in the utility sink was another dog dish, and on the shelf above was a bag of dog food. She peered down the stairs into the black that must be the garage, and as she was just about to ask him if there was a dog somewhere, there was a knock at the front door as it simultaneously swung open.

"Ethan?" A woman's voice called out. Aurora froze. Her first thought was this woman, with a key and the comfort to walk right in, must be a lover. Ethan dashed around the corner holding a shirt in his hand, an expression of shock on his face.

"Mom, Dad—what are you doing here?" he asked. She ducked behind the edge of the wall and held her breath for a moment.

"Have you forgotten I'm your emergency contact?" The voice was terse. And another male voice chimed in, catching Aurora's interest enough to sneak around the corner to peek. A couple in their mid to late sixties had let themselves in and were standing in the kitchen, the woman with her arms crossed, holding a colossal purse over her shoulder.

"Darla, go easy on him now, they told you it wasn't anything serious. He's obviously fine," the man said.

"I still don't take kindly to calls in the black of night saying my son has been injured and to boot you haven't called me!" her voice held the tone only a parent could take.

"Mom, I texted," he sounded apologetic as if scolded.

"You know I don't like to text," she cut him off.

"I'm sorry, I was busy, I was driving and..." his eyes searched wildly for Aurora, "Mom, Dad—this is Dr. Aurora Soileaux, the target in the case I'm working." Ethan stretched his arm out towards her as she sulked half behind the wall to the garage. He closed the gap between them, ushering her out of her hiding spot as anxiety zinged through her.

She did her best to smile while she wanted to melt into a puddle and ooze into a hole in the baseboard. His *parents?* Dear God. Her heart raced.

"Hello," Aurora offered her hand to shake as his mother's eyes honed in on her like a hornet. Caught completely by surprise, terrified as a deer in the headlights, her mind spinning like a merry-go-round, the only thing she could think to say came directly to her tongue. "Sorry if I'm intruding."

Shit. Aurora must have been twelve shades of red and looked twice as terrified because his mother took to her like a duck to water. Ignoring the hand offered to shake Aurora instead got a warm and inviting smile, and the woman hugged her hard, pressing her against her ample bosom like a long lost relative. She was slightly taller than Aurora, and though she wasn't fat, she was wholesomely filled out. She had salt and pepper grey hair, shoulder-length in large, draped curls, and smelled like sugar cookies. Aurora couldn't remember the last time a stranger had hugged her with such enthusiasm.

"It's such a pleasure to meet you!" his mother beamed. "He keeps his work at such arm's length. We are never privy to important people such as yourself." She squeezed with incredible energy and began to talk at such a quick pace that even Aurora lost her breath. Ethan kept trying to interject, but it was no use. She was like a dog with a bone. His father stood behind her, tapping his toes, hands in his pockets like it was a regular occurrence for his wife to latch onto perfect strangers.

It seemed like ten minutes before she exhausted herself from the frenzy of meeting a woman, alive and in the flesh, in her son's apartment.

"You know all you had to do was call me and tell me you were in the middle of something so important. I just would have liked to hear it from you directly that you were alright after whatever happened to land you in the hospital." She paused as if realizing she had forgotten the entire reason she came. "What did happen to you, anyway?"

"It was no big deal, just a little cut on my shoulder. We apprehended kidnappers."

"Kidnappers?" she snapped. Her eyes wide as they fixed on Aurora.

"Oh dear heavens, you poor thing," she exclaimed, clutching her chest.

"It sounds worse than it was, and I got extra attention since she's a doctor at Stanford, far more attention than I needed." Ethan was trying to downplay the situation and failing.

"You at least should still give me the courtesy of hearing your voice. I did raise you." His mother perked herself to standing as tall as she could and tilted her chin upwards in disapproval.

Ethan was already exhausted and shook his head in defeat.

"Ma, you know you would be the first person to know if anything awful happened, and it wouldn't be a phone call. They'll show up at your house." This statement brought another bout of anxiety-ridden chatter, and an exasperated interjection from his dad finally put on the brakes.

"Darla, we've been through this. The boy has a good job, leave him alone. We came to drop off all the boxes from our garage. We need to get to it so we can get to lunch on time." Tall, like Ethan, with the same curly brown hair and chocolate eyes, Ethan had all of his father's colors but more of his mother's features. His father took his mother by the elbow and started leading her back outside into the early July heat. As his father was almost out the door, he turned quickly, on his heel, and gave Aurora a quick handshake.

"I'm Mark, not that I ever get a word in edgewise, but I'm pleased to make your acquaintance." As he continued to usher his wife out, Ethan turned to Aurora, clearly distressed by the unplanned intrusion.

"It's very nice to meet you, and I'm thrilled Ethan has been in charge of everything for me, he's been wonderful." Mark shot Ethan a pleased sideways look, revealing he knew his son well enough to recognize their relationship as being more than strictly professional.

"I have to help move boxes, it shouldn't take too long," Ethan said, jitters bleeding through his ordinarily stoic demeanor.

"I should go sit with Bastet in the car and make sure she doesn't need the AC." He handed her the keys, and she trailed down after them, his mother snuck in another quick hug before Aurora could escape off the curb.

"It's so nice to meet you, take care now and when he comes to see us feel free to join him," Darla winked and smiled like she'd received a gift.

"Thank you. I'll remember that, and happy birthday, by the way." As Aurora said it, Darla's eyes lit up, and she clasped her hands in a gesture of thorough joy, turning back to Ethan, who looked like he wanted to crawl under a rock.

"About your birthday, Mom," Ethan started.

"Don't, don't, just don't, whatever you need to do is fine, we'll get together when you're free. I've had plenty of birthdays, and there will be plenty more to come." She began to chatter again as Aurora headed for the car, politely waving as she crossed the street. When she reached it, she heard Mark exclaim, *is that a new Tesla roadster?* Hearing his excitement made her grin and giggle to herself.

Ethan said something flatly back to him, of which she could only hear his tone, as she slid into the passenger seat, wondering if she should have gotten behind the wheel to keep the assumptions under control. *Too late now,* she thought.

She let Bastet out of the carrier and waited patiently in the car, petting the cat, enjoying her purring, wondering if Ethan had a dog hidden somewhere. There was so much about him she didn't know, so much she wanted to learn, curiosity was bubbling inside her.

It took a little longer than initially anticipated, but he was back in the car about twenty minutes later. He threw a small suitcase into the back beside Bastet's carrier and bent his giant frame in behind the wheel, sulking for a minute. She had left the key in the ignition, but before he reached for it, he turned to her.

"I'm sorry." He said with sincerity, "That was awkward and unexpected, and I wouldn't have come…"

She cut him off, "It's fine, don't worry about it. Your parents are adorable." He seemed like he was sweating as if something was bothering him, and he wasn't sure how to get it off his chest. Instead of unloading what was on his mind, he petted Bastet in her lap and started the car, pulling out into traffic quickly.

They drove in silence awhile, navigating the city streets faster than he had before. When they got across the bay bridge, headed out of the area on I-80 East, he finally asked, "North shore or south shore?"

She took a moment to reply, trying to gauge how soon he would come out of his mood and said, "North shore."

They were near Vallejo before he began to play with the radio, settling back into his seat more relaxed. Until his cell rang, and he unnerved Aurora answering it since it wasn't attached to the Bluetooth of the car.

"Hartman here," he was professional, but to her still sounded stretched thin. She wondered if he was in pain, she couldn't imagine him driving after taking a pain pill, so assumed that he was at least somewhat uncomfortable. She couldn't hear the opposite end of the conversation, and bent her ear as much as she could. He listened for a long time without response.

"Since when?" he asked. "With what kind of accuracy?" his tone darkened. "No, I'll handle it." His foot fell heavy on the gas pedal, and Aurora's heart started to race. "Hold on." Ethan put the phone in his lap and added in a few choice words as he changed lanes.

"Do you have your cell phone on you?" he asked her as he navigated towards an exit near a shopping mall.

"Yes, why?" she asked.

"May I have it?" he held his hand out. She fished it out of her purse and handed it to him, surprised when he turned it over in his hands, and promptly threw it out the window. "I assume you can afford a new one, yes?"

Her mouth dropped open, but she couldn't deny, the phone wasn't essential. She had a backup of the data and could buy a new one as she pleased. She wasn't sure if she should be angry or find the whole thing hysterical, so she laughed.

"Yes, I can get a new cell phone without financial burden, but it did have most of my personal information on it, including the code to get into the cabin we're supposed to be arriving at within a few hours."

"We'll figure it out. I need to get some things straight first." He picked up his phone again. "Tom, ping it again, has it stopped?" He pulled into a shopping center and parked in a corner spot in the shade. "Yes, Tom, I know there's a home office in Sacramento, I'd prefer not to get that far if we have a real problem. I said I'd handle it."

Getting out, he began circling the car, checking the wheel wells, crevices around mirrors, and the trunk even popping the hood and peeked beneath seats. She sat, curious but patient, while he fussed and inspected.

"What are you looking for?" she asked.

"A tracking device, an advanced one," he said. The thought made her heart skip a beat. "The guys that came after you, the cyber team believes they planted a tracking device on you somehow because we are giving off a beacon that they can pinpoint within twelve feet. I need to find it, remove it, and attach it to a semi headed for Vermont."

"So it wasn't my cell phone?" she sneered at him momentarily.

"Apparently not, sorry about that, it's always the most likely choice."

She continued to calmly caress Bastet, wondering how extensive the orders for her had been. The men who had attacked her the night before admitted, freely after they surrendered, that her mother had paid them quite handsomely to make her disappear, even if brute force was required. If it weren't for Ethan, she would be on a private plane headed for a yacht in international waters right now.

The situation had her heart racing. She couldn't lie. She was sure her mother, knowing her patterns, would not need a tracking device. That didn't mean her paid goons hadn't covered their bases. She secured Bastet back into her carrier and stepped outside with Ethan. "Well what about my purse? Could there be anything in my purse, or luggage?" she asked, not sure where to go next.

"You tell me," he said, still searching the exterior of the car.

"What are we looking for? Any kind of electronic device? Something stuck onto something? I'm not sure what tracking devices look like." She stood beside the car with her arms crossed, unsure of what to do. His phone rang again.

"Hartman," his tone was terse as he answered.

"Alright, so it wasn't the cell phone, I threw that out two miles back. What are we looking for?"

He went to the driver's side door, leaned his arms on the roof, and stared at Aurora over the top of the car. "Alright, I'll let you know," he said and hung up again.

"Who was that?" she asked.

"Agent Quillet," he said, unnerving her with his use of formal names.

"So, what does Tom think?" she asked, unwilling to give in to his mood.

"We're looking for something smaller than a nickel." He was doing his best not to be impatient and snappy, but truth be told, his shoulder was killing him. Whatever nerve was affected had started to throb, and the length of his collarbone along with half his arm felt on fire.

"Well, that narrows it down," she smirked at him, circling the car, trying to think of when it would have been accessible. It had been in the gated parking garage of the Avalon, which, even with security and entry codes required, wasn't foolproof secure. For the first time, she shifted her thinking. She tried to imagine someone sneaking around, trying to take advantage of a weak moment. Her thoughts ran through the events of the last twenty-four hours, minute by minute, and she realized her real weak point.

"It's Bastet," she said, shocked to even herself.

"What?" he asked. The sun and heat were straining him, sweat beading on his forehead.

"If my phone is gone and the signal is still with us, the only thing I brought from where I was is luggage and the cat. The luggage was never accessible outside the house, so," she looked to him, crossing her arms, knowing she was right, "leave the cat with me and take the luggage around the block. I'm willing to bet if I'm being tracked, it's because someone knows I take Bastet with me."

"Alright, I'm game, but I'm also unwilling to leave you and your cat with a tracker, so if we're testing the theory, you're leaving Bastet and me." He tossed her the keys and waved a hand for her to get in the driver's seat.

She sighed, "Alright, have it your way." She climbed into the car and fastened her seatbelt.

"Don't stop the car, go around the block and come right back." He sounded terse and, for the first time, thoroughly authoritative.

He watched her pull away, standing with the cat in the carrier on the ground beside him and dialed Tom back.

"Where's the signal, Quillet?" he asked with a snap. "Damn it," he cursed and hung up. A couple of minutes later, she pulled back up with a smartass grin.

"Alright, what's on the cat?" Ethan asked impatiently.

"Only a collar," she got out of the car as he stuffed the carrier in the back seat again. Once they were underway, she let Bastet out, and pleased, as usual, the cat curled cozily in her lap.

"Alright, take it off and chuck it out the window, we'll give it a couple of miles and see what comes of it. If you can land it in the bed of a truck or trailer, all the better." Aurora unbuckled the cat's collar and threw it out the window with force towards a pickup truck going the opposite direction. She wasn't sure if it landed in back or not.

Dialing Tom back he barked, "Where is it now?" without pleasantry. After a few intense moments of silence, Ethan rolled his eyes and hung up with nothing more than a brief one-word reply.

"So, is it still with us?" she asked.

"Nope, it's back at the exit where you just threw the collar out. Good call," though annoyance was in his voice and he didn't seem any more relieved. "How did you know that?" he asked.

"I didn't. Honestly, it was just a good guess, process of elimination," she replied.

"Then why did you think of it?"

"I suppose because my mother always knows my weaknesses, and she would know I would never leave Bastet for any substantial amount of time. Bastet has only ever stayed with Trent and me, and I routinely travel with her. She would have told those thugs to track Bastet to follow me."

Ethan was quiet, glancing at her, though mainly focused on the road.

"The only problem with that theory is that the Egyptian guards your mother hired, who are still in the custody of the FBI, with little to lose, didn't admit to a tracking device."

Aurora thought hard about what he was saying.

"And, why would they need a tracking device, if your mother knows your movements? If she can tell them where you would go next, she doesn't need to track your cat." She stared at him, his face unemotional and cold, focused only on getting her to the next stop. He felt again like a hardened federal agent to her, hands firm on the wheel; overpowering physical stature focused on only one task. He was right, and a shiver ran down her spine.

"I don't know. All I could think of was last night when I was on the back porch. In the dark, as I was enjoying the fresh air, I heard Bastet screech. She never screeches, and it worried me. Within seconds I was being attacked, so I guess when you pointed out weaknesses, the cat came to mind."

"She screeched how?"

"Like she was in a catfight, restrained or in trouble, I don't know. It sounded scary enough I tried to dash off the deck to find her."

Ethan's heart surged, bound up in his throat, almost choking him as possibilities crammed through his mind. If someone else had been there, with the cat, if she'd gone off to get it, he couldn't think what might have happened.

"Did it ever occur to you that the guys who attacked you last night might have just had coincidental, though excellent, timing?"

She frowned at him, "How so?"

"As in, perhaps there was someone else there to worry about, who also saw we would be distracted with the other two idiots, and decided to take advantage of the situation?" The more she thought about it, the more she considered it a realistic possibility. If there were someone covertly watching her, they would have seen her mother's goons and could have easily capitalized on the situation.

"Alright," she said slowly, "so someone was watching the people who were watching me?"

"Something to that effect, possibly."

"Shouldn't the FBI have found them?"

"Nothing is foolproof. It's a busy area with a lot of residents, people out a lot on the streets walking in an otherwise safe neighborhood. There were a couple of people that threw red flags, but nothing concrete."

"So, you were having the place watched?"

"There were some cameras put out, yes, in addition to tapping into Trent's cameras. Same thing that will happen where we arrive later tonight, a team will be dispatched to set up remote monitoring."

"You hacked into Trent's alarm system? Don't you need permission to hack into the cameras inside someone's home?" She scowled at him as though he had violated her privacy.

"It's more efficient, multiple cameras one person can watch instead of multiple people all getting tired and easily distracted. I don't care for the nerds on the cyber unit, but they have their unique talents. For your information, as long as the cameras inside aren't being monitored, we can do as we please with the exterior ones without a warrant. Thank Homeland Security."

She sat quietly, watching the cars pass, pondering how much more there was to her situation she hadn't realized. Her anxiety would have been very different had she known more, and she couldn't help but wonder if Ethan knew that, knew it was necessary to keep her calm by way of keeping information from her.

"If they'd found anything, I was with you already. My team immediately dispatched backup as soon as they recognized the guy was on your back porch. In fact, they called me and I didn't answer because I was headed out to talk to you. Had they not called Tom's cell as a second point of contact, he wouldn't have known what was going on out back when they were trying to drag you away. It's quieter to kidnap someone than you realize." She sulked down in her seat, snuggling Bastet closer, feeling exhausted with the whole situation.

"But they never *actually* saw the guy they were after, did they?" His lack of reply was all the answer she needed. She leaned her seat back, enjoying the warmth of Bastet purring on her lap. Ethan still looked too warm, even in the air conditioning, and she knew his sheer size must make it hard to stay comfortable. Her eyes felt heavy, and her head ached. She switched off the vents on her side of the car and leaned back, letting the hum of the car lull her to sleep.

Chapter Seventeen

By the time Aurora woke up, they had passed through Sacramento and were winding up the mountain roads towards Auburn. Bastet was kneading paws in her lap as the car bounced back and forth on the rough road under construction. Ethan seemed to have relaxed more, his grip on the wheel no longer reminded her of a vice and one arm leaned on the rest beneath the window. His face was no longer red as a beet, and the sheen of sweat had disappeared though she could smell him, clean and masculine, like spring water soap.

"How was your nap?" he asked flatly without looking over at her.

"Fine, thank you," for an instant, she felt guilty, "if you'd like to rest your eyes for a bit, I'd be happy to drive."

"I'm alright, thanks."

She scratched Bastet's ears absently, "You must be tired, as much as I am at least, if not more. How's your shoulder?"

"I've been through worse."

"That's not what I asked you though," she pulled a page from his playbook, and a twinge of a grin played on his face.

"I'm fine, it's sore but nothing I can't handle."

"It's a stab wound. It's throbbing murderously, isn't it?"

He leaned his head back onto the headrest and looked over at her, "I'm fine, I promise. Go back to sleep."

"I can't. I have to pee."

He sighed, "Ok, I'll hit the next stop."

She unbuckled and turned, putting Bastet back inside the plush carrier in the back seat and noticed his briefcase was beside it with a file folder sticking out, holding the photos she had looked at the day before. She took it, and as she buckled began flipping through them again.

"Anything come to mind since yesterday?" he asked.

On the photo of the man whose daughter was a patient she paused again, and pondered, knowing the eyeballs had referenced a child she dug farther back in her mind. She couldn't put a finger on it, but it bothered her to see him, she felt an almost physical discomfort in studying his face.

"Would it also help to have a photo of the patient who died?" he asked as he pulled the car off an exit towards a small shopping center with a couple of fast-food restaurants.

"Perhaps," she was staring at the photo, feeling nauseated.

Ethan pulled into a parking lot in front of an In N Out Burger, and when Aurora didn't look up, he put his hand out over the photos, closing the folder.

"That's enough for now. We'll make headway later. Go use the restroom, don't go anywhere else, and I know how ladies like to make best friends in bathrooms, but don't talk to anyone, please."

She nodded and got out. Making use of the facilities quickly she came back to find him on the phone. As she got back in the car, he paused the call.

"My turn, keep the doors locked." When he got out, he waited to be sure she did as he told her and strolled into the restaurant still on the phone. As soon as he was out, they swung around and got in the drive-through line.

"We couldn't just eat inside?" she asked.

"Car's safer, for now," he handed her his phone with a photo on it he had pulled up. "Does she look familiar?" he asked. As she enlarged and looked closely at the picture, her blood ran cold, and nausea welled up in her throat. She remembered. Closing her eyes, the memory came popping back to her, and a sadness sank into her all over again.

"Of course I remember, how stupid, I don't know why I didn't think of it sooner. Dr. Soileaux – it's my name, but it's also my dad's name. This photo, of the little girl who passed away, that was my dad's patient, not mine. That's why I don't specifically remember the case."

"Alright, you remember her, so what does that mean?"

She read through the notes again.

"His daughter, in the notes here, she had a very advanced form of cancer, and it mentions a Retinoblastoma." A chill had the hair on her whole body standing on end.

"What's that?" he asked.

"Cancer in the eye," she said slowly, thoughtfully, trying to recall the case. There had been so many patients over the years. "Can I have the list of other doctors murdered?"

"Sure, it's in the back in my briefcase, I'll grab it after we order." They pulled up to the window, and he ordered a double-double with extra cheese meal for himself before letting her order the single protein style. After they paid, he pulled around the front again and parked once more.

He ate the burger with gusto as if he'd missed breakfast, but she noticed, as she took small and delicate bites of her own so as not to get covered with sauce, that he wasn't using his left arm unless he absolutely had to.

"Your shoulder is sore; it's obvious." He glanced at her, irritated.

"Of course it is, I was stabbed last night, remember?"

"Why do you do that? Deflect that way?"

He sighed, "Sorry, it is sore, but that's how it goes, and I'm just tired. I've had a lot on my mind."

"Like me? I feel like you pretty much know everything about me now, right down to my nightmares, anxiety, and depression. Yes, I heard you talking to Trent about me. He's not as quiet as he thinks he is." His expression made it clear he thought she was unaware of how much he knew, and he looked somewhat apologetic. He squished up the wrapper from his burger, stuffed it into the bag, and fished for a handful of fries.

"I'm sorry if I come off short-tempered and grumpy, I don't mean to be. You're right, though, I did ask Trent about your nightmare. I was worried about you. You feel like telling me what it was about?" He turned to watch her picking at her lunch, unenthusiastic.

She thought he had forgotten or decided to let it go entirely and still wasn't sure she wanted to divulge everything about herself when she felt like she knew so little about him. Though she decided, if she wanted him to open up more, it probably wasn't going to help if she clammed up.

"It wasn't any single thing, specifically. It's more just a blur of moments that all run in the same emotional vein. I think my parents had this whirlwind romance before they were married and it was the opposite of what their lives turned out to be. They were very different people, and by the time I was born, their marriage was already falling apart. Rashida was always angry when I was a kid, and I think she resented me, we didn't have much of a relationship. She was happy with my older sister. They're so alike in so many ways, but Dad doted on me. We were very close, and it always felt like he was trying to invest more in me like he was making up for past mistakes." She spoke without really looking at him, and after wiping her hands with a napkin started absently picking at her chipping manicure. He relaxed back in the seat, munching on French fries, watching her patiently.

"That doesn't sound like enough to make you as upset as you were," his tone was concerned.

"I dreamed of a fight Rashida had with Donia when I was a child. It stands out because Dad was out of town, and it was the only time I remember them getting into it to the point they wrecked the house. I didn't find out until much later that Rashida had cheated on my dad, and Donia found out. Donia threatened to tell Dad because Rashida refused to buy her a car, which was stupid because Donia always got what she wanted. She's always been spoiled rotten. She got the car and kept quiet. It's a constant point of contention between us because years later I also found out about the cheating, only I didn't coerce a bribe, I just told Dad right away. I was so mad at her, but I was furious that he wasn't. He didn't care. Looking back, they were probably just keeping up appearances long before that anyway. The whole memory reminds me of losing him, of all the contention and bitterness left between Donia and me, and that was how the dream ended. I haven't spoken to Rashida since the week after Dad's funeral."

"Well, your morning puts my afternoon into perspective. I'm sorry if I took it out on you, my mom just sort of sets me off sometimes, that's all. I guess I should appreciate her more."

She laughed sharply, "If there's anyone that can relate to that it's me, though I'm sure it's not the same, your mom seems like she genuinely loves you."

"She does, so much so it can be smothering, but she's been through a lot, so I try to give her a break, mostly."

"She worries about your line of work. What's the rest of your family like? Do you have siblings?"

"Yea," he shifted a little in the seat to rest his arm against the door better. "I'm the oldest of four, and I have two brothers. Josh is three years younger than me, and Tim is five years younger than me, and my sister was ten years younger than me, but she passed away."

"That's very sad. I'm sorry to hear that. What happened?" A shadow came over his eyes as he stared out the window. "I mean, if you feel like sharing, you don't have to if it's too personal."

"It was a long time ago. She had cancer. For all I know, she might have been a patient of your dad's back at Packard. She died just after she turned eight."

Aurora's heart stalled, her throat tightened, and a part of her realized she had real feelings for this man.

"Oh, Ethan, I'm so sorry, that's awful. No wonder you're bothered, I'm probably a terrible reminder, aren't I?" She dropped the remnant of her hamburger into the cardboard and began stuffing it into the bag as trash.

"No, it's fine. I mean, yea, it's been on my mind more lately, but that's not your fault. I think about her a lot anyway. Is that all you're going to eat?" he asked. She shrugged, offering him her fries, which he took while he looked her over, clearly not happy that she wasn't finishing them herself.

"I'm a little carsick, to be honest, and I'm not much for hamburgers. I'm fine. I'm sorry all this is dragging bad memories up for you. Is there anything I can do?"

"No, nothing like that, it isn't you, it was just this morning—my mom," he leaned his head back and rubbed his forehead. "She was more upset that I didn't call her than she was that I was stabbed. She has this whole thing about needing to hear my voice, and it's smothering. She can be suffocating. My brothers are both married, and I wish they'd just give her a couple of grandkids to fuss over."

"Have you ever been married?" as soon as she asked, she regretted it.

"No, I haven't. I don't even date much, really, which is another point of contention for her and another irritating thing from this morning when Mom assumed you were with me as more than just an assignment. Which I guess, in a way you are, but not what she was thinking, hoping, whatever was in her brain. Crap, that all sounds terrible."

He snatched the trash bag and got out of the car to throw it away, and the rush of hot air sent Aurora's stomach tumbling. When he got back in, he buckled and threw the car into gear, the annoyance radiating off him again. It gave Aurora some relief that it wasn't all just his shoulder, and wasn't all aimed at her, though she now realized what she must represent to him.

"I'm sorry I said anything, I don't want you feeling like you're a bad reminder and it's not your fault my mom is overbearing. Speaking of reminders," he reached in the back and retrieved the briefcase roughly, setting it in her lap. "The list of other physicians will be on the side in a blue folder."

She buckled herself, opened the case, and began rifling through as he navigated back to the highway. When she found the list, she had to cross-reference pictures from the internet to be sure, but in a few moments, it all came flooding back to her.

She took a deep breath, "I remember her now. It was awful. I remember the case."

"If you can give me enough detail, I can get the ball rolling on getting anyone else as a next target into protection. That would be pivotal."

"I don't remember everyone on the case, though it should all be in the records from the hospital. There were probably twenty people in the viewing gallery. It was a research case. The child was only two, and at that age, she had already surpassed expectations for the kind of cancer they found. It had metastasized and was the worst case my dad had ever seen. I remember it keeping him up at night." She sat back, staring out the window, trying to keep her composure and fighting nausea from the road. She was impressed with Ethan's patience with her.

"She was a patient of his, and because of the gene sequencing he found in the tumors, she qualified for the clinical trial I was running. Dad had some kind of new laser surgical approach that had only been tested in twenty or so cases with mostly good outcomes. The equipment hadn't been completely cleared by the FDA yet. He had to get her into the research program to qualify for the surgery. He made it happen, even paying for some of the costs for travel for her family out of his own pocket. By the time he got her scheduled, the cancer had spread so far he had considered canceling the surgery, he was confident even with a successful outcome she would still die but the cancer encroaching on her eye was going to make her blind. It was a quality of life concern for him. He was torn, really upset about it, but I convinced him it was a valuable teaching opportunity for the upper echelon of students available to participate. Maybe that's my portion of the karma of it."

"I'm pretty sure karma doesn't work that way." He glanced at her as they began climbing into the mountains more, trees becoming thicker. Everything looked dusty, dry, and brittle as they sped along the winding highway.

"Well, the surgery didn't go well. Something with the laser malfunctioned, it sent out some kind of incorrect wavelength, and it ruptured the eye and burned a good portion of the inside of her frontal lobe before they got it under control. It burned the resident who was operating and one of the scrub nurses. Dad was devastated. She passed away before the next morning, and he blamed himself for robbing her parents of that little last bit of time with her, even if it were in the hope she wouldn't be blind. After that, he pulled his endorsement from the manufacturer of the laser, and I flunked the clinical trial, but I'm sure the conversation with her parents had to be one of the worst conversations of his life. He cried about it afterward, said he could picture me when he looked at that little girl, and he felt the pain of her parents. That's the kind of person he was."

Ethan became more and more uncomfortable as he had listened to her talk. He had told her she wasn't a reminder, but in truth, she was. It couldn't be helped. He pictured the hope his mother had, and the nights of endless weeping. Even now, twenty-five years later, he knew she still cried, knew she would never truly recover.

She told him just that morning how Aurora looked like his sister, Angie, or at least how she pictured his sister would look. It bothered him with the feelings he had for Aurora to look at her and think of Angie. His family had gotten past it, but they had never really gotten over it. It had been under his skin since then, making him helpless to wonder if things would have been different if they'd had a doctor like Aurora or her dad on Angie's case.

"I'm sorry to hear that," he couldn't muster much more at the moment. He pulled out his cell phone and dialed Tom. He rattled off all the information for the patient and asked him to have the parents tracked down. He was clearly in pain, holding the phone and the wheel and made Aurora nervous enough to yank on her seatbelt, which he noticed, and smirked at her.

"Tom's going to track the parents down, see where things are now. We'll know something by tomorrow, if not sooner."

"Well, that's reassuring, unlike your driving habits."

"My driving is fine."

"Typical male," she rolled her eyes, knowing she had another two and a half hours and the worst part of the highway yet to tackle.

By the time they reached Kings Beach, she was ready to get out and stretch her legs. The winding roads had taken their toll on her stomach, and she felt ill through and through. With only about ten minutes or so until they arrived, she straightened up and rolled the window down. As they turned onto Lakeshore Blvd, her heart felt lighter, memories from her childhood that she enjoyed bubbled in her mind to make her smile. Long days on the lake playing with David's son and two daughters, paddle boarding, water skiing, fishing, campfires at night with s'mores, this place was one of the only places that held cherished memories for her.

She pointed to the driveway in the dark, glad to get out of the car, and ran towards the panel by the garage door. Flipping it open, she was relieved she had a good memory for numbers as it lifted promptly, allowing Ethan to pull in quickly out of sight. As they unloaded, she let Bastet roam, setting up her litter box first in the garage. As David had two giant Irish Wolfhounds, there were dog doors throughout the house the cat could use to roam freely. Bastet jumped onto the long work table in the garage, curious of the fluttering moths swirling around the overhead light.

Inside, Ethan felt like he was checking into a hotel far above his pay grade. They shuffled bags upstairs into the master bedroom before she set out food for them both, opened a bottle of red wine for herself, and showed him around. The house had four floors, and a 'secret turret' Aurora said she wasn't yet prepared to share with him as she winked playfully.

The main floor had a library twice the size of Trent's and a separate office fully equipped with a drawing table and sofa set. Aurora explained that David's wife, Blanche, was an architect and had designed the whole house from scratch. There was also the kitchen, a living room, a formal dining room, and a sitting room full of plush white leather furniture that blended with four large sliding glass doors onto a deck that wrapped the entirety of the main floor.

On the top floor, in the master bedroom, was a lavish bathroom with dual full-size soaking tubs and a shower that looked like it could hold an entire football team. The closet was bigger than Ethan's entire bedroom, and it was adjacent to a large sitting room full of yoga and exercise equipment. Across the hall was a fully furnished children's room with three twin beds, two cribs, and a bassinette.

After she had walked him around the top two floors, they headed downstairs to a long hallway that had six bedrooms and four bathrooms. The entire story had a western theme, and each room looked straight out of the old west. The house was clearly used often for family gatherings and entertaining.

The bottom floor was the most impressive to Ethan, as Aurora flipped lights on he could see it was one giant room in the footprint of the whole house. There was a bar, a pool table, an entire wall of couches and lounge chairs, half a dozen flat-screen TVs, a ping pong table, darts, and a wealth of other small games. The best part was the edge to edge wall of sliding glass doors that opened completely to the lake on a private beach. The way the house was set naturally into a cove in the shoreline allowed for tall fences on either side to create a very private setting.

On the east side of the beach, a garage door separated the boat dock from an indoor mooring for a beautiful candy apple red speed boat and four colorful jet skis. A garage door separated the inside where the water toys were parked, but once opened, it extended out on a dock fifty feet into deeper water. The beach had some landscaping but mostly held to the terrain with a wide swath of waves lapping at crumbled granite sand.

There was a hot tub, a rack to hold paddleboards and kayaks, and a shed that Aurora claimed emptied in less than ten minutes for shade and beach chairs. As he stood at the edge of the dock, taking it all in, looking back up at the enormous house standing tall at the edge of the pristine lake, it all felt a little overwhelming.

By the time they had toured the mansion and were ready to call it a night, the clock was close to ten p.m. Ethan's eyes were heavy, and as Aurora shut off lights and set the alarm, he slipped upstairs alone. When she joined him, he had changed and was on the phone, giving the surveillance orders, providing the address. He outlined details without realizing she stood listening to him, sipping her wine.

She was mulling over the mess she'd fallen into, tired but relaxed and trusting him to keep her safe. Listening to him rattle off entrances and where things should be positioned before giving them the internet password chilled her. Every time she thought she had an evening to put it behind her, to explore this handsome new addition to her life, she found herself reminded why he was here.

"So when is all that going to happen?" she asked as he hung up.

"Sorry, I try to keep that stuff under wraps; I doubt you'll even notice them. You shouldn't if they're doing it right anyway, they'll have it in before morning."

"That's pretty quick. I guess I need to have Trent cancel my patients down the hill next week," she said it as she swirled the wine in her glass, thinking absently.

"Look, there's a lot to all of this, but we're making progress. Just hold tight, consider the time here a vacation. Catch up on some reading, binge watch a few shows, enjoy the sunshine, just try not to focus too much on what you can't control. That's my job. Let me worry about it."

He felt so professional, and as she looked at him, even out of his Fed suit in the athletic sweats and black shirt that seemed his usual choice for bed, she realized what she wanted from him was all personal.

She nodded, "Do you want to stay on this floor, or the guest floor below the kitchen?"

He thought for a moment, access out the front or sides would make more sense, having to get out where there was only access to water could cause an issue.

"Probably up here is the best bet."

"I can sleep across the hall in the children's room. The beds in there are surely too small for you, it would be miserable, and it sounds like you need your sleep to stay on your toes." He glanced across the hall again, something about the children's room gave him a bit of the creeps. He couldn't, for some unknown reason, figure out exactly why.

"This bed is the size of Texas, a few more inches either direction, and it would be Alaska," he said to her as he walked towards it.

"It's custom, as with most things in the house. I ordered it for them as a gift after their daughter had triplets. They already had two grandchildren, and Blanche was complaining on their second birthdays how her heart ached to keep them with her, but the bed didn't suit it. The drawers on the bottom," she slipped her painted toes beneath the dust ruffle and pulled out a long drawer, "they have feet that open and click into the frame so the dogs can sleep with them too, seven inches off the bed, so their feet don't get crushed."

Ethan bent down to examine the setup, curious at such a marvelous idea.

"Where on earth did you find such a thing?" he asked.

"Like I said, I had it custom made. I even had to order a custom mattress, comforter, and sheet sets for it. The whole thing cost a pretty penny." She sipped more wine. She had changed into her typical spaghetti strap short and tank combo but had a long-sleeved burgundy fleece robe on, tied loosely around her petite waist. Her hair was pulled into a ponytail at the nape of her neck, and as she sipped wine Ethan's mind drifted to their kiss on the ride home from the hospital.

"Custom made, where?" he asked.

"This is Tahoe, and there are woodworkers everywhere, some better than others. I just found the one I liked the most who lived down the hill and told him what I needed. I set out specific parameters and left the rest to him. It clicks together, something called mortise and tenon, so it was surprisingly easy to get in here. He gave me dimensions, and I ordered the mattress and bedding from a fancy place in Venice that specializes in custom upholstery."

As she talked, he had circled the bed. The wood was of an auburn hue and had been sanded smoother than a baby's butt, oiled instead of slathered in thick gloss. The headboard had a shelf with tiny glass doors, each with frame, grids, and knobs. The top had a platform that hung out over the bed and was surrounded with a four-inch railing, and on it were stuffed animals, a couple of large conch shells, and a model airplane. The footboard was ornately carved with a beautiful scene of a tree with a door beneath it, leaves swirling and spilling around as if tossed in the wind. To stand back and look at it was breathtaking and an incredible amount of work.

"Alright, I can't stand it anymore, this bed must have taken a year to make. It's none of my business, and you don't have to tell me, especially since you don't have an ounce of snotty rich brat in you whatsoever, but how much did this cost?"

She smiled at him genuinely, pleased for some reason, why, he wasn't sure.

"The bed was almost a hundred and fifty thousand. The mattress was twenty-five because I insisted on the highest quality materials and a thirty-year guarantee. The bedding was almost ten, but that's because I started with three sets and an extra waterproof cover in addition to several dozen shams in each size. Of course, I had to buy pillows to make it look as lovely as it is large."

"So you paid somewhere near two hundred thousand dollars for a bed, as a gift? I mean, you're a doctor, I'm sure you make a lot, I get that—you should, you work hard. But that kind of money?"

"I don't tell many people, but the majority of the money in the family estate was set up and managed by my dad. My mother, she had a lot coming in, she inherited plenty and earned more, as did Dad, but she was also the spender—vacations, resorts, shoes, clothes, cars, thousand-dollar dinners for two, you name it. She was never concerned about how to preserve it, only how to enjoy spending it. Dad had the bases covered with investments and longevity, and he set me up. I have never had a single rent payment or car payment. I own several properties that are rented or managed by an outside company and only earn me money. In the last ten years, with stocks and investments, interest and principal owed to me, not including liquid assets, I've outpaced the estate four to one. I'm worth far more than my mother."

He stared at her in wonder, not because he realized he was probably staring at a multi-millionaire, but because as she talked about it so casually, he was convinced none of it meant anything to her. She had expensive things, of course, but he had noticed already she wore no jewelry, no fancy rings, bracelets, or earrings regularly, and he had not seen a single label for a Coach purse or Louis Vuitton shoes. Besides the Tesla, you'd never know she was personally loaded just to look at her. Everything about her could blend in with any of his friends. Regardless, he was sure she could pour on the lavish to rub elbows with society's upper crust.

His admiration increased with the fact that with so much money, she must not *have* to work, would probably never have had to work a day in her life, but here she stood, incredibly accomplished. She had a hard-earned career. She had worked her ass off for every little bit of it and valued it. He thought about his own life, his time at San Diego State, where he earned a Bachelor's in behavioral science. He felt that had been an achievement, but standing in this house, it paled in comparison. He wondered why she would ever have found him attractive enough to have kissed him in the first place on that dark balcony.

"So, is the dog bed fold out thing big enough for me to sleep in?" He was relieved when she laughed, wholeheartedly, almost spilling her wine.

"No," she sauntered towards him, "it certainly is not. I mean, Dan and Davy are big, like ninety pounds each, but they sleep side by side. There's no way I'm letting you sleep in the dog bed."

"Dan and Davy, eh?" he asked. She put him at ease with how at ease she was.

"Yea, David is a big hunter. He loves chucker hunting and pheasant, lots of waterfowl, and he applies for an Elk tag every year. Plus, when he got them, they chased a raccoon into the basement somehow, it was a fiasco," she was giggling, her eyes sparkling, "so the dogs are Daniel Boone and Davy Crocket." Just thinking of it made her laugh even more.

"That's fun. Does that mean he has guns in the house too?" With that question, Aurora's face quickly changed, surprised he had jumped so fast from her mention of hunting to weapons.

"Yea, he does. But no one would find them unless they knew where to look."

"Alright, where would someone know to look?" he asked, and her eyes widened. It was an uncomfortable subject for her.

"Why does it matter?"

"I need to know. All I have with me is a single service pistol. People who hunt tend to have not only high-powered rifles but handguns and ammo in large quantities. I just don't want to get caught off guard, that's all." He kept his tone soft and unconcerned because he could tell she was on edge.

"If I tell you, can I trust you not to say anything to anyone or let on that I told you?"

"Of course, Aurora, that goes without saying."

"It's a big deal, I mean, a huge deal. David is very private about it, and he's like a father to me."

"I promise, it's only because I want to keep you safe, I just need to know what someone else could get to if something were to go wrong."

She stared at him long and hard, considering the reality and the consequence. Finally she headed out of the room, tilting her head for him to follow her. On the main floor, she took him into the library, which faced the front of the house, and switched on a small desk lamp just to drop the blinds and close the curtains. She set her wine down and switched the light back off, and taking Ethan by the hand she went to a corner.

She fidgeted for a moment with something in front of her, he couldn't see, and after a few small clicks, the entire face of the cabinet swung open. Still in the dark, she tugged on his arm, pulling him behind her into a room that smelled faintly of oil. She pushed him against a wall, and her hand flat on his chest had his pulse ratcheting up a couple of notches before she reached next to him to pull the cabinet closed. As it clicked, they were plunged into complete darkness for only a split second before she snapped on a light.

Ethan found himself in a room that was approximately eight feet by ten feet and was wall to wall guns. There were shotguns, semi-automatic rifles, three .30-06 hunting rifles hung up, handguns, knives, an arsenal all to itself. As he stared in awe, she stood squarely in front of him, and when he went to lean forward, she held him back against the wall.

"I know you're familiar with all of this in your role in law enforcement. I'm trusting you," she said sternly, "it's not something I often do. Please don't make me regret it." Her hands were flat on his chest, encouraging him not to move but not entirely meant to restrain him. He inspected the room, taking mental note of where the ammunition was astutely organized beneath each different firearm. There was a workbench that was meticulous, meant as an area to clean and maintain the weapons. He thought for a long while before responding, listening to her breathe, feeling her hands pressed against him.

"Do you know how to use any of these?" he asked.

"Enough of them, yes. He's taken me out pheasant and turkey hunting so I can use the twenty gauge and the bolt action sixteen, but we don't usually use that one, it's sort of an antique. I've used the hunting rifles at a range but never actually hunting, and I took a class one winter break on handguns so I can load and fire most of them with decent accuracy." She seemed nervous, but a vibe she was giving off was telling him it wasn't because of the weapons.

"Most of them?" he asked, and she nodded as he looked around, there had to be over twenty different handguns of varying brands and calibers. "That's a lot of handguns to be familiar with if you don't use them regularly."

"Well, I haven't practiced with any of them in a while. I thought that part of my life was over." She looked up at him carefully, gauging his level of interest.

"What part of your life?" he asked patiently, his gaze relaxed but fixed on her. She took a deep breath and closed her eyes.

"I figured you were going to look it up," she paused, studying him.

"Look what up?"

"The Gearhardt bludgeoning," she was waiting for a reaction, and when he didn't give her one, she crossed her arms and took a deep breath. "Dad was never much into guns or hunting, but David has always been comfortable with all this." She waved a hand around the room and turned away from him as if she was afraid her face might reveal too much of what she was feeling.

"So you said, but I'm guessing there's more to it than that."

"After a merger that my mother orchestrated with a company she was working for went south, in a horrible way, she tried to threaten some of the upper management into cooperation. She started to receive threats, so she hired private security to protect us. Probably from the same company as the guys that stabbed you. They're elite, expensive, supposed to be the best of the best, but also slightly illegal in the US. She sent us to Mexico City with them until things smoothed out only instead of resolving anything diplomatically, she took action to cripple those who opposed her. I still don't know all of the details. By the time things were over, the President and the CEO of Gearhardt International Industries were both found bludgeoned to death, along with their families. Seven people from the two families were killed and I would like to think Rashida didn't have anything to do with it but…"

"You're a brilliant person."

She chuckled and said, "I don't know that intelligence has anything to do with it. Dad evacuated us unexpectedly from Mexico City in the middle of the night with David's help. It was the only time I've ever seen Dad with a gun. We stayed here for the entire summer, and I remember it being one of the best times of my life because Rashida never joined us. David and his son spent that summer showing me how to use the guns, taking me to the range. His daughters went too, so it wasn't as intimidating, and that fall, I went hunting with them for the first time. Donia refused to go, but Dad encouraged me, David encouraged him, and though I don't shoot regularly and haven't hunted in probably six years, I don't regret any of it."

He thought, staring out into the room, she might never stop surprising him.

"So, is it alright with you if we sleep in the bed big enough to park a tank on, together? I mean, you have to promise to keep your hands to yourself," he grinned in jest, "but it would make me feel better."

She looked up at him with her head still level, her eyelashes curling against her lids thick and pretty and smiled. Leaning her head against his chest briefly, she took a deep breath and exhaled slowly before leaning back, nodding.

"Yes, that's fine with me, and I'll do my best to behave." She winked as she squeezed his hand before flipping the light off and leading him back out. Before she turned the desk lamp on, he heard clicking, indicating she had locked the room again.

"Just so we're on the same page, if something does happen and you need to hide, that's where you need to go. Don't hesitate, don't think twice, if I tell you to run, you run, but if I tell you to hide, that's where you hide. Alright?" She nodded, leading him upstairs.

She finished the little bit of wine she had left, leaving the glass on the bathroom sink as she was brushing her teeth, and retired to bed. She let Ethan turn the lights out before he crawled in next to her, though still five feet away. With the fourth story windows open, the bedroom door closed, and a man with a gun strapped to his chest stretched out within arm's reach beside her, for the first time in a long time she slept like the dead.

Chapter Eighteen

Deputy Bill Wilson had been an Idaho Sheriff for almost forty years, and he'd seen a lot, but he'd never seen anything like this before. A smell had been coming and going throughout a neighborhood on the west side of town for a couple of days, there had been several calls, but they weren't able to pin down exactly where it was coming from, until today.

When the call came in about four in the afternoon that neighbors had finally pinpointed which house the smell was coming from, the idea of a dead body in the July heat had been almost enough to make him turn tail and retire. When he got there, his initial assumption of how bad the situation was, paled in comparison to reality.

The smell in the house, with all the windows and doors closed, was enough to knock someone straight to vomiting, and it was clear why it had been severe enough to filter out through the sealed home. The Mentholatum he wiped on his upper lip and around the entrance to his nostrils barely put a dent in the overpowering stench. He had forcefully opened the front door, only to open the windows closest to it that he could reach and went back outside to call for backup.

When a buddy of his, Deputy Carl Martin, arrived about twenty minutes later, it had aired out a bit, but not enough to avoid rolling nausea. They went in, holding their noses, anticipating the worst, and found it.

The house was spotless, almost sterile in every room as they moved through the three-bedroom house until they reached the closed master bedroom door. Bill held his breath, anticipating a mess, and swung it open to reveal a private mortuary. As the smell backed Bill off, Deputy Martin rushed in to open a window, audibly gagging.

Placed meticulously on the bed was a dead woman. Dressed in a lovely pink silk dress, draped in what, at one point, must have been beautiful flowers. She had rotted to mold. They both went back outside for a few minutes, to call in a forensic team, and catch their breath.

When they went back in, able to go closer to the bed to examine the carcass, they realized a small, even worse decomposed body was carefully wrapped in the woman's arms. Exposed bones, darkened and festering flesh, still held the image of a mother and child holding one another in love. When the Deputies went back outside to wait for the forensic team, they looked to one another in dismay.

"What do you think that's all about?" Bill asked.

"I don't think I want to know. Looks like mother and daughter to me? Maybe suicide?"

"Sounds terrible."

"Smells terrible."

"I've been doing this job too long, Carl, these moments—they either keep me awake for months or make me wonder why they don't."

As they sat in the squad car, air conditioning blowing full force, they were surprised the first car that pulled up wasn't a county forensic team. A couple of guys in suits with dark sunglasses stepped out, and as they approached the vehicle, Bill turned to Carl with a look of intrigue.

"They look like Feds, am I right?"

"Kinda hard to miss," Carl responded, "I wonder what this is all about."

The suits stepped out of their car and quickly shook hands with the Deputies. The driver of the black suburban introduced himself as FBI Agent Jack Thompson and asked why they were there.

"Dead body, Agent. Some timing you have. I arrived on the scene about forty minutes ago. Stuff like this needs backup, so I called, and Carl joined me. He got here about twenty minutes ago. Neighbors have been complaining on and off for over a week about a smell, finally found which house caused it. You gentlemen can help yourselves." Carl waved a hand at the front door and at the same time fished out the Mentholatum, offering them some. Agent Thompson passed, but the other Agent took Carl up on it, with a distinct look of disdain.

A few minutes later, the two came back out, clearly unnerved, Agent Thompson on the phone. They both kept their distance from the cruiser while the Deputies soaked in the air conditioning, shielded from the balmy Idaho heat. They'd been taking bets on how the Feds had beat their team to the punch.

Thunderstorms had been building in the distance, and as they waited, the wind kicked up, scattering debris along the ground. An ominous feeling crept along Carl's spine as lightning snapped against the horizon and thunder encroached. Agent Thompson stayed on the phone as the other Agent approached the window. Carl rolled it down for him.

"Deputies, the federal government will be taking charge of the situation and investigation here. You're welcome to stay to sign any required documentation, but we'll ask kindly that you not enter the home again."

Carl nodded. They were both silently relieved. They would be home in time for a well-cooked meal tonight instead of buried in a mountain of paperwork.

In the background, Carl could hear Agent Thompson on the phone, and Bill couldn't help but eavesdrop to the best of his ability.

"Yes, Agent Hartman, it will take some time to confirm, but our initial assessment leads me to believe that Mrs. Heraldson is deceased inside, with the skeleton of a small child draped over her, which we believe to be her daughter. Mr. Heraldson is nowhere to be found, and the power has been shut off, indicating he's been gone for some time now."

Carl wasn't sure if it was the storm swelling on the horizon, the memory of the stench, visualizing what they had seen inside, or just the fact he was tired of being in law enforcement. As he drove away, he was glad the case wasn't his to investigate and decided he'd had enough of this line of work, it was time to call it quits.

Chapter Nineteen

The shimmer of sunshine off the lake out the window was dazzling, making Ethan squint as he headed for the kitchen for a second cup of coffee. Aurora was still asleep, and though he had been initially worried about the late morning he was relieved she was still in bed for the moment, allowing him to get a grip on where the case stood.

He'd received an email that the father of the patient Aurora had identified in the photo was Declan Heraldson. Mr. Heraldson's residence was in a remote town a couple of hours drive north of Boise Idaho, and though agents were on the way, they wouldn't arrive until late afternoon. Now that he had a reason to believe they'd isolated the killer, all he had to do was pick up the pieces and figure out what the trigger was. If this person was the killer, his daughter had died almost two years ago, what was the catalyst for him finally acting out now?

Ethan had spread out on the dining room table, pages haphazardly scattered as he worked, confirming orders had been completed, reviewing backgrounds, and details on new information. The tracking device found on the Bastet, who was currently curled up and purring in Ethan's lap, had been identified as one found commonly in spy shops across the country. It was a simple device but required some rather specific software to function, and it had been expertly hidden inside the collar. It needed expensive equipment that required a fair amount of skill to operate.

As information began trickling in about the suspect, Ethan's anxiety skyrocketed. He had walked off his job at a slaughterhouse four weeks ago and was terminated as a no-call no-show. His bills were all overdue, and the power company had shut the power off for nonpayment a month prior. DMV records listed one paid off car, and another that was due to be repossessed by the bank in his wife's name. She had no history of employment for nearly three years, congruent with the timeline of losing their daughter.

The small town they lived in was an area that flourished on livestock and farming with a decent tourist economy for hunting, and there were several weapons registered to him in the state. There were overdue taxes, a lien against the house, and multiple credit cards in collections. The most frustrating part was trying to figure out, then, with maxed credit and significant collection actions without a job, how the guy was getting around so easily. Traveling required funds, and it didn't look like this guy had any.

Ethan was typing out an email for Tom to start checking campgrounds between Idaho and the first murder in Colorado when Aurora came tripping downstairs. She was still in her robe, hair tousled, padding around in fluffy pink slippers. She cruised past him with nothing more than a wave as she darted for the coffee machine.

"Did you enjoy sleeping in this morning?" he asked. Bastet jumped off his lap to trail at Aurora's feet meowing.

"As a matter of fact, yes. I think it was far overdue. Are you finding everything you need? There's plenty of food, and I have a special delivery order in mind for this evening, just for you." She bent to retrieve the cat, setting her on the counter in the small pantry off the garage. Opening a can of cat food, she turned it upside down into a dish and stroked the cat lovingly as it began to feast.

"Yes, everything is satisfactory," he said, sipping more coffee.

"Fabulous, then I'm going to have some coffee and curl up with a book, maybe go out later and get some sun before a sunset bath. You'll let me know if you need me?" She breezed by, raising her mug in cheers. He raised his in response and was glad she seemed in excellent spirits as he turned back to his laptop.

Aurora held to her plan as the day wore on. She sped read nearly an entire romance novel before spending a couple of hours on the beach out back, seemingly napping. After that, he found her engrossed in a medical journal thick as a brick, the cat sleeping in her crossed legs. She came down a little after two and put a variety of snack foods in front of him, of which she packed half onto a plate and retired back upstairs with for herself. By five, she had poured a glass of the previous night's red wine, stating she was getting into the bath, and he was to stay out of the master bedroom.

While listening to the water running into the tub, he almost missed the buzz of his cell phone.

"Agent Hartman, this is Agent Thompson, from the Boise office."

"Glad to make your acquaintance. Did you find anything at the Heraldson residence?"

"Yes, it will take some time to confirm, but our initial assessment leads me to believe that Mrs. Heraldson is deceased inside, with the skeleton of a small child draped over her, which we believe to be her daughter. There's no trace of Mr. Heraldson, and the power to the home is off, indicating he's been gone for some time now."

"Shit," Ethan hung his head, "you're sure the child is with her?"

"Yes, skeletal remains are quite obvious."

"The kids been dead for two years, he would have to have exhumed her, you're absolutely positive?"

Thompson paused for a moment, seeming to take in the gravity of the situation.

"Yes, there's definitely a child with her. The remains have been in the heat for weeks. We don't have a cause of death for either of them as of yet. Of course, only DNA or dental records will confirm identities, but that would be the initial presumption, wouldn't you agree?"

Ethan sighed, "Yes, I agree, I wish I didn't. Thanks, keep me informed of the progress."

He hung up the phone, cursing fate and whatever foul play had been in action. He now had confidence he knew who the Hypocrite killer was, and probably why. That still only brought him to the beginning of a trail he knew had been cold for weeks, and would possibly leave him too far behind to track to an end, before it was too late.

After filling out a couple forms, reviewing requests to the coroner's office in Idaho, and digging into the funeral home hired to bury Candice Heraldson, the deceased girl's name now starting to stick with him, he was ready to call it quits for the day. The sun had reached the top of the trees to the west and was slicing across the lake, throwing golden reflections against the ceiling of the dining room.

Bastet had made a spot in the chair beside him and had taken to crying at him every so often when she felt ignored. He would pet her and return to his work and had found her, generally, a nice distraction. By six-thirty, he had been sitting too long, his shoulder ached from typing, and as he pushed back from his chair to stretch it against the wall, Aurora came downstairs on the phone.

"Yes, please, extra chips and salsa, and make sure there's extra wet sauce. I'll make it worth your while, I promise. Thanks, Julio!" she hung up and refilling her wine glass looked up at him.

"Your shoulder is bothering you, yes? Don't lie to me. It affects how much I trust you." She came around the counter towards him, smooth and graceful, relaxed with a rosy hue from the heat of the bath radiating on her cheeks.

"Right now, everything is bothering me," he tried not to sound grumpy, but it wasn't far from the truth. He always hated being behind a desk, and he hadn't been to the gym in over a week. His eyes were strained and tired, his head ached, and truthfully his shoulder was killing him, though he honestly couldn't believe it was all from the small stab wound.

"Dinner will be here in about a half-hour, give or take ten minutes, burritos plus some from J's – I know the owner, so he's sending someone to deliver. I think you'll be quite pleased. In the meantime, I'd like to look at your shoulder. As long as the wound closed up, I think a swim would be good for you." The way he tilted his head reminded her of a curious puppy and had her laughing. "Come on, sit, here," she shuffled him into a shorter chair at a table on one end meant for children, and he frowned at her.

"You're too tall for me in a regular chair. Take your shirt off, every time you argue with me, I'm withholding a serving of chips and salsa." He obediently slipped off his shoulder holster, then his grey polo, and she began peeling back the bandage at his collarbone. After setting down the dressing and the wine, she stood facing him, scrutinizing the area then lifting his arm. As she swung it up and down, in and out, she asked him which positions hurt, and though he tried to pretend none of them were painful, she caught him wincing.

"I warned you not to lie to me, next time I'll hold back dessert. The wound looks alright, and it's closed nicely, but I think you have some residual swelling, causing some pressure on the nerves. You need a swim, then some ice. I don't suppose you brought swim trunks?" She questioned him, tossing his shirt back to him as he shook his head, no.

"Downstairs, in the room on the far end," she pointed, "there's a dresser full of clothes. Top three drawers are for men, and I guarantee you'll find a suit, probably with the tags still on, that will fit you. Go, get one." She shooed him away, flapping her hands as she went to get dishes out. By the time he had rifled through what seemed like half a department store's worth of new clothes and found a suit, she had set the corner of the dining table for two.

"Alright, let's go," she grabbed her glass of wine and headed downstairs, shuffling him ahead of her. On the bottom floor, she pointed, "There's a bathroom in there, under the stairs, go change."

"You're awfully bossy all of a sudden," he smirked at her.

"You haven't seen anything yet, trust me," she turned and began opening the sliding glass doors to the beach.

When he came out of the bathroom, he saw her standing at the far end of the dock, fifty feet out from the beach. Her hair was shimmering, blowing in the wind, the thin canary yellow, soft cotton summer dress billowing around her ankles. Stopping to admire her, he could imagine hanging the scene on a wall as a painting, so picturesque in the golden sunshine of late day.

He walked out after her, feeling the plastic decking beneath his feet smooth and warm. When he reached her, she smiled at him, and it seemed the world stood still. The air was fresh and clean, and she was so stunningly beautiful he couldn't help but smile back. She stirred something in him.

"So, how flexible are you?" she asked.

He shrugged, "Flexible enough, I think, why?"

"Can you still touch your toes with that shoulder as sore as it is?"

"I think so," he bent over, and before he knew what hit him, she had shoved him from behind, and he was diving headfirst into the lake. He hit the water less than gracefully with the lack of warning, and on top of the sheer shock of the seven-foot fall, it was far colder than he had anticipated. The chill stole his breath as he swirled to recover to the surface. As soon as his head was above water, he could hear her laughing uncontrollably.

"That's for my phone," she put her hand on her hip and sipped more wine. He tried to splash her, unsuccessfully but found he still couldn't help smiling from ear to ear. As he swam back, the cold seeped into him, and the weightlessness of the water did feel good. By the time he had his feet back on solid ground, he almost wished he could stay in and swim. Aurora sat on a lower portion of the dock about twenty feet from shore, toes dangling in the water, arms behind her leaning with her face turned up to the dying rays of the sun.

He swam to her, treading water at her feet, watching her sip with a sly grin on her face.

"You think you're so funny, don't you?" he asked.

"I didn't think it was funny when you threw my phone out the window, but I laughed anyway, no point in making mountains out of molehills. And for the record, yes, I think it's funny." She sipped, and he splashed her feet, hanging onto the side of the dock next to her. "I also know the cold water will do wonders for you, and I wasn't sure I was going to convince you once you dipped your toes in. It's cold, yes?" She smirked, and he grabbed her ankle, toying with the idea of pulling her in.

She shrieked, laughing, "Don't!" she shouted, "I just took a bath!"

He let her go but found the idea of swimming with her quite tempting. She yanked her feet out of reach and stood back up on the dock.

"If you wanted company, you should have come to swim when I was out here earlier. Now you have to wait. You should do one more lap to the end of the dock and back. I'll grab you a towel. Dinner will be here soon." She stood up, admiring his physique, and headed back for the house.

He swam back out to the edge of a rocky spot bordering the west side of the house, amazed how cold and warm currents flowed and swirled in such a large lake. The water was crystal clear, as his feet touched to the top of a sunken rock to stand, he could see how quickly the shoreline receded to deep water. Within sixty feet of the shore, the depth had to be near fifty feet, deep azure swallowing the bottom. A breeze rifled through the trees and across the surface, fresh and warm. The sheer rugged beauty of the lake astounded him.

Swimming back to shore, he could see the ridgeline of the mountains and admired the trees, tall and majestic. When his feet touched the sand, it was littered with small stones, rough and sharp. He looked up to see Aurora standing with her toes in the waves holding a large red beach towel under one arm. She smiled at him, and he realized she might have an insight into things he didn't even know he needed. The brief swim had relaxed him and had helped him far more than he wanted to admit.

"So we're even? The phone for a push into the lake?" he smiled as she handed him the towel.

"I suppose," she smiled back as she eyed him top to bottom. It was the first time she had seen him with such a small amount of clothing on, and it had her blood pressure rising. Every inch of him was perfect. "Dinner is here, so let's get to it before it gets cold." She turned and headed back towards the house, and as he watched her go admired the view every step of the way.

Upstairs he pulled his shirt on as he inspected what seemed like a feast she had set out. There were burritos, chimichangas, a giant bowl of chips and enough salsa to match, quesadillas, sauces galore, and sopapillas. He hadn't realized he was hungry until he saw the spread. As she sat and set her wine in front of her, he realized she had poured him a giant glass of soda.

"You got me soda," he said, astonished.

"I pay attention. It's not hard." She waved a hand at the chair beside her as she shoved it back with her foot. He sat, not sure where to start on the enormous amount of food. She started pointing at things, telling him what each dish was.

"J's is my favorite Mexican food at the lake, as authentic as it comes up here anyway, and I like leftovers. Mexican food is one of those things that is just as good the next day as it is when you order it." He filled his plate and began pouring on sauces at her recommendation, in full agreement after a couple of bites. The food was terrific.

They ate and talked, she asked about progress on the case, he lied. He wasn't sure she needed to hear the reality, and having a mouthful of food made it easier to dodge her questions. He asked if she was getting bored, or if she'd need to be in touch with anyone that she couldn't contact on his cell. He had hoped to put off replacing her phone as long as possible and was glad she didn't seem concerned about having it with her again.

"Trent knows to call you if he needs me for patients. I have the computer in David's office to check email and search as needed for anything, so no, the lack of my phone isn't a major inconvenience."

"That's good."

"I will need to call Trent tomorrow to check on things, but I can use the house phone too."

"Use mine, please. I'd prefer you not call any of your regular contacts from this number."

"Alright," she looked at him deep in thought for a moment. "So that tracking device, how scary is that? I mean, if this person had that successfully planted on Bastet, does that mean I'm more at risk?"

He thought hard about how to answer, not wanting to get caught in a lie, but not wanting her to know the whole truth either.

"Let me worry about that. One of us is enough. Today brought in a whole load of new information, and we're getting close, but you being worried isn't going to help anything."

She sighed, clearly displeased with his response but accepting of it.

By the time they finished eating, it was almost eight. The sun had slipped behind the mountain, and the haze of dusk had surrounded the house. She sent him upstairs to 'shower the lake flake off' while she cleaned up the kitchen. He wasn't sure what she meant until he was standing in the running water, trying to scrub off tiny, flat, black pieces of something that were hard to peel off even with a fingernail.

Bastet had accompanied him upstairs, and he found himself oddly self-conscious nude with the cat peering at him as he dressed.

"You're like her spy, aren't you?" he asked the cat, wondering why he felt the need to talk to her. When he finished, he scratched her head as she sat on the edge of the tub. "You go and report back to her on all you see, don't you? That's how she knew you had that tracker on you, isn't it?" The cat purred loud enough to drown out the breeze and shoved her head hard into Ethan's hand.

"Are you bribing my cat for my secrets?" Aurora came into the bedroom, swinging a new bottle of wine in one hand and a nearly empty glass in the other.

"If she could talk, I might," he shot her a sly grin.

"Thank heavens that she can't. She's my only real confidant. She could get me in trouble." Without even standing close to Ethan, she could smell him, fresh and clean, intoxicating. "Feel like watching a movie?"

"Depends on what movie," he ran a brush through his damp curly hair, and she found it difficult not to watch him.

"I'm up for anything except horror movies or depressing movies. I have enough sadness to deal with in real life. I don't need to watch it on TV. As for horror movies, they are either so cheesy I want the wasted two hours of my life back or so realistic and freaky I have nightmares for three months, neither outcome is agreeable. Other than that, I'm up for pretty much anything." His mind had strayed to watching a horror movie with her. The thought of her in his embrace or jumping into his lap at a fright had him considering ways to convince her, in the future, to watch a screamer with him.

"How about a comedy? I never could turn down laughter," and for the time being, he figured he could settle.

She smiled, turned on her heel, dropping the wine and accompanying glass on the nightstand she went to a large armoire facing the bed and swung open two cabinet doors to reveal an impressive television. From the shelf inside, she grabbed two remote controls before jumping back onto the bed and crawling toward pillows that she subsequently gathered and piled for her comfort.

As he approached the bed, unsure how comfortable she intended to get, she gestured to the wine glass as she flipped through titles.

"Would you fill that and hand it to me, please?"

Pouring her another glass, he watched her peruse through movies with Jason Sudekis before deciding on Masterminds. The glance she flicked him sought approval, and he nodded.

"SNL greats and Zach, always a safe choice," he said

She patted the bed next to him and propped up more pillows as a spot for him to get comfortable without being within reach, and curled herself beneath a throw blanket with her arm resting on the mountain of bedding she had piled high. Having chatted dinner away, with the stress of the day still swirling in his mind, the distraction of a movie was welcome. The sun had disappeared over the horizon, and a dusky purple glow was fading over the lake, lights from the south shore twinkling in the distance.

He felt tired and ready to relax, but his shoulder kept him from getting comfortable. Aurora immediately noticed he was antsy.

"Here," she set the wine glass on the headboard and pushing him forward moved the pillows behind him. "Put your thumb or your fingers into the waistband of your pants," she held his elbow then slid a small pillow underneath his forearm before pulling a larger one underneath his side. The pressure of the weight of his arm was instantly relieved.

"You're pretty good at what you do, aren't you?" he rested his head back.

"I hope so," she smiled and picked her wine back up. "Speaking of which, let me get some ice for you." She clumsily clambered off the bed and retrieved a slushy ice pack from downstairs. Adjusting it on his shoulder, she settled back in after once again topping off her wine glass.

The movie was funny but wasn't enough to hold his attention through the weight of the fatigue he was feeling, and before it was halfway over, he was fast asleep. She watched intently, giggling, holding her breath, trying not to disturb him but found herself watching him more than she was focusing on the movie. She hadn't been this comfortable with a man in a very long time.

She sipped the wine, studying him, every inch of him was perfect. From his high forehead beneath tousled bark brown curls with his deep-set dark eyes behind short thick lashes, his long nose, and pouty mouth over a strong jaw, he was flawless. He was handsome in a boy-next-door kind of way that was all the more attractive with his sheer size. Sound asleep and relaxed next to her; she could still see the ripples of muscle beneath the thin cotton shirt resting on his chest.

All I want to do is touch him. I'm going to have to lay off the wine if I'm going to behave myself.

She switched off the television and sat beside him in the dark, Bastet curled at her feet purring while she listened to Ethan breathe. Even with the weight of the wine, she wasn't yet ready to go to sleep with the clock having edged just past ten. Her mind didn't want to turn off. Thoughts of the dangers surrounding her, and how she was going to deal with patients, and the case she planned to bring against her mother for her attempted kidnapping jumped through her disorganized psyche. Something that looked like a bird or a bat zipped past the window, and she became lost in the view outside.

Memories of being at the lake seeped in, reminding her of her childhood and the pieces of it she missed. She missed her dad, and the shimmer of the water almost disguised the flash of Ethan's phone. It buzzed on the bed between them, so she tapped it to silence it without waking him. A text message in green read *'motion detected, exterior west side, unable to validate cause, recommend perimeter sweep'* and Aurora's heart skipped a beat.

It is Tahoe, she thought, *trees are billowing in the wind and there are raccoons and coyotes, no one knows I'm here, it's probably nothing.* She tried to convince herself, but her pulse wasn't cooperating. Another message flashed in *'confirm receipt of contact.'*

Well crap, I don't know his passcode.

She swiped the screen open and was shocked when it didn't even ask for a code. She was just starting to reply, wondering what she should say when an odd noise caught her attention. If she didn't know any better, she would have thought someone was in the kid's room across the hall.

But no one could have gotten in the house, surely, without disturbing us, she thought.

The alarm was set, and everything was locked. The house was dark and otherwise quiet as another snapping noise came from the room across the hall. Aurora held the phone, put her wine glass down, and carefully snuck off the bed so as not to disturb Ethan.

Shrouded in darkness, she tiptoed carefully around the bed. As she came to stand in the doorway to the bedroom, looking directly across the hall through the children's room, her heart hammered against her chest hard enough for her to lose her breath as the silhouette of a man stood illuminated through the curtains.

Outlined in the shadow from the one faint tawny streetlight out front, he knelt on the roof of the front porch outside, working on removing the screen from the window.

She froze, her blood turning to ice in her veins. Her feet refused to cooperate with her. The phone flashed again and glancing down at it she saw a message questioning if local authorities should be dispatched.

What was I thinking?

The figure in the window moved, and she jumped back to the bed to Ethan. Shaking him, he roused immediately.

"Ethan, there's someone outside," she could barely contain her voice as he sat up.

"What?" she handed him his phone.

"There's someone on the roof out front, trying to get in the window to the kids' room across the hall." She was shaking, her body not cooperating with her demands to breathe.

Ethan's gun was out of the holster in his hand before he even read the messages on the phone. He had his arm around her waist, pulling her beside him, and as he headed for the hallway, he shoved her against the wall beside the door behind him leaning to look out.

"There's no one there," he said in a whisper.

Oh God, is he in the house already? Aurora's heart was in her throat, taking up enough room she couldn't get air into her lungs. Her fingernails dug into the arm Ethan had outstretched to keep her back.

"I saw a shadow," she gasped, "it was a person I swear, outside, doing something to the window."

Ethan's phone was dialing now, ringing on the other end. The voice of a woman answered *'command'* in a calm tone. A loud smacking sound echoed through the house as if something metal hit a window.

"Dispatch, critical level three," Ethan spoke fast and immediately hung up.

"What does that mean?" Aurora whimpered, but Ethan shushed her, pulling her around the corner and down the stairs with him. At the bottom, he immediately swept the room with the gun pointing out in front of him, and Aurora was terrified that her knees were seconds from buckling as shadows danced around them. Yanking her around the corner and into the study, he pressed his hard body against her as he examined the dark room intently.

"Remember what I said? Hide," he whispered to her in a deep and grumbling low tone that sent terror through her. She didn't question him, didn't think twice as she darted towards the corner to unlock the safe room. Within seven seconds, she had it open and was sliding inside. Pulling the shelf closed behind her all she could see was Ethan's silhouette through the study door before she was engulfed in pitch-black darkness.

She rested her forehead against the cold plaster of the wall, her hands trembling, and her stomach so sour she worried she might vomit as her mouth watered. She knew the light couldn't be seen from outside, but her fear kept her from turning it on until the morose thought that someone might already be inside sent an icy finger from the grim reaper sliding down her spine. Snapping it on, she spun around to an empty room, terror seizing her rib cage so tight she couldn't get a deep breath.

Of course, there's no one in here. It's a safe room. I'm losing my mind.

She couldn't hear anything outside, had no idea who had been on the roof, or what would happen to Ethan, and as she stood alone in the small room filled with guns and smelling of oil, she cursed herself.

I hate being helpless, I hate feeling weak, but I'm surrounded by weapons, so why do I feel powerless?

As soon as her hands steadied enough that she thought she could handle a magazine, she retrieved a Glock from inside a large drawer where David had several handguns. It was the smallest one available and made the most sense for her to control and use. She loaded it and turning herself to face the door, tried to prepare for the idea that if anyone but Ethan knocked from the outside, she would need to be prepared to use it.

As soon as the click of the door to the gun safe snapped through the room, Ethan's anxiety level dropped a couple of notches. Aurora was safe and, hopefully, hidden until she didn't want to be. Having her out of his way, he felt far more confident he could subdue whoever was creeping around the house. He listened and with strained ears thought he heard the sound of something above him, though it could just as easily be a squirrel as anything else.

Local back up was on the way already, but he wanted to catch this guy, and if he'd been on the roof out front, he had to be close still. Ethan turned and went out the front door, the chill of the night taking him by surprise compared to how hot the day had been. There were no lights, no unusual sounds, and nothing seemed out of place as he stayed alert following the wall to the west. The breeze ruffled the trees, crickets sang, somewhere not too far off an owl hooted, but there was no sign of people to be seen.

Staying against the house in the shadows, he crossed the garage door. He couldn't see if anyone was on the roof above him, but there was no sign of footprints and no indication of anyone having used a ladder or other assistance to gain access to the overhanging roof. As he rounded the corner on the west side to peer around towards the lake, the feeling of having eyes on him iced his spine, sending the hair on the back of his neck up on end.

It was too dark to see accurately in the shadows beneath the trees, but he could sense someone, and could feel a heavy, menacing stare. He scanned his surroundings, sweeping from behind him out across the road and through the underbrush and trees out to the lake, and as his head turned, he caught a new sound. Something electrical, whirring and buzzing, whizzed past his head. Before he could get his bearings on what it was, a bright flash blinded him temporarily.

Dropping to his knees, he blinked, trying to get his vision back. The sound continued away from him, and as he regained his sight, the first thing he could see was the stroboscopic light on top of the Sheriff cruiser pulling in the driveway. Red and blue flashed across the house, but he turned away, trying to use the light to focus on anyone who might be hiding in the distance. The skipping and jumping swirling lights illuminated a hundred feet out but were too inconsistent for him to identify anything.

If there had been anyone there, they were most likely getting away now as two more cruisers pulled up behind the first, and officers started streaming out.

"Agent Hartman, I presume?" An officer with a weapon drawn approached him from the first car.

"Yea," Ethan was more lackluster in his response than he intended to be. "You guys have a pretty hot response time," loosening his grip on his gun he wasn't yet ready to holster it as he walked around the side of the house.

"What's going on?" the Sheriff asked.

"Not sure, Dr. Soileaux said she saw the silhouette of a man on the roof through the window upstairs. Remote surveillance team reported movement but wasn't able to confirm what caused it. I came to check things out, and something buzzed by my head about thirty miles an hour, flashed a light that blinded me, and I didn't see where it went."

"Drone?" the Sheriff asked.

"Makes sense, though I'm not sure what the goal would be. I want your team to canvas the area. Make sure no one is hanging out hiding."

"Sure, I've got a K9 unit on the way."

"You always have this many guys just chilling and ready for a call?" Ethan was walking around the back deck, satisfied the wraparound porch was empty but still scanning the darkness around the house intently.

"It's income village. Do you see these houses? High expectations," his attitude told Ethan they'd all seen more than their fair share of complaints and were sufficiently staffed to handle the demand. "You want us to start inside or keep to the perimeter?" he asked.

"Keep to the perimeter, but I want neighbors on each side alerted." Ethan finally holstered his weapon and went back around the front inside. Flipping all the lights on, he was silently disappointed he hadn't gotten a shot off at the guy, if it was even who they were after. Turning into the study to let Aurora know the coast was clear, his cell phone buzzed in his pocket with an incoming call from Sheila.

Sheila? Who the hell is Sheila, I don't know anyone named... Oh, right. Never mind.

"Trent, what's up?" Ethan answered calmly.

"Aurora's blood pressure, among other things, what is going on?" he asked.

"What? How did you know?"

"Aurora's on the other line. She called me from that little room no one is supposed to know about scared out of her wits, she's hysterical."

"Shit, tell her everything's fine, she can come out now. I'm in the study waiting for her."

"Ok, call me back as soon as she's calmed down," Trent disconnected, and within twenty seconds, the bookcase was swinging open as Aurora rushed out, gun in hand, into Ethan's waiting arms.

"Whoa, hold on, let's put that away first," grabbing the hand she held the gun with, he quickly put the safety on and set it onto a chair. She was sweating, sobbing so hard she seemed like she could barely breathe and shaking like a leaf. Falling into his arms, he was at first afraid she might faint.

"Oh my God," she sobbed.

"Hey, it's ok, you're ok, everything's fine. Slow down," Ethan cradled her as she quaked and cried, clutching at him as though he might vaporize into thin air.

"I was so afraid," she said between raspy sobs into his shirt.

"Try to take a few deep breaths. You're safe, everything's fine."

"I don't care about me!" she squealed and shoved back from him. "I was terrified you would get hurt!" Smacking him feebly in the chest with her fist, she pulled herself back against him in one fluid move. Her show of emotion touched him, and he was and unsure of what to say.

"I'm fine. You don't have to worry about me. I can handle myself." He almost laughed, but the level of distress hanging on her had him holding his tongue. His cell was ringing again, and as he pulled it out, he opened it and handed it to her.

"It's Trent. There are some Sheriff Deputies outside searching the property, so I'm going to help. You stay inside, ok?" He tilted her face to look up at him, her honey irises awash in green flecks and sparkles of gold as she hiccupped through deep breaths, fighting back the tears. She nodded.

"Talk to Trent, stay here," he dropped a quick kiss on her forehead and spun away. He could hear her answer the phone behind him, and before he was out of earshot, heard her ask why Trent's contact was saved as Sheila.

Shit, too late now.

Greeting the Deputies who were swarming around the house, he began organizing a sweep of the area. Within thirty minutes, Ethan felt confident the Hypocrite killer, or someone else with ill intent to enter the house, had been there but had successfully slithered back into the night undetected. The Deputies handed off a report of the areas secured and said their goodnights as he closed the door.

Aurora had retired up to the master bedroom again. He could hear her still on the phone, and a rainbow-colored light was spilling into the hallway. He secured the bottom floors and turned off all the lights before heading up to her. Closing in on her, he could hear her portion of a conversation that stopped him in his tracks just outside the door.

"I don't like the medication. I never liked the medication," she paused. "Yes, Trent, I know it's as needed. Do you forget you're talking to a doctor? I don't want the stupid Pexeva either, you know what I need, what I *actually* need? Yoga, tea, meditation, sleep, this creepy killer behind bars, and my mother in a casket. I'm allowed to be upset by all of this. It's scary!" Her tone was sharp, and there was a long stretch of quiet. Taking his chance to interrupt without making it seem like he'd been eavesdropping, Ethan rounded the corner calmly.

He found her sprawled out on the bed with an empty mug beside her that had a little paper tag hanging out of it on a string. In her hand, at the moment was a glass of wine, nearly empty. He wondered how those two had come to fruition and paired as he went in and slipped his shoes off. Bastet greeted him with a head bump, and he returned the gesture with an affectionate rub as Aurora sat up.

"I have to go, honey. Ethan's back, and we both need some rest. Thank you, I love you. I'll call you tomorrow." She clicked off the call and tossed the phone towards Ethan on the bed. He watched her down the rest of the wine before setting it aside and climbing beneath the covers.

"You alright?" he asked as he tossed decorative pillows to the foot of the bed.

"I don't know what I am," she flopped on her side, facing him.

"You need anything?" he slid in beside her, still in his shirt and pants. Her eyes inspected his expression, coursing over what felt like every detail in his face.

"So much I can't even put it into words," she whispered as she stared at him reflectively. He wasn't sure how to respond, so he didn't.

"So that you know, I put the Glock in the top drawer of the desk. You should put it back tomorrow. The safety is on, but I left it loaded. We checked out the window. The screen was off, looks like someone was trying to break the lock or jimmy it so it couldn't be locked again, maybe to gain access at a later time. I'm not sure it was the guy we're after. It could have just been a random attempted burglary." He had settled flat on his back but was watching her face as he spoke.

She looked numb and didn't seem to have any emotional response whatsoever. She blinked her puffy red eyes and reached out across the bed for him. He stretched his arm out and met her hand, sliding her long, soft, thin fingers between his. Without saying anything, she reached behind her and snapped off the light before scooting closer to him in the bed. Close enough to hear her breathing, close enough to smell her, he remembered her frantic behavior at the idea he was in harm's way. Thinking of her conversation with Trent, he wondered if he pressed her if there was a medication she actually should be taking.

"You sure I can't get you anything? Do you have anything you can take to help you relax or sleep?"

She took a deep, steadying breath, and in the darkness, he wondered if she was again fighting tears as she said in a quivering and hushed voice, "Nope, you're enough."

Chapter Twenty

Trent texted Ethan first thing the next morning, a long and arduous message about how Aurora should be taking medication to manage the panic attacks and should not be allowed to sleep too much. He was apprehensive about her and had been through traumatic incidents in the past with her. The thought crossed Ethan's mind, with the intense concern from Trent, if she'd ever been suicidal in the past, but he couldn't bring himself to ask. It felt too personal.

Standing at the side of the bed sipping coffee, he watched her chest rise and fall in a constant and relaxed rhythm. He felt uncomfortable knowing next to nothing about severe anxiety or clinical depression, but he just couldn't see how sleeping soundly could be a bad thing. Letting her rest, he went back to work and checked on her diligently every thirty minutes.

The fifth time he checked on her, he was surprised to find it was almost as if she had fallen into a deeper sleep as she had started to snore. Bastet stayed faithfully at her side, purring, curled up on the pillow next to her head. At two in the afternoon, he started to wonder if she'd gotten up and taken something to make her sleep and decided if she didn't wake by three, he would wake her up just to be sure she wasn't in a coma.

She sulked down the stairs at quarter to three and without making eye contact with him, padded into the kitchen. Seeming uninterested in the coffee, she went for a box of teabags and ate a banana as she watched the hot water sputter out.

"I was starting to wonder if you were ever going to wake up," Ethan stepped back from the laptop he'd been examining with eyes so tired they were nearly crossed and went to join her. He was trying, in vain, to hide how worried about her he had become.

"Maybe some part of me was hoping I wouldn't," she curled up her nose at him and took another bite of banana. The comment didn't settle well with him. He didn't know her well enough to gauge if she was joking or hinting at something more sinister bothering her. Coming around the center island in the kitchen to stand next to her, he towered over her. Waiting for her to make eye contact, he held his tongue until she locked eyes with him.

"That's not funny," he said in a gentle but sincere tone, wanting her to know he was concerned.

"It wasn't supposed to be," she said, matter of fact. She turned with the full steaming mug as if to maneuver around him, and he stuck out his arm, catching her gently by the waist. His stomach soured with stress, but he had to know if she was clear-headed.

"So you're going to worry yourself sick about my physical wellbeing, and I'm going to worry myself sick over your mental wellbeing. Is that how this is going to work?" He tugged her back and turned to face her, trapping her between his arms leaning on the counter with his hands behind her. She frowned, wrinkling her forehead. Setting the cup down, she rested her free hand on his forearm affectionately.

"Why would you be worried sick about my mental wellbeing?"

He didn't want to be having this discussion with her, had a sneaky suspicion she was going to get pissed at him for it, but he still felt like he needed to hear it from her. He needed to know she was alright, through and through.

"I heard you on the phone last night with Trent, sounded like he wanted you taking some kind of medication. He told me a few days ago that sleeping is a precursor to depression and anxiety that you sometimes struggle to control. It doesn't do me much good to be here worrying about your physical wellbeing if you're not taking care of yourself."

She had continued to eat, and with the last bite of banana tossed the peel over her shoulder onto the counter behind her, still chewing, she put both her hands on his arms and leaned back, looking at him thoughtfully.

"You're so different," she finally said.

"Is that good or bad?"

"Good. Mostly. I mean it is, but I guess I'm not used to it. I like that you're upfront, even when you're saying something I don't like, and it's a strike against you." He got the impression she was referring to him accusing her of kissing him because she'd had too much to drink and, well, other things in that same conversation. "I don't know what you heard or what Trent told you—*yes*, he did tell me he texted you—and I'm sure it was out of the best place in his heart, but he's not always right. He knows me well, but he does better when he can see me, touch me, read body language. Do you want to know the most amazing thing about therapy that replaces medication?"

Ethan shook his head slightly, unable to look away from her.

"It's permanent," she stood up from the counter to lean into him. "Medication has its place in the world, I will never argue that, but when it comes to mental wellness, medication is often overprescribed and poorly used. Therapy, which I have had plenty of, trains people how to handle stressful situations, how to manage anxiety, depression, grief, and a wealth of other negative things that *most* people wish they could handle better. I've been on meds, and I needed them when I was. I've been through a lot, but I've learned to cope. You'll see it the more you're around, but for now, you need to trust me to manage myself."

Her hands slid along his arms in a personal gesture that felt almost intimate, and he stood up, dropping them to his sides so she could more easily walk away if she wanted. She didn't. Instead, she leaned closer to him, a small smile curving up her cheek to form an adorable dimple.

"I was scared to death for you last night," she whispered as she wrapped her arms around his waist. "I realize there are probably going to be more moments like that if you're around, and I'm going to have to deal with it. I know if I don't want to, I don't have to, but I am *allowed* to be scared, worried, terrified. It's *alright* for me to feel that way about someone I care about, perhaps more deeply than I care to admit yet. I will learn to manage it. It's just new."

She looked up at him with steady golden eyes reflecting glints of copper and emerald as she rested her chin against the hard plane in the center of his chest. His gut clenched. Heat trailed along her hands as she slid them up his back to rest in the curve between his shoulder blades. He was caught unable to answer her in any way verbally and struggled to keep his body from answering for him as she pressed herself against him.

I need to work more on cause and effect. What was I expecting? To ask a personal question and get an impersonal response?

He scolded himself silently for his choice of words remembering the way she had kissed him, then how he had kissed her back, and last but not least, how she had reached for him in the bed they were sharing and held his hand late into the night as she slept.

Rein it in Hartman. It isn't Love Island Bachelor in Paradise.

"So you're taking care of yourself? No more talk of not wanting to wake up."

"Yes," she smiled sweetly, "I'm sorry if it bothered you, I didn't mean it like death." She flicked her eyes to the ceiling before burying her face in his chest.

Forcing himself to stand taller, he put his hands on her shoulders, but not wanting to push her away coldly, opted for a friendly hug and patted her on the back before shuffling away.

"Alright, I'll trust you," he said, heading for the fridge to round up something for a late lunch. "You do know you slept until almost three in the afternoon, though, right?"

"Yes, again, I'm sorry. Believe it or not, it feels good to sleep, and I'll tell you a secret if you promise not to tell Trent. Or, Sheila?" she eyed him ruefully.

"It was his idea," he defended himself, and relief zipped through him when she laughed.

"I don't want to know," she waved a hand as she grabbed her tea mug. "Regardless, most of the instances Trent has burned into his memory that I was sleeping, I actually wasn't. Now, I'm going to take a bath."

She breezed past him on the way back upstairs, and he considered he might have mistaken her body language and demeanor simply because of his concern for her. He watched her climb the stairs and resigned himself back to digging through files. The records from the coroner in Idaho had arrived only moments before she had come downstairs. Photos of the home of Declan Heraldson, detailing what looked more like a tomb than a master bedroom, were spread on his screen.

The grim scene was disheartening. The more he dug into the background of the family, the more depressing and personal it became. The Heraldson family had endured a similar fate to his family. Only the little girl they lost was much younger than Angie had been. After another forty-five minutes reviewing the sad history of the man, he was fairly certain had been on the roof the night before, he was ready to call it quits. When he heard the drain begin to empty the tub upstairs, he snapped his laptop shut.

His stomach was getting the better of him since all he had done for the majority of the day was snack, and though cooking wasn't his forte, heating leftovers was doable. Busying himself in the kitchen, he almost didn't notice Aurora coming back downstairs. She seated herself at the counter on the island, where there were a couple of barstools without saying a word.

"You look tired," she said, leaning on her elbow with her face squished against her hand.

He wanted to tell her about the Heraldson's. He wanted to open up about how much this case was under his skin. He wanted her to open up about what she'd been through with her family. More than anything, he wanted to ask about her relationship with her father. Instead, he just opened a bottle of cabernet and poured her a glass.

"I'm fine," he managed to smile, if even a bit wearily.

"Bags under your eyes come with the territory?" Unlike him, she had none. She looked refreshed, wrinkle-free, as soft but firm as an orchid petal.

"Most of the time."

"You want to talk about it?"

His mind said yes, but his mouth said, "No."

He retrieved a plate of food piled high from the microwave and slid it in front of her before joining her when the plate he'd piled twice as high for himself beeped its completion.

"Thanks for heating up dinner."

"It's not as good as cooking, probably better."

"You don't cook?"

"I can use a grill. I make tri-tip, have a special recipe for lemon rosemary smoked turkey, have a great technique for cedar plank salmon but cooking with measuring spoons and spices, no."

"Sounds very Guy Fieri." When he glanced over at her with his mouth full, his heart nearly stalled. Strands of her dense dark chestnut hair drifted in front of her cheek with the rest tucked behind her ear and tumbling down over her shoulders. Her complexion was more than rosy, presumably from the bath or the first sips of red wine, and her lips, full and luscious, were a seductive strawberry color from the spicy chili pepper she had been sucking on in compliment to the tostadas.

"I would be honored to think I could compete with the likes of him," Ethan made a conscious effort to slow the rate at which he was shoveling food in his mouth.

"How's your shoulder?" she asked.

"I'm surviving."

She sighed and said, "At some point, you're going to give up the big tough guy routine and just be honest because that's reasonable, right?"

"Nope," he shot her a quirky look and attempted to evade her reaching for the collar of his shirt. She had better reflexes than he'd anticipated and with three fingers yanked hard to reveal the bandage on his shoulder. Grabbing hold of her wrist, he pushed to keep her away and was surprised at the strength she employed to resist him.

"Let me see," she leaned into him, and her fierce determination had him so surprised he relented. It didn't help that his arm was aching, on fire, and had been for most of the day. She nitpicked over the wound, pressing around it and running her fingers over it while he munched tortilla chips.

"Do you need to amputate?" he asked and shot her a comical look. She slipped her hand down around the front inside of his arm just above his bicep and, with her long middle finger, delved between the muscles. As she pressed harder, a fiery surge of electrical pain seared down his arm ending in his fingers, and he recoiled.

"How far down your arm does that hurt?" she asked as he grabbed her fingers to push her away.

"Into my fingers, crap knock it off," he snapped. She didn't persist but instead stood up and retrieved a cup of ice from the freezer.

"It's not good that the nerve pain goes all the way to your fingers; it means the swelling is still severe deep in the tissue." Without asking, she put the ice directly on the tender spot above his collarbone and pressed through a towel. Holding it steady with one hand, she sipped wine with the other, studying him as he tried to ignore the heat between them. There was a chemistry that couldn't be denied, thick, and hovering in the air.

"So ice is a cure-all?" he asked, barely glancing up.

"No," she laughed, "but it will help. What you actually need is a strong anti-inflammatory and to take a break twice a day and go for a swim. Tomorrow?"

"Sure," he sucked down the last of his soda and leaned back in the chair, resolved to let her hold the ice against the wound that felt as if she were driving a hot iron under his collarbone instead of cold. She was watching him closely, judging his reaction, and it took a decent amount of discipline not to let her see how he felt she was torturing him.

"So when was the last time you saw the Cubs play?" she was trying to distract him, and he appreciated it. Buying into her diversion, they began chatting about sports, the players, famous games, opinions on who was going to the series that year, and before long, he found himself at ease with her again. Before she had melted through the ice, it felt like he was sitting with an old friend.

"I think it's good for a while. Now you need to take a hot shower. Run water over it as hot as you can stand, and it should help you rest better. I'm going to go fish out some anti-inflammatories if I can find any, and that should help too."

She waved him upstairs as she busied herself, cleaning the kitchen, and he couldn't help but notice her scent followed him as he went.

I have to stay focused. I can't be this distracted. Maybe I need a cold shower.

Half an hour later, he was dry, dressed, and surprised how the shower had done wonders to loosen his shoulder. The only light in the bedroom was from a stained-glass lamp on the opposite side of the giant bed, and the colorful shades it threw in the room were soothing. Before he could flop into bed, Aurora was closing the door behind her with the glass of cabernet in one hand, a bottle of water in the other, and the half-full bottle of wine tucked under an arm.

"How's your shoulder after the hot shower?" she asked.

"The shoulder is still sore but not as bad. I'm sure it will heal and be fine, the ice helped."

"This will help more, here," she wiggled to get the wine bottle out and handed him two pills and the bottle of water.

"Anti-inflammatories?" he asked, and she nodded, smiling.

"And, after you've taken those, I'm curious if you have any interest in astronomy." She was looking him over, head to toe, as if trying to read his mind. He swished down the pills, barely taking his eyes off her.

"Astronomy as in stars?" he asked, frowning.

"Yes, astronomy as in stars."

"I used to camp a lot, so I've enjoyed my fair share of the night sky, but I can't say I've ever been much into astronomy."

"Well, it's one of my favorite things and something I look forward to every time I come here." She hesitated, studying him, considering the expression on his face and his body language. "You know you're getting a lot of my secrets just by being here. More than I would share with anyone else after such a short time."

"I feel honored," his face was sarcastic.

Walking past him into the anteroom full of exercise equipment, she motioned for him to follow her as she shut off the lights. His heart stalled in the dark with her, not knowing what she was doing.

As his eyes adjusted, he could tell she was fidgeting with something against the ceiling and, with a sharp click, lowered an attic ladder he would never have known existed into the center of the room. As the stairs descended, he wondered how he had missed it, the turret she had not yet shown him.

She took his hand and led him up the narrow, rickety, creaking stairs through the small opening. At the top, a tiny round room opened, reminding him of a short and stocky motor home. Pillows and blankets littered the floor in no particular order, and a shelf above them had a large padded area.

"Watch your head. You don't have shoes on, do you?" she asked.

"No," he said as he crouched, taking in the space. She pulled the stairs closed behind him with a loud snap.

"There are a few stairs, here," she was still on her hands and knees, leading him to one side as she crawled, carefully holding the glass of wine. The room was octagonal and made entirely of windows, built into the angle of the roof, entirely facing the lake. As he crawled after her, he could see the ceiling made entirely of glass. The whole top of the turret was panels of windows. At the top of the four long, stubby stairs that had no railing was a flat area that was wall to wall cushion except for a short shelf at the head. They couldn't have stood up. The glass was only three feet high before the panels formed a dome over them, he could have touched the top if he stretched up on his knees.

Aurora set the glass on the shelf and settled herself with her knees crossed, watching him take in their surroundings.

"This is the turret, isn't it?" he asked.

"It is, it was my dad's idea, years ago when they built the house before I was born. He was a fanatic for astronomy, and he loved this lake. He loved the open space and the darkness. He knew so many constellations. We used to make s'mores on the beach then come up here with all the kids, and he would sip port with David pointing out all the stars in the sky, telling stories as we snuggled together. David has three children, a son and two daughters, and I am in between them all in age." He could tell it was a cherished memory for her.

"It's pretty impressive. No one would know this was here."

"That was the idea, they had the paneling in the ceiling staggered, and the fire sprinkler is a fake. It's what I pulled on to get the stairs down. There's a metal hook that most people wouldn't even realize is meant to open it, and now you know both the big secrets of the house." He had made himself comfortable, sprawling out on the cushion, staring at her as she talked.

"It's incredibly creative," as his eyes continued to adjust, he could see why the spot was so appealing. It was on the roof, set back far enough that it wouldn't be visible until several hundred yards out on the lake, and by then could easily be mistaken for an odd window or skylight. No one would see it from the lower floors or swimming on the private beach. It was set to the side of the main roofline so neighbors couldn't see it, and being on the back was impossible to detect from the front.

Aurora sipped more wine, opened one of the rollout windows, and settled beside him with a pillow under her head, feeling nostalgic.

"So, you know a lot about constellations?" Ethan asked, enjoying the quiet and the breeze. The view was breathtaking, soaring pines waving in the breeze encircled them, twinkling stars littering the sky.

"Not like my Dad, but I learned a thing or two for sure." She sat up on one elbow, admiring him in the darkness. Looking up, getting her bearings, she slid closer to him, put her head beside his, against his shoulder, and pointed. "See that bright one there, just in the corner of the third panel from this grid?"

He tilted his head and murmured, "Mmhmm."

"Follow it," her hand slid over him. "See those three stars there?" he nodded. "That's Apus, the bird of paradise." She continued to show him Hercules and then Scorpio. "That one there, that's part of Ursa Major."

He interrupted her, "Wait, I know that one—that constellation is the big dipper."

She giggled, "Actually, the big dipper isn't a constellation. It's an asterism."

"What?" he looked at her in disbelief.

"It's just an easily recognizable pattern of stars that are often part of a larger constellation." He turned his head, feeling her hair tickle against his cheek.

"You mean to tell me the only constellation I've been able to find routinely throughout my life isn't really a constellation?"

She laughed and sat up on her arm again to sip more wine.

"Are you disappointed?" she asked.

"It's life-altering," he teased, "I feel like a fool, my joy of the night sky was based on a lie." She threw her head back and laughed. It was the first time she'd heard him being openly sarcastic.

"Ok, how about this—have you ever been able to find Cassiopeia?"

"That sounds like something you catch in a swimming pool that makes you itch," he said. She laughed out loud, rolling towards him, burying her face in his right shoulder.

"No," she enjoyed the feeling of being close to him. "It's from Greek mythology. It loosely translates to 'the queen.' Look, there," she pointed. "It starts with these five stars, one, two, three, four, five." As her fingers traced the sky and her arm leaned over his, he caught her hand, lacing his fingers into hers, pulling her towards him. She was too enticing to resist.

"From Greek mythology, I take it the queen must have been beautiful," his eyes met hers, intrigued and intense.

"She sure thought she was, she was vain, boasting of her beauty. There's a whole story about it. She claimed that she was more beautiful than the Nereids, sea nymphs, who happened to have a sister Amphitrite, who was married to Poseidon. Of course, being a loyal and defensive husband, Poseidon sent the sea monster Cetus to destroy the city of King Cepheus, Cassiopeia's husband. Cepheus and Cassiopeia had a daughter, Andromeda."

"That name sounds familiar," he blurted.

"Yes, well, it's one of the most famous rescue stories of all history. Cepheus and Cassiopeia chained their beautiful daughter Andromeda to a rock by the sea as a sacrifice to appease Cetus. Before she could be consumed, she was rescued by Perseus."

"Perseus beheaded Medusa, didn't he?"

"Very good, I'm impressed."

"My grandfather was super into those seventies movies, and there was one with Kirk Douglas where the guy used a reflection to kill Medusa, that's the only reason I remember." Even in the dim, his sly grin lit her heart.

"I suppose there are worse ways to remember Greek mythology," she chuckled.

"I don't honestly remember the mythology part. I just remember the love story."

"You're just full of surprises, aren't you?" Her head was nestled into his shoulder again, and she could hear him breathing, he traced his fingers along her arm lightly as it rested across his chest, sending electricity dancing through her. Pulling her arm over his neck, he propped up on one elbow, slowly leaning into her in the moonlight. He paused, just as his lips brushed hers, contemplating cause and effect so before he could decide against the kiss, she stole it.

Bringing her mouth to his, she licked into it, savoring the shape and feel of his lips. He was clean-shaven, and his jawline was soft, flawless skin she caressed with her hand. Feeling his breath against her, she settled beneath him, drawing him down on her, twining her fingers in his hair. The intensity of the moment had her whole body vibrating with anticipation.

As his weight came down on her, she welcomed the strength his embrace surrounded her with, cradling her head on his arm. Alone in the starlight she soaked in every movement he made, every caress, his mouth wandering lustfully in hers, lost in desire. She ran her hands over his body, trailing along every crease between each muscle. His lips grazed her neck and collarbone, slowly mapping every curve as his fingers traced down from her shoulders, exploring along her waist and hips, firmly pulling her thigh closer to him.

Her heart skipped, her breath went ragged, she trembled all over as he whispered hotly, slowly in her ear, "You are so incredibly beautiful." She couldn't breathe, and as his lips met hers again, his kiss made the world around her spin out of control. She relaxed beneath him, letting him lead her, unfolding herself to his desire. Running his fingers down her arm, he pulled on her wrist, tucking it under the arm that her head was cushioned on, holding her gentle but firm, opening her like a flower.

Holding her attention with his lips and captive with his touch, he caressed her belly, sliding her long dress up to bare her legs. Every meticulous move he made tantalized her, sending shocks through her body. She kissed him fiercely, and he shifted, slipping the solid massive muscle of his thigh between her legs. Dizziness overtook her as his fingers snuck first beneath her dress to cup the perfect globe of her breast, his thumb perking her nipple taut, before gliding back down past her belly button into her panties.

She inhaled sharply, gasping at his touch, and surprising her, he pushed up to look at her, to watch her face change as his fingers found their way into her most intimate, wet folds. As she lost control of her breathing, clutching his forearm with one hand and tugging hard at his back with the other, his expression changed. He smiled ever so slowly, indulging in her enjoyment.

She moaned as he slipped his fingers deeper inside her, heat radiating from her hips, she rocked against him, helpless under his weight. He kissed her again, his mouth finding her nipple pinching playful and sultry as his fingers aroused her from inside. She bucked beneath him, arching in pleasure, nearly hyperventilating as he drove her mad with desire. Pressing down hard with his hip, he held her, focusing his energy with a skill that impressed her as no man had before.

Feeling him hard against her sent an entirely new thrill through her. Just knowing *this man* wanted her made her feel fulfilled somehow, sexier than ever. Panting, quaking, he brought her to climax and held her there, obviously thoroughly enjoying the way she tensed uncontrollably, clutching him. Reading her like a book he gently eased back, still kissing her, running his hands over her thighs, she found herself helplessly under his control. Satiated and limp beneath him, he could have had anything he wanted from her. She would have been powerless to refuse even his darkest desire.

Expecting the moment to be only the beginning, she found herself lost for words when he merely rolled onto his back, tucked her under his shoulder, and caressed her arm lightly. He radiated contentment, showing just as much satisfaction as she felt, which left her confused.

"Is that it?" she asked, breathless and quivering.

"Was it not enough?" he asked in a rhetorical tone, he knew very well what he'd just done.

"Of course, I mean," she stuttered, wasn't sure what to say, her mind was still recovering from the sparkles. "It was amazing, you're impressively good at that, but," she paused, studying him in the moonlight. He was calm, relaxed, appeared pleased, and looked at her as if he'd just enjoyed a lovely dessert.

"But what?" he asked without expectation.

"Don't *you* want more?" The smile that spread across his face was worth a thousand words.

"Of course I do, you have no idea how much, trust me, but all in due time. Before we get there, I want to know that once we do, I get to keep you." Her astonishment must have been apparent. "I also like to be better prepared for certain things." He pulled her in and kissed her, melting her all over again.

"A federal agent who likes to be prepared," she flattened herself on his chest, listening for his heartbeat, "go figure."

"On that note, in the thread of being prepared, we should probably head back down. Especially after last night. For how private and secret it is up here, it still isn't someplace I would care to get caught off guard." He squeezed her and rolled her over the top of him closer to the stairs, sitting up, he shuffled her down. She found herself still dizzy, lightheaded, and fluttery all over.

After freshening up, she joined him, already halfway to sleep in the gigantic bed and thought back to when he had told her she would have to keep her hands to herself. She hadn't taken him literally, but climbing in beside him found it difficult to stay away.

The struggle was real. She wanted to climb in his arms, had never had a man do what he had just done. *I guess there absolutely is a first time for everything* she thought, as she welcomed another night's sound sleep.

Chapter Twenty-One

Ethan woke up at the crack of dawn with a pounding headache and the hard-on from hell. Aurora was still asleep beside him in the bed as big as Texas, peacefully, but she hadn't slept a second in his dreams. She had haunted him from the moment he had drifted off. He tried to stretch and found his shoulder stiff, and a new shooting pain was searing down his arm. Grumbling, grumpy, and not ready for the day, he slipped away and into the shower.

He couldn't get her out of his head, couldn't focus on what work he was supposed to be starting on for the day. He let the hottest water he could stand run over his shoulder as he rubbed and stretched, irritated and tired. The night before had only served to use up his last ounce of will power, if she came at him again, he would be defenseless, and it left him annoyed with himself.

Of all the stupid things to do, he wasn't sure why he had chosen that route. He should have just kissed her or kept his hands to himself entirely, or maybe not even gone up in that romantic little room in the first place. He was sure she had done it on purpose, with a plan she knew would be against his better judgment, but he'd let her do it anyway, and *damn it he wanted her.*

Stepping out of the shower in nothing but a towel, a small part of him was as much horrified as he was turned on. Aurora sat cross-legged on the edge of the tub, sipping coffee with a second cup waiting for him beside her. She stood up, handing it to him with a smile she hadn't used on him before. *Damn it, damn it, damn it.* He sipped, feeling like he deserved the uncomfortable scorch of the liquid on his tongue.

"Good morning," she said, sweet as sugar.

"Morning," he didn't do an outstanding job of hiding the gruff.

"Your shoulder is bothering you. By the look of the way you were rubbing your neck, so is your head. I know it's because of me, the way you were sitting all day yesterday, and the day before, hunched over a laptop." She was fixed on him and had no intention of letting him out of her sight. She wore a calf-length flowing periwinkle blue skirt and a simple white skin-tight tank top. He wanted to curse her, to tell her he couldn't be in charge of her case anymore because she clouded his thinking. Instead, he stared at her like a dog that hadn't eaten in a week. It took a conscious effort to keep his tongue in his mouth.

"Not really because of you, because of someone after you. I didn't sleep great, that's all. I just need some caffeine."

"You're protecting me, it's the same thing, and I hate it when you lie to me."

He was sure he looked like a deer in the headlights, but since he had turned into the closet to slip on his clothes, he was at least glad she hadn't seen his face.

"I'll be fine. If it doesn't go away in an hour or so, I'll take some Tylenol." *Or maybe take a cold shower, or an ice bath, or a plane ride to the North Pole.*

"My dad trained in conventional western medicine, but he was a big believer in holistic approaches as well, as long as they had proven results. I want you to let me work on your neck and shoulder this morning." He almost choked on his coffee. He didn't feel like walking around all day with a hard-on was going to cut it, and he knew if she laid a finger on him, he'd be a lost cause.

The look of determination on her face when he went back out had him wincing, he knew how to pick battles with a woman, and this just wasn't going to be the hill to die on today. She held her hand out to usher him back into the anteroom, and he cringed.

"How long is this going to take?"

"As long as it takes," her tone held finality.

He didn't like the sound of that, but sucked down the coffee and shuffled ahead of her, trying to brace himself. She had already laid out a variety of triangle cushions, foam rollers, and floor mats that looked as though they belonged in a physical therapy office. A sturdy massage table was in one corner, only ten inches or so off the floor, and another massage chair sat beside it.

"Wait," his mind caught up with the situation, "you were watching me shower?"

She shrugged and made a face like a kid who'd been caught with a hand in the candy jar, "Guilty as charged."

He just rolled his eyes. He was in way over his head.

"Sit here first," she pointed to the massage chair, and so finishing his cup of coffee, set the mug down and straddled the cushion, face down in the padded ring. "I'm going to use, at different points, hot and cold stones. I have a little crock that keeps the stones hot on one side and chilled on the other, so don't let it startle you."

He said, "Alright," thinking, *I'm so screwed.*

She circled him, touching his back and neck, sliding her fingers down his spine in such a way it felt very professional. He could tell she was checking large and small muscles, pressing the discs of his spine and neck. She lifted his arm next, putting her fingers into pressure points on his shoulder, he tensed expecting pain, but when none came, he relaxed again. He tried to focus on how he felt not what she was doing as a distraction and, after a few minutes began to relax.

Using her elbows and the base of her palms, she began kneading and massaging, applying some kind of warm thin oil that smelled of herbs, fragrant but light. She worked up and down his back before going to his shoulder, maneuvering his arm she supported its weight while finding muscles and tendons he hadn't realized were sore.

"Take several very slow deep breaths through your nose." her voice was soothing, soft. As he did, she turned his arm, pinning it against him with her leg, sliding her fingers along his collarbone and up to his neck, she caught muscles that seared red hot with pain but only for an instant. Before he could recoil or react, using ice-cold stones, she found pressure points and almost magically released the tension.

"Keep breathing," she caressed her hand lightly over his neck.

She moved his arm three or four more times in different directions. Each time finding a way to slice through pain and create relaxation and flexibility before finally using her elbows to massage his back, almost lulling him to sleep. Moving to rub his head, he was surprised how specific her movements were, finding tension in his scalp with her thin, delicate fingers. Every move she made melted him a little more.

"Alright, tough stuff, rollover here, onto the floor, face up." He wasn't sure how long he had been facing down, and though he felt buttery and limp, dreaded having to look at her and face what reactions he might have. As he stood up, he became light-headed and swayed a little. She guided him to the floor, seeing his unsteadiness.

"What exactly do you call this besides heavenly?" he asked, sighing as he sank.

"Oh, lots of things mixed together, some old Chinese medicine, some European techniques. I bet you didn't even notice the acupuncture, did you?"

"Jesus, you stuck needles in me?" he couldn't tone down the shock.

"Don't worry about it unless I hurt you. Then I want to know." Leaning back onto a squishy piece of triangle foam covered in some kind of non-slip microfiber, he was putty in her hands. She put a cylindrical cushion behind his neck and tucking his right arm tight beside him began to pull and stretch his left arm, all the while working her fingers into crevices between muscle and bone. She was using hot stones of varied sizes now, had made a small pile of them beside him she was going through one by one.

He closed his eyes, leaving himself at her mercy, relaxed and at ease, but knowing it was only a matter of time before she would arouse him and surely notice. She worked on his neck first, stretching it and rolling it side to side before moving on to his chest and torso. Her hands expertly gliding along his pecs and abs came to rest on the inside of his hip, digging in to find a tight, sore tendon. Just as he began to worry that he wouldn't be able to contain himself any longer, she straddled him, rocking her hips sexy on top of him.

His eyes shot open, and his hands clamped around her waist, his breath catching as he realized she wasn't wearing any panties.

"Aurora," his breath was thin, and his voice didn't sound like his own. She smiled at him, such a look on her face he would have thought she'd successfully stolen a fortune from a high-security vault. He shook his head, no, in a vain attempt to stave off her advances but quickly found himself in no position to argue with her. She leaned forward on him, crushing her mouth to his, hungry and insistent, she reached behind him and unclipped something causing the triangle to collapse like a rocking chair, dropping him back.

His body balanced inches off the floor, and in a swift movement with her leg, she hooked his pants and slid them down before he realized what she was doing. She was kissing him like he was air, and she'd been at the edge of drowning. Pulling on his neck and putting her weight on his lap, she rocked him upright again, and with a click behind him, he was supported once more.

She caught him, skin on skin, completely unprepared, and unable to argue. His heart slammed in his chest, as soft and wet, she pressed against him, instantly hardened and aching. He groaned, utterly out of willpower. She was drinking him as if she was parched, her lips hot and unyielding. Grasping her hips with his hands, he tried to push her off, but she'd wrapped her legs around him and cupping his face in her hands, she made him look up at her.

"No," she whispered, "I want you, and I will have you, and then I will be yours." She rose up, keeping his melted chocolate eyes fixed on her, and came down on him in a hot rush. He gave in. It was too much. He wanted her too desperately. She looked at him like a harlot who'd landed the biggest client in town, unrelenting and triumphant. She had changed as she aroused him; dominant with an air of ownership, she tugged him to sitting. Her stamina was beyond anything he had expected as her fit figure continued to glide over him. She looked him in the eye. She was terrific, every bit of her, and *damn it* if she was so determined to have him, why was he fighting it?

Lifting her with him, he rolled, pinning her to the floor he let go of his inhibitions and drove into her. She cried out in pleasure, raising her hips to meet his thrusts, clutching at his neck, running her fingernails down his back. She said his name, moaning and breathing hard, letting loose little sounds of delight. He kissed her hard, and his hands closed on her hips as he tore her tank top off over her head, his mouth found her breast and sucked. He couldn't get enough of her fast enough. She arched up into him, gasping and clinging, pulling his hair as she lost herself with him.

"You feel so good, don't stop, don't ever stop," she said before she laced her tongue into his mouth, breathless and starving for as much as he could give her.

Sweat rose between them, salty but sweet. He looked at her, a glimmer of hesitation in his eyes, but she squashed it, running her fingertips along his side and down the sexy, solid muscle V of his abdomen, and it was enough. At that moment, the way they looked at one another secured trust between them. His hands slid beneath her and wrapped in her hair, cradling her head as he exhausted himself in the joy of her.

Sprawled out flat on the floor, windows wide open and without shades, utterly naked, he lay panting on top of her in the wavering amber light through the trees. She was like nothing he had ever known, unbridled, full force, undeniable, and complete bliss. She caressed him with her fingers, her nails sending chills through him she squirmed beneath him and managed to roll him over. Flat on his back with knees bent; he was still warm inside her as she leaned on his bent legs. Her skin was damp like dew, sparkling, and beautiful.

"I'm not done with you yet," she grinned at him as she rocked her hips again. He closed his eyes, trying to catch his breath as she slid in long leisurely movements on him. She reached behind her, sliding her fingernails down his inner thigh, sending chills through him. Slow, sensual, tantalizing, and relentless, still wet, she kept him hard as iron. His blood began to boil once more as her breathtakingly beautiful body glowed warmly over him, eyes of liquid molten gold unwavering.

For a long time, he kissed her sweet and soft, stealing her breath, running his big hands over her learning every curve. Her hair tumbled around his face, sweeping across his chest as she moved, and he ran his fingers into it, breathing deep the sweet scent of her. He felt so wholesome to her, even in the throes of passion a gentleman as his fingers brushed her breasts tenderly exploring. She began to moan, to vocalize the ache she had for him, for something only he could provide.

"You're so different. You feel so good." She whispered in his ear, saying his name she buried her face against the solid steel of his neck lingering as she trailed kisses along his salty skin. He curled her against him and rolled to be on top of her again, keeping her legs around his waist. Her eyes drifted south over his perfect, beautiful chest and flat stomach to the muscles of his hips, watching as he slid in and out of her so controlled, so purposeful.

His eyes never left her face, and when she looked back into them, they had turned dark, heavy-lidded, and lustful. She was breathing hard with her mouth open in anticipation of his kisses. As he bent his mouth to meet hers, it lingered only briefly before trailing down her neck along her collarbone, along the flat velvet skin between her breasts, then sucking gently around her belly sending flutters through her. Quivering, she ran her fingers into his dense brown curls as he continued to slide his hands around her, gripping her bottom firm as he buried his face between her legs. As his mouth latched onto her most sensitive wet folds, she cried out, but he slowed, taking his time finding just where he needed to be.

Patiently he built a fire to burn in her belly. As her body clenched, she gasped and panted with little noises of pleasure as he indulged her. Drawing her steadily closer and closer to climax, his hands gripped her stronger, holding her in place as she bucked beneath him. Crying out his name with her fingers tight in his hair, she came in a pulsing blaze of heat, shuddering, spent, and utterly satisfied, clinging to him like a leaf to a tree in a storm.

He let her legs fall, stretched her out flat on the floor as his hands coursed over her, and his lips continued to caress their way back to her breasts. Breathing far too heavy, enjoying him like she'd never enjoyed anything else in her life, she admired his broad shoulders, the thick muscle of his neck and arms as he hovered over her. She was putty in his hands as they came around her with his mouth locked on her nipple, pinching and teasing with his lips. She could feel him pressing against her again, silk over steel between her legs, and she gripped his broad shoulder with one hand, his hip with the other inviting him in. His lips met hers, salty with her own taste. He slammed into her, capturing her in a rapture that sent her over the edge again, clinging to him. He was her pinnacle of ecstasy as he thrilled her, thrusting into her over and over before finally finding his euphoria in climax.

Enervated, he relaxed on her, and they melted into one another, quiet and content in each other's arms, silently knowing they would never want anyone else again.

Aurora had known from the moment she opened her eyes, watching Ethan walk away to the bathroom, that she had to have him, and she had to have him *today*. Her dreams had been lustful and seductive, and she woke with a fire in her belly that wouldn't be sated any other way. As she watched him rock his head back and forth, rubbing his neck, she knew exactly what she wanted and how she was going to get it.

What she hadn't known was that it was going to surpass her wildest dreams. Ethan was perfect, from his well-honed body of solid muscle and his creamy cocoa eyes right down to the way he curled his toes as she touched him. She could barely contain herself, and by the time she had moved in on him, thirsty and determined she knew she would never want someone that way ever again.

Pinned beneath him, with the early morning light filtering through the trees spreading dancing shadows across the floor, she felt whole, complete. She had dragged him back to bed, managing to keep him from putting more than boxers back on, and was sprawled on his chest stark naked, enjoying the feel of his warm skin on hers. She could hear his heartbeat, and it soothed her.

"I'm probably going to get fired. You know that right?" he said.

She laughed, curling her hands behind his arms, legs intertwined with his. His hands were so strong but so gentle, trailing over her bare back.

"It's not funny what you do to me," his voice was light, but she sensed the sincerity of it, his insecurity.

"Well, that makes two of us. And I don't see how you can get fired, you haven't actually done anything illegal, and I'm still in one piece, so you've done something right."

"It's fraternization."

"We don't work together, so not quite."

"Insubordination," he insisted.

"Did you disobey a direct order?" She slid up on her arms to hover above his face, aching to kiss him again. He sighed, shook his head, reached for the sheets to wrap her as she resisted, pulling him sideways to her again.

"You know what I mean. Jesus, what am I going to do with you?" he kissed her neck again.

"Take yourself off the case, let someone else deal with it, we'll fly to Venice."

"You would say that, but I can't, my life isn't like yours. I can't pick up at the drop of a hat that way." She took a deep breath and sighed heavily.

"No, you're right, I honestly can't either. It sounds so appealing and maybe someday, but not now. I know as soon as we leave this room, you'll be back on your laptop, and I'll be left to my own devices once again, waiting for this all to end so I can have my way with you without worrying about consequences. Right now, can we just settle for a nap and deal with it at lunch?"

"Nap? You think we're going to nap when you have no clothes on?" He smiled as he pulled her, laughing, back to him, wrapping her in the sheets tight against him, putting off the real world for just a little while longer.

Ethan was watching the ceiling fan spin, half dozing and half-dreaming when his phone startled him just after eleven in the morning. Aurora was tucked comfortably under his arm, still nude, warm and soft with one leg sprawled over him, seeming to be asleep. When he checked the caller ID, he made an exasperated, grumbling noise.

"Who is it?" Aurora asked sleepily.

"My mom."

She tilted her head up to his face. "Answer it. You said yourself she has a thing about needing to hear your voice."

"Yea, but that's the problem," he grumbled.

"Oh, stop it, seriously, there are plenty of people that would give their eye teeth to have their mom calling them. Answer it." He grimaced at her sideways, rolling his eyes before answering.

"Hey Mom," he sounded less than thrilled, and she went immediately into a rambling chatter. Aurora could only hear a little bit now and again as Ethan grunted "uh-huh" and "sure" occasionally throughout the conversation. After ten minutes or so, as Aurora was just getting bored enough to drift back off to sleep, she heard her name. Without a reply, Ethan slid her off his shoulder and sat up with lightning speed. Startled by his reaction, she sat up, wrapping the sheets loosely around her, and gave him a dirty look.

"What's that for?" she asked. His face had suddenly changed as he looked back, walking away from her, obviously avoiding the possibility of her hearing the conversation.

"No, Mom," he paused, "and, yea, I mean it is, but no, we're not." Pausing again, he continued to walk towards the closet, ignoring Aurora, "I explained that already, no, it's just not."

"Ethan?" Aurora shouted. He turned sharply, at the closet door, and put his finger over his mouth to shush her. Her mouth fell open, shock rocketed her to her feet, and she dashed across the room to him, dragging the sheet with her. He tried to close himself in the closet, but her foot slipped in the way just in the nick of time.

"No, Ma, I gotta go, I'll call you back later," he paused, spinning away as Aurora pushed her way into the closet. She reached out with her free hand, pinching the back of his arm.

"Ouch!" he swatted at her fingers, catching her hand as she gave him a dirty look, whispering to him, "did you just deny me to your mother?"

"Ma, no, I pinched myself, I'm fine, I have to go, I'll call you later." He held Aurora's hand, keeping her at bay, "love you too, Ma." Ending the call, he slipped the phone in the pocket of his pants and quickly scooped Aurora up, tossing her over his shoulder like a rag doll.

"I heard my name," she squirmed and kicked to no avail, "what was that all about?"

"Don't worry about it," he plopped her back onto the bed and grabbed a shirt he began pulling over his head.

"I don't deserve to know what your mom is asking you about me?"

"Not until I feel like answering her and answering her truthfully. If the time ever comes that I feel like answering her, she'll probably be asking you instead of me anyway, so don't worry about it."

Aurora scoffed at him, but she honestly wasn't sure what to say to that. After pondering a moment it occurred to her, it made sense, he was a grown man who probably kept most of his sex life off-limits to his parents, and that's pretty much all they had so far. Bastet jumped onto the bed beside her, meowing loudly and rubbing her soft fur against Aurora's bare back, obviously hungry.

Ethan padded downstairs, poured a cup of coffee, and buried himself in work. He was more motivated than ever to get the case wrapped up. If the morning had shown him anything, it was that there was a real possibility there would be something to explore with Aurora once the serial killer hunting her was behind bars. He had a lot to do before then, sitting down, he was determined to put his personal feelings out of his mind and make progress. Smiling to himself, he thought the sooner he could make that happen, the better.

Declan stood on the beach barefoot as the sun set over the western horizon behind a haze of wildfire smoke so thick it blurred the edge of the world between solid and sky. It was hot. The July day had nearly hit triple digits, and after being burned the night before by almost being caught, he had decided a break in his tension was overdue. He had anticipated the final stages of his plan would be easy, and the challenge that had met him had thus far only frustrated him.

It would be any day now the neighbors would begin smelling his last victim, ripe as caviar left in a hot car. He needed to step back, rethink his approach, discard his jumbled and failed plans and form new ones entirely. This pig that had holed up with Aurora was throwing a real wrench in his ability to finish what he'd set out to do. There had to be more holes. There were always ways to track and trace, divide, and conquer. He would find them.

Tomorrow.

Tonight, with the fresh air of the mountains swirling around him and Jack Daniels pulsing through his veins, he was in the mood for something else. He hadn't once in his entire marriage so much as looked at another woman whether his wife was fulfilling her commitments or not, but she was gone. She hadn't been taken from him by luck or chance either. She'd chosen it. It felt like she'd divorced him.

Under any other circumstance, he would have grieved her for the remainder of his days on earth, but she'd left him, forsaken him. 'Til death do us part had released him from his commitment. The sand, still hot from the scorching sun, tickled and scratched at his toes. He turned to walk back from the beach to his small shanty cabin across the street. The night was lively with people, the Fourth of July holiday only a couple of days away the lake was swarming with tourists.

Families, couples, college girls in shorts with their plump little fannies dripping out. It was almost too good to be true and indeed too good for him to resist. He was restless. He needed to flush out some of this dirty energy so he could focus on completing what he'd come to do. Deciding the evening would be better with another drink, he slipped on his flip flops and traipsed across the street to the convenience store.

After grabbing a couple of mini bottles of Jack and a large Coke, he promptly poured out enough of the soda to make room for the Jack and emptied the mini bottles into the cup. Standing on the side where the bathroom was, in the dark, it didn't take long. Before midnight he had a perfect little minx, stumbling from too many margaritas, knocked unconscious in his arms.

Poor girl, she drank too much, she needs someone to take care of her until she's flushed the alcohol from her system.

He carried her through the bushes where there were no lights, then pulled her through the back window of the small shanty cabin he felt was way overpriced for what he was getting. He tied her up, enjoying the sounds she made, the way she whimpered as she started to wake up before he choked her back unconscious. Her breasts were perky, her lips were plump, and she was young and firm all over. Three times he found his release with her, and by the time the sun was rising, he let her wake up all the way so that he could enjoy the terror in her eyes as he extinguished the light from them entirely.

Rolling her onto the floor, clearheaded again, he considered the changes to this plan and the need for adaptation. As he fell asleep to the rising sun, it came to him, and he knew where he could capitalize on the holes the Fed had left for him.

Chapter Twenty-Two

Ethan's phone flashed lightning bright against the pine ceiling of the master bedroom, waking him just after midnight. Sitting up, he could tell Aurora was sound asleep beside him. Snatching the phone and his flashlight, he unsnapped his shoulder holster for quick access to his gun and started downstairs. He paused at the landing to look at the message, *'intruder alert, level one, garage entrance'* blinked across a green background.

As he reached the bottom step, he could hear the flap of the dog door. *What the hell?* Bastet shot past his feet like a bullet.

Coming around the corner, he trained his flashlight at the bottom of the door between the kitchen and the garage. A thin, petite, bleached blond woman in a sparkling emerald sequin cocktail dress was crawling through the dog door, with some difficulty, on her hands and knees.

In a calm yet authoritative tone, with the flashlight in her eyes, when she looked up, he said, "freeze, federal agent." The woman let out a shrill, high pitched shriek, screaming Aurora's name, numbing his ears. She clasped her arms above her head and planted face-first onto the tile just inside the door, squirming to get through without using her arms. Ethan immediately smelled alcohol.

He crossed his arms, rubbing his sore shoulder as the lights in the kitchen went on, and Aurora came running up behind him. This woman, whoever she was, obviously wasn't a threat, and he just wanted to go back to bed.

"What the hell is going on?" Aurora demanded. Her expression changed from surprise to anger as she caught sight of the woman on the floor, and she clapped her hands over her face. "In the name of all that's holy, Donia, what the fuck are you doing?"

"Aurora!" the drunken woman tumbled through the door finally, scrambling off her hands and knees to stand, lunging at Aurora, arms wide as if to embrace her. Aurora sidestepped her, slipping behind Ethan, which left him no choice but to grab her intoxicated sister before she fell, yet again, on her face. She tripped before he steadied her against the counter in the kitchen, and she plopped herself into a bar chair on the backside of the counter.

She was wearing stiletto heels far too tall to manage in her inebriated state, which she promptly began unbuckling to remove once she sat down. Aurora seethed at her, arms crossed, face vermillion, and furious.

"What are you doing here, Donia? What is wrong with you? Crawling through the dog door in the middle of the night dressed like something straight off the pole. For crying out loud, it's a Wednesday night! You aren't even supposed to know I'm here. How did you find me?" Aurora's temper was bubbling, and for how much Ethan wanted to retreat, he remembered the night she had cold-heartedly slammed the face of an Egyptian assassin into the deck without a second thought. He figured he'd better stick around, just in case.

Donia was still catching her breath, sneering at Ethan as he leaned calmly on the counter across from her, unaffected, patiently observing.

"Answer me!" Aurora snapped.

"Lily told me, though she shouldn't have had to, you should have told me yourself," Donia whined.

Lily was David's youngest daughter, and Aurora had to wonder if he'd explained the situation to her or if she'd possibly just overheard a conversation he'd had.

"Do you not remember last time we spoke you chastised me for getting myself into such a mess, to be hunted by a serial killer? Are you seriously so dense you fail to realize the entire point of me being here is so that no one knows where I am? You're lucky he didn't shoot you!" Aurora pointed at Ethan.

Donia dropped the shoes carelessly to the floor and went to retrieve a glass of water, suddenly exuding an attitude worthy of a teenager in a tantrum. She shot Ethan a wary look, examining him head to toe, as she filled the glass at the refrigerator beside where he stood. She swayed as she turned back to the chair, and he could see her face, mascara that had run and smudged, eyes puffy, crimson, and swollen. Her makeup had smeared, and deep lines beneath showed a woman who looked much older than she undoubtedly was.

Aurora went to Ethan, "Can I have your phone, please? We need to call her a cab and get her out of here." Without a word, he handed it to her, and she began looking for a phone number.

"You don't want to see me at all?" Donia's voice cracked slightly, upset.

"I don't care to see you like this, no." Aurora was terse, but as she looked up, she could see tears rimming Donia's eyes as she hung her head in her hands. "Why do you do this, Donia? What is it? You can't ever call me, make plans with me, spend time with me when you're sober, and have your shit together, but I'm supposed to take all your negativity and be your support whenever you need it. I'm over it."

Ethan felt the emotion of the moment shifting, he could see Aurora's hand tremble, see her breathing change, and Donia began to sob. He wasn't sure what to do, but he knew what he didn't want to have happen, and he for sure didn't want to get caught in the middle. He went and stood beside Aurora, gently placing one hand on her back reassuringly he reached carefully and took the phone back, she hadn't dialed yet. He slipped it into his pocket and, taking her hand, gingerly leaned in to whisper to her. Her body tensed.

"I know you're upset, but she obviously has something going on she needs to unload, it might be good for you two just to talk a little. I'm here, and I'm not going anywhere. I don't know her at all, I still don't know you all that well, but I know enough to see you're stronger than her and you already know you're allowed to block toxic people from your life. Maybe this is your chance to make peace with the situation. Get some closure."

She leaned into him, just briefly, and squeezed his hand. When their eyes met, he could see the torment, the stress, and anxiety in them, but she nodded. He caressed her back before retreating to the living room, where he could still monitor the situation without being *in it*.

"So, what is it?" Aurora tried not to be rude, but she wasn't sure she was up for dealing with her sister.

"Why do you think I need something? Why is it you think Mom and I are on the same side? Do you think she doesn't despise me just as much? I've been calling her, and she hasn't called me back in days. She doesn't care about me any more than she does you," Donia blubbered.

"Why is it you always take her side? You constantly defend her and treat me like she's right. Do you know what she did? Last week?" Donia shook her head and sipped more water, wiping her already scarlet eyes with the back of leathery, wrinkled hands. "She sent Gerhardt after me."

Donia's face paled, she sat back in her chair, shaking her head, tears overflowing.

"No way," she squeaked.

"Yes, she did," Aurora's emotions began to bleed out.

"Why? For what?"

"If it weren't for E-," Aurora caught herself, trying to keep the personal out of the situation, "Agent Hartman, I'd be on a yacht in international waters right now. She wanted them to kidnap me; they admitted to it."

"Shit, of course, she did. She always hated your independence," Donia hung her head.

"Yet you called me that same morning to tell me how ungrateful I was. You scolded me for landing *myself* in such a mess. None of this has been my fault Donia, but you know who made it worse?" Aurora demanded, leaning over the counter, voice rising. "Rashida!" she shouted, "the grand Rashida Soileaux decided I couldn't take care of myself, that even the FBI couldn't care for me, so she sent men to forcefully remove me against my will."

Tears were streaming down Donia's face now, her head hanging in her hands, her shoulders racked with sobs.

"I should have known. I should have seen it, the way she called me last week. Her façade of feelings wasn't genuine. I fell for it. I fall for it every time. She's manipulative, and I never see it. I'm sorry," Donia said.

Aurora stood in shock.

"That's why I came. I wanted to apologize. Randy dumped me. I slept with Jillie's boyfriend a month ago, and she found out, and she told Randy, and my life has fallen apart. I can't do anything right, and I know it's all my own fault. Jillie was the last friend I had, and I don't know what's wrong with me. I was so jealous of her. I'm just a disgusting mess, but I thought of all the people who could forgive me, maybe you could. I'm so sorry, Aura."

Aurora stood stock still in the kitchen with her arms crossed. Her stomach rolled and heaved, tingling as it did hula hoops around her waist. Her emotions were in shreds. Donia deserved everything she had coming to her. Everyone knew it. Jillian Smith had been her best friend through thick and thin since she was in junior high school and was the only person who had maintained a good relationship with her. It was the last straw, and it was apparent Donia knew it. At the moment, Aurora wasn't sure she wanted to give the inch her sister was sure to take a mile with instead.

Donia sat and sobbed, disheveled, drunk and disoriented in the white kitchen light, a total wreck. Aurora had been so angry, so bitter, and so ready to discard her from her life, but over the edge of the couch, she could see the back of Ethan's head. She thought about his family, what he had been through, how they had managed to be supportive of each other. Though she wanted to cut ties and move on, she realized, if there was anyone she was cutting ties with, it was her mother. Donia was her only family.

"I'm sorry, I'm going to go, you're right, I shouldn't have come," Donia slipped awkwardly off the stool and tottered as she picked up her shoes. Aurora walked around the counter tentatively, contemplating if she wanted to let her go or not. She was tired, emotionally, physically, and in her soul. But she couldn't quite bring herself to cast her only sister aside.

Donia tripped towards the front door, and Aurora followed her, reaching the entry Ethan was at her arm as the front door swung open.

"I'd prefer that you stay inside," he whispered, one eye on Donia.

"I won't go off the front porch. I want to see her get home safely."

"You want her home safe how about I call the Sheriff?" Aurora nodded as Ethan pulled out his phone.

"Donia, wait," Aurora stepped quickly out the door behind her sister. "Ethan's going to call someone for you to get you home." Pulling the door shut behind her, Aurora caught her sister by the arm. "Sit, wait for someone to come, alright?"

"Why? I walked here. I can walk back to the Hyatt."

"You walked all the way here from the Hyatt in those heels?" Aurora was stunned. Her sister couldn't usually get in a car that wasn't a limousine, let alone walk anywhere, especially more than a mile from the beach hotel.

"I did. After I danced all night, hoping anyone would pay any attention to me." Aurora pulled her down onto a swing on the front porch. "I don't know what I was thinking. I don't even like Jillie's boyfriend; he's chubby. But we went out on the boat, and the way he looked at her versus the way Randy was looking at me, I got so jealous. He was doting on her like they were happy."

And you just couldn't stand that it wasn't you, never happy enough with what you have, Aurora thought.

"I thought I would be married by now, some socialite somewhere in the golf club hosting parties as the trophy wife. No one wants me. I'm washed up, wrinkled, sagging and old, and Mom cut me off from the bank account." It was the first time Aurora had heard her talk that way, ever. She was always confident, boasting, self-centered, and full of herself despite a lack of achievements. The two sat quietly for a minute, letting the fresh, crisp mountain air clear their heads. After a long pause, Donia rested her hand on Aurora's knee,

"After losing Randy, I guess it hit me I'm not sure why I do most of the things I do. I'm sorry. I miss you, and I miss Dad, and I guess I only listen to Mom because she's the only one that will talk to me. You have your career and your friends that love you for who you are instead of something you're pretending to be." She hung her head, and in the moonlight, Aurora could see the creases on her, wear and tear from too many years of sun and partying.

"My life isn't all rainbows and sparkles," Aurora was trying to be positive; it wasn't easy.

"At least you have a life. You have your patients and your degree, like Dad, you were always so much like Dad. You never needed us. You've always been on your own two feet."

"Remember that summer after my third year of college, when I wasn't sure I wanted to keep going?" Aurora squeezed her sister's hand as she laughed.

"Of course I do. It was probably my favorite summer of all time. That fake I.D. I got you, the clubs and the beaches and the parties, staying out late just the two of us. It was the time of my life. Not what my life is like now, constantly on the hunt for the next guy who will dump me. And then you left, back to the real world and onto things bigger and better and I became jealous, like I always do. Mom never liked either of us, really, but you were Dad's favorite. He was bound and determined not to screw up with you the way he did with me."

"That's not true," Aurora sat forward.

"Of course it is," Donia swayed. "Mom got what she wanted out of me. I was the vain one who always wanted to shop and have my hair and my nails done, her little trophy. You were Dad's pride and joy with your dedication and commitment and your test scores and how you excelled at everything. You deserve it, though, you know. I never did." Donia's voice cracked, and tears began to surface again.

"You know feeling sorry about it now isn't going to fix anything," Aurora scolded her gently.

"Are you sure?" she asked, "because I was hoping if I could show you how sorry I felt you'd let me fix things with you. Forgive me? Please?" Aurora's heart swelled to bursting, angst and regret seeping into her. She wanted to, but she just wasn't ready. She needed to see more.

"Come back, in a couple of days or a week, when this is all over, we'll spend some time. Right now, I just, I can't..." as Aurora spoke, Donia was on her feet, holding her shoes in her hand. Aurora stood up, started to walk with her, trying to hold her back.

"Donia, wait for a ride," she said as she heard Ethan open the door behind her.

"I don't want a ride. I need the fresh air and time alone." Donia hugged her, and Aurora found it suddenly, strangely, hard to let go.

"It has to be forty degrees out here, it's cold, you can wait." Donia had peeled away from her, and as she attempted to pursue, Ethan had her by the waist.

"Donia, wait!" Aurora called out, but Ethan's grip was unrelenting. He was like a statue come to life, hard as stone strong as steel. She wasn't going anywhere he didn't want her to, her petite frame was powerless in his arms. He pulled her back inside as Donia went out onto the road and disappeared to the east of the house, shuffling clumsily with her head down. Aurora tried to pull away, squirmed, and twisted, but Ethan dragged her in, locking the door behind her as he let her go.

His face was stern in the dim light spilling from the kitchen.

"I called the Sheriff's office, they've sent someone to get her, they'll find her on the road and make sure she's alright. They had an excellent response time last I had to call," he tried to sound reassuring.

"I can't just let her go like this, she's drunk, she's barefoot, she can't take care of herself."

"The Sheriff will take care of her," he insisted.

Aurora lunged to try and get past him, doing her best to shove him out of the way, only accomplishing bouncing off of his unmovable frame. She found her temper rising, his easy control of her and the situation had her blood beginning to boil.

"So what?" she snapped, "because she hasn't been good to me, I'm not allowed to stick up for her? All that's left is blood, so she's not supposed to mean anything? You can't relate to any of it having your *perfect* family, can you? Your doting mother, who actually loves you, your dad, who's still around when you need him. Your normal, I'm sure, wholesome brothers for every holiday and birthday prevents you from seeing how unwilling I am to let my sister—however poorly she's treated me—put herself in harm's way?" She was seething, hissing, and ready to strike out at him even as he loomed over her like a giant, ushering her unwillingly back towards the living room. That made it all even worse, how vastly dominant he was over her, how she was powerless to overcome him physically.

"Aurora," his tone was firm but soft, trying hard to back her off the ledge she had perched herself on, with his unfortunate encouragement. "Calm down. She won't be alone for more than a block."

"How dare you tell me to calm down, you were the one who told me to let her stay! You told me to talk to her, and now you want me to watch her walk into the cold dead of night alone. Get out of my way!" she screeched, shoving at him as hard as she could, and when she made no progress, she stood back and lashed out, slapping him hard across the face.

The loud crack her flat hand made against his cheek shocked her, and his hands were around her wrists before she could recoil. Twisting her arms behind her, he had her off her feet. Walking her back to the couch, he planted her flat on her back, crushing down on top of her.

"Get off of me!" she squirmed, wiggled, fought, and even tried to scratch, not making any difference. Ethan said nothing, holding her firm and pressing her into the plush cushions he restrained her without hurting her. His bodyweight alone was more than she could hope to manage. His face only inches from hers; he showed no emotion, no sign of temper or anger.

"Is this part of your assignment? To tell me how to live my life, then keep me from living it?" She was unraveling, fighting against him for all she was worth making no progress at all as he remained stoic. He moved both of her wrists into one massive hand. Still maintaining control over her, he leaned up on one elbow, patience steadying him. As she wore herself out, her physical resistance waning, tears began to seep up in her eyes. He waited, observing her as she drained emotionally.

When she stopped pulling to get away from him, he asked, "Can I let go without you slapping me again?"

She scowled at him, still angry, the answer in her eyes.

"I'll wait," his voice was frustratingly controlled and light. She twisted her shoulders, trying to square herself against him, realizing for the first time that for how strong and overpowering he was, he had remained gentle. She didn't hurt anywhere. He hadn't even made her wrists burn. His hips and torso pressed against her, his legs crossed over hers, preventing her from moving though not pressing hard enough to hurt. She felt exasperated by the whole situation, cornered and frankly thoroughly pissed.

"Wait for what, my sister, to come back?" As soon she said it, the significance hit her like a punch in the gut. At least her sister *could* come back. His sister never would. She relaxed beneath him, letting tension between them fade, trying desperately to read his eyes. He looked away from her, something in him blocked from opening up to her. She took a deep breath, exhaling slowly, trying to curl her fingers around his arm behind her back, where he still held her. He shifted off her slightly, loosening his grip.

When she was able to pull her hand from behind her, she reached for him, especially regretting her actions when he winced as she brought her hand, even slowly, to his face. The light pink spot on his cheek stood out in the pale light, a reminder she had lashed out in anger, and he had responded with patience. Her heart sagged, ashamed, and full of regret. He wouldn't look at her.

"I'm sorry," she whispered, caressing his cheek. She could feel his weight still, leaning on her careful not to stifle her. His strength, the sheer mass of his thigh between her legs, his arms encasing her, set her insides simmering. She caressed his cheek, ran her fingers through his hair, and forced his face to get him to look at her.

"I'm sorry, really, I lashed out angry without thinking and that was awful of me to say, I didn't mean it that way." She whispered again, coaxing him to meet her eyes, his expression pained her, she had hurt him. Her fingers ran along his neck and shoulder, gently dragging her nails over his skin, sending sparks through him. She turned herself, raising her hip to cup against his torso like a puzzle piece. The muscles of his back were taut, intense, and holding him away from her. She tugged on his neck, curling her arm behind him as she squeezed him.

His face lowered to her, and she grazed his cheek with her lips, circling the red spot she had left. Painstakingly slowly she kissed his face, doing her best to undo the damage she had done, and kiss by kiss his body softened. Heat radiating from him soaked into her, warming her from the outside cold as he relaxed onto her. Her legs intertwined with his, drawing him over her. When his breathing slowed, she turned his face and, with the airy touch of a butterfly, passed her lips over his.

Opening herself to him, holding him against her, she could feel his heart pulsing in his chest like a kick drum, steady and reliable. Fingers in his hair, she rolled her head back and invited his kiss as she embraced him. Hesitant at first, as her nails set electricity through him, he leaned into her, licking into her mouth. Welcoming him, she clung as if she'd fall if he let her go.

Pressing down on her, something desperate deep inside overtook him, a need for her and what only she had to offer. He kissed her with abandon, disregarding everything around them, lost in her. Her lips curving around his, the taste of her still fresh and light, the silky softness of her skin consumed him, burning in him something he couldn't extinguish. She moved against him with wanton desire, sexy and hungry.

With every ounce of willpower that he could muster, he held her back. Breathing heavily, he went up on his elbows, burying his face in her shoulder, smelling her fresh and spicy, wondering how long he could manage this game they were playing. Her arms came to her sides and he laced his fingers into hers, sliding his face down to rest on her chest.

"I'm sorry, all I do is screw up, I'm so sorry," her voice was weak. He shot upright, looking down at her intently.

"You've nothing to be sorry for. I want you. I can't help it. I don't want to be sorry for it, but it's getting in the way of what I'm supposed to be doing here. I need to focus, get this case wrapped up, but I can't if we're constantly," he realized he wasn't sure what to call it, what was going on between them, "doing this, whatever we're doing." He stood up, pulling her with him.

"I'm sorry," she couldn't look at him, "I feel like I'm just jumping from one mistake to another."

"Stop it," he pulled her behind him, shutting off lights.

"No, really," she traipsed lightly after him, "I should never have said those things about your family. You all have things figured out way better than mine."

He just sighed and hurried her towards the bed, shutting off lights behind her.

"It's never black and white, no one, no family is perfect. Sometimes we all just make due, and you've had a harder time of that than most. Just try to prioritize right now, your sister isn't the most important problem on your plate to handle. Keeping you safe and in one piece is. She shouldn't have been here, she puts you at risk and though I care, don't mistake my actions for disregard, she isn't my responsibility. You are."

She sat on the bed in the dark, staring out over the lake. She was worried about her sister, about herself, about Ethan and how he perceived her, if there would be more between them in the future or if she would end up becoming her own worst enemy.

Chapter Twenty-Three

When Aurora woke the next morning, Ethan was already downstairs, head down in his laptop, and on the phone. She desperately wanted to talk to him, to work through what had happened the night before, but she could tell by the tension in the house that wasn't what he wanted. She did her best to stay out of his way and instead called Trent. After three pastries she didn't need, two cups of coffee, a pedicure, and a two-hour conversation with Trent, she gave up.

She wanted Ethan, wanted all of this to be over, but in the meantime, she knew admiring him from afar would have to keep her appetite at bay until she could devour him all she wanted without messing things up. She caught up on reading, spent a good portion of the morning on the beach, and by three had decided she wanted Italian food for dinner.

Downstairs she felt a pang of anxiety interrupting Ethan even to ask about ordering food.

"I thought we could do Italian for dinner? There's a restaurant that does a pretty good job of calzones I like. Does that sound good?" He glanced up at her briefly and nodded shrugging.

"Sure, that's fine."

"I also think we should get some more groceries, is that something you can pick up or should I get it from eCart and have it delivered?"

"Deliver it," he answered without looking up.

His short responses, the way he was laser-focused on his laptop, and the array of gruesome new photos she had not seen before, didn't want to see, spread across the table gave her the impression she wasn't getting more from him. Deciding it was best not to poke the bear, she secluded herself in the office, picking out groceries and ordering delivery for dinner on David's laptop.

It hadn't even dawned on her that it was the Fourth of July. Deciding even though the situation wasn't prime for jovial partying she still couldn't let the holiday pass without some kind of celebration, so she ordered a fancy red white and blue cake for dessert from the grocery store bakery.

When she finished, bored, and already having absorbed too much sun, she curled up on the couch with Bastet and a comedy movie with Seth Rogan, longing for Ethan to join her, trying to be patient. By seven, she was relieved beyond belief to hear the laptop snap shut behind her. Glancing over her shoulder, trying to be sly, she saw him filling up a water glass, headed upstairs. Before she could follow him to see what he was doing, the doorbell rang. Hopping up to get it, she recognized the logo on the car through the window as the local grocery store.

"Groceries are here," she called to him, though he was halfway back down the stairs already.

"Wait," he was more on edge than she expected him to be, and before he opened the door, was careful to check out the window, and to her surprise, unclipped the gun from the holster on his chest.

He only opened the door enough to allow the grocery bags inside, and before Aurora could tip the delivery girl had locked it closed on her.

"No, wait, I need to tip her," she shoved a twenty-dollar bill at him, surprised when he didn't immediately open the door again. "Call her back. I don't want cruddy produce. They work hard for their money and deserve a tip."

Begrudgingly he opened the door again, called the delivery girl back, and handed her the money. Locking the door behind her again, he grabbed a couple of bags and headed for the kitchen, she picked up the remainder and followed him.

"Is everything alright?" she asked. Ethan took a deep breath that had her nerves on high alert.

"At the moment, things are fine, but I got some new information today, and I just want to be extra careful."

"Alright," her heart sped up, "what new information? Careful how?" she asked.

"Don't worry about it, just do as I say, please. Don't answer the door without me, stay in the house unless I'm with you, that's all." Chills ran through her. "Right now, I'm going to go use the exercise equipment in the anteroom and take a shower. I'll be down shortly." He left her to finish putting groceries away.

The change in him, to see him more professional and colder unnerved her. She felt as though she had just cracked his rough exterior shell for good, and suddenly it was back, twice as thick as before. She unloaded the groceries and decided if the evening was going to be remotely tolerable, she needed wine.

Popping a bottle of Barbera open as Bastet danced around her feet, the doorbell had her coming nearly unhinged. She went to the foot of the stairs and called for Ethan. He didn't respond. She stood there, calling again, looking out through the glass of the front door at the small figure standing outside. Figuring he must be in the shower and must have known she was expecting dinner to be delivered, she peered out the window and made a decision.

Seeing only one car, one young woman, and bags to match her order, she opened the door. A college-age girl offered her the food with a warm greeting and a pretty smile. It smelled amazing. Aurora fished out cash for a tip, and as she held it out, noticed the girl was looking around behind her.

"Thanks," she said with a smile as she took the cash. "Um, this is kinda weird, but there was this guy on your curb when I pulled up, just past the bushes there." Aurora's heart started to pound. "He caught me as I was coming out of my car, and he said if you were alone that I should give this to you." The girl fished in her pocket and produced a small ivory envelope that bulged in the middle.

"He said if there was a guy with you not to give it to you, I hope it doesn't get you in trouble with like, your husband, or something." She looked so innocent, so honest. Aurora took the envelope with trembling fingers.

"Thank you," Aurora looked around past her, hoping to see someone. There was no one outside as far as she could tell.

"He seemed super nice, and he paid me forty bucks, and he said if you had a guy with you that I should just keep it and throw it in the trash."

"Yes, it's fine, thank you. Have a nice night," Aurora closed the door on her but watched her walk back to the car and was sure to see her get in and drive away safely. Ethan's words came back to her as she began to sweat. Whatever was in the envelope, he wasn't supposed to know about it. She took the take out containers to the kitchen counter and slipped into the pantry to open the note.

The envelope had no name, but as she tore it open, a gush of disgust wrapped in terror ripped through her. A simple, dull yellow note was inside with a portion of a fingernail stapled roughly to one corner, blood dried and cracking as the letter slid out of the envelope. She covered her mouth in a weak attempt to prevent the cry of fear from escaping. She didn't have to read the words to know the fingernail belonged to her sister.

The note read:

The polish is such a pretty emerald green, such a shame for your sister to waste even a dollar on something just to make a point. If you want to see her ever again, you will leave your knight in shining armor without speaking a word of this, and meet me on the dock at eleven p.m. sharp. Don't be late. At edgewater, if there's observation by anyone else, I will end her.

Aurora's heart thundered, threatening to shatter her rib cage. She clutched the note in horror, hoping at any moment that she would wake up, but it wasn't a dream. Her mind swirled a thousand miles a second. Ethan had just told her she needed to be extra careful, but he had also let Donia walk into the night alone, he was responsible for her, not for her sister. Did that make it right? He said he had called the Sheriff, what had happened?

She needed time to think, time to decide, she wasn't sure about anything. She reread the note, committing every word to memory, and then read it twice more. It didn't flow. Something was wrong with the terms used. Shouldn't it have said *'at the water's edge'* or *'at the edge of the water'* instead of edgewater? *Shouldn't that be two words?* As she mouthed the words to herself, it hit her. Edgewater and Observation. Dollar and Point.

Oh no, he knows where David and Blanche live.

As if the hand of evil itself passed through her, she went snowflake cold, felt as if she were falling like one, drifting aloft in a dizzying storm. How could the killer have found her, found her friends so easily? Her faith in the protection of the FBI, her faith in Ethan, was suddenly shaken to the core. It made her feel alone, vulnerable, exposed, and unable to escape.

The killer only wanted her. Everyone else was just collateral damage. She couldn't allow it. The thought of anything sinister happening to David or Blanche was too much for her to stomach.

She stuffed the note back into the envelope and slipped it into her pocket. She chugged the first glass of Barbera to steady her nerves, knowing she had to get through the rest of the evening without Ethan suspecting anything. She went out and poured herself more, leaning against the counter, stunned and unable to believe the reality.

She had a piece of her sister's finger in her pocket.

Nausea swept through her, and she was nearly hyperventilating, she knew she had to get a grip and get it quick. Ethan was going to be back downstairs any second. She scurried to collect the food, set plates out on the table. She had to act normal, but catching a glimpse of herself in the reflection of the window, she had a feeling, no way was that going to happen.

Setting out serving spoons, she heard footsteps on the stairs and felt like her heart might jump out of her throat. She knew, with absolute certainty, he was going to take one look at her and know she wasn't alright, but the screech from Bastet distracted her. The cat bounded through the kitchen from the dog door, and a blur of fur darted in front of her before she realized what was going on.

A squirrel.

The cat had captured, subdued, dragged inside, and released in the house a small grey squirrel. Her nerves already fried, Ethan at the foot of the stairs, Aurora let loose with a scream that could have curdled milk and hopped onto a chair in the dining room. Bastet hissed, peeled furiously around a corner in a furry blur, and was on top of the squirrel again. The sound was dreadful.

I didn't even know squirrels could make noise!

Ethan came sliding around the corner of the foot of the stairs to see her standing on the chair, clutching her glass, soaked in wine she had just spilled all over herself in total hysteria. The cat and the squirrel were ravaging each other underneath the dining table in what seemed like a duel to the death. He darted to the pantry, retrieved a broom, ran to open the back door, and as Aurora deafened him again with a scream from her toes, swatted at the cat and the wild rodent beneath her feet.

A couple circles around the dining table and Bastet, clearly the predator of the two, had the squirrel herded outside and off the deck to an unknown doom below. Ethan slammed the door, turned to face Aurora dropping the broom, and began to laugh as if he'd never catch his breath. The whole ordeal lasted less than a couple minutes but snapped the last thread of calm Aurora held together.

"Are you alright?" he asked through the laughter, helping her off the chair. She was shaking, thoroughly terrified in more ways than she wanted to share with him, and wasn't ready to deal with any of it. She nodded, still trembling, tears stung her eyes and not for the reason Ethan seemed to be willing to accept.

"I don't know where Bastet learned how to hunt squirrels but what a trick. I'm impressed." He realized the extent of how badly she'd been unnerved and said, "It was just a squirrel, you're alright."

From the moment he had first touched her, his arms had felt good. Reliable and gentle, secure, and reassuring, but as she stood leaning on him now, tears beginning to overflow her eyes, his touch was foreign. She was questioning everything she had felt for the last week and a half, and she couldn't hide the weight of it all. He stopped laughing, steadied her, pulled her against him, and studied her face.

Oh no, he's an FBI profiler, he's going to read the whole situation out of my eyes.

"Are you okay?" he asked again. "Are you hurt? What am I missing?" She shook her head, set her wine glass down, and slipped away from him. "Aurora, where are you going?" he asked.

"I need to change," was the only response she could muster in a hoarse voice. Tears streamed down her face freely. Turning away, she slipped upstairs, hoping for some much-needed solitude.

Changing her shirt, she slipped the note into a drawer in the bathroom to hide it, to give herself time to decide what she was going to do. She composed herself, washed her face, and took deep breaths, trying to calm down. As she stared in the mirror at herself, the entire ordeal came to a threatening head.

David and Blanche had been family to her as long as she could remember. She loved them and would not allow them to be dragged into this mess worse than they already were. The note, she hoped, was a precursor, a hint or a clue and not an indicator she would find them in the aftermath of some terrible fate. Chastising herself for even coming here, she fidgeted with her cell phone to call them, prayed they were alright and that nothing evil had already befallen them.

The call went to voicemail, killing her hope.

She cared for Donia, whether she wanted to admit it or show it, they had grown up together, and her sister was, in whatever small or indirect way, important to her. Donia had come last night with the intent of a genuine apology, for the first time in her life. Ten years older than Aurora, less accomplished and secure, the gesture had held real meaning. She *wanted* to believe her sister loved her. She *wanted* to think they could be friends again, be close again. Ultimately that's what it came down to was what Aurora *wanted* to believe.

She also wanted Ethan. She couldn't explain it, couldn't understand where it was coming from, but she was drawn to him, and he was something for her no other man had ever been. She didn't want to betray him, and for how silly it seemed as a grown woman, she didn't want to disobey him.

She also wanted him to live.

She remembered being locked in the safe room, holding a gun with trembling hands, anticipating his return, terrified through her soul that he might not. Images of him lying unconscious and injured had overwhelmed her. For how much she appreciated the feeling of him being protective of her, she *hated* the idea of him in harm's way on her behalf.

As she remembered the night before, in vivid detail, her decision became clear. Ethan had chosen to allow Donia to leave. He had prevented Aurora from making Donia stay, had made his choice on who needed protection, and that was all that was left for her to do also.

She had to choose who she wanted to protect, who she wanted in her life if there was to be any future at all.

Steadying herself on the bathroom counter, she took a few slow, deep breaths, grabbed her messy wine glass, and headed back downstairs.

Ethan had finished setting out silverware and opening takeout containers, and when he saw her, he walked towards her. Putting his hands on her shoulders, he studied her though she didn't look up to him right away.

"Do you have a deep-seated fear of small rodents that I need to know about?" he asked, jestingly.

"No, it just startled me, that's all."

"Enough for tears?" he brought her chin up so that she had to look at him.

"I guess you just had me on edge from what you said," she lied.

"Ah, yet you answered the door to dinner without me anyway," he caught her.

"I called for you, and you didn't answer, I didn't want her to leave, it was a tiny college girl, alone." He held her in check briefly as she squirmed to get away but ultimately released her. She went and sat at the table, feeling morbid and disgusted. He sat beside her, clearly aware of her distress but seemingly unable to pinpoint from where it stemmed.

"Alright," he said as he scooted his chair in, "I'll let it slide this time, but not again. Don't answer the door or go outside without me, please."

She nodded as someone under oath or in custody for a crime would.

"Are you sure you're alright? You still look pretty rattled," he asked as he slid a calzone onto her plate. The idea of food suddenly nauseated her.

"I guess I had a bit of a sour stomach, to begin with, and what you said gave me some anxiety, then there was the squirrel," she trailed off.

"Yea, it got a little 'Christmas Vacation' in here for a few minutes for sure." He was dishing himself a hefty serving of bowtie pasta, seeming not to notice her lack of appetite. She sipped more wine, feeling the first real effects of having chugged a glass only twenty minutes earlier. Realizing that if she wasn't going to tell him because she intended to go after her sister, most certainly to her doom, that she probably wanted to be at least awake to get to the boat, she slid the wine away from her.

Ethan ate with gusto while she picked at her meal pathetically. When he finished, she stood up, covering her plate with plastic wrap and sticking it in the fridge. She tidied up the table as he stood to help her, examining her with new eyes.

"Is that all you're going to eat?" he asked. She avoided looking at him directly.

"I'm just not very hungry, and I feel a little queasy, I'm just tired I guess and need to go to bed."

He set his plate in the sink, and as she turned to go back upstairs, caught her by the arm.

"How much have you had to drink?" he asked, frowning at her.

"Not enough to feel like I do," he turned her towards him, looking her over meticulously, seeming to notice something wasn't right with her but unable to put the finger on what.

"You don't seem yourself," he said, pulling her into him. Her arms felt limp, her hands unresponsive to what her heart wanted; she blocked herself to him. Turning her face away, she resisted his advances to hold her. For the first time, she felt vulnerable, unsure, and unwilling to allow him to comfort her. He felt like a stranger again, like the first time she had seen him in the office at UCSF.

"I think I just need to go to bed," she pulled away and went upstairs as he watched her every move.

Ethan could see it. He could tell something was wrong. Perhaps he was too hard on her, or he'd sent too rough of a message the night before. She had changed since that afternoon, though, he could tell. He just couldn't understand why. Her touch felt icy, and as he watched her slip away from him upstairs, it was clear, whatever was going on in her head wasn't for sharing. He put the rest of the food away, cleaning up the kitchen with his mind in overdrive. Whatever was bothering her, it wasn't just a tousle between Bastet and a squirrel.

He climbed the stairs at half-past nine, fireworks popping in the distance over the lake, expecting to find her watching them or stretched out reading a book. Instead, the room was dark, and she was in bed. He stood at the giant picture window watching the brilliant colors burst in the sky, the booming rounds resonating with each new set of bright flashes. Keeping an eye on her while he took in the show and the view, he waited to see if she would get up but with nothing otherwise amiss, figured perhaps she really wasn't feeling well and chalked her behavior up to a sour mood.

Chapter Twenty-Four

Aurora had changed into yoga pants and a long-sleeve sweatshirt. Knowing she would be going out to retrieve her sister in less than two hours, knowing she didn't want to wake Ethan as she left, she wanted to be as prepared as possible. She rested in the dark, eyes closed, listening to Ethan come in and ready himself to crawl in beside her. For the first time since she had met him, she was praying he wouldn't reach out and touch her. It hurt. The whole situation was like acid burning its way through her.

She wanted to tell him but didn't want to risk David or Blanche, her sister, or him. She wanted to be loyal and do whatever it would take to rescue Donia, but her heart was still bitter from years of dispute. She had found happiness and trust in this man, and so didn't want to further put him in harm's way, whether it was his job or not. She wasn't sure what lengths Donia would go to for her if her sister felt strongly enough about her to be her savior if roles were reversed, but that was Donia. Aurora knew she was a different person, cut from a different cloth, and it didn't matter what Donia would do for her, she knew what she could and could not live with doing for her sister. She also knew it was probably a death wish to go after her.

Her mind raced like a mouse wheel out of control.

What was she doing? Was she going to walk into the arms of a serial killer willingly? If she didn't, where would that leave her? Could she live with herself knowing she had a chance to save her sister that she gave up? She thought of her father, considered her mother, thought of her whole life, and her stomach churned. Maybe Donia was already dead, could she live with that? Checking the cheap watch she had found in a drawer and snapped on, she found herself missing Trent's cuckoo clock.

A whole new round of anxiety started up. What would Trent say? What would he tell her to do? If she died, how was he going to feel? *Was she going to die?* She didn't want to die. Her mind spun, swirled and dived, and in the process decisions were made, last minute, that she hoped would be her safety net, if it even mattered.

As the clock edged on eleven, she snuck out of bed, stood beside it, listening to Ethan breathing to be sure he didn't wake up. She picked up her shoes to be as quiet as possible and snuck to the bathroom. She had no idea what was waiting for her, but she knew she had to play both sides to her advantage, if at all possible. Sliding the drawer open ever so carefully, she took the note out and placed it on the counter.

She hoped, with any luck, that if Ethan woke to find her missing, he would see it and have an idea of what had happened. She knew, very well, she could get on a boat and in very little time be back in a car on the way to God only knew where, but at least this way he would know where to start. With Bastet at her heels, she slipped downstairs and yanked her shoes on facing the glass doors to the beach.

This house had held so much joy, and so many beautiful memories for her. She hated the idea it could be the end for her. She thought of David and her dad, of how much she had shared growing up spending summer nights here. In a matter of moments, it would be obsolete, she had made her choice, and now she needed to do the best she could with it. At precisely eleven o'clock, without seeing a boat, she opened the door and began walking down the dock anyway.

She knew there was surveillance, knew someone would see her, but she couldn't risk letting the chance to see her sister again pass her by. They had so much to put behind them. Rushing to the end of the dock her heart nearly leaped from her chest as a boat sliced through the water towards her. Pulling up with the driver's side closest, barely slowing enough for her to get in, she obediently stepped on board at the instruction of a dark-haired man who promptly, as her footing caught the floor beside him, slammed her in the side of the head with something hard, knocking her out cold.

Aurora wasn't sure how long she'd been unconscious, but when she woke up, her hands and feet were bound, she was lying flat on the floor of a boat, her head was splitting with pain, and she was freezing. The side of her head was throbbing, and as she took stock of her surroundings, realized Donia was beside her, either asleep or unconscious herself. The boat was moving fast, and as her eyes adjusted in the dim running lights, she could see a short and stocky dark-haired man driving.

It was too late to panic. She had made her decision, and now she only had to decide how she was going to deal with it. She wiggled closer to Donia, shoving her with a knee, trying to wake her up. She didn't respond. Aurora wasn't gagged, but she was sure there was no one to hear her scream anyway. She thought about trying to call out to her sister to rouse her, but she was confident it would only alert their captor to her consciousness.

Think, there has to be an angle or a weakness. This man lost his mind because he lost his daughter, think! She demanded of herself.

She tried to gauge how long they had been traveling, and how fast, but she had no point of reference and no idea what kind of boat they were in or of what speed it was capable. She was already chilled to the bone when the driver cut the engine.

As he turned, she failed to close her eyes in time, and he laughed. In the quiet of what she was sure was the center of the lake, there was no hope of anyone hearing them.

"Don't lie to me. I hate that." She found her own words echoing in his voice as he stood above her, pulling her up roughly. She said nothing.

"You were the most prized, final challenge for me, and you were difficult, but worth it in the end." He had picked her up and set her on the back of the boat. "Do you remember me?" he asked.

She looked at him intently, ice flowing in her veins, anger billowing from her soul. After all, she was the daughter of Rashida Soileaux, if her mother was capable of turning a blind eye to things like murder, then so should she be.

"Of course I do. Your daughter had cancer she was born with and had no chance of survival. My father stuck his neck out to get her the best care that could be offered." The punch came out of nowhere, sending Aurora reeling. Blood filled her mouth as stars clouded her vision.

"Bitch," he screamed. "You have no idea what she had and what we went through. The hospitals, the pretentious doctors, the lazy nurses, the stupid technicians, and all the dirty staff, it is your fault she died!" His voice roared so loud, her ears rang.

Aurora hadn't been ready for the level of hate he spewed, but as she got her bearings, she knew she would have to be prepared to anticipate his next move. Blood oozed out of her mouth, running down her chin in fast streams.

Wake up, Donia! She had no idea how she was getting them both out of the situation now if she could at all.

"Your father, your astute and well educated, high and supreme father. I trusted him, my wife trusted him, and you know what we got. I know you do!" he was yelling in her face at the top of his lungs spitting and shaking. "One of you killed her. I thought I cared which one, I thought I wanted to know so I could make sure that woman suffered the most but after I killed the second stuck up, self-centered, holier than thou wench I realized—I don't care." His rant had rolled back to a nasty and cold statement with an undertone of disgust.

He had a hold of her shirt, twisting it tightly in a fist at her chest as he shoved her against the cold leather of the seat of the boat, crushing his knuckles against her tender sternum. She could see the blood from her face dripping on his dark skin, where he held her, and he didn't seem to care if he noticed at all.

"I know it was a woman because when he came to tell us what had happened, he said *'she'* when he described the person using the machine. I watched you all walk out together. None of you even looked upset, none of you cared. My girl, my beautiful baby girl, was gone, and all she was to you was a test case, a research project, collateral loss in the name of progress." His face had twisted, and he had swiftly shifted from a cracking, unsteady voice of loss to spitting through clenched teeth.

Aurora shook her head, no, "It isn't like that with patients, I never felt that way with any of my patients, neither did my dad, there's no such thing as collateral loss, it's life, all precious life." Her voice quivered, tears surging up uncontrollably as she stammered through bloody lips. He peered at her silently as predator peers at prey before striking, shooting daggers through her heart.

"My wife, my sweet Eda Jean, she was all I had left, and I watched her wither. I watched her heart shatter, and her body fail around her after our girl was taken. Our sweet Candy, and it was all your fault. You stole from us, the last little bit of time we had with her. You and your blood money clinical trial."

She did her best to gather herself, but she began to shake. Between the chill of the night air and the terror coursing through her, she began to understand what a mistake she made.

"The laser," she spat the words out through drying, sticky blood almost involuntarily, "the laser malfunctioned. It wasn't the technician's fault. It was a clinical trial, a hail Mary chance. My dad, he canceled his endorsement right after the surgery. So did I. He felt terrible, he cried." The blow from the back of his closed hand sent her reeling this time. She felt something in her nose snap a little, a crunch, and her head bounced hard off the fiberglass of the boat before he whipped her back to face him.

"Your daddy dearest never knew what it was to lose a child, did he?" He sneered at her, holding her by the hair with his ugly face only inches from hers, she could smell him, nasty and rotten.

"We don't get to choose who fate calls out. Let my sister go. She isn't who you wanted." It was all she could think to say. Life got to choose. For all the time she had spent trying to save people, *children*, she knew more than anyone she had no power in the grand scheme of life. Just like the teenage patient she was supposed to operate on who killed herself the night before her last surgery, she had no power to save those who were set in the stars to knock on the doors of heaven.

How ironic, she thought, *to be standing at deaths' door accepting the reality of fate.*

He shook her abruptly, grabbing her face with steel fingers as her head bobbed helplessly, looking past her into the dark for some reason. She could still see Donia unconscious on the floor then looked up to the stars wondering if she'd done the right thing. Were they both just going to die?

"I'm going to enjoy giving fate a helping hand tonight," he pitched her backward hard, and if it weren't for the way he held her legs and a rope bound to her tied hands, she would have been overboard, tumbling into the water. Blood ran across her face, tasting metallic and thick. Her nose was full of it, congealed and clotting. As she lay over the back of the boat, she thought she heard a sound, faint like an engine. Before she could identify it, a towel was over her face, and a stream of water covered it.

She struggled to breathe, turning her head she fought to keep her face free, to no avail. Her attacker swung her legs up, kicking her hard so that her feet landed in the water. Her hands, secured by a long rope, attached her to the back of the boat as the motor kicked on. Her heart raced, threatening to render her unconscious before he could cause her more harm.

The boat began to move, slowly this time, at a trolling speed used for fishing and her body, held tight only by the rope around her hands, slid farther into the water. It was cold, stealing what small amount of air she could still find beneath the towel before more water poured over her face. She kicked, twisting, feeling like she was drowning. The more she struggled, the more she slipped into the water.

Heraldson was cursing her and enjoying her misery, her panic. She could vaguely hear him talking in a vile and angry tone as he yet again poured more water over her face. She realized he was waterboarding her. The more she fought the towel strangling and drowning her, the faster she slipped off the back step into the water. Her choices were to breathe the stream of water coating her face or slip into the depths of the icy lake with her hands and feet bound.

Desperate to be free, twisting, and turning, she tried to pull herself up by the rope binding her, but he only let out more slack. She was submerged in the water now. Her body was flailing off the back of the boat as she fought to keep her head above the surface and the towel caught in the wake.

Her life flashed before her eyes and the last face she saw clearly was Ethan. She pulled with all she had left in her, lifting herself one last time above the surface, and was lost beneath the water. It seemed like a long time her body refused to give up before finally succumbing to unconsciousness, but as the cold, black water overtook her, she slipped away.

Chapter Twenty-Five

Ethan wasn't sure what woke him up, a sound, a chill, a dream, or a premonition, but as soon as his eyes opened, he could hear the gurgle of a boat motor, too close. As he sat up, the flash from his phone lit the room like lightning. Cold air off the lake was wafting in the windows, and he could smell fresh spray. As he snatched the phone, the number sent panic through him. It was the cyber-surveillance team. He leaped to his feet and dashed to the window to catch only a glimpse of white curling wake spreading away from the shore in the back of the house.

He answered the phone, skipped the greeting, barked for them to send backup and dispatch the Coast Guard, and began running down the stairs three at a time. He yelled for Aurora, but he knew already, without even the lack of her response, that she was gone. In only a thin black cotton shirt and his running sweats, he dashed downstairs through the game room towards the boathouse.

Snatching keys to a jet ski off the ring inside the door, he jumped off the edge of the indoor dock, heart pounding like it would break ribs if the damn garage door went up any slower. He tossed his phone in the center beneath the seat as the engine fired up. The instant he was able to sneak under, he sped out, narrowly avoiding slamming into the boat parked just outside, still moored to the dock. The moonlit air was frigid. The nights were nothing like northern California, and the temperature had dropped to a brisk fifty-two degrees since sunset.

His knuckles were white on the grip of the throttle as he stood up to look as far as he could. Eyes still adjusting he searched, with only starlight and the fingernail moon to guide him, he felt blind. Shooting straight out and away from the shore, a sense of panic caught him. He had no idea what he was looking for, no life jacket, nothing to keep warm, and his GPS would be useless as soon as his phone got wet, which was only a matter of time.

Several hundred yards from shore, he forced himself to stop, hearing only the gurgle of the motor he cut it, praying without the engine noise he would be able to hear another boat. The slapping of the water against the sides of the jet ski was all that remained. The night was still as the water rocked him back and forth.

His head whipped side to side, searching, begging as he strained to hear or see anything that might give him an idea of where the boat carrying Aurora had gone. Doubt swelled in him. What if it was a diversion? What if she wasn't even on the lake but instead had been whisked away by car? He looked back to the house, and it was dark still. Drawing on endless hours of training and years of experience, he forced himself to stop, to calm.

All there was to hear, see, or feel was the water. Rolling, pulsing, freezing, black, and seemingly endless water, and that's when it hit him. Wake. The boat had to leave a wake, and in the still and silent night, it would be the only thing causing ripples in the perfectly calm water. It rolled sideways, undulating in long and lazy waves transverse beneath him. It could only be coming from one direction, so starting the engine, he twisted the throttle full open and followed the waves.

He sped forward, the mountain air stinging his face, numbing his fingers and forcing him to steel himself against shivering. Minutes passed like days as he raced across the open water as fast as the engine would carry him. The shoreline had become only a silhouette of the horizon as the depth of the water under him felt threatening. He lost the wake beneath him in the speed, so he released the throttle and immediately cut the engine, closing his eyes to listen.

This time, above the washing of the water around his feet, he could hear a thrum, a low and throaty engine sound, and as he opened his eyes, he could see, just barely in the distance, a glimmer on the surface. Firing the engine up again, he opened the throttle, surging across the water as the jet ski thrust caught and darted through the midnight.

His eyes were blurry, dry, and stinging. Keeping them shut, he opened them only briefly to be sure he was still closing on his target. The dim light of the speedboat was lost occasionally against the twinkle of city lights behind it, causing his heart to hammer uncontrollably. *I'm not losing her*, he thought, *not tonight.*

He raced on.

Seeing the faint light in front of him glow brighter, then begin to fade again, he realized his target was aware of his pursuit. The throttle wouldn't turn anymore, and at top speed already, even on water as smooth as glass, he feared he wouldn't overtake the boat in time to stop whatever was happening on board.

"It's expensive, which means it's fancy, it has trim," he could hear Aurora's voice, see her tan complexion smiling in his mind, her gold-flecked eyes dancing. His fingers traced the handles of the jet ski searching for the button. When he found it, he felt the lift and thanked heaven.

Closing fast on his target, he realized it had slowed tremendously, and his mind searched for reasons for the change. As he neared, his worst fear was realized. The boat was trolling, with no one at the wheel, and why would there be, in the center of Tahoe, there was more than enough room to roam.

Instead of steering, the shadow of a man perched off the back held the Bimini rail with one hand and controlled a rope with the other. Someone was in tow, in the water, being dragged, and Ethan's heart surged into his throat, refusing to imagine, but still knowing, it had to be Aurora. The silhouette of the devil himself had the rope looped around the tow cleat, loosening it little by little.

Dear God, if she hasn't drowned already, please, I'll do anything, don't let her die. The prayer rose fast from Ethan's heart, without forming words in his mind as he swerved the jet ski towards the back of the boat. As it became clear the man controlling the rope was aware his time was running out, Ethan watched in breathless horror as his hands rose above his head, showing he'd let go of the line.

Less than twenty-five feet from the back of the boat, Ethan pulled the emergency kill switch out of the ignition, used as much of the forward thrust left in the motion of the jet ski, and dove into the inky water.

The cold was sharp enough that his lungs immediately ached to take a breath, the shock of the chill raced through him, but he forced his muscles to cooperate and swam. Eyes open, it did no good; the crystal clear water was as dark as hell. In the pitch-black, as he dove with all sound drowned out, all light beyond reach, he stressed himself to the limit and prayed.

His body was aching, his lungs ready to burst, disorientation threatening to consume him he searched. Swinging his arms wide and refusing to give up, a glint caught his eye. He wasn't sure if it was a color or a trick of the moonlight, but he twisted himself painfully deeper and to the left, and just as he thought madness would overcome him, he felt rope.

The rough and callous edge brushed against his forearm, and he lunged, spinning his arm in the hope of snaring the long lead, and he did. Feeling dead weight at the end, he pulled, fought for all he had left in him to the surface, dragging what he prayed was still the living, breathing love of his life, to air.

Breaching the surface, he gasped, taking in enough breath to regain his strength he pulled, one arm over the other, barely maintaining his head above water as he struggled. It felt like forever, as if he were raising her from the floor of the lake inch by inch. Finally, her figure appeared, limp and lifeless, pale as he'd never seen her, face down the rope held her by her wrists.

Lunging, he grabbed her head by the hair, trying desperately to get her face above water first. She didn't respond. Searching his surroundings with air stinging his lungs and water searing his eyes, he located the jet ski thirty feet away and swam with all his strength, pulling her with him as best he could while keeping her head above water. Halfway to the jet ski doom loomed over him, *I'm never going to make it,* he thought, *she's already dead.* The bitterness of the possibility weakened his spirit, but the feel of her skin against his hardened his resolve.

He was no quitter. He was never going to give up on her.

Reaching the jet ski after what seemed like swimming the English Chanel, he found himself forced to let her dangle so he could right himself on the seat before pulling her onto his lap. He slid back, flopped her lifeless figure face down over the seat, pushing on her back first in the hope of expelling as much water from her lungs as possible.

Rolling her over to an awkward position, he plugged her nose, planted his mouth on hers, and did his best to revive her. He stood up, sliding her beneath him on the seat he fought to keep her straight, to keep them from tipping over, pressing on her chest and breathing again into her lungs, his lips clamped on hers. He began to shake, the cold of the night overtook them both, some part of him snapped.

"Aurora!" he screamed, his voice sounding unfamiliar, threatening. He slapped her face, rolled her onto her side, refusing to believe she was dead. He leaned over her and bringing her hands down, untied the rope. It slithered into the water and sank as he lifted her and draped her over his knees.

Starting the jet ski, he turned towards the north shore. He wasn't even sure where he was, wasn't sure how far he had come, or where he should aim to return. Wind whipping through his ears, feeling like he would be a solid block of ice before they got back, the memory of her voice came to him.

Remembering the sweat on her skin against his was so real, so tangible, the warm feel of how soft she was. He looked to the sky and found the constellations, found the big dipper, 'an asterism' he could hear her laugh, and using its handle he aimed towards where the house should be on the shoreline.

Minutes felt like hours, speeding along on the water in the night. His mind raced through the case, her kiss, his sister, the killer, her laugh, and her touch, his family and hers, like his life was flashing before his eyes. As the silhouette of trees became more defined, within a couple hundred yards of the shore, he could see the red and blue flashing lights, and he felt her move.

Her hand closed around his ankle, and the muscles of her abdomen tightened as she struggled still face down across his thighs. He let go of the throttle, leaving them bobbing in the water.

"Aurora," he lifted her to face him, feeling stiff and frozen, numb and shaky, "talk to me, say something."

She coughed and sputtered, said his name weakly as she choked, her arms searched for him, closed around him, and her fingers dug into his back. He swung her legs over his and around him, held her fast against him as he twisted the throttle again. She began shaking violently, gasping as she clung to him. Aiming for the flashing lights, going as fast as the engine would take them, he held onto her as tight as he could, gliding across the surface of the lake.

When the house came into clear view, he aimed straight for the beach and slammed the jet ski into it hard enough to knock them both against the handle bars. He wanted to be swift, strong, and in control but found himself clumsy and numb, so cold he was having a hard time moving. He awkwardly eased her off the jet ski, the sand beneath his feet felt warm compared to the icy water and chill of the wind.

"Stay with me, don't give up," he said to her through his shivering.

Stumbling, struggling, but refusing to quit, he clambered up on to the deck. He set Aurora down on the stairs and threw open the lid to the hot tub. It hadn't been on, was not at full temperature, but even being in water that was eighty-five degrees would be better than the hypothermia threatening them both.

He pulled her up, with his last ounce of energy, and slid her into the warm water. She was struggling to breathe. He could hear her lungs raspy and rough, and her hands wildly searched for him in the dim light, afraid she was again slipping beneath the surface. He climbed in after her, securing himself in one corner he pulled her against him, put his arms around her to be sure her head could rest and still be above water. The heat stung, made his entire body tingle with a searing, painful sensation.

She was gasping, fast, and short hard breaths, and her fingers curled around the collar of his shirt. She must have been feeling as much shock from the warm water as he was, but he knew she needed it. Cupping his hands, he splashed water up onto her head, pouring it carefully over her hair.

"Aurora, talk to me," his hands ran over her body, searching for other wounds but finding none. She seemed unable to hold herself up, leaned on him weakly, and still sounded like she was breathing through a straw. Her throat seemed to clog, and she heaved violently, sending icy fluid out of her mouth to spill down the back of his neck.

He leaned her over the edge, and her body convulsed again, spewing what looked in the dark like thick mucus onto the step of the deck. She wheezed, physically drained, and entirely spent. He held her secure, face down but with his arms still around her. As her breathing began to ease, the pressure in her lungs relieved, she reached for him, sinking into the water against him.

Her head rested on his shoulder, and his only comfort was in the feeling of her breath against his cheek.

"You're alive," he said in a harsh whisper, "sweet Jesus, I'm so thankful you're alive."

She rested against him for only a brief moment before lights in the house flashed on. David must have arrived as officers swarmed the downstairs. Ethan waved his hand up to get their attention over the half top of the hot tub.

They came out, guns drawn, flashlight beams trained on them with David trailing behind, but as they approached, he heard the calls for medics as a relief. David was at the side of the hot tub reaching in within seconds.

"What happened?" David demanded.

"She almost drowned, she had water in her lungs and was unconscious." Ethan was finally starting to catch his breath in the warmth of the water.

"Get blankets," David said, "she can't get out until she can stay warm. Get the paramedics into the living room. We have to get her upstairs."

Ethan could tell the local authorities had been dispatched first, based on their pea-green uniforms. The local Sheriff's swarmed the scene. His people, though late, must have understood how dangerous the situation was, as there had to be a dozen officers already where he could see them.

Within seconds they came down with blankets, and he helped wrap her up, nervously watching as they whisked her away.

Even at his advanced age, David managed the scene with authority, much to Ethan's relief.

"Get her upstairs, no one is to touch her until I say so," he barked, "and get this man checked out as well." He pointed at Ethan, who was waving them off, clumsily climbing out of the hot tub. Coming up beside him, David offered a blanket and began rapid-fire questioning.

"How in the hell did this happen?" He said in a surprisingly calm tone. "I got a call twenty minutes ago that authorities were on the way here and I needed to come let them in, that the FBI had alerted them of an intruder. I nearly had a heart attack." He was shuffling in beside Ethan, hurrying them along.

"She took off," Ethan found himself feeling more winded and spent than he expected.

"What the hell?" David demanded. "Why and to where?"

"I don't know for sure. I woke up, and she was gone, and I heard a boat, so I followed my gut."

"For the love of all things holy," David began to curse and was upstairs ten steps ahead of Ethan. Aurora was on the couch, still wrapped in blankets, and Ethan was surprised by the ownership the older man was taking of her.

"Back away!" he snapped tersely. "I am her doctor, and all of you will assist me or get the hell out." Ethan sat in the plush chair at the end of the couch where he could see Aurora and watched as David worked on her. Her color was terrifying, pale with ashen lips like violets, but she was breathing, and her eyes followed David well.

"We have to get you out of the wet clothes love," David said to her in a professional tone, and Ethan knew she wouldn't argue. David shook a blanket out and snapped his fingers at a female deputy who promptly began helping her remove her wet clothes from behind the blanket, draped loosely to protect her dignity. David gave instructions to his wife, and by the time Aurora's clothes had come off, Blanche had appeared with a long sleeve shirt and pants she handed to the Deputy.

"Are you hurt anywhere else?" he asked her. She covered her face lethargically and Ethan noticed the discoloration of the bruises just starting to bloom. "Having a hard time talking?" he asked, and she nodded yes. "Do you think you've aspirated vomit, or is it just lake water?"

"Lake water," she tried her best to whisper in a raspy tone.

David secured supplies from the paramedics, still spouting orders as quickly as they could react. He had an IV line in her forearm before Ethan even realized what he was doing and had attached a bag of solution he had his wife squeezing.

"Alright, we'll start with this, get the heating blanket. I'm more concerned about hypothermia at the moment than I am about her lungs." He stood up and went out with the paramedics to the ambulance.

Everything was in motion around Aurora, as a Sheriff finally honed in on Ethan.

"Are you Agent Hartman?" he asked. The name on his badge was Deputy Livingston.

"Yes," Ethan answered.

The Deputy handed him a cell phone with a call already in progress, and as Ethan answered, he realized his phone was still in the jet ski.

"Boss, what's going on?" Tom's voice was a relief.

"I'm still trying to figure it all out myself. She just took off, willingly from what I can tell. I woke up and heard a boat only seconds before the cyber team called my cell, but she was already gone."

"They said they caught her on the camera out back, walking to the end of the dock and a boat cruised by, and she just hopped in, do you have any idea why?" Tom sounded rattled for the first time since Ethan had known him.

"Maybe, have you been in touch with the Coast Guard?"

"Yea, local LEO's did the dispatch, but I picked up communication with the team a couple of minutes ago. They're looking on the lake now, we used your GPS, but it didn't last long. We're sending over a photo of the boat from the camera, but it's not a great one, just a side profile. We watched you pull her in off the jet ski, but she didn't look good, is she alright?"

"They're working on her, she's alive."

"What happened?"

"He tried to drown her, effectively did drown her, I found her unconscious. A rope tied her to the back of the boat, and he was dragging her right before letting her loose to sink."

"Shit."

"Yea, I'll second that notion."

"Are you alright, boss?"

"Yea, cold, but I'm fine. It's like winter up here at night, it's ridiculous. Hey, I have to catch up with the Sheriff, tell the fourth floor to do me a favor, and be faster next time. She shouldn't even have been outside. They should have called me sooner."

"There was some weird delay in the loop, they're trying to figure out why right now boss. They called as soon as they saw her."

"Well it wasn't soon enough. Let me know what the Coast Guard comes up with, I'll call you later."

Standing up, Ethan handed the cell back to the Sheriff and said, "I'll be right back. I need to put on dry clothes." As he walked past Aurora, her eyes followed him briefly before squeezing shut. She had started to shiver again. Running through the night in his mind, he was baffled, couldn't get a grip on why the hell she would leave, why she would willingly walk into the arms of someone she knew wanted her dead.

I was right beside her in bed for crying out loud!

Anger started to boil up in him, annoyed with her risking her own life and not saying a word to him. He didn't want to admit it, but it hurt she didn't trust him. Pulling on a dry shirt and jeans, just as he was starting to think he had no idea who she was, the note on the bathroom counter caught his eye. His heart stopped. The little yellow square of paper still had the fingernail stapled to it, crusted with smeared black blood. As he read it, ice curdled the blood in his veins.

Staring at himself in the mirror, all the pieces he missed, all the time he wasted, this was all his fault. He had become so wrapped up in her that he hadn't seen the forest for the trees. Of course, the killer would know about her sister. Of course, the killer would have just as much reason to hurt Donia and use her against Aurora. His gut clenched, his heart throbbed in his ears, he felt like a fool.

He wanted to punch something, felt sick, his guts churning in knots as the pieces slipped into place in his head. Donia had been there, just the night before, and he had only focused on Aurora, not just *allowing* but *encouraging* her sister to walk off into the night alone. He had never followed up to be sure Donia was retrieved, or had arrived safe. He'd been too wrapped up in Aurora, too concerned about what was between them.

Heraldson must have been watching, must have known there would be a slip up eventually. He'd been patient that long already. What was another week or two? It had paid off. He had seen Donia, taken her, done God only knows what to her, used her to get to Aurora, and Ethan felt entirely responsible. He left the note on the counter. He needed to call Tom to get it into evidence as soon as he could.

Downstairs the house had thinned out, only two paramedics and a handful of officers remained in the front room. He dashed downstairs and out to the jet ski to retrieve his phone, which luckily was still dry and working and immediately called Tom back.

"I need a forensic team, fast, he got to her here," he didn't even say hello.

"Sure, boss, I'll get the order out. What do you mean he got to her?"

"Her sister, she has to be with him. Either on the boat or he has her stashed somewhere, he pulled a fingernail off of her and left Aurora a note. I don't know how she got it and she's not talking yet. I'll send you a picture. Look harder at the tech, get the best guy we have, we're missing something." Ethan hung up before Tom could say anything else. As he started across the living room towards Aurora, the look on David's face stopped him in his tracks. Twisted with anger and grief, he looked up at Ethan while listening to something Aurora was whispering as he clipped together pieces of some kind of mask with tubing.

"I need everyone out," Ethan flagged the Sheriff team and paramedics, holding the front door open, leaving only David and his wife. "I'll be back to discuss the situation with you in a few minutes, but I need to get some information from her first." He did his best not to slam the door, and when he turned back to her, it took everything in him to keep his temper under control. She and David were speaking in French, obviously for privacy reasons, and it irritated Ethan.

"English," he snapped at her, interrupting them. "How did the note get in here?"

"The food delivery," Aurora's voice was thin, strained.

"This isn't the time for this, she needs a breathing treatment and medication, and she needs to rest," David tried to block Ethan from coming closer, unsuccessfully.

"He has Donia, doesn't he? Did you see her?" Ethan loomed over the couch; his sheer size authoritative. Aurora nodded her head. "Is she alive?" he asked.

"I don't know, I think so," she began to cry, and a piece of Ethan's heart broke at the same time anger boiled over.

"Damn it, Aurora, what were you thinking?" he demanded. "Why wouldn't you tell me what was going on? I get it, he threatened you and said not to tell anyone, but you had to have known you couldn't do any good by yourself. Don't you trust me? You walked into the arms of a maniac, are you suicidal or something?" he was beginning to yell. The whole situation felt so personal.

"That's enough!" David stood up defensively. "She needs medication in her lungs. You can talk to her again when I'm done and when you can be professional." Ethan glared at him but quickly realized he was right.

Walking away, shaking his head, he went up and retrieved the note, snapping a quick photo of it he immediately sent to Tom. Back downstairs, he dropped it, wrapped in tissue, onto the table beside the couch, and went out to the Sheriff team. David continued to work on Aurora, with a mask over her face. He spoke to her in French while she breathed deeply, her nose and eyes showing new signs of significant swelling and bruising.

Outside, Ethan coordinated a search team, communicated with the Coast Guard, and provided photos and other information from the cyber tech team. As orders went out, his phone started ringing off the hook. He only answered it when he saw Tom's number.

"Boss, we found the problem."

"I'm listening," Ethan wasn't in the mood for a guessing game.

"The team, they found shadow surveillance. The delay in the loop, it's because the signal was being routed through another server before hitting here. This guy, he hacked in, he's crazy good. I called Chang, the stuff we found this morning only scratches the surface, makes the tracker and the hacking into the cameras look like child's play, a hobby. He's been watching her every move since you left town, and the signal is bouncing. Chang doesn't know how to shut it off, but he's working on it."

"So it's all been a game? An emotional, cat, and mouse."

"It's looking like it. Like he could have had her anytime he wanted."

"But I was in the way, so he needed a way to draw her away from me voluntarily. So he used her sister."

"It's a bit beyond sick."

"And he still has Donia," Ethan was distracted by a tap on the shoulder. "Hold on," it was David's wife, and she looked as though she'd just seen a ghost.

"Agent Hartman," she sounded terrified, he nodded. "I know I should stay out of this, but I couldn't help myself, we've been so close to the girls for so long. I," she stuttered, looked away from him and took a step back as though she wanted more privacy. "I read the note on the table."

"I'm sorry, I shouldn't have left it where it could be upsetting," Ethan started in the house, but she caught him by the arm.

"No, I think I can help you," he looked at her, confused.

"What do you mean?"

"David said Aurora told him some of what this man, this killer, said to her. She said he wants her to suffer, wants her to hurt and feel anguish the way he felt when his daughter died. That's why he took Donia, so she could feel responsible and feel the loss."

"That's what we're also gathering, yes. I'm sorry you've been through all of this," he did his best to keep a gentle, even and professional tone. He wasn't sure he was achieving empathy.

"Well, you see, the note—it's a hint at our address, and she knows it."

"What makes you say that?" Ethan's blood ran cold.

"Well, I don't speak much French, a word here or there," her voice was low as if she didn't want anyone to overhear, "but I think I heard her tell David she was worried about us and that doesn't make sense. We haven't been involved in any of this. And, maybe I'm reaching," she paused with uncertainty but seemed to gain confidence when Ethan squared to face her, interested and focused.

"The note, the way it's written doesn't make sense, but David and I live on Dollar Point, at the corner of Edgewater and Observation Drive. The way the killer used Emerald and Knight— only people who live on Tahoe and know Tahoe well would know the history of Lora Knight and Emerald Bay. I like puzzles so maybe it's all in my head but it's just too much of a coincidence for me not to say something." Ethan's gut clenched.

"What's the address? Is there anyone home, at your house, right now?" he asked.

"It's 25367 Edgewater Drive. It's empty except for our dogs," fear was thick in her voice.

"Thank you for telling me, I'll take it into account," he nodded, and she went back inside as he turned back to his call with Tom.

"Make progress on the tech, get whatever feed he has canceled and cross-reference it with 25637 Edgewater Drive, see if there's anything hacked into both residences."

"On it," Tom hung up, and Ethan turned to the Sheriff.

"Get in touch with the Coast Guard, and if they haven't found him already have them search Emerald Bay, I have new information that leads me to believe he would dump her there." One of the deputies turned away and spoke into his radio, asking for Coast Guard dispatch.

"I need one of you to take me to Edgewater Drive," Ethan demanded.

"I can take you," Deputy Livingston spoke up.

"Leave a team here, I'll be right out." Ethan went back inside to Aurora, calmer, and more focused. She still had a mask over her face, and David was pushing some kind of medication into the line in her arm with a syringe as Blanche sat at her head, stroking her hair and face gently. She still looked awful. Ethan went to sit beside her, everything in him conflicted and confused. He wasn't sure how to feel.

"Does she need to go to the hospital?" he asked David.

"I'd prefer she not, I think she's safer here with less exposure to additional pathogens. The greatest risk once her hypothermia resolves is infection. Her lungs are irritated. She needs antibiotics, steroids, and rest. Hopefully, that will be enough. If she takes a turn for the worse, I will have an ambulance take her in, but I'll stay with her until I feel she's out of the woods."

Aurora looked at him, weak, with sadness in her eyes.

"He hit you in the face, didn't he?" Heat crept up in Ethan but he kept it in check as she nodded. David cursed under his breath. "Did he say anything you think would help find him?" She closed her eyes and, after a moment, shook her head, no.

Ethan looked up to Blanche but said only, "I'm going to go look for him, and Donia, I have a hunch I need to follow. The Sheriff is leaving two units here, so there will be four Deputies guarding you. Keep the house locked, keep the lights on, and the shades drawn. I'll be back soon."

As he stood up, Aurora's hand brushed his knee, and he found himself aching to stop, to hold her, to comfort her, but he kept walking. His phone began to ring as a distraction, and seeing Tom's name, knew he had the answers he needed. Before he reached the door, Blanche caught him and not realizing what she was doing until he was stepping outside, she had slipped a house key into his hand. His gut was telling him she was right, and he had to end this tonight.

Chapter Twenty-Six

Declan Heraldson pulled the boat up to the East side of Fannette Island in the center of Emerald Bay at just after midnight. Things hadn't exactly gone as planned for his final adventure, but if the night panned out, David and Blanche Fournier would be easy targets, and the pesky FBI Agent would be a bonus. He wasn't sure Aurora had survived, but he wasn't sure she hadn't. If she had, he would enjoy watching her misery when she found out he killed her sister despite her best efforts to sacrifice herself. He would better yet enjoy seeing her agony at the soon-to-be charred remains of her dearly beloved friends, the Fournier's. He would most of all enjoy seeing the torment in her eyes to learn he demolished Ethan Hartman into nothing more than dismembered body parts and mist. He pondered what it was that thrilled him more, the chase, the takedown, or the aftermath. The final climax would be to watch her cry at the funerals before he killed her for real.

If she survived, he reminded himself. He was getting carried away in the joy of her suffering without even knowing her fate. There would be plenty of funerals to enjoy, one way or another.

How ironic, to be looking forward to funerals, he thought. He hated funerals, always had, and he swore it was what put his poor Eda Jean over the edge. They were all he had, his wife and his daughter, and watching his Eda Jean wither after Candice died had broken something in him. Finding Eda Jean dead with a suicide note, a bottle of pills, and a bottle of rum had released him. He had nothing else to live for, and he wanted to make sure the people responsible had nothing else to live for either.

He swung the boat wide, letting the waves push him close to the largest rock he could safely slide against, and without ceremony or consideration, he rolled the body of Donia Soileaux off and onto it with a dull thud. Her head made a louder sound than he anticipated, and he smiled a little as the boat scraped the rock before pulling away again.

That should keep the Coast Guard busy for a while.

Turning the speed boat back towards his ultimate target, he enjoyed the wind in his face, the cold sting of it in his ears whipping through his hair. With the running lights off, using only landmarks along the shore for guidance, the shimmer of the moon on the lake took him back to happier times. He hadn't asked for much out of life. He only wanted food on the table and a decent home in a safe neighborhood where his daughter could play. His union job at the slaughterhouse paid the bills and had the benefits, and his tech hobbies funded their vacations, they were all doing well until Candy got sick and things fell apart. He wondered, staring up at the stars, if Dr. Soileaux had any idea whatsoever that her own mother had funded his pursuit of her demise.

He pulled the boat up to the dock two houses down from the Fournier residence on Edgewater Drive, careful to pay attention to any lights or movement. There was none. Opening his case, he took out one of his drones, smaller than the palm of his hand, and as it took off, slipped his backpack back over his shoulder. He guided the drone using a tablet, watching it slice through the air away from him.

The slick little devices with their quiet approach and high-resolution cameras had kept him easily one step ahead of the law, and tonight, he was confident they would help him finish what he started. He watched the screen as the drone flew up and over the house, circled it, and verified there was no one there, yet. He walked the short distance to the back fence and marveled at how comfortable rich people became. The gate wasn't even locked.

He let himself into the backyard, knowing the dogs were curled up safe and cozy, probably asleep inside. The first place he anticipated his company to meet him was at the dock, expecting him, of course, to arrive by boat. He had already carefully set explosive charges every twelve feet on the floating dock so he would be able to pick and choose which one to set off and when. With any luck, this law enforcement thug she'd been hiding with would be in the group to arrive once he set off the alarm. Now he just needed to find a comfortable place with a good vantage point to sit and dispatch the rest of his drones. With their high-resolution cameras, he'd have the perfect three-dimensional view of the demise of Aurora Soileaux's favorite person.

He was excitedly looking forward to enjoying watching her face when he sent her the photos and video he planned to capture momentarily. Nothing could please him more than being able to see her distress as she got a good look at the death of her new beau.

He was calmly trotting through the immaculate landscaping as he sent the drone ahead of him to scour the path. As the wide stone stairs opened to the patio, he sent the drone up to the second floor to get a better look at the expansive backyard for a place to sit, but through the giant picture windows facing the lake, something caught his attention he wasn't expecting.

Through the tall pane, he could see a man standing inside, watching, in a uniform. Changing the camera settings of the drone, he could see the figure clearer, someone in a Sheriff's uniform was standing in the living room, watching the backyard over the lake. He paused, curious why he hadn't seen a marked cruiser of any kind out front. *Why were there no lights or sirens, and how did they get inside, in the dark?* This man was a kink in his plan. With someone already inside, then there was no longer an alarm set. Dropping the drone back down to eye level to explore the back door, he switched the camera to infrared, and just as it caught a hot spot, obviously a person, a booming voice broke the silence.

"Freeze, federal agent, put your hands on your head." Ethan had found him first, and fury lit Declan. *How did they beat me here?* He seethed. He wasn't going that easy. Holding down a button on the side of the tablet for the drone light, a high-powered LED flashed bright, slicing through the darkness like a sword. Ethan was ready; he had closed his eyes briefly and didn't lose his vision. Declan rushed him, drawing a knife out of his waistband, bending to take Ethan out at the hips with his shoulder like a linebacker. As the two flew backward, they tumbled down the broad stone stairs crashing at the bottom painfully.

Ethan outweighed him but had lost his gun in the tumble, catching sight of the knife only in time to prevent it from sinking entirely into his leg. The blade sliced the inside of his thigh as he shoved back on Declan, struggling to keep the blade at bay. The light of the drone threw shadows, and as they rolled, Ethan could see the insanity in Declan's eyes, he wasn't going to allow capture. As they tumbled again, Ethan trying to get him in a chokehold,

Declan slammed the handle of the knife into his shoulder, sending shooting pain through his fingers, loosening his grip.

Unable to hold him in check, Ethan twisted, securing the arm with the knife and transferred his weight back on top of Declan, who wrapped his legs around Ethan's waist. The two were at an impasse, wrestling with sheer muscle power, but Ethan had more training, sharper skills, and his gun was back in reach. If he let go of the arm holding the knife, he could get to it, though he wasn't sure in time to avoid a dangerous stab wound. Just as the choice became critical, a growl rose from behind them. Before either knew what was happening loud barking backed by vicious teeth had them scrambling as David's wolfhounds pounced like the guard dogs they were trained to be.

In the brief flurry of fangs and fur, Declan's attention was absorbed, and Ethan was able to retrieve his gun, turning quickly, doing his best to avoid hitting the dogs, pulling the trigger with a prayer, the bullet hit his mark. Declan went down with a wound in the shoulder, and the dogs never let up, thankfully trained to handle gunfire, they had Declan pinned by the throat, face down.

Deputy Livingston was on Declan with cuffs before Ethan could get his bearings. Blood was pouring from his leg, and he realized the wound was worse than he initially thought. Adrenaline had kept him focused, but now with Declan subdued, lightheadedness was rushing in. Deputy Livingston was calling for backup as Declan yelled beneath him, angry and in pain. The dogs growled and sniffed at Livingston and his captive, circling them with mistrust.

With Declan under control, Livingston turned to Ethan.

"You alright?" he asked.

"I'll be fine, he just caught me in the leg," Ethan was sitting up, pressing against the gushing gash in his thigh.

"You need me to call for a bus?" Livingston fished out a flashlight but before he could get a good look at Ethan's leg a shot rang out. The Deputy slumped, staggered and fell towards Ethan as two more shots were fired. Ethan's immediate instinct was to return fire and still in the dark, head-spinning, dogs jumping and barking, he fired blindly in Declan's direction from behind the Deputy.

Declan had pushed himself to his knees and fished a small pistol out, firing from hands cuffed behind his back, and as the Deputy sank onto Ethan, there was no choice left. Ethan swung his gun and rapidly fired four shots to prevent Declan from injuring the Deputy further or being hit himself. The clang of metal against concrete was clear as Declan fell forward hard, the bone of his skull hitting the pavement with a sharp smack.

It was over; only there was a massive amount of clean up. Ethan rolled Livingston off him, trying his best to evaluate where his wound was. Livingston groaned, at the edge of consciousness. Grabbing the radio off his shoulder, Ethan barked emergency orders into it, trying to figure out how badly the Deputy was injured. Finding the flashlight, he evaluated the hole in Livingston's upper torso and applied pressure, feeling his own energy wane.

Refusing to give up, he held on until additional Deputies arrived, only minutes before Blanche and an ambulance. A paramedic stepped in to wrap Ethan's leg while they loaded Livingston into the first ambulance.

"There's another ambulance on the way, this should hold until they get you situated, but I'll stay, they're staffed to handle the officer." The young paramedic tightened a bandage around Ethan's leg.

"I'm fine, go with the Deputy," Ethan huffed.

"He isn't going anywhere," Blanche interrupted. Ethan hadn't noticed how tall she was. Her frame was almost too thin with beautiful, shining silver hair. Kneeling beside him, he saw for the first time how fatigued she seemed.

"How is Aurora?" he asked her without a second thought.

"Resting comfortably, for the moment. David won't let the ambulance leave until her oxygen saturation comes up, her lungs are still struggling, but she's stable. He is with her, and that's her best bet." The dogs had come to sit beside her, affectionate and protective, and she absently petted one.

"Officers," Ethan called to the deputies securing the scene. "Has the Coast Guard located the other victim?" A short and stocky officer with pale skin and white-blond hair answered as he walked towards them.

"We don't have confirmation yet on the status, but we believe they did find her, we're waiting on identity." Ethan's heart skipped a beat, his head swirling. If Aurora lost her sister because of him, it would devastate her, he was sure she'd never speak to him again, and he would never forgive himself.

"Does that mean she's dead?"

"No," the Deputy shook his head, "she's unconscious, so they just aren't sure if it's the right person or not. They haven't located the boat yet."

"It has to be near here somewhere. Heraldson was back here too fast to have used another form of transportation." Ethan tried to sit up but quickly felt flush and dizzy. The paramedic put a hand on his shoulder to encourage him to lie down and turned to the Deputy,

"What's the ETA on the next bus?" he asked. "He's bleeding badly enough that if it's more than two minutes out, we should take him in a cruiser."

"What?" Ethan asked, but his vision was blurring, a ringing settling into his ears.

"Lie down and shut up." Blanche's voice was terse but protective, "Do as they tell you. It doesn't matter how tough you feel. You have a pallor two shades shy of a corpse."

One of the dogs stood up, licking his face as a flashlight cast shadows over him. The warm, slobbery wet, rough tongue reminded him of his Basset hound, Murphy, who had passed away only a few months previously, and his mind flashed to memories. He relaxed back onto the concrete, and beneath the heavy scent of puppy breath, fell unconscious.

Ethan woke in the hospital, nurses and doctors scuffling around just outside a thin curtain that separated him from the rest of the emergency room. His mind was fuzzy, not only because he'd lost a substantial amount of blood but because they'd given him something, perhaps for pain, or a general sedative. He vaguely remembered being unsuccessfully combative in an ambulance, without doing any damage.

His leg was throbbing, felt swollen, and his arms were tied to the side rails with restraints. Calling for a nurse, he was relieved when a middle-aged woman immediately swung the curtain back.

"Welcome back, Agent Hartman," she smiled.

"Why am I tied down?" he asked, his mouth felt dry and fuzzy.

"You're the size of an ox and stronger than one. When you came in, you were altered, disoriented a little, and you were reaching and grabbing. Nothing to be ashamed of or regret, you were just confused. It was for our protection." She began undoing the Velcro around his wrists.

"I'm sorry," he said sheepishly.

"Don't be. It happens all the time. Dr. Fournier's wife was here, so at least she was able to communicate for you."

"Is she still here?"

"No, I think she went to get your wife," he was high, but he was pretty sure he wasn't so high he imagined her response.

"Did you say, wife?" he asked.

"Yes, I assumed the woman you were talking about was your wife, sorry, is it a girlfriend?"

"I have neither," he frowned at her, "what was I saying?"

"You were worried about someone you said you loved and needed to be sure she was alright, and that she knew you were alright, pretty common, that's all." She began checking his blood pressure and other vitals, typing something into a computer. He didn't even want to imagine what he'd said being a couple quarts low on blood and under whatever medication they'd given him.

Before he could successfully backtrack in his memory to whatever he'd said, the curtain swung open again, and he was shocked to see Tom stroll in with Jansen behind him.

"Boss, how the hell are ya?" Tom asked, smiling with a smartass grin.

"I'm in the hospital. What do you think?" Ethan wanted to be pissed and irritated, but he was too sedated.

"I think you're the badass who just wrapped up the Hypocrite case with the kill shot and the future scars to prove it."

Ethan looked at him as if he had two heads.

"How did you get here so fast?" he asked.

"Fast?" Tom frowned, "we took a puddle jumper plane, so that helped, but it's nearly six in the morning."

Ethan realized he had slept for almost the last five hours. The sun would be coming up outside.

"What's the status? Did they find Donia? Is Aurora ok? How is the Deputy who was shot? Heraldson is dead, yes?"

"Take it easy," Tom was relaxed, hands in his pockets jingling change he slowly explained everything as he leaned against the gurney. "Dr. Soileaux is stable. Her sister was recovered from Emerald Bay and is resting upstairs. They expect to keep her for a day or two under observation for concussion and risk of infection, but all signs indicate she'll make a full recovery. Deputy Livingston is due out of surgery any minute now. He had a collapsed lung, and the bullet shattered a couple of ribs, but he is also expected to make a full recovery. Declan Heraldson is in the morgue, thanks to you."

Ethan relaxed, taking it all in, his mind catching up with the details blocked by the swift progress of the last few hours.

"Drones," Ethan said, closing his eyes. "The asshole was using drones."

"A customized version of the DJI Mavic Air Quadcopter, to be specific." Jansen piped in. "Chang was able to figure out that's how he was getting all his information. They're small, quiet, easy to miss, and have an excellent range with multiple camera settings." Ethan shot Jansen an annoyed look. It *was* annoying this cyber-geek seemed impressed with a psychopathic killer's tech hobbies.

"You need some rest, boss. We'll be back to get you once you have a doctor sign you out with a clean bill of health. It's going to be a long day," Tom bumped Jansen with his shoulder as he turned to leave.

"Tom wait," Ethan interrupted. "I have a favor to ask, can you make a couple calls for me?"

"Sure, boss, what's up?" Ethan's head was swirling. Knowing Heraldson was gone, and Aurora was safe made him instantly impatient to make things right. He could only pray it would be enough.

Chapter Twenty-Seven

Tom decided breakfast would be a great way to kill a couple of hours while Ethan rested, and the forensics team gathered up enough information to wrap things up, or his stomach had decided it for him. He dragged Jansen, who was claiming a protein shake and a nap were a better idea, out to eat insisting, what better place to eat in Kings Beach than King's Café?

As they sat enjoying the meal, he made notes, caught up on emails, and decided he was willing to risk certain things in his career for a good friend. Since Jansen had slipped Tom some secret intel about a moment between Ethan and Aurora (only slightly hidden by a couch in the front room) that had been caught by the outdoor front surveillance camera, Tom had been preparing for the worst. Damage control wasn't out of the question; it just took more than Jansen could offer in the way of cleanup.

If it hadn't been for Jansen, who had destroyed the evidence and sworn himself to secrecy for tickets to a couple of Giants games, Tom wouldn't have been prepared for the situation. Thankfully he was. Tom and Henry Chang had come up through the academy together, and he was the first choice, naturally, to call when things got more advanced than Jansen could manage. Tom also wanted someone he could trust, and he knew Henry would keep things in confidence.

As he polished off his plate of scrambled eggs and saw Henry's personal cell number light up his phone, he knew the conversation would be interesting, at the very least.

"Quillet," he answered hoping Jansen would think it was a work call and not question the conversation.

"You were right," Henry obviously wanted to keep the conversation short and sweet.

"When am I ever wrong?"

"Don't get cocky. I used *your* Onyx credentials to take care of everything. I updated the loop settings, so it looks like all along it was set to feed and not save. And I deleted all the files, overwriting them with loops of the last ten minutes of footage."

"Was there something there to begin with?" Tom was confident there was a video of Ethan and Aurora that wouldn't be appropriate for anyone else's eyes. However, he hadn't shared what he expected would need to be erased. He wanted to know if Henry watched any of the videos recorded by the FBI, or on the drones.

"I don't know, and I don't want to. You asked for a favor, you got it, leave it at that."

"I know the drill. I appreciate it, trust me, I owe you one, thanks."

"No, I'm getting married in two months, and you're my best man, remember? As long as you show up and don't screw up the speech, we're even," Henry snickered.

Tom laughed, said, "Deal," and hung up. Jansen eyed him suspiciously but had apparently decided he was better off not knowing. There were some lessons in the FBI you picked up on over the years, and knowing when to keep your nose out of someone else's mess was a valuable one.

"Did the data from the drones get downloaded?" Jansen asked, hinting he had some idea what was going on. He had been there when the forensic team handed the backpack from Heraldson to them only a couple hours earlier, with fifteen drones inside.

"There was no data. It was all on some type of live loop feed, Heraldson watched but didn't save anything," Tom didn't look up. He knew even as good at lying as he had become if there was a giveaway it was always in the eyes.

"Makes sense, video like that takes a lot of storage and is hard to manage." In his own way, Jansen was signing off on what Tom was doing, and for what it was worth, it made Tom feel better. In situations like this, there was always a price to pay. Whether it was for hiding the truth or accepting it, nothing came for free. Having Jansen buying into the consequences gave Tom his loyalty, one way or another.

Tom slapped his card down for the waitress, "This one's on me. Thanks for not making me sit in the car listening to you snore."

"No problem. You get to drive back while I'm going to be home for a late lunch, so I figure we're even."

Tom shrugged as his cell went off again, this time it was the team from the Bay Area currently engrossed in picking apart Rashida Soileaux's Santa Cruz beach house.

"This is Agent Quillet."

"Agent Quillet, this is Special Agent Jennifer Brown, DEA. It's a pleasure to make your acquaintance." Her light and airy voice was not what he was expecting.

"Good morning, I was expecting Agent Perez. I'm sorry. What can I do for you?"

"Actually, I'm calling because of what I can do for you."

The conversation advanced into a mountain of information he had not previously been aware of, and as the pieces rapidly clicked into place, his priorities shifted just as fast.

Ethan wasn't sure how much longer he had slept by the time Tom came back in. After a quick check by the doctor again and a signature he was back in blue hospital scrubs, for the second time in less than ten days, being wheeled to the front doors in a chair much too small for him.

Inside the standard-issue black SUV, he pushed the seat back all the way. The nurse had given him a stiff last dose of some kind of pain medicine that had his head feeling light and bubbly, but having his leg bent still sent a sharp pain through his thigh.

"How are you feeling, boss?" Tom asked, cheery enough to be annoying.

"I'll survive."

"They give you a good shot of something to keep the pain at bay for the drive home?"

"Something," Ethan leaned the seat back and buckled.

"Good, you're going to need it to keep you off the ledge, there's a lot I have to tell you."

"Yea? Get to it then."

"First of all, I called ahead to the Agents still at the Fournier summer home and asked them to pack your things for you discreetly. I don't think it's a good idea for you to go back inside."

"What?" Ethan frowned, thoroughly displeased the decision was made for him without discussion. As Tom began to explain the tip from Jansen from the FBI surveillance camera, the drone footage of the anteroom, and his call to an old friend, the blood drained from Ethan's face.

"Are you fucking kidding me?" Ethan was in shock.

"I'm not, but only you know if there was fucking involved if you know what I mean, and I think it should stay that way," Tom shot him an all-too-serious look.

"Jesus, Tom, I don't even know what to say," Ethan felt sick, utterly humiliated and embarrassed. He had no idea Heraldson had been recording them for days through the open windows. He remembered the steamy moments with Aurora and felt naked.

"Don't say anything, that's the entire point. It's also why I think you need to lay low and just go back home with me. Being around investigators who are actively looking for anything out of place will surely notice your feelings for her. I'll explain you aren't well enough to finish the case, use your injury to your advantage and give you some time to figure things out on a personal level, later. It's better that you not even let the idea of anything between you surface."

Ethan thought for a long time, contemplating the situation. It wasn't a position he wanted to be in, risking his career, but apparently, it was too late. Aurora probably hated him anyway, after all, he was pretty pissed about her going out alone and hadn't gone easy on her, and he had almost gotten her sister killed. He wasn't even sure she wanted to see him anyway, and with the tension so thick, he knew Tom was right.

"Alright, you're right. Just tell me you didn't stick your neck out far enough to be on the chopping block beside me."

"There's no chopping block. It's handled, trust me. But there's more…" Tom continued to tell him about Rashida and her connection to Heraldson, which only made Ethan sweat worse. Tom was right, again, he was glad he'd had that last dose of pain medicine.

"Christ, her own mother?" Ethan felt green.

"Yea, not pretty. The DEA had been tracking her a long time for criminal charges in conjunction with the FDA. There's an open investigation concerning her illegally providing patient data for a kickback on the profit of the clinical trials, the only hope I have is that Aurora didn't know anything about it. The FDA thinks Rashida used her husbands' passwords to obtain the records."

Ethan's stomach churned, even more, knowing what Aurora would have to face in the coming days, even weeks, and the hurt he'd left her with on top of all of it, stung the most.

They pulled up in the shade behind another SUV across the street from the Fournier summer home at just after eleven in the morning.

"I'll be back as quick as I can, take a nap or something alright, just promise me you won't get out of the car?" Tom unbuckled, tossed Ethan his sunglasses, and paused to wait for a response before opening the door.

"I'm living proof smart people do stupid shit, but this isn't one of those examples. I'll stay put." Ethan wanted to go inside to see Aurora, almost as much as he wanted to hide.

Aurora woke in the dark to familiar voices, her chest still feeling like she'd been breathing hot coals. She was asleep in the guest room with the darkest curtains, drawn to block out daylight, and wasn't sure what time it was. Bastet was sleeping beside her, warm and soft, but when she heard the scratch of dog claws on the hardwood from the floor above her, she decided she should get up and close the door.

She felt weak and had a medication hangover, but wanted to see what the commotion was about upstairs. She slipped on some sweatpants and a short sleeve shirt from the pile of her things on the couch in the room and headed up in stocking feet. The kitchen was a zoo of people. David and Blanche had apparently offered to feed half the County Sheriff's office and a full team of FBI investigators.

Zach, Lily, and Sophie—David and Blanche's three grown kids—were herding small children around as Davy and Dan followed them hoping for scraps of food. Seeing the room, the people in action warmed Aurora—it felt like home.

When David caught sight of her, he nearly dropped his plate to rush over.

"Aura darling, how are you feeling?" he asked, embracing her kindly.

"I'm doing ok," her throat felt scratchy, and she coughed and wheezed to talk, but considered since she had almost drowned the night before, she was doing pretty well. David held her a long time, rubbing her back and told her in French how much he loved her. It made her miss her dad terribly. Blanche and her daughters joined in the hug when they noticed she'd come up, and it felt like a family reunion had started.

Aurora ate a little bit, answered what questions she could for the Agents and the Sheriff, heard the news that Donia and Ethan were both in the hospital but doing well, and was relieved to see Tom come in a short time later.

"Good morning Dr. Soileaux," Tom smiled at her, pulling a chair up beside her.

"Good morning," she couldn't quite bring herself to call him Agent Quillet, it felt weird to her.

"How are you feeling?" he asked.

"Like an idiot, but otherwise, I'll survive."

Tom laughed a little, "All is well that ends well. I'd like to catch up with you and Dr. Fournier, in private if possible." Her nerves instantly went on edge, but she nodded and got up to lead him into the library. David closed the door behind them and went to sit beside her protectively.

"I wish I could bring better news this morning, but I think it is best to get you caught up face to face before information starts to get out in pieces," Tom said.

She nodded, with a lump in her throat, as David reached for her hand.

"It's about your mother," Tom almost looked uncomfortable.

"I'm listening," Aurora was confused, her mouth went dry. Tom had slipped his jacket off and got a chair up closer to her in an attempt to be less authoritative, but he wasn't sure it was working.

"When you and Donia went missing last night, the Bureau reached out to your mother to notify her of the situation. It's standard procedure. Try as we did to get in touch with her, there was no response, so after two hours, they sent local police to knock on her door. I'm sorry to have to tell you, she was discovered dead, in her Santa Cruz home, a little after four this morning."

Aurora's face went white. Shock chilled her as she inhaled sharply.

"What happened?" she asked.

"We held off on notification because of the situation in which we found her. It appears Declan Heraldson, before coming here to pursue you, murdered your mother first."

"But I don't understand, what did my mother have to do with any of this? She's not a physician. I thought he was after doctors because of his daughter?" Aurora's voice quivered.

"We weren't sure at first either, but she was found with a lot of documentation we felt the need to verify before this conversation."

David groaned, cursed a little under his breath, and Aurora looked at him, confused. His eyes betrayed him. He knew more than he had let on.

"What was she found with?" Aurora was becoming agitated.

"Declan Heraldson had uncovered a link between your mother's finances, tied to the clinical trial you and your father were working on, and the equipment that killed his daughter. We're still trying to verify, but the DEA was on scene a little while ago. We believe your mother was illegally using records from patients you and your father were treating to interfere with the funding of the research."

Aurora's head began to spin.

"Damn it," David cursed aloud, "Aura, honey, your dad never wanted you to know. You had no part in it, and he knew that. He had the proof of it, but he was working with the DEA when he and your mother split up. Your mother wasn't only cheating on him, and he left her long before he got sick because he found out what she was doing." Aurora was finding it hard to breathe, squeezing David's hand as if she might fall off a cliff should he let go.

"What? I, I... don't understand," she stammered. Tom looked to David, unsure how much else to say.

David piped in, "She made some poor financial decisions during the last recession. Things went very badly for her, financially, and your dad began to pull away. He didn't know what she was up to until it was too late. He waited too long to turn her in, which made him an accessory of sorts. The whole thing was a mess, but once he got sick, none of it mattered, and he just wanted you and Donia to know how much he loved you."

"He could never have seen this coming," Tom reached out and put his hand on Aurora's shoulder. She didn't look well.

"That night, the men who came to get me at Trent's," she gasped. "They weren't there to put me into safe hiding. They were there to keep me from saying anything I might know that would incriminate my mother."

Tom was impressed by how fast she put the pieces together.

"She had invested in the company that was doing the trial and stood to make a great deal of money if it was successful. Your dad didn't know until after Heraldson's daughter died, he was sick over it, just sick," David's voice was rough, angry.

"Of course he was," she whispered, remembering everything under a new light.

"Your dad was a good man, darling. He had the best of intentions in everything he did."

"Unfortunately, there's a little more that I think you should hear upfront, to be prepared," Tom wanted to get everything out of the way.

Aurora didn't think it could get any worse, but she nodded, trying to stave off trembling.

"Your mother tried to bribe Heraldson a few months ago to stay quiet. His wife committed suicide, and he became manic. He exhumed the body of his daughter and created a shrine to them in the house he left behind in Idaho. He approached Rashida shortly after that with all the information and threatened her. When she wouldn't cooperate and bribed him, he accepted the money. Then he used it as a means to kill the other physicians, and she knew he was coming after you too."

Aurora was roughly hyperventilating now, David rubbing her back in an attempt to soothe her.

"She never told me. She knew all along and she never told me." Uncontrollable tears welled up and she felt like she might pass out. "I hate her. I'm glad she's dead."

David wrapped his arms around her, squeezing tight enough it hurt while she let all her emotions drain out of her.

There was a knock at the door, and David's son Zach swung it open with a concerned look on his face.

"Dad, the DEA is here, and they want to talk to you," Zach sounded worried.

"I'll be right there," David said, letting Aurora go. "It's ok darling, I was helping them, years ago, there's nothing to worry about, they finally just have their proof and want my statement of corroboration." He stood up and walked towards Zach. "Take care of her, don't let her out of your sight, and if she starts having trouble breathing, I want to know immediately. Zach nodded and went to Aurora on the couch.

Tom stood up, brushing her shoulder reassuringly, and said, "I'll let you have some privacy."

Zach sat down beside her, hugging her as his dad had. She had known him all her life, he was only a few years older than her and she knew very well their parents had silently hoped for years they would become a couple which they had both avoided, he was like a brother to her. At the moment, his arms were kind and feeling like her world was collapsing, she was grateful for him, grateful for all of them.

"You know what I think you need? Some fresh air and sunshine," Zach smiled, helping her up on her feet. As they walked out, she noticed a suitcase by the front door. Still wiping her face she let him lead her outside to the front porch, setting her into the swing she had been in only two nights before with her sister. He was right; the sun felt healing.

"I'm not going to ask what's going on. I figure I'll hear it all in due time. Do you need anything?" He hugged her close, curling her legs up in his lap. She shook her head, burying her face in his shoulder, tears seeping steadily from her eyes. All she wanted was for all of this to be over so she could move on. And she wanted Ethan. She'd been a nervous wreck knowing he had gone after the suspect, in the middle of the night, basically alone.

David had dosed her with a reasonably potent sedative the night before, it had been the only way she'd been able to sleep, but now that the day was nearing noon she was worried again. She didn't like knowing he was in the hospital. More often than not, injuries were downplayed, and she was hoping that wasn't the case.

Rocking back and forth lazily on the swing Zach just held her, rubbing her arm and holding her, giving her time to recover. She appreciated the comfort accompanied by the quiet, she wanted space, but she also didn't want to be alone. As she calmed, she was glad to have his ear; to have someone who knew her life well enough that she didn't have to explain things.

"Donia and I, we haven't seen eye to eye in a long time, you know?"

"You and your irresponsible party-girl sister? Imagine that," he joked.

"She came here the night before last. Her drunk, sorry ass crawled through the dog door," it sounded so ridiculous to say it out loud now.

"Just when you think you've heard it all," he laughed.

"You know, even though she is ten years older than me, I thought she'd never grow up. I thought she would always be our mother's daughter. She's always been so selfish, self-absorbed, shallow, even vain at times. But she was different with me Wednesday like she hasn't been before. Something happened with her boyfriend, and she uncharacteristically admitted it was all her own fault."

"Yep, heard all about that one, oy," Zach took a slow, deep breath.

"I'm sure she deserved getting dumped. I'm not sure she deserved to be abducted by a serial killer, and now Mom is dead. The whole thing is just so much irony it's hard to feel bad about it."

"Rashida's dead?" he asked in surprise.

"Apparently, and I think, from what your dad said, she royally had it coming."

"No shit," he paused thoughtfully. "You know I think that's the first time I've heard you call Rashida mom in over twenty years."

She laid her head on his shoulder, thought long and hard about growing up, about what she'd been through and how she felt.

"I guess so," she looked up at him, this childhood friend who knew her so well. "The word 'mom' always felt so personal and sweet. I hated calling her that. I guess I've subconsciously felt like because she gave birth to me, she still deserved the title of mother."

"Because she never really loved you, it was too hard to call her mom." Zach finished her sentence artfully. "I get it, I think it's fair. It would be silly to say she deserved more. No one liked her, not even my mom, and she likes everyone."

"Really?" Aurora was astounded. "She never acted as if she didn't like her."

"Oh yes, she did, just not around you or Donia." Zach began to tell her stories she had never heard, her head resting easy on him, his arm draped over her. She never saw Ethan through the tinted windows, sitting on the passenger side of the black SUV across the street, but when Tom came out with the suitcase, her interest instantly peaked.

He set it aside for a moment, came over to shake her hand.

"Dr. Soileaux, it's been a pleasure working with you, and I'm glad you're safe. I'm sorry about your mother. If you feel the need for any kind of crisis counseling or assistance, please don't hesitate to reach out to us."

"Thank you, but Tom, where is Ethan? Is he still in the hospital?" she had sat up, concerned.

"His injuries are such that he's been released from duty. I had the agents inside gather up his things. If they forgot anything, we'll be in touch."

"So he's headed back, just like that, he's not coming here again?" Aurora's heart faltered. She had so much she wanted to say to Ethan.

"No, we need to get him back home to rest," Tom had already begun to back away, calm and serene. He wasn't sure if she knew Ethan was in the car or not, but preferred not to make her aware if she hadn't figured it out. He waved as he crossed the driveway, picking up his pace just before reaching the car. He tossed the suitcase quickly in the back and had the car in gear before Aurora stood up for a better view.

"How'd she take it?" Ethan asked as they drove away.

"Like a champ," Tom said as he buckled his belt.

"Don't lie. I could see her on the front porch."

"Yes, that's unfortunate, sorry about that. She cried, but I get the impression she's tough, she'll be fine." Tom knew it was under Ethan's skin she'd been sitting with another man. Before they were on the highway, Ethan couldn't hold it anymore.

"Who was the guy she had sitting with her? In the swing?" he asked.

Tom sighed, "David's son, Zach, I think his name was, and don't ask me anymore. I don't know anything else anyway."

"I made an absolute mess of this one, didn't I?" Ethan sounded bitter. It was a rhetorical question, Tom knew, and so didn't answer.

Throughout the five-hour drive, they discussed the entire case, front to back. Ethan confided in him entirely, figuring he knew the majority anyway, feeling embarrassed. By the time Tom dropped him off at home, he felt like a complete and total loser who had just screwed up so royally he'd lost the girl of his dreams. Only time would tell if he'd lose his job too.

Tom tried to cheer him up, to keep him on the bright side, but it didn't work. When Tom dropped him off at just after five, Ethan looked thoroughly defeated.

"You'll have at least four days to recover before you have to worry about the office or anything else, just stay put, don't push it," Tom said as he dropped the luggage beside the couch.

"You do know that's not how worrying works, right?" Ethan flopped into bed, sour hearted and Tom just sighed.

"Well, do your best anyway," before he turned to leave Ethan stopped him.

"Hey, I forgot to ask, did you get a hold of Theresa? Was she interested?"

"I did, and she is, she's coming by tomorrow. I'll show her around, get the paperwork done, and her backgrounds started. If all goes well, she'll be on board by the time you're back to full duty."

"Thanks Tom, I appreciate everything."

"Of course, boss, I'm sure you'd do the same for me." Tom slipped out, locking the handle of the front door behind him, leaving Ethan in silence. As he stared at the city skyline, all the mistakes he'd made began to press in on him. He decided if there was anything to learn from the situation, it was not to repeat the mistakes of the past. Pulling out his cell phone, not because she always got upset when he didn't call, but because she knew him better than anyone on the planet, and at the moment, he couldn't think of anyone he wanted to talk to more, he called his mom.

Chapter Twenty-Eight

Sunday morning brought with it sunshine and clear skies, and a feeling of closure Ethan couldn't get off his chest. He hadn't heard so much as a peep from Aurora since he'd left Tahoe and it had been driving him absolutely insane. His investigative mind had raced over every minute detail there was to consider, a dozen times.

Maybe her phone hadn't backed up and saved his number since she had to restore it? Maybe she was just too busy with Donia and friends? Maybe she had fallen ill from her near-drowning. Maybe she was angry with him for the way he'd snapped at her the night he pulled her out of the water, or maybe she was upset that he hadn't taken proper precautions to prevent her sister from being kidnapped in the first place. Maybe she felt like she couldn't trust him and decided it was a deal-breaker. Maybe she had just decided there wasn't enough between them, or that he wasn't someone she considered permanent in her life. Maybe, maybe, maybe, just maybe he'd go crazy thinking about her.

Making it worse was the image in his mind of seeing her on the front porch with Zach, resting in his arms snugly being comforted. Ethan wanted to be the man comforting her, not some other guy. It made the feelings he had for her more powerful, all that much stronger and real. He wanted to call her, to reach out to her, but what Tom had said kept him at bay. After everything, he'd met her in a professional capacity and used poor judgment in his actions with her, a lack of self-control. Reaching out to her, if his contact was unwanted, additionally put his career at even greater risk than it already was.

Another day without talking to her and the distraction it was causing him might cost him his job anyway. His leg was healing, but he felt like a tear in his heart was painfully widening.

With an empty apartment, he needed a distraction and was thankful it came in the form of an early morning call from his mom.

"Hi, Mom," he said solemnly, and she immediately honed in.

"Darling, I can hear it, you sound depressed. You're not doing well, is it your leg? How are you feeling?"

"My leg is fine. It's healing like it's supposed to, I'm not bad, just not in a great mood."

The silence spoke volumes as to whether or not she wanted to touch on the subject.

"It's the girl then, isn't it? The doctor. Have you talked to her yet?"

Ethan sighed, "Yea, I mean, no, I haven't talked to her and, I guess, yea, she's on my mind."

"Have you even tried to call her?"

"No, it's not that simple."

"Most things in life that seem complicated turn out to be far simpler than you would expect. Are you worried about making it personal? More personal than it already is, anyway."

"Sort of," he wished he had his mother's optimism.

"What about Tom? Or that new assistant you hired, Theresa? She was close to the doctor, wasn't she? Maybe she could shed a little light on the situation for you?"

"I don't know. I don't feel like it's a good idea to drag other people into my messes more than is necessary."

"They're your friends, Ethan, and they care about you. It might be nice just to talk to them about it, especially Tom—isn't there 'guy code' or something? I could put your father on the phone."

Ethan laughed a little, and it felt good. "No, Ma, it's not like that with guys."

"Oh, well, whatever you say. All I know is sometimes doing nothing at all puts the first nail in the coffin, which is why I'm calling. What are you doing today? I wasn't sure when you were planning to go back to work, and I was wondering if you could come up for a bit? I would love to see you, as would your dad, we have something for you."

"Um, I was planning to go back tomorrow, maybe not the whole day, but at least to try. I'd come up, but I have to figure out how to get my bike back first. What do you have for me?"

"It's a surprise, and I know how you are, if you start nagging me, I'll hang up on you because you know how hard it is for me to keep a secret and I don't want to spoil it."

The smile that gave him warmed him enough to try and go, "Let me make some calls and see if I can get my bike back. I'll let you know."

"Alright, sweetheart, I hope we'll see you soon. I have lunch for you if you can make it."

"Thanks, Ma, I love you."

"Love you too," she hung up.

Ethan got dressed, realizing it was nice to have a reason to and called Tom. He was in luck, and Tom was ready to get out of the house and agreed to drop him off to get his motorcycle. He typed out a quick text to Trent asking if he was around then saved the contact under the correct name instead of as Sheila. His heart skipped a beat after sending it, wondering if Aurora would be there or not. He didn't want to ask. If it was meant to be, then it was meant to be.

Tom picked him up less than a half-hour later, and they were on their way south of the bay. They mostly chatted about the case, filing paperwork, media coverage, getting things back to normal, and onto the next covert killer. As they got closer to Trent's, it was clear something else was on Tom's mind as he became quiet.

"Spit it out," Ethan said, "I can see the wheels turning."

"Have you talked to the doc since you got back?" Tom wasn't sure Ethan wanted to talk about it.

"Nope."

"Have you tried to call her?"

"Nope, why?" Again, the silence spoke volumes. "Tom? You were the one who said I shouldn't go in, that I should stay away from her for a while. For better or for worse, that message was sent and received, loud and clear. I don't even know if she wants to talk to me, and with everything that's happened, you were probably right, it's a bad career move to chase her. The ball is in her court. If she wants to talk to me, she knows where to find me."

Oh, she wants to talk to you, Tom thought. "For the record, I said to stay away from her in the presence of other FBI professional investigators who make their living noticing things. I never said you should stay away from her entirely. I don't think

303

shooting her a text that you would like to talk is exactly chasing her."

"It's been three days, and I'm sure she needs time. She's been through a lot. I don't want to be one more thorn in the ivy."

At that, Tom couldn't argue without conjecture, which he didn't think was healthy. As they pulled up to Trent's, he held his tongue, wished Ethan well, and shot off a text message to keep a promise to a new friend. Ten minutes later, Ethan was pulling out of the driveway, wondering if Aurora was hiding upstairs. He wondered if Tom was right, wondered if he should have asked about her, and had his anxiety bubbling up all over again. With only the road to distract him, it was going to be a long drive.

The traffic was light being a Sunday, and with his leg still sore, he stuck to 101, contemplating if he would be ready to take Highway 1 on the way back. He enjoyed the scenery of the coast highway tremendously. The curves of the road beneath the motorcycle, the way it hugged the road, and he figured it would do him good to get a little ocean air in his lungs before the end of the day. By noon he was pulling into the driveway at his parent's house in south Ukiah.

As soon as he swung the door open, the smell of homemade pasta greeted him, and as he dropped his gear on the chair in the front room, a sense of home pushed the stress from the last two weeks to the back of his mind.

"Anybody home?" he called as he headed towards the kitchen and was surprised to be greeted not by his parents but instead by a small ash grey puppy loping towards him clumsily. "Well, hey there, where did you come from?" He bent to rub the pup's ears as his mom snuck around the corner, watching him with a smile.

"He found me at the farmer's market and told me he needed to go home with you," she said as she came to stand beside him. Her hair was down, soft billows of salt and pepper silver curling around her shoulders.

"Did he now?" Ethan smiled, picking the puppy up, extra skin covered in soft fur cuddling against him, licking enthusiastically.

"I know how much you've been missing Murphy lately, and I hate that you're in that apartment all alone. I was picking out tomatoes, and he got away from his litter and was at my feet with those big blue eyes. All I could think of was you like he spoke to me."

"You worry too much, Ma," Ethan leaned over and hugged her warmly as the puppy squirmed in his arms.

"I miss you too much is what I do, you don't come up often enough. This big case with the serial killer after all the doctors, it's over, right?"

"Yea, it's over," he surprised himself that he sounded almost disappointed.

"You say that like it's a bad thing," he met his mother's eyes and could tell she could see right through him. "It's because of this doctor, isn't it?"

"Sort of. Well, no, I mean, I'm glad the case is over, and I'm even more relieved we wrapped it up with Aurora safe, but yea, I guess it just didn't end well, that's all."

His mom went in and retrieved a can of soda out of the fridge before pouring a glass of iced tea for herself. She joined him in the living room as he sat on the floor to wrestle with the puppy. Handing him the soda, she settled into the couch, watching him intently.

"You're upset. I can tell, you know," she said as she eyed him over the glass. He didn't look up at her for fear of what she would see in his eyes. He knew she could read him like a book. "Tell me about it. Why didn't it end well?" she asked.

He sighed heavily and rolled the puppy on his back to scratch at his belly.

"I forget how sharp puppy teeth are," he yanked back a finger the dog had playfully chomped.

"Don't evade me, Ethan. You cared for this girl, what happened?"

"Damn it," he snapped the soda open and chugged some of it. *How does Mom always know what to say and when?*

"I'm waiting," she said, surprisingly patient.

"You said it already. I care about her. Maybe more than just care about her, I can't honestly describe it. There was just something between us from the moment I saw her, and I thought it was all me, but then," he hesitated, not sure he wanted to describe to his mom the mind-blowing electricity that had been between him and Aurora.

305

"She likes you, and she showed you." She sat forward on her elbows to pet the puppy, jumping and licking at her knees. "Well, who wouldn't like you?" She smiled at Ethan as he sucked more soda down. The can wasn't going to outlast the conversation, she could tell. It was a sign of stress for him, and it had been since he was in high school. He might not know it about himself, but she did. The more anxiety he felt, the faster he drank.

"I thought she liked me," he said in a heavy tone. "But I don't think she trusted me, in the end. She didn't come to me when I thought she would, and she got herself in trouble, and I was pretty hard on her for it."

"That's your job, though, to protect people even when they don't know what's best for themselves. Have you talked to her at all?" She shook a toy at the puppy, keeping her eyes on Ethan's face. She could see the sadness in him, and it shot through her like an ice pick.

"No," he said with sad eyes. "I don't feel like I handled myself well, not professional, and it would be even more unprofessional of me to intrude in her personal life."

She thought hard about it, his job was essential to him, but she knew, perhaps more than he did, his career wasn't going to be there for him when he grew old.

"So you two became involved, somehow?" she waited for him to meet her eyes over the can of soda.

"Yea, Ma. Are you going to make me give you the play by play?"

"No, but I am going to make you consider why it would be different now than it was during the case? If you crossed those lines and she was fine last week, why does the case ending change any of it? Professional is professional, but what becomes personal stays personal. If you care about her, you owe it to yourself as much as her to at least reach out and allow some kind of closure. Maybe she feels like your status as an Agent with the FBI prevents her from reaching out to you. You don't know until you talk to her."

He was lying flat on his back with the puppy circling his head, batting it playfully back and forth as it lunged at him.

"I don't know. I'm pretty sure she's pissed at me. It just doesn't feel quite right, like me calling her is imposing on her, pressing her in some unwelcome way."

"Maybe," when she said it with a light tone as if that might not be a big deal, he frowned and zeroed in on her eyes. "I'm certainly not recommending you harass her, but wouldn't you just like to know for sure how she feels? She's a grown woman, a quite accomplished one from what I understand, so it doesn't seem unreasonable for her to stand her ground without feeling threatened. It's just a phone call." She shrugged and got up, walking into the kitchen she called back over her shoulder, "Take it from an accomplished and independent woman that sometimes it takes a man with enough balls to impress us by not giving up."

He chuckled and continued to play with the puppy. Their conversation changed from the subject of Aurora to family and the goings-on around the small town. He ate lunch with her and his dad, who joined them only a few minutes later. It felt nice to be home, and he was glad he made the trip.

Four hours later, his mother insisted that he leave his motorcycle at the house and take her car, to return within a day or two to trade so he could take the puppy home. He was pretty sure it was a ploy to get him to come home again, as much as it was to get the small hyper dog out of her hair sooner. The reality was, it was probably better for him to drive the car anyway as his leg had begun to throb by the time he was ready to leave.

He said his goodbyes and tucked the dog into the front passenger seat to keep him company and headed back to the city. It was early, and he had nowhere to be, and even though he realized the dog was going to be welcome company, it made him admit to himself he wished he had Aurora waiting for him at home.

～

Aurora dragged herself out of bed at quarter after ten and trampled into the kitchen for coffee in her pajamas. It had been three days since she had nearly drowned in Tahoe and her life felt like it was never going to get back to normal.

She had spent Friday and Saturday with the Fournier family recuperating, and Donia had joined them, soaking up all the attention over her irreplaceable fingernail, but had surprisingly shown an enormous amount of empathy as well. They had a few long discussions on the beach, some heart to heart healing moments, and Donia had promised to be a better sister in the coming years. For some strange reason, Aurora believed her this time.

They had gone through a good deal of their mother's affairs, and to the shock and horror of everyone, it had been much worse than anticipated. There had even been some phone calls and interview requests from the press, and Aurora had found it difficult even to begin planning a funeral service. She'd been more than relieved when Blanche had volunteered to take on the daunting task, even if she seemed to enjoy the idea with a slightly dark bit of humor.

So here she was, on a Sunday, cases canceled for another two weeks with nothing but a pile of errands she didn't feel like handling. In all of it, the worst part had been, she couldn't get Ethan off her mind. He hadn't called, hadn't sent any kind of email or text, she wasn't even sure he wanted ever to see her again and after all, why would he? She hadn't trusted him when it meant the most, had practically put him into direct danger to protect her and he'd ended up stabbed, again.

She couldn't blame him if he hated her, but it hurt her heart to miss him and some part of her needed closure.

She decided that even if he never wanted to see her again, she needed him to know how much she cared for him. She just wasn't sure how to go about achieving that communication in a way that would satisfy her without upsetting her worse. In the short amount of time they'd spent together, he'd put a permanent mark on her heart.

She stumbled to the couch with her coffee and peeled open a magazine, sipping while she stared at the pictures, not absorbing what she was browsing. When her phone lit up with a text message from Trent, her heart skipped a beat.

'Guess who is coming to get his motorcycle this morning?' Trent's message read.

'How soon? Did he ask if I was there?' She replied.

'No, honey, he didn't. Does he need to? Are you not going to find him and tell him how you feel?'

Her insides squirmed. It felt strange. She had felt so close to Ethan, and now she felt torn apart, shut out. Her only fear was rejection itself, and she wasn't sure she could get through a conversation with him and deal with him telling her he didn't want to see her.

'You know it's bad enough that I think I know how he feels, that I think he doesn't ever want to see me. I'm not sure I can handle any proof. Rejection's not on my list of things to deal with today.' Aurora texted with her bottom lip pinched in her teeth painfully.

'Sweetheart, nothing is worse than not knowing. It's like a wound that won't scab. You're better off with a scar than something that bleeds without end.' Trent replied.

Shit, he's always right. She frowned.

'Ugh, when did he say he was coming?'

'Just said he's on his way.'

'Alright, I'll be there as soon as I can.'

She showered in a whirlwind, probably spending too much time on how she looked and was halfway to Palo Alto when Trent called.

"You missed him, honey," his voice was sour. She just sighed.

"Maybe it was meant to be."

"Oh shut up, you know that's what losers say when they don't win," he scolded her.

"Whatever, he hasn't called me, he probably hates me."

"We've had this conversation, it's *exhausting*," Trent dragged the word out like a yawn. "I'm just going to say, he said he was going to see his parents, and he was walking better but not normal either, so maybe you should call him now before he kills himself on that dreadful donor cycle."

Aurora chuckled, but she was right back at square one. The call-waiting buzzed on the Bluetooth.

"Trent, honey, I have to go. Theresa is calling on the other line."

"Well, good, maybe she can talk some sense into you," he snickered as he hung up. Aurora flipped the line to the incoming call.

"Tee-ta!" she squealed.

"Hello, darling," Theresa laughed. "What are you doing this morning, my love?"

"I'm driving around for no reason. I was trying to catch Ethan at Trent's house, but I guess I've missed him."

"Oh, well, I was going to invite you for brunch, but it sounds like we have more important things to handle. Tell me all about it." And so Aurora did, happy to have her ear and her reassuring heart. As she turned the car around, headed back to her apartment in the city, she learned Theresa was far more than just reassuring. She was turning out to be an ace up Aurora's sleeve.

Just before the sign for Dillon Beach came into view, the puppy roused from sleep on the front seat and yipped loudly, followed by a rolling puppy wail. Ethan reached over and put a reassuring hand on him, wiggling the extra skin as he admired the soft coat again.

"You ready to run around a little bit, buddy?" Ethan flipped his blinker on as the puppy crawled across the center console into his lap. Leaning on the side armrest of the window, the dog peered outside and drooled on the glass. Veering onto Highway 1, he realized how much he missed the ocean, missed the beach. Maybe the day had turned out to be therapeutic, even if it hadn't taken Aurora off his mind.

Less than a half-hour later, he was setting his shoes on a picnic table, sinking his toes into warm sand, watching the little dog chase seagulls across the dunes as he tripped on his wobbly paws. Ethan grabbed a stick and lured him along the surf, careful to keep him out of waves deep enough to topple him. His grey fur was shiny in the sun, and his ears flopping and dangling made Ethan smile. *Yes, my mother might be a pain in the ass, but she knows me better than anyone else in the world,* he thought.

They walked the length of the beach together while Ethan threw sticks, trying to figure out a name for him. The sun began to boil the bottom of the clouds with a cotton candy pink sunset as the sky reddened and darkened. His mind drifted, began to run through the last two weeks again, but the beauty of the Pacific sun soaked through him, lifting his spirits. As they reached the end of the beach where the rocks jutted out from the bluff, the dog ran around a large outcropping, disappearing momentarily. Ethan's heart jumped with worry. Ignoring his sore leg, he picked his pace up to a jog to get the pup back in sight, whistling, only in time to see he'd found a friend.

The dog had climbed rocks up to a dry spot and was jumping on a woman in a billowing, flowered pink skirt and a loose coral shirt that hung off one shoulder low. Her face was turned away as paws accosted her, but he could hear a laugh, and there was an instant familiarity. He whistled again for the dog, and as she turned, his heart stopped dead in its tracks, his lungs unable to fill with air.

It was Aurora.

Sitting back from the crashing waves, she was barefoot on top of a rock, and as she looked at him, locked eyes with him, time froze. He didn't know what to say, didn't know what to do.

Jesus, she's going to think I'm stalking her.

Her shock was genuine but less severe than his as she gingerly got up. The dog was back at his feet, jumping and barking playfully, but all Ethan could do was stare as Aurora stood carefully and made her way off the rock.

Watching her walk towards him, he couldn't move, was in total denial, his mind unable to grasp and react, his heart hammering in his chest like a buzz saw. He couldn't run, he felt trapped, like nothing he could, or would do, would be the right thing and yet she walked towards him, her face unreadable. When she was close enough that he could have reached out to touch her, she bent down and picked up the puppy, snuggling him close as he squirmed lively in her arms, trying to lick her face. The swelling on her face had gone down. Mottled black still hung beneath both her eyes and over the bridge of her nose, yellowing at the edges. His gut clenched. He hated that she'd been hit, it brought out an anger in him and a protectiveness for her.

"Hey Captain America, who's this little guy?" she asked with a bright smile. Ethan stared at her then stared at the dog, forcing himself with every muscle in his body fighting him, to react.

"I think I'm going to name him Dillon."

"After the beach?" she didn't miss a beat. He nodded as she put the dog down.

"What are you doing here?" he asked out of sheer shock. "I mean, it's the beach, you're at the beach, but this beach, why are you at this beach?" *Damn, it just shut up!* He told himself to hold his tongue, and she smiled a shy grin, taking another step closer to him.

"It's a long story. I talked with Theresa. She said you sought her out and hired her to be your personal assistant. She starts tomorrow, yes?"

He nodded but kept his mouth shut for fear of sounding like a dumbfounded moron because that's how he felt.

"That's incredibly sweet, Ethan, it means the world to her to feel needed and useful, and it means a lot to me to know you did something like that for her, probably because of me, I assume." She stopped for a minute, looking hard at him, squinting in the fading sun. The rays of light slanting sideways across the horizon played off the bottom of watery grey clouds and mixed with the crimson of the sunset bled shades of amethyst into the sky. The reflection from the heavens and water highlighted every perfect feature of her face, and the golden emerald flecks of her amber eyes danced as she stared at him. Her beauty held him captive all over again. He wasn't sure what he would do if the conversation ended with her saying goodbye forever.

"Theresa said she talked to Tom, on Friday, she saw him in the office when she was setting up her desk, and they had a conversation about you, and about us." Ethan thought he might vomit his heart out, knowing what Tom knew, what he might have, *could* have said.

"I um," she put her hands on her hips, fingers pointed downward, and swayed to one side, looking away from him. "I wasn't sure you ever wanted to see me again. I, ah, figured you were pretty pissed at me for taking off like that and, rightfully so. I figured I owed you an explanation. I still owe you an explanation, for what it's worth, I just didn't know if it mattered or not or if it would change anything. I didn't think you wanted to hear from me, so I guess it was nice to have Theresa tell me that Tom thought I should call you." She wouldn't look up at him. He couldn't read her face but could hear a nervous tone in her voice over the breeze off the ocean, the crash of the waves.

"I wanted to. Honestly, I tried. I picked it up and changed my mind a dozen times or more. I was confident you hated me, I'm still not sure what you think, I mean, you risked your life for me.

I've lost count how many times, and then I just couldn't bring myself to face having to hear it from you."

He stepped forward, his body loosening. Watching tears crack through and wash over her broke his heart.

"I just wanted you to know it wasn't because I didn't trust you, I did, I *do* trust you. I was just so conflicted because you barely knew me, honestly, and I had started to care about you so much, and you were shot at and stabbed because of me, and I didn't want you risking your life for me again, or *ever* for Donia, I guess. Then I was thinking about David and Blanche as well as Donia and what would happen. She hasn't tried to talk to me like I mattered to her in so long, and maybe it's a weakness, but I missed it, the way she used to care. We were close once. I imagined her looking at me wondering why I would choose you over her by risking her life telling you about the note, and the whole thing was just rotten, and I'm sorry." She had begun to cry a full-hearted, covering her face with her hands, through to her soul sob. "I'm just so sorry, Ethan, I don't know that I can ever make it up to you."

He had reached for her, grabbed her hand, and pulled her closer to him, and by the time she finished talking, exhausted from putting everything emotional on the table, he had her in his arms, his face in her hair as he held her. Sobs shook her petite frame, but her arms came around him, her hands flat on his back hanging onto him as if she would be washed into the ocean if he let go.

"Don't, just don't," he whispered as he kissed her temple. "Please, for the love of God, stop crying. I can't take it," he said into her ear.

She inhaled sharply, pressing her face to his chest.

"I'm the one who is sorry. I royally screwed up every step of the way, letting you too close too soon—it was unprofessional, and it clouded my judgment. I should never have let Donia leave like that. Things would have been different, so incredibly different if…" tilting her face to his, they locked eyes with tears moistening her long, thick lashes.

"If I wasn't already so damned in love with you," he choked out.

She was breathless, staring up at his coffee-brown eyes squished up in distress, she clung to him as if the waves would wash the ground right from beneath her feet. Her words were soft, but as she wrapped her arms around his neck and told him she loved him, their lips met, hungry and desperate. He kissed her as if the world around them ceased to exist, holding her so tight it hurt, he lifted her off the ground, and she wrapped her legs around him, clinging to him for dear life.

She wasn't sure how long they stood there, locked in each other as if there was nothing either of them would ever need again. But roused by Dillon's bark, she pushed back, still lost in Ethan's unwavering gaze as the puppy boisterously made his disapproval of the lack of attention known. Hugging her again before putting her down, Ethan couldn't bring himself to let go of her, but she knelt and scooped the dog off the sand. He was tiring and seemed pleased to be carried in her arms as they began to walk together.

"I still don't understand, how did you know to come here?" he asked.

"Trent texted me when you went to pick up your motorcycle. He's been bugging me to reach out to you, so when he told me this morning you were coming, I tried to get there in time but didn't make it. Then he told me you mentioned you were going to see your parents. By chance, Theresa called, and when I told her where you were going, she called your mom."

"What?" Ethan stared at her, confused.

"Yea, Theresa called your mom, she didn't have any trouble finding your mom's cell number since she is your emergency contact. They hit it off quite well, and she said this is your favorite place, that she had a sneaky suspicion you would be here with the new puppy sometime late this afternoon so, I took a chance."

"That's quite the chance," Ethan was floored.

"I guess it felt good to me to have a little bit of fate's hand in action." She winked at him, rubbing Dillon's head lovingly, leaning into Ethan as they walked back along the beach towards the rest of their lives together.

Read more of Ethan, Aurora, and Tom in the upcoming series *Weathering The Storms*, coming soon.

ACKNOWLEDGEMENTS

Two down, dozens to go.

Thank you to my Mom, as always, for helping me persevere. For putting up with my confusing rants and helping me work through the twists and turns. For endlessly fostering my creative process and never telling me to give up. For letting me discuss the sexy parts without making me feel like a naughty freak, and without blushing. For always eating what I serve without complaint. I love you.

To my husband, your favorites are my favorites, and I know I found a new way to discuss those favorites, thanks for not making it weird babe. Go Cubbies! I love you.

To my daughter, for going to bed on your own and letting me have the dark of night to weave my tales and spin my stories. I'm proud of you, of who you are, and who you are becoming and the leaps and bounds you take every day. I don't deserve you. I love you.

To my old friends and new, who have jumped into this process with me without hesitation and have been a never-ending fountain of encouragement, thank you. I love you all.

LOOKING TO CONNECT?

Website:
www.NatalieNeverman.com
Facebook:
https://www.facebook.com/natalie.neverman.5
Instagram:
https://www.instagram.com/natalie.neverman/
Email:
Natalie.Neverman@yahoo.com
Natalie.Neverman@gmail.com

Made in the USA
Columbia, SC
09 October 2020

22471531R00176